A World of
Our Own Making

A World of
Our Own Making
A Sequel to Walden Two

Michael Shuler

Golden Word Books
Santa Fe, NM

Library of Congress Control Number 2019951283

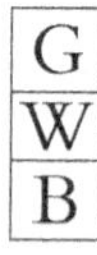

Published by Golden Word Books, Santa Fe, New Mexico.

ISBN 978-1-948749-51-0

To B.F.S. (aka T.E. Frazier)

Acknowledgments

This book would not have been written without the encouragement and support of many people. *I thank them all,* although first I would like to thank Dr. Stephen Ledoux with whom I first discussed writing a sequel to Skinner's *Walden Two* in 2014. He seemed to have more faith in the project than I had. He encouraged me to continue writing, and when I presented him with a tentative manuscript, he responded quickly and thoroughly with many helpful suggestions. This novel would never have been written without his support. The first chapter of the novel is based partly on his book *Running Out of Time.*

Two others who were also deeply involved in improving the novel were Werner Matthijs of Leuven, Belgium, and my daughter, Dawn Kutza, who read the manuscript and helped me to put the female journalist in a better light. Her advice improved the novel considerably. Werner Matthijs meticulously edited the novel, correcting typos and other errors, and offered many eminently valuable suggestions. He suggested a word here or a clause there that vastly improved the point I was trying to make. His notes were so detailed, and had so many helpful comments and suggestions, that I felt that he was here with me as I went through the novel and made changes. While his primary language is Dutch, he helped me immensely with my English. I can't thank him enough for his support and kind words.

I should also thank his group of Belgium Behaviorologists—the "BBs," including Jo, Patrick, and Sven—who read the manuscript and discussed it during their monthly behaviorology meetings, which they describe as their 'happy few' (HF) meetings. Werner also passed the manuscript along to many other interested readers in Belgium, including his wife Cornelia, and to Hubert De Mey in the Netherlands, and all were kind enough to take the time to read the novel and contribute comments. Werner's support is greatly appreciated.

Finally, I would like to thank my wife, Cathy, for her patience with me during the writing process. I was often preoccupied with ideas for the novel during our daily walks rather than listening or contributing to our usual conversations. I'm sure she missed my full attention as much as I would miss hers.

An early version of the novel was formally peer reviewed for the *Journal of Behaviorology*. The six reviewers differed as to whether or not it was appropriate subject matter for publication in a scientific journal. However, all reviewers thought it should be published as a novel. Some reviewers offered very helpful suggestions. One of particular note was Traci Cihon of the University of North Texas. I changed the gender of one of the main characters at her suggestion, and named the character after her. Of course, my indebtedness to B.F. Skinner, whose scientifically grounded ideas permeate the novel, goes without saying. Any remaining errors in the novel are my own. All royalties from this novel will be donated to The International Behaviorology Institute (TIBI, at www.behaviorology.org) to support efforts to solve global problems scientifically; please consider joining or helping in other ways.

Preface

This novel is a sequel to *Walden Two,* a novel that B.F. Skinner wrote in the late 1940s. As a sequel, it imagines a network of cooperating Walden Two communities spread around North America and elsewhere. They are all grounded in *behaviorology,* the natural science of behavior. They operate with a worldview that advocates experimentation with cultural practices using scientifically grounded principles of behavior, while reducing or completely eliminating the current ubiquitous use of coercive practices. This experimentation provides the foundation of societal activity in these Walden Two communities. The communities pursue increasing self-sufficiency, and each produces unique art, products, services, and technologies (although some redundancy necessarily exists).

Dr. Fred Burris narrates the story. Dr. Burris is a Walden Two-trained behaviorologist and the grandson of the original Burris from Skinner's novel. Because he grew up in Walden Two, he differs from his grandfather by being a direct product of Walden Two's educational contingencies. Dr. Traci Jensen, who gives the opening remarks to the visitors in Chapter 1, is also one of the community's behaviorologists. Other characters are introduced as the story proceeds. (Readers can discover more about behaviorology in the articles and books described at www.behaviorology.org or in the Suggested Readings at the end of this book.)

One of several differences between *Walden Two* and this sequel concerns the writer's viewpoint. Skinner wrote from the viewpoint of a visitor to the community. This is a very effective and common device to help the reader identify with the narrator and see the community from this vantage point. This author instead thought that writing from the viewpoint of one of the community's current behaviorologists might be more interesting, as it allows the reader to see the community from the point of view of a member who grew up and studied behaviorology there, and thereby understand better how they think about behavior.

This sequel features applications of behaviorological science to human affairs. Before this, many readers may not have ever heard the word "behaviorology." For example, the author was very interested, and widely read, in the science of behavior for decades but had not heard or read of behaviorology until reading (in 2014) Stephen Ledoux's 2012 *American Scientist* article, "Behaviorism at 100." The point of making this sequel available is to expand the reader's awareness of behaviorology as an immediately and widely applicable area of scientific knowledge of substantial importance to humanity's future. As the cover of Ledoux's 2014 textbook states, "Behaviorology is the natural science of *why* human behavior happens, a natural science to help build a sustainable society in a timely manner."

Hopefully, for humanity's benefit, general audiences will become more familiar with behaviorology and will help generate interest in and support for this field and this discipline. Thus, the point of this novel is: (a) to bring the science of behaviorology, and its possible application to cultural and societal questions, to readers who might be concerned about humanity's future; (b) to point out the many advantages of a network of self-sufficient, Walden Two-like communities; and (c) to enable more people to become familiar with the 100-year-old natural science of behavior now known as behaviorology.

I did not want to write this novel myself; I wanted to *read* it, and, as opportunity arose, to help put some of these ideas into practice. I had watched for a sequel to *Walden Two* ever since reading Skinner's unparalleled vision in 1971. My original hope was to spur other behaviorologists to write a sequel while I offered some ideas. Some of my initial writing on the topic occurred in exchanges of correspondence with my daughter as she was away studying at college and graduate school.

I wanted to see Skinner's original story brought into the twenty-first century, so I imagined a network of such communities as a viable community-based alternative to the current corporate-dominated social structure. These communities would be a feasible way to secede from corporate-dominated societies, rather than futilely trying to change them through feckless political activities. But in order to secede, communities *must be* self-sufficient, and the people in them must be able to join together in harmonious cooperation—this is where the natural science of behavior comes in.

Skinner originally wrote his *Walden Two* in part as an effort to bring his natural science of behavior to a wider audience and, certainly, to get people thinking about the possibilities and benefits that such a science could bring to society. He established the way of life in his Walden Two community as experimental; there is no predetermined best way to do anything. The members were encouraged to try new and creative ways of doing things, and these would be available for selection by consequences. Many professional readers have seen this as the most important message of his Walden Two community. Skinner also implied that, as a community, Walden Two would divide and eventually subdivide into many communities.

In an updated version of the original *Walden Two* concept, we can imagine many such cooperating communities the products of which are intellectual or perhaps clinical, as well as physical. For example, different communities could specialize in different disciplines and fields (e.g., behavioral medicine, education, genetic research, behavioral safety, diplomacy, applied behavior analysis, neuroscience, interventions for autism or other disabilities, and so on). They would openly share their results with others in the network as well as with the scientific community at large.

Skinner once wrote that if he were to rewrite *Walden Two*, he would make it more heterogeneous. So, for example, a sequel today might deal, at least briefly, with elderly members, autistic members, handicapped members, and so on, while depicting various prosthetic environments designed to circumvent their difficulties and enhance their lives. And while Skinner used a Dewey-type teaching method, up-to-date communities could feature more recent, experimentally validated processes and procedures such as programmed and computer-assisted, instruction, along with precision teaching methods such as those outlined by Skinner's daughter, Julie Vargas, in her 2013 book, *Behavior Analysis for Effective Teaching*.

With our current corporate-dominated consumer society, often dysfunctional government, and growing disparity in wealth, a perfect time may have come to try to generate new interest in Skinner's vision, the vision that a natural science of behavior can contribute to the planning and activation of non-punitive, non-aggressive, self-sustaining communities that try to consume no more than they need, pollute as little as possible, and take the future of the human species, as well as the rest of life on the planet, into account. The members of these communities can be happy and productive and even "self-actualized" although a better term, perhaps, would be "Walden Two actualized" or even, as Stephen Ledoux suggested (in a personal communication) "contingency actualized." Such a reinforcing culture could bring people to their full potential. In these ways, a *Walden Two* sequel should generate greater interest and discussion about both behaviorology and its actual and potential engineering applications, especially with respect to culture and solving global problems.

We are all controlled by the world in which we live, and part of that world has been and will be constructed by men. The question is this: Are we to be controlled by accident, by tyrants, or by ourselves through effective cultural design? The danger of the misuse of power is possibly greater than ever. It is not allayed by disguising the facts. We cannot make wise decisions if we continue to pretend that human behavior is not controlled, or by refusing to engage in control when valuable results might be forthcoming. Such measures weaken only ourselves, leaving the strength of science to others .... It is no time for self-deception, emotional indulgence, or the assumption of attitudes which are no longer useful. Man is facing a difficult test. He must keep his head now, or he must start again—a long way back.

    —B.F. Skinner

     Freedom and the Control of Men

Those who reject the scientific conception of man must, to be logical, oppose the methods of science as well.

    —B.F. Skinner

     Freedom and the Control of Men

1

When Frazier died in 1990, an obituary in the *New York Times* read in part:

T.E. Frazier, the Champion Of Behaviorism, Is Dead at 86

Thomas Eliot Frazier, 86, died peacefully on August 18, 1990 from complications arising from leukemia. He was credited with founding the first Walden Two community near Canton and published widely in the natural science discipline now called behaviorology.

In his research and his voluminous writings, Dr. Frazier advanced the belief that individuals could better understand themselves and build a better world by systematically modifying human environments in accordance with behavioral principles he discovered in his research. By becoming a behaviorist in the late 1920s, when the discipline was in its infancy, Dr. Frazier helped to shape behaviorology as both a laboratory science and a cogent philosophy.

Over the course of his long career, he worked on projects as diverse as machines that teach, utopian communities, missiles guided by pigeons, temperature-controlled environments for infants and the education of the severely retarded. Some of these contributions earned him the reputation of a profound thinker while others caused him to be seen as a cold manipulator of humanity whose ideas could have disastrous consequences if they fell into the wrong hands.

"All human beings are controlled," he once told an interviewer, "but the ideal of behaviorology is to eliminate coercion, and for people to apply controls by changing the environment in such a way as to reinforce the kind of behavior that benefits everyone. Fascism and other authoritarian political systems are capable of applying the new technologies emanating from behaviorology," he added, "and the challenge to democratic society is to develop it first. The society that adopts the technology first will have the competitive edge, and if ours is not the first, we shall be in danger."

Personally, I knew little about Frazier. Much of what I do know about him came from Grandfather Burris, who first visited Walden Two in the mid 1940s. But I did meet Frazier on several occasions when I was a young boy and found him to be very charming. He always made people feel that he was genuinely interested in them, and I truly believe he was. I remember him talking to me when I was very young with the same respect that he would give to my father, or any adult for that matter.

My grandfather once told me that Frazier always listened intently to people, as if he were trying to glean what "contingencies of reinforcement" had produced their repertoires. This was part of the technical terminology that Frazier developed. He read widely in history, philosophy, science, and literature, and always kept up with events happening around the world. He was educated at Harvard but left academia to pursue his interest in planned, sustainable, prosocial communities that would maximize the behavioral repertoires of their members.

He was not only interested in all aspects of Walden Two, but also culture in general.

My grandfather wrote about his first encounters with Frazier and Walden Two in his book, *Walden Two*. Over time, he and Frazier became close friends—at least to the extent that one can become the close friend of a genius. While Frazier always made people in his company feel that they were on equal ground with him, you somehow knew this was not the case. It did not take long to realize that his intelligence was on the extreme end of the normal curve, yet he politely remained in your intellectual comfort zone while probing you as if you were the most interesting person around. It was only when you heard him conversing in depth with others on so many diverse topics that you understood the extent of his intellectual breadth. While he was clearly a polymath, he spoke with people about topics and on a level to which they were accustomed, and he had a knack for finding this level quickly. He seemed especially to take delight in understanding the common person; perhaps because he was so far removed from them.

My father once told me that he overheard Frazier telling Grandfather Burris that, once you condition prosocial behavior in common people, they can be "quite delightful." We both found that amusing. I suppose Frazier enjoyed other people the way many of us enjoy our animal companions, keeping in mind that we can truly love our animal companions, even though we do not consider them to be our intellectual equals. Frazier was not a product of Walden Two, so perhaps we can excuse his idiosyncrasies.

I do not wish to write here extensively nor expansively about Frazier. Even Frazier considered himself a locus where unique variables came together to produce the person we call "Frazier." He did not put himself in any special class of scholars or intellectuals. He believed, as his science would dictate, that he was just the product of a unique genetic and environmental history, as we all are. So I have come to this point to bury Frazier, not to praise him. I believe this is what he would have wanted. For far too long we have been giving people credit or blame for what we now know is the result of environmental variables. This was Frazier's main point. This is why he began Walden Two: to demonstrate the possibility of arranging environments that will produce the kind of behavior most favorable to not only the survival of our species, but also the happiness of our species.

Grandfather Burris died several years after Frazier, in 1996. But perhaps I should wait until later to tell his story, since I will devote part of a chapter to dignified dying. My purpose herein is to inform the reader about the science behind the model community that led to the proliferation of Walden Two-like communities that now pepper North America and elsewhere.

*   *   *

Dr. Traci Jensen stood at the podium in the conference room shuffling her notes, and when the polite applause subsided, she began:

"Good evening ladies and gentlemen. Welcome to Walden Two. My name is Traci Jensen; I am one of many board-certified behaviorologists here. I have my doctorate in behaviorology and teach graduate level courses in this subject to students both inside and outside of our community."

Dr. Jensen looked over the top of her reading glasses at the small audience of visiting science journalists. "May I have a show of hands, how many of you were familiar with our communities before being assigned to come here?"

All hands went up, as expected.

"Now, how many of you are familiar with behaviorology—one of the main sciences behind our communities—or believe you know something about it?"

Only two hands went up.

"Very well," Traci said with a smile. "I hope to change that today."

She continued, "I also currently serve on the board of planners here. We hope to make your visit here pleasant as well as informative. I know some of you will be staying with us for a few days, so please feel free to make yourselves completely at home. We will do all we can to make you comfortable, but please let us know if we can assist you in any way. I would like to make a few remarks before you begin exploring our community tomorrow; I think this will help you to better assess it, and I promise to keep the technical jargon to a minimum. We may have to introduce some technical terms later when you actually visit the community, and then only if needed to elucidate an important concept. My talk should take no more than thirty minutes. Incidentally, this talk is very informal, so please feel free to ask questions during my talk. If you raise your hand, I will take your question, but I may continue to complete the point I am making before calling on you.

"As you know, Walden Two was the first of many such communities, all of which are based upon very similar principles, and all of which are networked together via a heavily encrypted intranet connection. Note that I did say *intra*-net. We are relatively self-sufficient and each of our communities provides its own unique products and services—with some redundancy, of course. For instance, several of our communities specialize in veterinary science training, the training of companion animals, and also in the education and training of companion animal trainers. I know many of you are already aware of some of the other products and services we offer, so I won't go into them here tonight. Since many of you are science journalists, I would like to begin by addressing one of the main sciences that underpins Walden Two and all of our other communities. I don't believe you can fully understand our communities without some appreciation of the primary science upon which they are based; namely, behaviorology. I imagine most of you are at least slightly familiar with some of the technologies produced by this science since they have been applied piecemeal in many societies. It has improved everything from the treatment of animals to human working conditions and education, and, as you will soon see, it has been used to produce viable non-punitive communities.

"Several of our communities offer graduate level courses in behaviorology to people outside of them; it is just one of the courses we offer and it provides a part of our income. We would like to see *everyone* benefit from this science and we believe it is a win-win relationship. Therefore, tonight I will give you a brief overview of behaviorology. I certainly can't give you a crash course in the *science* in a thirty-minute talk of course—if I could do that, we could shorten our graduate programs considerably—but I would like you to leave here with a better understanding of the main science upon which our communities are based, and possibly allay any preconceived fears that you may have about that science.

"So first, let's consider the name of this science. Though the *name* 'behaviorology' was initially rejected due to euphonic concerns—some simply did not like the *sound* of this name—it was eventually accepted and adopted as a perfectly suitable name for this discipline. 'Ology' translates to 'the scientific study of.' Biology studies life forms and processes, geology studies the elements and properties of the earth, and behaviorology is the scientific study of behavior. Therefore, 'behaviorology' is the proper and accurate name for this science, since our subject matter is *behavior*.

"You see, behaviorologists study behavior *in its own right* and infer nothing inside the organism other than a nervous system and any biochemical processes and anatomical structures needed to support that behavior. Since the subject matter of behaviorology is behavior, it is important for us to define it. For our purposes, we can begin by saying that behavior is anything that an organism does: it is running, crying, building nests, flying, pinching claws together, playing the violin, speaking, swallowing, eating, spouting water from blowholes, and so on. All of these behaviors are mediated by the nervous systems of various organisms. Rocks and plants do not behave simply because they lack the requisite nervous system to do so. Again, behavior is anything that an organism does, or anything that happens inside the organism; for example, the firing of neurons is also behavior. Our job, as behaviorologists, is to try to determine what causes behavior to occur.

"Now, people in the past have looked for what they considered to be the 'purpose' of a bit of behavior. Ethologists, for instance, may study certain behaviors of a species in their natural environment and—after carefully describing them—try to determine the survival value of that behavior. They may say this survival value is the *purpose* of eating, fighting, or nest building, say. Behaviorologists, on the other hand, study the behavior in context and attempt to determine all of the controlling variables for it. The contexts of behavior are the stimuli that precede and follow the behavior. Of course, much of our behavior actually does have survival value, but this is not the 'purpose' of behavior. 'Purpose' implies a *future* cause of behavior and has the etiology of behavior exactly backwards—as I hope you will learn over the next few days. Simply put, the dynamic interactions between behavior and environment, and the effects these interactions have on behavior, is what behaviorologists investigate.

"Now," Traci said, looking around the small audience, "psychology, on the other hand, translates to the study of the, well, 'psyche.' 'Psyche' is an old word originally meaning the human 'mind,' 'spirit,' or 'soul.' Here is the problem: For a discipline to be called a natural science, it must first subscribe to naturalism, a philosophical viewpoint according to which everything arises from *natural* properties and causes; all spiritual, supernatural and non-natural explanations are excluded. Yet psychology still adheres to internal and fundamentally metaphysical explanations of behavior; and I'm not speaking here of physiological causes; but rather of 'minds,' 'selves,' 'personalities,' and so on. As one of our professors of the history of our science has pointed out, psychology broke from philosophy by adopting empirical methods, but it fell short of becoming a natural science by not fully adopting naturalism. Although it avoided *theologically* mystical causal agents, it nevertheless maintained or introduced mystical *secular* indwelling agents—such as a 'mind'—as causes of behavior. Many, to this day, blame Descartes for this mind-body dualism.

"Here is an important point I would like to make concerning the utilization of behaviorology in our communities," Dr. Jensen said, looking out over the audience, "Without the experimental approach of *this* science, we believe our communities would founder, like all non-experimental communities before us, and like, in our opinion, *most* societies outside of Walden Two today. While many societies have achieved greatness, there always seems to be a compensatory downside. As T.E. Frazier, the man credited with starting this very first community based on behaviorology noted: "Science has been successful wherever it has been applied, let us apply it to human affairs."

"He argued that the natural sciences have increased our understanding of other parts of nature to the point where we understand them far better than we understand ourselves. As a result, we find ourselves in possession of great scientific achievements, artifacts, and technologies, which we are using with stone-age brains and ancient outdated conceptions of humankind. And while we steadily gain control over nature and understand it better through our sciences of physics, chemistry, biology, astronomy and others, too many of us still see humankind as distinct from nature, as if we were somehow observing nature from outside of it, rather than being immanent with nature.

"Even some otherwise intelligent people, who accept the reality of human evolution, still believe that humans are somehow qualitatively separate from the other animals in some fundamental way—by suggesting that we have free will, for example. But at what point in our evolutionary history did this non-natural 'free will' enter into the natural nervous system? At what point did a non-natural 'mind' or 'self' enter into the natural nervous system? Just when in the history of life was the chain of natural causation supposedly broken? Are these supposed to be emergent properties emanating from the Law of Cumulative Complexity, which I will touch on later? Behaviorologists, on the other hand, do not believe that the chain of natural causation was ever broken; we believe that we are continuous with nature; an intrinsic part of nature."

Traci paused briefly at this point to allow all of this to register with her listeners before continuing. Then she glanced at her notes and continued.

"Because many neural behaviors, the kind we call 'thoughts,' often precede our motor behavior, we often feel that an inner version of ourselves is causing this behavior. Behaviorologists call this 'agentialism,' which is putting an agent inside the body to explain the external behavior. By 'external behavior' I'm talking about the behavior that everyone can easily observe. This is in contrast to the private behavior that only the person him- or herself can observe. Examples of private behavior would include thinking, feelings, and emotions, along with all other private sensations. What is curious is that people don't feel it necessary to explain the inner self, and instead think of it as an initiating cause—some kind of autonomous agent that causes our behavior to happen.

"But an inner *agent* is not causing our behavior; if anything, it is inner *behavior* that is causing *more* behavior in a chain-like fashion. Therefore, we behaviorologists call it 'chained' behavior, since one behavior either elicits or evokes the next behavior in the chain. But this inner behavior also needs to be explained. And like emotions and feelings, thoughts happen at just the right time to appear to be an *initiating* cause of the motor behavior that follows it. However, if we trace any behavior's causes back far enough, we find that all behavior is caused eventually by external variables, including, of course, those external variables that selected our bodies through evolutionary processes.

"Behaviorology is still a relatively young science with a very complex subject matter. It was less than fifty years old when Frazier began Walden Two, but it has steadily grown. It is now over a hundred years old, and shall undoubtedly continue to develop and add to our understanding of human behavior and human affairs. It is by no means complete. No science is. But like all *natural* sciences—and therefore unlike psychology—behaviorology brooks *no* metaphysical explanations. It deals exclusively with real, natural events. These events can be observed and detected by the methods used in all of the other natural sciences.

"Psychology may finally be beginning to doubt some of these fictitious, inner agential causes of behavior. And, as new information comes in from physiology, they are trying to redefine these inner agents in *physiological* terms and asserting that this is what they meant all along. But remember, behaviorologists have *never* accepted these kinds of hypothetical constructs—we have always insisted that behavior should be studied *in its own right,* and this has given us a great advantage in our search for the actual causes of behavior. The discovery of the natural causes of behavior greatly facilitated the treatment of behavioral disorders and helped to improve educational practices and human relations in general.

"Now, granted, psychology has adopted some of the *methods* of the natural sciences, but it did not adopt the insistence of the natural sciences on dealing only with natural events. This insistence is what makes the natural sciences so successful. Let me give you a possible explanation as to why psychology did not adopt naturalism earlier. Since the behavior of other humans and animals has always been a part of the human environment from our beginning—that is, we have *always* had other behaving humans and animals as part of our environment— behavior has undoubtedly always been a paramount concern.

"It was, and is, important to be able to predict, to some degree, the behavior of other people and animals with which we interact. Therefore much of our early language must have been about behavior and its causes. But we have been talking about behavior and its causes long before we developed methods to understand it in a scientific way. And our ancestors came up with numerous creative but false explanations for it, including stellar and planetary influences—which, fortunately, very few educated people consider as causes today. Nevertheless, many of these prescientific conceptions have permeated most, if not all, human languages, and still remain a part of them to this day. Once these concepts were inculcated into our language they continued to influence how we think about human behavior, and some investigators have tried to study these prescientific concepts using scientific methods."

Traci looked out over the small audience while she spoke and only occasionally glanced at her notes—other than this, her talk appeared to be completely extemporaneous. She is a very articulate speaker with no superfluous "um's" and "ah's." Her voice is very clear and she presents confidently with nearly perfect diction, making excellent eye contact with her listeners. This is no accident. Special audiences here at Walden Two have carefully shaped her elocution by providing the all-important differential feedback during her early education. She has also learned to discern the interest level of her audiences with great accuracy and can quickly adapt her speech to recapture waning attention; she did not want to lose her audience at this point in her talk because she knew the importance of explaining the main science behind all of our communities—a science that is still little understood even by natural scientists in other fields. She was hoping to help change this. It was especially important to explain this science to *this* audience. She knew this audience would disseminate the concepts she was explaining on this day to many others. She took a sip of water from a cup beside her and continued.

"Science is a set of methods that have developed over time for teasing out the causes of natural phenomena. It is important to note that science is also *behavior*. Think about this for a moment. We have generated rules over many centuries to govern our 'scientific' behavior—rules that increase our chances of successful investigation. An important tenant of science is that researchers must begin with natural phenomena, *real* phenomena that exist in nature. And a scientific discipline must adopt this tenant, along with other scientific methods, before it can be called a natural science.

"But, as I've suggested, prescientific thinking about human and non-human behavior has admitted mystical entities and explanations early on in the investigation of the causes of behavior, and names for these putative entities have entered into the vernacular of many cultures. They have been with us for so long, and are so familiar to us, that most people accept them without question even to this day. Since prescientific thinking posited internal explanations for behavior, these faulty concepts entered and remain in our language as 'spirits,' 'psyches,' 'minds,' 'selves,' 'souls,' and so on, and psychology became the 'study of the psyche or mind.'

"Early thinkers could not break out of this zeitgeist, and some contemporary thinkers are not doing much better. Although psychologists have been using empirical methods and advanced statistical analyses that give psychology the appearance of being scientific, they continue to allow prescientific reified internal entities to remain in their discipline. These metaphysical entities have been their problem for well over a hundred and fifty years and have hampered their progress. Surprisingly, it is only recently that neuroscientists—who were not immune from these prescientific concepts—have begun to discount many of these fictitious inner agents. And as they step away from the explanatory fictions of psychology and begin to adopt behaviorology, they find themselves advancing much more rapidly.

"So let me be clear about this, psychology is *not*, by definition, a natural science, and this is why it has often been called a 'soft science.' What it needed to do in order to become a natural science was to complete its break with theology and philosophy and abandon any of their prescientific, metaphysical entities. Instead, psychology only renounced the theological, mystical, 'spirit' or 'soul' cause of behavior—often believed to be influenced by the gods—and adopted the secular mystical 'mind' cause of behavior, which was believed to be more autonomous—at least with respect to the gods; but this 'mind' is, nonetheless, a mystical entity. Contemporary psychologists now use the term 'cognition' for the putative internal *processes* resulting from these reified mystical entities. And, once again, they are not talking about neural processes, but rather, so-called, 'mental' processes that a dualistic view of human nature entails."

At this point a man seated near me in the back row raised his hand, catching Traci's attention. "Yes," she said, pointing to him.

"Why, then, do you suppose contemporary psychologists still entertain these internal explanations?" he asked, as he stood up. "What can they accomplish by believing that these—'mystical entities,' as you call them—have real existence if in fact they don't? It seems to me that they would have abandoned these concepts long ago if they were not somehow useful in explaining behavior."

"That is a very good question," Traci said. "We can surmise that the break from these prescientific assumptions was prevented by some early successes brought about by statistical predictions. These successful predictions may have strengthened their 'belief' in these hypothesized internal agents. But if one studies *any* lawful phenomenon long enough, one can usually make accurate predictions in spite of any fictitious causes one may invent to explain it. For instance, our ancestors could predict the regular movement of the sun quite accurately yet they attributed its movement to a spurious chariot that pulled it across the sky. And like the chariot, a fictitious inner agent inside an organism is an explanatory fiction—an unparsimonious and unnecessary hypothesis that future scientific researchers will one day only find amusing, as behaviorologists now do. The sun will continue to rise, and people and animals will continue to behave, with or without our theories about them. But if we want to influence natural phenomena, we must first determine the 'causes'—what scientists refer to as the 'independent variables'—that actually influence them.

"But to your point, sir, behaviorologists would say that it would only take a few successful yet coincidental predictions to maintain psychologists' behavior of talking about these adventitious inner agents. But, like the chariots, they are completely unnecessary and add nothing to our understanding of this natural phenomenon. Many of the predictions of psychologists involve what we would call behavior-behavior predictions. That is, predicting one behavior from another. For example, two of the most touted successes in psychology are: prediction of academic success based on the outcome scores on I.Q. tests, and predictions of future behavior based on personality tests, both designed by so-called psychometricians. Note again the 'psychic' root of this word that translates to 'measuring the psyche.' The successes of these statistical behavior-behavior predictions reinforce 'belief' in the reified concepts of intelligence and personality, although these successes clearly exemplify behavior-behavior correlations."

The man stood up again. "But isn't that useful information?" he asked.

"Yes, of course," Traci answered. "But behavior is the *dependent* variable in the natural science of behavior. We must always account for *both* of the behaviors involved in these correlations. While behavior *can* be predicted to some extent from previous behavior, this is clearly a case of correlation without causation. No science-oriented investigator would say that a high score on an intelligence test *caused* future academic success; only that some as not yet mentioned independent variables caused both the high score *and* later success; intelligence per se cannot be manipulated as an independent variable. Intelligent behavior, as a dependent variable, must be accounted for in other ways. I hope this answers your question?"

"Yes, well enough," said the questioner before sitting back down.

Traci paused briefly again after making this last point to again allow her remarks to sink in. "I apologize for the density of this talk," she said, "and I hope you will bear with me just a while longer. And please don't feel bad if you are not catching everything at this time; I can assure you that I do not give this talk to all of our visitors—just to the science journalists." There was a small chuckle from the audience. She spotted me sitting at the back of the room and I gave her a small nod of approval. She then continued.

"Certainly some people—and other animals as well—inherit genes that produce nervous systems that form synapses more rapidly, or arborize additional dendrites, thereby forming more connections, or produce additional receptors — perhaps even some with greater affinity for their neurotransmitters, or have larger structures such as the hippocampus, or form thicker myelin sheaths, or are superior at neurogenesis. All or some of these may result in faster or longer lasting behavior change that can superficially be described as 'intelligence.' But this is not some non-natural inner trait called 'intelligence.' These are all very natural structures and processes that have resulted from one of the three biologically relevant selection processes: in this case, natural selection.

"Being educated people, you are certainly familiar with natural selection, and possibly somewhat familiar with operant conditioning. Unfortunately, when many people think of operant conditioning they think of the early experiments with rats pressing levers, or pigeons pecking disks, for food. Our communities notwithstanding, these people seem to believe that operant conditioning can only account for the behavior of 'lower' non-verbal organisms, and that verbal organisms require a different accounting. But verbal behavior is nonetheless behavior, and it can be accounted for in the same way as any other behavior—by finding the independent variables of which it is a function. In the 1970s, behaviorologists began to understand the operations and variables that bring about what are called 'equivalence relations.' If you are not familiar with this research I hope we can touch on it later. But the concept of equivalence relations goes a long way toward explaining what have traditionally been called 'language' and 'cognition'; and also how the functions of many stimuli can be transformed by verbal behavior."

A woman interrupted Dr. Jensen and asked, "Surely you don't believe you can account for *all* behavior at this time? For instance, do you believe you have found all of the variables that account for the complex behaviors investigated by cognitive psychologists?"

"Of course not," Traci answered. "But neither have they. Describing a phenomenon is not the same as explaining it. And inventing internal cognitive mechanisms to account for behavior is no solution at all and actually makes our job unnecessarily difficult. Just as creationist explanations of human origins hindered the search for our true origins by giving us a mythical pseudo-explanation, cognitive science is hampering our search for the natural causes of behavior. Because of this, Frazier once called cognitive science the 'creationism of psychology.'

"Frazier also pointed out that behaviorologists are in an awkward position; as scientists, we are always in the presence of the most complex phenomena that we are expected to explain. He compared it to giving a physicist of a hundred years ago a modern electronic device and saying, 'Okay, you say you have a science of electricity, explain that!' Yet this is what is expected of us. Many sciences began their early investigations into their subject matter by breaking it into small pieces, so to speak, and moving them into the laboratory for study, while we, on the other hand, are expected to explain everything about behavior at this moment in time, or else concede that such a science is not possible. Even though early physiologists, anatomists, and geneticists learned much about human physiology, anatomy, and genes by studying simpler organisms, early behaviorologists were harshly criticized for working with simple organisms in simplified environments. Some critics disparagingly and unfairly called these early studies 'rat science.' In hindsight, and with many subsequent investigations with *human* subjects, we can now clearly see that behaviorologists were on the right track after all. The same simplification tactic that was used in all of the other sciences was valid and applicable to the study of human behavior.

"But," Traci continued, "just because a science—any science—cannot yet explain *everything* within its purview does not mean that it must forego applying what it knows to be pragmatically true. Therefore we take a pragmatic approach and simply apply what works. And the application and success of the technologies produced from our science continue to bolster our overarching theory. And like the early physicists we are steadily advancing methodically and cautiously, but will not fall into the trap of trying to explain complex behavioral phenomena that are still under investigation.

"Once we have discovered the independent variables of which behavior is a lawful function, we can manipulate these variables in ways that produce beneficial behavior change. By adopting both naturalism and experimental methodology, behaviorology has steadily advanced and is producing a technology that can now be applied to help solve some very important problems of humanity. We believe this highlights the difference between the natural science of behaviorology and the non-natural discipline of psychology. Our strength derives from our science-grounded technology; that is, we have a science that tells us how to intentionally produce the very *behavior* we need for survival and happiness. One large advantage is that we can see and measure the outcomes of our technology, and continually make adjustments if necessary.

"Now," Traci continued with a conspicuously feigned sigh while looking over her reading glasses, "in case you haven't guessed, my point in mentioning all of this is that, while psychology with its often *mystical* explanations for behavior reigns *outside* of our communities, behaviorology with its natural science approach reigns *within* our communities. We see this difference as paramount to our success. You see, since many of humankind's problems involve *behavior*, and our science is telling us what independent variables must be changed in order to bring about changes in behavior, we can move ahead on solving many of these problems.

"With our rapidly expanding human population—composed of individuals who are exposed to unique, haphazard, and sometimes counterproductive contingencies—we can no longer afford to wait to apply those parts of the science we already know to be effective. For example, overconsumption, excessive procreation, pollution, violence, and so on, all involve behavior. Behaviorologists don't try to address people's 'attitudes,' 'opinions,' 'beliefs,' 'perceptions,' or 'feelings' about these things. We address the independent variables causing the actual behaviors that contribute to these problems.

"People often say they are happy with their current behavior and that they don't want to change it; that they enjoy, for instance, driving large vehicles that consume large quantities of gasoline that pollute our breathable air and contribute to climate change. Many psychologists will say that we need to change people's 'attitudes' about this, or reduce their 'apathy.' But what if I told you behaviorology could help humanity produce prosocial behavior that was incompatible with this problematic consumptive behavior *without reducing their happiness, and perhaps even enhancing it?* What if we could use our science to produce prosocial behaviors that people would enjoy just as much as their current asocial behavior? This is a win-win. It would be good for the individual, our culture, and our descendants, if all of us would behave in ways that help sustain our planetary resources, like clean air, water, and uncontaminated food—all of these are necessary for large mammals like us. This is a big promise but we believe that by working with other natural scientists, we can deliver.

"And finally, I will end by saying, since our communities are informed by behaviorology, our educational system is designed using behaviorological principles. You will witness these first hand as you tour our community, especially our formal educational centers. I would argue that even people who say they don't like the idea of being 'controlled' by a technology emanating from a science of behavior, would nevertheless want the best possible teachers, educators, and instructors to teach their children; but these best teachers, educators and instructors must be using some of the various techniques uncovered by behaviorology if they are any good at all. We didn't invent these techniques; we discovered them through behavior analysis and improved upon them.

"What many people can't seem to imagine is how our science can be used to *help* humankind. We hope to demonstrate this for you as you tour our community over the next few days. Also remember that science is only a refined set of methods for investigating a subject matter; it cannot take away something that we never had; I'm referring specifically to free will now. And it cannot control a subject matter that is capricious. But always remember, if behavior *is* truly capricious, then there is no hope; we will be destined to continue down previously traveled roads—possibly to extinction.

"Well, I will conclude on that happy note," Traci said. "I know this is a lot to digest and I sincerely hope that I have neither bored nor overwhelmed you. If I have convinced you of the importance of this science to our success, then my talk today will have served its purpose. And while I have avoided going into the actual *science* of behaviorology, we do intend to elucidate some of its important features and point out its applications as you begin to tour the community tomorrow. We can explain all of this much better as you visit different areas of Walden Two where we can show you how it has informed our methods.

"Tomorrow's breakfast will be served beginning at seven o'-clock in the dining area of the Watson Center. Previous visitors have told us that they found our meals quite satisfactory, and we think you will enjoy them too. You will find the Watson Center marked on the map of Walden Two provided to you. If you don't have one, or a copy of the itinerary for the week, please pick them up from the table at the back of the room on your way out.

"Oh, and one last thing for you to think about: One of the most asked questions about our communities is, 'Who decides what behavior to strengthen?' I will hold my answer for later, but let me hint at my response to this question: I can only say that the question is misleading. I will explain why later.

"Thank all of you for coming, and again, I hope you enjoy your stay here at Walden Two."

With this, Dr. Traci Jensen gathered her notes, nodded politely to the small audience of science journalists, reporters and writers, and left the podium.

The following morning, we would begin to take the journalists on an educational and fact-finding tour of Walden Two. Little did we know at that time that one of them was actually working for a formidable political group hoping to undermine public opinion of our communities. As things were going in the world these days, we expected as much.

2

Around 7:30 the next morning, I carried my breakfast tray to a round table in the cafeteria of the Watson Center where a few of the visiting journalists were already seated and involved in a quiet but animated discussion. The journalists were divided into two small groups of three. Traci had one group, and I the other. This was the small group I was to assist in the tour of our community. When I approached the table, one, whose eye I had caught, looked up and said pleasantly, "Good morning Dr. Burris, won't you join us?"

"Of course, thank you," I said, placing my tray on the table and sitting down, "and please, call me 'Fred.' I trust you all slept well last night? Are you finding your breakfasts satisfactory?"

"Yes to both," he answered, apparently expressing the consensus of his colleagues. "We were just remarking that this seems more elaborate than we expected from a small community, more like something we would find in a nice restaurant. I'm afraid we were expecting something a little more spartan."

"We were wondering whether these muffins were purchased locally or made here at Walden Two," said another.

"Oh yes, they are made right here by our chefs," I said. "We find them even more palatable than you do, I suspect, since we have acquired a taste for much less sodium and sugar than most people outside of our communities. And we can rest assured that they are stuffed with nutrients and fiber. Everything that we consume here is carefully thought-out and guided by the latest nutrition information. It's our chefs' job to work with our nutritionists to make healthy foods palatable; together they combine an array of nutritious ingredients with fresh spices and seasonings to produce the most agreeable flavors. I'm sorry if I sound like one of your commercials for gourmet spaghetti sauce, but kitchen chemistry is an art, like all cooking I suppose. Moreover, we rotate the various food groups and ingredients to ensure we are eating adequate varieties of nutrients, including ample amounts of fiber, of course, for good health."

"Well, *I* am impressed," said a woman bearing the nametag: "Martha Thompson." "Your breakfast selection appears to be very healthy. The cantaloupe is perfectly ripe and the soufflé is delicious. With my harried job, I'm used to grabbing a quick, often-processed, fast food breakfast. I'm quite aware that most of what I eat is not healthy for me, and I've got the waistline to prove it. Even though I've written articles about nutrition and know better, it's just too convenient!" At this point, she reached for a handful of purple grapes and began to consume them with obvious gusto.

"I am so glad you like it," I said. "That soufflé is a favorite here for many. Our chefs are not trying to produce products *to sell*. They could easily prepare food that would be 'addictive' to our members by pumping it full of artificial flavors, added salt, sugar, and fat. That, unfortunately, is what happens when conflicting interests arise in societies. One interest may be to maximize profits, and another to maximize health. We have only one concern in Walden Two. I'm afraid, however, that far too many people in society at large are addicted to unhealthy foods. Obviously, that's not at all their fault. The human genome has not changed in the last century but human waistlines have.

"Our members possess a similar genome, of course, but they don't have to fight urges deliberately created by a food industry that designs and engineers food products to addict consumers. Many of these foods are loaded with extra sugar, fat, and salt and are even engineered for texture to produce a pleasant 'mouth-feel.' It is typically only after people realize—often too late—that these food products are detrimental to their health that they try to eliminate them from their diet. And it is only when sales go down and these companies begin to lose money that they change their products to healthier versions—assuming, of course, that healthier versions are what people are willing to purchase.

"Here, good health has always been one of our highest concerns. Sales in the marketplace do not dictate our nutrition policy; nutrition science does. I'm afraid we are also witnessing what happens when cultures around the world get so large that food has to be heavily processed for distribution and increased shelf life. Our communities have returned to the tried-and-true small local organic farming and gardening; it produces a healthier effect and does not leave us at the mercy of for-profit food distributors. An added benefit is that it reduces pollution created by the transport of food. I should add that we also work with local farmers and have local exchanges."

Each of our visitors was wearing a nametag with his or her affiliated media outlet on it. The man seated to my right offered his hand saying, "Dr. Burris—excuse me—Fred, I'm Paul Johnston with *American Scientist*, to my right is Clifford Douglas from—is it *Newstime?*—and next to him is Martha Thompson with *Discover*. As I'm sure you are aware, we are science journalists for our respective magazines."

We shook hands all around.

"I've not heard of *Newstime*, Mr. Douglas. Is that a new publication?" I asked.

"Yes," he said. "Actually I write freelance, but this particular article about your communities just happens to be for this publication—I just thought it would be appropriate to add it to my nametag."

"Ah, very well," I said with a smile. "I look forward to reading your article, and yours as well," I added, looking around at the others. "We enjoy seeing how we are perceived from the outside."

"Then I will be sure to send you a copy," Clifford said. "But I gather that you have a rather low opinion of the food industry, am I correct? Many people would agree that we should respect freedom of choice. Do you agree?" he asked, sounding rather like a devil's advocate. "We believe it is the consumers' job to educate themselves about nutrition, and then purchase those products that meet their own concerns? And shouldn't we be free to choose even unhealthy foods if we so desire? What if someone simply chooses to live a short happy life, for example? Who's to say this is wrong? And if people quit purchasing a product, businesses will quit producing that product and try to produce what people want. Isn't that free market capitalism at its best? Shouldn't we each be free to purchase whatever we desire?"

"Ah yes, 'desire' and 'free choice,'"—I had heard this so many times before—"but where did that 'desire' come from?" I asked him. "Did you create your own 'desires?' Or were you subjected to advertising or perhaps given samples of products engineered in the laboratories of the food industry, specifically designed to reinforce consumption and purchasing behavior? Perhaps you were unlucky enough as a child to have parents who were uninformed of the long-term health hazards of these foods.

"We are 'free to choose' among a variety of foods here at Walden Two, Mr. Douglas, and our other communities as well, in the sense that we have a wide variety to choose from. But we can always be confident that these foods are healthy and nutritious for us. We know exactly where they came from and how they were grown. You mentioned that people should be allowed to make unhealthy choices, but remember, when people make unhealthy choices they are not just hurting themselves. Not only do our healthcare costs go up, we must also allocate resources to aid them in sickness and disease; but more importantly we would lose close friends and community members to illness or death. We do not need to settle for a short happy life; we can have a long happy life."

"That makes sense, of course; I believe I see your point," Clifford said, but then he added a little cynically, "I can see where smaller communities cannot afford to lose too many members."

The others looked a little surprised by his comment, but I brushed it aside.

At this point, several of us again visited the breakfast bar and returned with tea or coffee. In addition to black tea, Martha had replenished her plate with more fresh fruit and a piece of toast. Many people had entered and departed the dining area but we remained talking; or rather *I* remained talking; after all—they were here to write about Walden Two, and it was my job to present and explain our philosophy and cultural practices to them and their readers. Many people falsely believe that if science is used to inform cultural design it must necessarily be cold and unfeeling. Why should this be? Why couldn't science be used to inform us of ways to enhance human happiness and give us the feeling of more freedom? Science is not a monolithic *entity*, and it should not be equated with its *products*—the products of science come from its technologies. But it is the *products* of science—the spacecraft, orbiting telescopes, and particle accelerators—that most people think of when they think of science. Science should be thought of, rather, as a body of knowledge and a collection of the most effective *methods* for observing nature and finding out how it works. As such, however, it does not exist outside of the scientific repertoires of behaving people. Science is a very complex set of methodical behaviors, and its effectiveness is the very reason these scientific behaviors were selected.

As we settled down with our beverages, Paul asked, "That was a very nice talk given by Dr. Jensen yesterday. Has she been here long?"

"Yes," I said. "She was born here in Walden Two."

"She seems very bright," he added. "Was she educated here also?"

"Oh yes, but don't let that mislead you. Traci, like many others, has traveled to several of our other communities for specialized instruction. There is a lot of cross-pollination, so to speak, between our communities. She also speaks several languages fluently, including German, French, and Spanish. Recently she took a year's sabbatical and stayed in one of our communities in Belgium where she quickly added Dutch to her repertoire."

"And where exactly is that community?"

"About fifteen kilometers west of Brussels," I answered. "We have several communities in other European countries as well."

"Interesting," Paul said. "I wonder if I might get a chance to speak with Dr. Jensen at some point?"

"Oh, I'm sure of it," I replied.

I was not sure of Mr. Johnston's marital status, but I detected an interest in Traci. He was not the first. While Traci is quite amiable and engaging, she often comes across as sexually aloof.

Martha Thompson is a pleasant woman in her late 30s to early 40s. She told us she had recently divorced and had two children—ages twelve and fourteen—who were staying with their father for the week.

"I am trying to get my children to eat better," she assured us. "I noticed some young children a few tables over who were eating what appeared to me to be very healthy breakfasts. I didn't see any sugared cereals anyway," she laughed. "Could you explain how you convince your children to eat such nutritious food?"

"Oh, actually that's easy for us," I said. "They began eating well from birth and have acquired a taste for these healthy foods. Also, they have not been subjected to consumables engineered for addiction. And, once they become verbal, they are instructed in self-management techniques. This education begins very early and teaches them valuable behaviors that apply in many other areas of their lives. Then too," I added somewhat humorously, "there really are no junk foods available here for them to eat."

"Do they ask for foods they see in commercials?" she asked. "When my children were younger, they drove me crazy asking for this or that new cereal or flavored drink."

"Oh my, that must have been unpleasant for all of you," I commiserated. "Our young children do not watch commercial television. Now, our older children do watch isolated commercials, but only for instructive purposes. Modern commercials serve as good examples of the current state of the advertising industry's art of persuasion. Our older children analyze these commercials looking for principles of conditioning they have learned about in their studies in behaviorology. They have learned that the conditioning techniques used in advertising typically involve attractive models that appear to be enjoying consuming various products while pleasant or popular music plays in the background. Commercials often feature exciting or exotic places and people, or pair humor or status symbols with their products. Similar conditioning techniques are also involved in all propaganda and the children are quite good at picking this out."

"And commercials are closely targeted to their audiences," Paul added. "That targeting *itself* is a science. I recently read a book by Albert Bandura in which he stated that even some highly rated television shows were discontinued because they had captured the wrong audience for the advertisers."

"Oh, of course," I agreed. "An example of this targeting are the beer commercials designed for men—often shown during sporting events men are known to watch—depicting beautiful women appearing to be making themselves available to those men who consume a particular brand of beer. These are old and very effective techniques involving modeling and respondent conditioning. Respondent conditioning—sometimes also called, 'Pavlovian' conditioning—is the procedure of pairing a neutral stimulus with a stimulus that already elicits some response—a pleasant emotional response, for instance.

"After several pairings, the previously neutral stimulus will elicit a similar pleasant emotional response. For example, a product such as a particular brand of automobile that has been paired in commercials with various pleasant emotional stimuli will come to elicit some of these same pleasant emotions; its actually quite simple and straightforward conditioning. This is how many 'desires' are initially created by well-crafted advertisements. We believe too many unfortunate people who are exposed to these conditionings have lost their ability to make good rational choices.

"People's so-called 'desires' often arise from well-known principles of conditioning that are used for the sole benefit of these companies. You must remember, the neural mechanisms involved in conditioning undoubtedly originally evolved because they were advantageous for our ancestors in their natural environments—natural environments that did not play tricks. But unscrupulous people who understand how these function can now appropriate these neural mechanisms and behavioral processes for exploitation.

"So, after the initial 'desire' is created and people move on to sample, say, non-nutritious food products engineered in a laboratory, a sort of addiction takes effect and a pool of reliable new customers develops. People don't complain about these controls on their behavior because they are often convinced, perhaps by the advertising industry itself, that advertising is not very effective and that these advertisers are only showing us what products are available. If this were actually the case, why not just show the products without the beautiful models and music? And, of course, most of us would like to believe that we are too smart to be affected by such chicanery. Many people scoff at the brand loyalty of others while blithely adhering to their own, never asking themselves where this loyalty originated. But even when you show people the direct relationship between their exposure to advertising and their increased consumption of these products, they often attribute the increase to other factors; no one wants to appear 'weak-minded,' you see? And the fact that we don't purchase everything we see advertised might convince us that we are in control; and this is exactly what vendors and advertisers want us to believe."

"But how effective are these commercials really?" Clifford asked. "I don't watch much television, but still, I don't feel like commercials have any effect on me at all, other than annoyance. In fact I usually mute the television during the commercials."

"I think you would be surprised," Paul said to Clifford. "There is one thing business does not do, and that is waste money on unprofitable ventures. Ventures must show demonstrable returns or business will abandon them. I agree with Dr. Burris on this."

"And the fact that businesses have been using advertising for *so many* years," I said, "attests to its effectiveness. They are in possession of the sales data and they know *exactly* how effective advertising is. It is obvious to all of us that it must be affecting *some* people, 'Just not us,' we say. Collectively, billions of dollars are spent each year in the United States—by far the largest advertising market in the world—making commercials and purchasing airtime and print space to subject viewers to them. Of course, the vendors' behavior is just as lawful as any other behavior and is maintained by the success of these practices. Though I would not be surprised to learn that *they* think of it as psychological chicanery."

"Oh yes," Paul agreed. "After all, I know they have dabbled in other techniques that were not overly effective, such as 'subliminal messaging,' where advertisers tried to obscure the message, or present it so briefly that the person was not aware that they were being conditioned. I actually wrote an article about this several years ago."

"Exactly," I said. "And advertising is ubiquitous and is squeezed into anything that people might be known to look at, including such things as roadside billboards and blimps. Advertising quickly invaded the Internet when vendors realized this was where people were spending their time, and the interactive nature of computing allowed them to insert snippets of code into home computers to track browsing habits and target potential consumers. Again we have a technology used to promote consumptive behavior.

"But what some call, sometimes pejoratively, 'techniques of *persuasion*' include aspects from some of behaviorology's areas of expertise. In fact, the advertising industry studied many of our early procedures and methods of conditioning; they then co-opted them for their own use in order to create artificial 'desires' for their various products. The advertising industry, of course, now has its own research labs, well funded by business and undoubtedly better funded than we are.

"Well then," I said, "to *our* way of thinking, this is not good for humanity in general and is not the most effective use of the 'science of persuasion.' Frazier imagined how we could best use these conditioning techniques for the benefit of *all* humankind, not just the few wielding it. You will see this theme throughout our community. We will use any effective technology if it benefits everyone. Ask yourselves what would you do if you were in possession of a science of behavior that is telling you how to arrange environmental contingencies to produce behavior to specification? Is increasing sales and profits for vendors, possibly at the expense of the health of consumers, the best use of this science?"

"Of course not," Clifford answered somewhat huffily. "But this kind of thing is the price of freedom. We can't just ban commercials or advertisements because we feel—or even *know*—they are exploitative; they are covered under the First Amendment like any speech. People don't have to look at them if they don't want to. And if these vendors have the money to waste trying to influence our buying habits, well, we don't have to like it, but that's just the way it is."

"Well, maybe that's the way it is," I said gently, "but that's not the way it has to be. While such speech may be free, it is not mandatory. Over the last several decades, behaviorologists have produced technologies that could easily be employed to improve any number of areas, such as regular and special education, child rearing, government, penal rehabilitation, the treatment of behavioral disorders, companion and service animal training, and even diplomacy. But these technologies are not being put to good use in societies around the world today. Instead, certain behavioral technologies have been usurped by the few to exploit the many.

"When the techniques of persuasion fell into the hands of private business and the public relations industry, the best thing they could think to do with them is to use them, through in-home mediums, such as radio, television, and the Internet, to sell their wares to people. Who would have dreamed that people would even tolerate commercials interpolated into a movie that was originally designed to be watched uninterrupted? These interruptions ruin the *flow* of the movie. Movies are designed to generate emotions, excitement, and anticipation that continue to build as stimuli flow from scene to scene. Commercials break the flow of stimuli and allow the emotions to dissipate. In fact they may generate counter emotions."

"But commercials pay for the expenses of the programming and airtime," Clifford said. "People can always purchase movies on a variety of mediums and watch them uninterrupted, if that's what they want."

"That's another story, but don't miss my point," I said. "Behaviorology has produced, and is still producing, very effective methods of changing behavior. And these methods can be put to good use in a variety of areas. This behavioral technology can be used to both increase humankind's happiness and improve our chances of survival as a species, but this will only happen if it is in the hands of those whose contingencies compel them to do so. We have engineered these prerequisite contingencies directly into our communities. But others can use this science as well to help reduce population growth, produce a better educated public, reduce overconsumption and increase prosocial behaviors in general while decreasing antisocial behavior of all kinds, all while increasing overall well-being, happiness, and the feeling of freedom. We are simply arguing for a better use of the technologies generated by behavioral research.

"Don't you see how we could avoid the wasteful conditioning and counterconditioning used by various private power structures?" I said. "Many modern advertising agencies have gone so far as to use the very sophisticated technologies of neural science to detect the activity of the nucleus accumbens— the acknowledged pleasure center of the brain—of volunteers to see which commercials are most effective. Here you have science used to the detriment, we believe, of the general population. Think about this, we produce a technology of behavior and then one of its biggest uses in society is to increase the consumption and overconsumption of products; consumption that benefits only businesses and their stockholders and often harms the rest of us. Here in Walden Two and our other communities we have avoided all that."

"With the widespread availability of the internet," Paul said, "people can now access information all around the world. This seems to me like a game-changer since many young people are turning to it for information. Television is practically a relic to the current generation, don't you think?"

"To a degree yes," I answered. "But don't underestimate television's power to influence. It is still an information source for many and has several channels offering programming specifically designed to attract young viewers—including cartoon channels for the very young. Commercial television still does what it was designed to do, and that is to capture audiences and sell them to advertisers, period. There are other businesses—as you alluded to earlier, Mr. Johnston—such as Nielsen's Ratings, that determine who, and from what socioeconomic group, is watching what. This provides the targeting information you spoke of. They then sell this information to advertisers so they can target sales mainly to those audiences most likely to purchase their products. You can read a history of the privatized media system in the U.S. by Robert McChesney, for example, to see how this came about."

"Oh, believe me, I have," said Paul. "And now, modern cable-boxes can track viewing behavior and gather much more accurate information for advertisers. If you engage with any modern media you should expect that your personal information and habits are being collected and distributed to other businesses for more accurate targeting."

"Of course," I agreed. "If a particular broadcast program happens to inform people, well, perhaps I may be too cynical, but I believe that would be incidental to its main purpose. Screenwriters are commissioned to produce entertaining serial programs that will keep people watching and coming back. Game shows are created where people can vicariously win money or prizes along with the guests, and movies and sporting events are shown specifically to hold the audience's attention, all while businesses interpolate advertisements designed to 'influence' potential buyers. Do you see the lost potential here and what is happening to your society?"

"I do," Clifford said somewhat indifferently. "But one gets inured to this sort of thing. Most people of any intelligence avoid all of this by searching out alternative sources of information and entertainment. But, I will admit, when I'm not re-searching or writing, I'm a television news junkie."

"Then I'm sure you are well aware that even your news programs are in the ratings system," I reminded him. "And many of your news anchors are groomed and selected for audience appeal, with advertisers now vying for this precious airtime. News must now be even more entertaining or sensational in order to attract viewers for advertisers."

"Oh, of course," he said. "That's why I often record the news and watch it later when I can fast-forward through much of it."

"I hope you don't think we are complicit in any of this," Martha said somewhat defensively. "I think I can speak for all of us in our business when I tell you that we try our best to deliver the most accurate information we can to our readers. We have spent many years learning and honing our craft and try very hard to get our facts straight. In fact, that is why we are here at Walden Two, to acquire accurate facts about it. But how our respective media bring in revenue is something we have little control over. And even *we* don't like some of the powerful conflicts of interest brought about by private and corporate ownership of the media. But you were speaking of what sounds to me like treachery in advertising; what is wrong with designing commercials that are appealing to viewers? And how are advertisers being deceptive by using these 'techniques of persuasion' as you call them?"

"A classic example of this," I said, "is the tobacco industry's use of persuasion techniques that, up until the 1970s, targeted both adults and children, to get them to first try and then hopefully—their hope anyway—become addicted to smoking. They made smoking look very appealing by using well-known actors and attractive models likely to evoke emulation, and depicted them in various pleasant environments and situations enjoying the inhalation of smoke. Not unlike the food industry now, the tobacco industry used persuasion techniques designed to get people to sample their products so later addiction would produce reliable consumers. They obfuscated the evidence of the harmful effects of smoking right up to the end, causing untold numbers of premature deaths, lung diseases, and heart diseases that destroyed countless numbers of lives, not only the lives of the smokers themselves, but also of family members who had to watch the suffering and slow demise of a loved one. When it was discovered, through recovered internal memos, that certain cigarette companies were well aware of the harmful effects of smoking, but were nevertheless deliberately genetically engineering tobacco strains with *extra* nicotine to addict more customers—those who dared sample this product—a class-action lawsuit took them into court. The only reason that the tobacco industry doesn't advertise today is not because it is illegal, as some may imagine, but because tobacco companies would have to compete with anti-smoking public service announcements that, by governmental legislation, are mandated to occur if cigarette commercials continue. This would, in effect, counteract their pro-smoking commercials, essentially costing them money."

"But that is an exception, is it not?" Clifford responded. "That product just happened to turn out to be extremely dangerous."

"Yes, but it was known to be dangerous for many years prior and this information was withheld from the public and buried by tobacco companies. It also clearly demonstrates the effectiveness of advertising; if people can be persuaded to try a product that is initially aversive—you must admit, smoke is not pleasant when first inhaled by a neophyte—they can easily be persuaded to purchase and consume food products that are *not* initially aversive; in fact they are quite pleasing because they have been engineered that way. And we now know that the excessive consumption of some of these food products can be just as dangerous as smoking."

"Do you then believe advertisers have a detrimental effect on fair and honest reporting?" Martha asked. "I have friends in other news media who tell me they have had certain report-ing curtailed at the requests of advertisers."

"Oh, I'm sure of it," Paul jumped in. "I have read of spon-sors who have threatened to withdraw their sponsorship for any number of things shown or reported on commercial tele-vision."

"I think we will all agree," I said, "that, if the media actually is the 'Fourth Estate,' as it is often called, whose purpose is to inform the public, then journalists should be schooled to the highest standards in unbiased reporting and then should not be hampered or threatened by corporate or governmental in-terest groups because of 'unfavorable' reporting. Unfortu-nately, as Mr. Johnston has just said, this is not the case. Public radio and television have each been threatened by advertisers, business, and by certain business-oriented members of Con-gress, to have their funding curtailed *even when* they were re-porting accurate information that happened to be unfavorable to business interests.

"I say '*even when* they were reporting accurate information' because if the reporting was false, businesses could either sim-ply refute it, or sue for libel. The euphemism for reporting that puts business in an unfavorable light is that the news outlet is not 'business-friendly.' This would include reporting on cor-porate crime, corruption, or malfeasance, for example. This is precisely why corporations fund *public* media: once you subsi-dize something, you can exercise control over it by threatening to defund it.

"Businesses don't have to worry about this kind of negative reporting in the privately owned 'business-friendly' corporate media. So if business doesn't directly own a particular media outlet, say, for example, PBS—the Public Broadcasting Sys-tem—it at least wants to subsidize it and thereby control its content. It can do this by directly withholding its own funding, or by having business-friendly politicians in congress—usually

those that business Political Action Committees helped elect—
threaten to withhold *government* funding also.

"To justify this, they sometimes begin by convincing their
constituents that public media is showing lewd art, or endors-
ing homosexuality, or undermining religious beliefs with science-based programming—things known to offend the values
of some conservative members of the population. In any case,
they threaten to defund public media by striking from two an-
gles, government and corporate support. This has the effect of
reducing unbiased reporting even in *public* broadcasting and
virtually guarantees the skewing of public information. Consequently, media content is often skewed toward the particular
views and interests of the sponsors.

"And what about the elephant in the room?" I asked. "In
the US, we have one popular television news outlet known to
have been created solely for the purpose of propagandizing
one particular political party's views, while discrediting all
opposing views—usually by using straw man arguments or
commissioning weak representatives for opposing arguments.
People surveyed who are 'informed' by this outlet can be
shown to hold many *demonstrably* false views on many key issues, but viewers will insist that they have not been influenced
by their exposure to it, all while repeating its talking point arguments nearly verbatim. This station's propaganda technique of presenting one view strongly and often, and the
opposing view weakly and sparingly, was so effective that
other news organizations have begun to emulate it to different
degrees. Unbiased news reporting is virtually dead in privately owned media."

Paul set his empty plate aside and sat back comfortably in
his chair, "Some corporations," he said, "have also proposed
subsidizing public shortfalls if cities will allow them to advertise
on public vehicles such as police cars, and even in school text-
books. But have you ever noticed how many *people* have become

walking billboards? They not only walk around wearing clothing with various company logos and product names, they *pay* to wear them. Who would have thought?"

"Yes," I said. "Ironically, since these people are not conspicuously coerced to do so, they *feel* free—but are they?"

"Of course they are," said Clifford. "Why should we think otherwise? If these people are not *coerced* into wearing the logos of their favorite automobile or motorcycle, or even their favorite soft drink, then they are free to do as they please. I must say, I'm not at all sure what you're driving at."

"Just this, Mr. Douglas, behavior can be controlled by techniques other than coercion," I said quite earnestly. "And much more effectively. This is what our science is telling us, and this is what we are trying to tell others. Freedom is an illusion, Mr. Douglas. The best we can do is to free ourselves from coercion and aversive forms of control. It is possible to design cultures that will accomplish this, as we have done here, but we can never free ourselves from *all* forms of control. So, first we must recognize these other controlling variables—and that is precisely what behaviorology has been doing for the last hundred years."

"How do we prevent any society from devolving into totalitarianism?" asked Paul. "I'm no longer certain that democracy alone is enough. Just look at some of the things happening around the world today. You were speaking of techniques of persuasion, Dr. Burris, what happens when these techniques are used to influence elections? I find it hard to believe it's sheer coincidence that middle and working-class people always seem to elect the very kinds of people who have been exploiting them all along."

"You have asked precisely the right question," I said. "Frazier pointed out many years ago, that the first step in a defense against tyranny is the fullest possible exposure of behavior-controlling techniques. He was speaking of all forms of control by any power structures whatsoever, which would include, of course, governments and large domestic and global corporations. But with the ascendency of nationless global corporations, I believe his advice is extremely apt here.

"You see, governments have historically used punitive control—fines, imprisonment, floggings, public executions, and so on—that are obvious forms of behavioral control. But private corporations and governments are now using not so obvious, but nonetheless effective, methods. People don't complain about these methods because they are *not* obvious and they therefore *feel* free, even when they are being exploited. This is what I was talking about earlier, and of what I hope to convince you. Who does not believe that their own beliefs and desires are self-determined and true, while those of others with whom they disagree are the result of false propaganda?

"As I alluded to before, even if you were to show people data—for instance, from pre-propaganda and post-propaganda questionnaires—demonstrating that their exposure to randomly chosen propaganda has changed their beliefs, most of them will continue to argue that it had little or no effect on them. They often say that they have *always* held these beliefs. And they *may* be telling the truth. We all hold latent contrary or contradictory beliefs to some degree. It is the job of propaganda to strengthen particular latent beliefs or predispositions that propagandists wish to manifest, while leading us to believe these beliefs originated from within us; and they certainly appear to.

"That is why we offer our courses in behaviorology to everyone, both inside and outside of our communities. We want to reveal these exploitative, manipulative controlling techniques. Everyone should have at least a high school science level appreciation of this subject, so that they can help spot and prevent misuses of this knowledge, as well as not fall victim to those misuses. Always remember that the most effective techniques of control are those that don't seem like traditional forms of control at all; that is, they are not overtly coercive and therefore we don't resist them. Nevertheless, we mainly teach our science because we want all of humanity to benefit from it; after all, it *can* be used beneficially and wisely, as in our case."

"So what's the solution?" Paul asked. "How do you convince people that they may not be as free as they thought?"

"Yes," Clifford added assuredly, "You will never convince someone like me that I do not have complete free will."

"Perhaps not," I said lightly, "but I will not give up on you just yet, Mr. Douglas. You see, our beliefs have no bearing on reality itself; the best we can hope is that our verbal statements comport with and accurately describe reality. The scientific method can only increase the accuracy of our statements about reality. Whether behavior is determined or not is an empirical question, and the evidence is steadily mounting. I do not expect you to change your long-held beliefs in one day, Mr. Douglas, but I do hope you see the value of changing them when the data warrant it. Behaviorologists recognize that many of our beliefs involve Pavlovian conditioning and language, and also what are now called 'equivalence relations' by some and 'relational frame theory' by others.

"This understanding comes from relatively new research findings in our field and is *very* relevant to language, cognition, and symbolic thinking in general. These theories are also particularly relevant to propaganda techniques. It is imperative that our science does not fall exclusively into the wrong hands; this is another reason why all people need to understand it. I often wonder how many of those people who have been critical of a science of behavior, and who have contracted emphysema or lung cancer due to smoking, would now happily trade their disease for a little educational conditioning by one of our behaviorologists.

"Incidentally, all of our community members are well trained in behavior science and the conditioning techniques used by our communities, and understand them well. We took

Frazier's admonition to heart; we fully expose all of our *own* controlling techniques too. It is not difficult for our members to determine who and what is working in their best interests. And please don't be frightened by the word 'control' as I am using it here. You are, in a very real sense, controlling my behavior right at this moment by your nods, questions, and other signs of interest; knowing this does not bother me in the least. Always remember that people are controlling each other's behavior all of the time and always have been—at least the way we are using the word. Until people become familiar with the science, they will not fully understand the processes involved; we want to remedy this."

At this point, Clifford's phone began to vibrate and he glanced at the screen before saying, "Excuse me. I know this is somewhat rude, but I must take this call. Sorry." He left the table and moved out of hearing range. I could see a distressed look on his face and he appeared to be reassuring someone of something.

I turned to the remaining journalists and returned the discussion to where we began. "To get back to our food, our desire for food here at Walden Two is not created by unaccountable special interests. By learning about food nutrition and then tasting various fresh fruits, vegetables, seeds, nuts, berries and other natural foods, prepared with spices and seasonings and cooked or baked to bring out flavors, we develop strong tastes for these healthy foods. Taste for food is acquired quite early in life—sometimes even in the womb by what the mother consumes—though it can and does change throughout one's life. I think if you ask anyone here, they will tell you that they find our food quite delicious, and don't feel like they are missing out on anything.

"With our chefs always on the lookout for new foods and flavorful, nutritious combinations for us to try and consider for adoption, we have more freedom to pursue other things since we don't have to waste time worrying whether some profit-driven business is trying to addict or poison us by adding substances later found to be harmful. Food is enjoyed here, but it is not the obsession it is for many outside of our communities. A big advantage of this is that our healthcare costs are much, much lower than in society at large. We do not have the diseases produced by obesity and overconsumption of unhealthy food products. Obesity has been associated with a metabolic syndrome that can lead to coronary artery disease, Type 2 diabetes, hypertension, and stroke. And I can assure you that we do not feel deprived of food or the pleasure of eating it; we have acquired tastes for healthy foods that are every bit as satisfying to us as, I'm sure, your foods are to you.

"Now, I realize some might argue that neither business nor government nor our behaviorologists should be using the techniques that a science of behavior has discovered to 'persuade' anyone of anything. They would prefer that we sequester this science of behavior. People often say to us, 'I don't want my behavior controlled by anyone but *me!*' But you must understand that, scientifically, that is not possible; our behavior is controlled all of the time. By 'controlled' we mean environmentally determined by the independent variables—the contingencies—that make behavior happen. Our behavior is always determined, regardless of whether we are aware of the determining variables or not. You don't have to be aware of these determining variables for them to have their effect. I insist that all of us are using controlling techniques all of the time, although most of humanity are using them intuitively and haphazardly. Why not take the time to understand what a science of behavior can tell us, learn it well, and then use it wisely to enhance human happiness?"

We had long ago finished our breakfasts and Clifford had returned appearing a little agitated. My guests appeared eager to begin their tour of the community. All, apparently, understood this, and we seemed to move in unison at this point. We stacked our plates and stood up.

"I would like to begin by showing you our children's learning environments," I said. "Just follow me this way please and we'll deposit our trays on the rack by the door on our way out. I didn't mean to be overly critical of your cultural practices; I'm sure you've heard the old saying, 'Any jackass can kick down a barn, but it takes a good carpenter to build one?' Well, please allow me to show you Walden Two."

3

We walked as a group toward our first educational des-
tination, the nursery, and sat down on a bench circum-
scribing a round table in a shaded area just outside. I wanted
to take this opportunity to explain the rudiments of operant
conditioning to my guests. They were obviously intelligent and
the nature of their occupation made them very inquisitive and
therefore receptive also. I began by describing how we take advantage of early childhood education opportunities. Indeed,
we begin rather early, when our infants are still in their aircribs.

"Education in our communities literally begins in the aircrib," I told them. "The aircrib, as you will soon see, is a temperature and humidity-controlled space where our infants sleep
mainly, but there is plenty of opportunity here for them to learn
an important lesson: that behavior produces consequences.
When certain programs are activated in the aircrib, moving or
vocalizing in particular ways will produce music, colored lights,
sounds, recorded verbal behavior, and many other consequences known to strengthen human operant behavior.

"We do not have specific behavior requirements at this age;
any acceptable operant behavior will do. 'Operant behavior,'
for those of you unfamiliar with it, is what many people refer
to as 'voluntary behavior,' as if there were an internal agent
inside each one of us volunteering the behavior freely. I believe
Dr. Jensen did a laudable job yesterday explaining our position
on this issue. We, on the other hand, call this behavior 'operant'
behavior because it is a type or class of behavior that *operates*
on the environment and produces consequences. That is, the

behavior produces a change in some of the stimuli comprising the person's immediate environment, and this stimulus change feeds back into the person's nervous system to effect a change in it. These changes to the nervous system result in changes in future behavior. The accumulations of many such changes eventually produce the complex behavior patterns comprising the repertoire of the adult. Extra-parental contingencies can change the behavior of children to such an extent that it becomes unfamiliar to parents over time, as any parent who has sent a child away to college can attest."

"How does this differ from the reflex?" Paul asked.

"Operant behavior is quite different from reflexes," I said to him. "Reflexes, often called 'respondent behavior,' as opposed to 'operant behavior,' are responses said to be *elicited* by stimuli that come *before* them, that is, by antecedent stimuli. Many people refer to respondent behavior as 'involuntary behavior.' We are all familiar with our doctor tapping on our patellar tendon and the knee jerk that follows. Note that neither the tap nor the knee jerk alone is called a reflex, it is only when both occur together that we speak of a reflex. In the case of the reflex, the stimulus change—tap—comes first, then the response—knee jerk. In contrast, a salient feature of the operant is that a stimulus change *follows* the behavior and may change the probability of that behavior occurring again.

"Operant behavior changes the environment in some way. It is also important to note that operant behavior can come to be *evoked* by antecedent stimuli; notice we don't say 'elicited' in the case of the operant. So while reflexes are *elicited* by antecedent stimuli, operant behavior can—through conditioning—come to be evoked by previously neutral antecedent stimuli. Let me give you an example of this: If a child's request for candy is typically reinforced only when a particular parent is present, say, the mother, then the child's request for candy will come under the control of this antecedent stimulus—that is, the mother. So in this case, the child's request for candy will most likely only occur when the mother is present. If requesting candy in the absence of the mother is never reinforced, let's say that the father never reinforces the request for candy, the mother alone will come to *evoke* the child's operant behavior of requesting candy. Again, it is important to understand that operant behavior is not elicited by the antecedent stimulus; it is evoked by it.

"And why is this distinction so important?" Paul asked.

"Simply because, unlike the antecedent stimuli that consistently elicit a reflex from birth, the antecedent stimuli that come to evoke operant behavior are mostly learned. It might help you to think of the antecedent stimuli of the operant as cueing the *availability* of the reinforcer. If the behavior occurs when the cue is present, the reinforcer is likely to follow the behavior. If the behavior occurs in the absence of the cue, the reinforcer is not likely to follow. Therefore it is important that our behavior comes under stimulus control of these cues. If our operant behavior was not cued by antecedent stimuli in some way, we would be wasting time and energy behaving in ways that would not produce the reinforcing consequence."

"Well, that makes perfect sense," Paul said. "If a child were to say 'candy' all day in the absence of a person to hear it. . . ."

"Yes, if this persisted, the child would probably be considered to have a behavior disorder," I said. "Cues for operant behavior are ubiquitous and are very important to successful responding. The most consistently successful responses—those most likely to produce a reinforcer—are those responses that are under good stimulus control. If you were not at this moment present as a cue for my speaking, my speaking would go unreinforced. Actually this is not quite true in this case; you see, *I* would hear myself speaking and this would have the same effect as thinking out loud; but I'm sure you get my point."

Some children were leaving the nearby education center.

Martha smiled at them and gave a little wave; they smiled and waved back. I could see the look of a mother on her face; they must have reminded her of her children when they were a bit younger. Martha turned to me and asked wistfully, "How important is the environment as opposed to genes in determining the child's personality and intelligence, Fred? Is it nature or nurture that is more important? Have behaviorologists weighed in on this issue that seems to consume some social scientists?"

"I hope to address this in good time," I said. "Of course, the short answer is that both are equally important. The body, especially the nervous system, is the substrate that is changed by experience. And nervous systems can differ from person to person. But once the nervous system has formed, environment takes over; and this is what behaviorologists study. When many people think of the environment, they are often thinking of their static surroundings, and they wonder how—if the environment is so important to learning—two people, who share the same environment—in this static-surroundings sense—can be so different.

"But it is not the static environment that effects the behavior changes we are talking about. When behaviorologists talk about environmental contingencies they are speaking of a *dynamic interaction* between behavior and environment. They are talking about an environment that changes *as a result of* operant responding. Two children can share the same environment, for example they can grow up in the same household and go to the same school, they can even be identical twins, but they can experience very different contingencies of reinforcement. For example, one child can receive much more social attention for her behavior and, as a result, learn many new behaviors that produce good things; while the other child receives little attention, remains passive, and produces few reinforcers. One of these children could even receive reinforcers non-contingently; that is, the parents could give her reinforcers without her having to do anything. They could hand-feed her, get and give things to her, and so on, essentially robbing the child of the opportunities needed for her to learn to obtain them for herself.

"This is bad parenting, and we often say these parents 'spoil' the child. As a result of these very different contingencies, the twin girls will behave very differently even though they may have genetically identical nervous systems. It is these dynamic behavior-environment interactions that shape and maintain our behavior. When you walk you change your position in the environment, when you pull on a drawer it opens, when you ask for a glass of water you receive it, when you turn on a faucet, water comes out. It is the consequences of these behaviors that select, strengthen and maintain them. If these consequences cease to follow the behaviors, the behaviors eventually also cease to occur; we call this last process 'extinction.'"

"When you speak of *reinforcers*, or more specifically, *positive reinforcers*, may we assume you are talking about the strengthening effect some consequences have on behavior?" Martha asked. "I recall from one of my courses in psychology that a positive reinforcer that follows operant behavior will cause that behavior to increase in frequency."

"That is correct," I said. "Although if the behavior is already occurring frequently due to a history of reinforcement, the reinforcer may just maintain the response at its current rate."

"Then negative reinforcement must be the opposite?" she enquired. "It must be the same as punishment, right? I never quite understood this."

"This is a common mistake, even among psychologists," I said. "But to 'reinforce' means 'to *strengthen*'; a negative reinforcer *strengthens* the behavior that either removes it, or mitigates it. When you step outside into the painful bright sunlight, you are likely to squint and turn away, or shield your eyes with your hand, or put on dark sunglasses. These operant behaviors of squinting, shielding, or putting on sunglasses *mitigate* the brightness of the sunlight. Therefore we say that the reduction in brightness *nega-*

tively reinforces the behavior of putting on sunglasses, squinting, and so on. Notice that we are reducing or subtracting some aversive stimulus; you are therefore more likely to put on sunglasses the next time you enter bright sunlight, and the operant behavior of putting on sunglasses is what is reinforced. The 'negative' in 'negative reinforcement' refers to the *subtraction* or reduction of stimuli—behaviorologists therefore sometimes call it 'subtracted' reinforcement in an attempt to make this even clearer. The important point to remember is that it too *strengthens* behavior."

"And do behaviorologists have a new name for *positive* reinforcement?" she asked.

"Yes. 'Added' reinforcement, of course. Because these reinforcers increase the frequency of—or maintain the current rate of—the associated operant behavior when these stimuli are *added* to one's environment. For example, you may turn up the volume of your stereo when your favorite song is playing; you are adding or increasing stimuli; and the increased intensity of your favorite song will reinforce the operant behavior of turning the dial."

"And I recall that punishment is defined by the fact that some stimuli reduce the frequency of the behavior they follow," Martha said confidently. "I and most of us learned firsthand about punishment from our parents in our childhood," she added with a smile.

"Yes," I said. "And just as there are two kinds of reinforcers, there are also two kinds of punishers. In this case, and in contrast to reinforcers, both kinds of punishment *reduce* the frequency of operant behavior. There are aversive stimuli that are *added* following some operant, such as a slap or frown, and there are stimuli that are *subtracted* following some operant, such as removing a toy from a wayward child. These are called 'added punishers' and 'subtracted punishers' respectively."

Clifford sat silently. He seemed to be a little nervous and distracted. I was not sure what he was thinking about but, while he did seem to be listening, he didn't seem particularly interested in our discussion. At least the others, being good science journalists, wanted to learn more about the science behind our communities. I expected nothing less from them and I was doing my best to inform them. A common problem upon first meeting others is that one doesn't know their personal history and therefore it takes a while to determine how much they already know about a topic and how quickly they learn. I was used to people here at Walden Two who, because of their conditioning histories, unabashedly ask pertinent questions that would evoke the answers they need in order to respond appropriately.

At this point, a small girl around six or seven approached us. She paused for a moment, looking quickly at each of us to make sure no one was at that moment speaking, before saying, "Hello!"

"Hello, Abigail!" I said. "Folks I would like you to meet Abigail, she is one of the young students here at the school."

Everyone said hello. Martha adopted her "motherly" expression again.

"Are you helping Ms. Graves today?" I asked.

"Yes, Dr. Burris, Ms. Graves wanted me to ask you if you would be bringing your guests into the classroom before the end of our school day. We could see you outside of the classroom window," she explained.

"Please thank Ms. Graves for me, but tell her we will be visiting the nursery first. And thank *you*, Abigail."

"I will tell her," she said as she was turning away; then she stopped abruptly and turned back to the journalists, saying, "Goodbye, it was nice meeting all of you." She then walked a few meters and disappeared through the classroom door.

"What a lovely child," Martha said. "Just adorable. And so polite."

"Isn't she?" I agreed. "All of our children are equally polite. But we must give much credit to our contingency managers and educators."

Paul gave me a concerned look. "You have mentioned 'contingencies' and 'contingencies of reinforcement' several times. Could you define precisely what you mean by this so we can better understand this concept? I have heard this expression before but am not sure I understand exactly what is meant by it. I gather this concept is vital to fully understanding your communities?"

"Yes, certainly," I said. "And don't feel bad, many people have trouble with this concept. While it is one of the most important causes of behavior, actually it is not that difficult to understand. A *contingent* relation is the same as a *dependent* relation. If an open drawer *depends* on one pulling on it in just the right way, then this is another way to say that an open drawer is *contingent* on the behavior of pulling on it in just the right way. That is, the drawer will not open unless one pulls on it properly. Many desirable outcomes—those I have been calling 'added' or 'positive' reinforcers—will not happen unless we operate upon our environment in particular ways. Outcomes such as open doors, water coming from a faucet, clothes folded and arranged neatly in drawers, perfectly cooked and seasoned soup, are all contingent on particular behaviors that produce these things. So if one were to ask, 'What behavior does an open drawer *depend* upon' or, equivalently, 'what behavior is an open drawer *contingent* upon?' one would say 'pulling outward on the handle of the drawer'; because pulling outward on the drawer handle is the operant behavior that produces the open drawer—it depends, or is *contingent*, upon the behavior of pulling.

"Imagine all of the things that you would like to happen in a day. For example, perhaps you want your laundry cleaned and folded, or you want dinner prepared and on the table; these things just don't magically happen; their occurrence or production is dependent—again, we say 'contingent'—upon certain operant behaviors that must occur if these things are to come about. And the expression 'contingencies of reinforcement' just implies that there are, in general, many contingent relations between reinforcing outcomes and the operant behaviors that produce them; that is, the outcomes will not occur unless the behaviors occur. These are additional examples of the dynamic interactions between behavior and the environment. Perhaps now you can see that it is the environmental consequences that select and maintain our operant behavior. *We* do not select the behavior that will open a particular drawer; the mechanics of the drawer select the behavior that will open it.

"But I should also point out that there are often many physically *dissimilar* operant responses that will produce the same consequence; there are many ways to open a drawer, for example, including using one's left hand, right hand, foot or teeth. We can even ask someone else to open the drawer for us. And as I mentioned before, we may squint, shield our eyes with our hand, or put on dark sunglasses to mitigate the bright sunlight. Notice that all of these operant responses have the same outcome—for example, reducing the bright sunlight. Since these topographically *dissimilar* behaviors can produce the same *outcome*, we do not define an operant by its form, but rather by its function—that is, by a common outcome.

"Can you see how drawer-opening behavior belongs to a class of operant behaviors defined by a common outcome? We probably never open a drawer exactly the same way each time since many dissimilar behaviors will produce an open drawer. So, operants are often better defined by their outcomes—or, again, by their *function*. Since topographically disparate operant behaviors can be functionally equivalent, we can therefore define an operant class by a common outcome. For instance, we could define one operant class as 'all those responses that open a drawer.' The important thing to remember here is that the outcomes which reinforce operant behavior would not occur without the behavior occurring—we therefore say that they are *contingent* upon the behavior. We describe all of these behavior-*dependent* relations as 'contingencies of reinforcement.' Does this help clear this expression up for you? Or not?"

"I think I'm slowly getting there," said Paul. "But how does this operant behavior differ from what we have been tradition-ally calling 'voluntary behavior'?"

"It is very different," I said. "You see, operant behavior—or we simply say 'the operant'—is selected by its consequences; that is, by the change the behavior produces in the environment. There is no homunculus of any kind inside the person's body 'volunteering' the behavior. The concept of contingen-cies of reinforcement highlights the real controlling variable—the consequence—that is reinforcing the behavior. The very expression, 'contingencies of reinforcement,' once understood, makes clear what is causing the behavior to repeat. The lexicon of behaviorology allows the scientifically educated and astute listener to quickly identify what variables are actually deter-mining the behavior of interest."

"But how can something that *follows* operant behavior strengthen it?" Clifford asked a little petulantly. "Clearly the cause is following the effect. I believe Dr. Jensen alluded to this in her talk yesterday, but I didn't understand it."

"Ah, indeed she did," I replied, a little pleased to have Clif-ford joining the conversation. "The reinforcing consequence of an operant response does not strengthen *that* particular re-sponse, but it can, and does, strengthen synapses that were in-volved in responding. Thereafter responses similar to the reinforced response are more likely to occur when the environ-mental conditions—'cues' or 'evocatives'—are similar to those present when the response was reinforced. Our neurobehav-iorologists now better understand and can describe the cascade of biochemicals that cause the remodeling and restructuring of synaptic connections between the neurons involved in a par-ticular operant behavior. In some cases genes are switched on in the neuron that will produce the proteins needed to remodel and restructure the neural connections involved in the behavior. We have always been aware of the increase in rate of responding following reinforcement, now we are actually seeing the changes in the nervous system that account for it."

Martha said, "Surely not all consequences of operant behavior have a strengthening or weakening effect upon that operant behavior, correct? I can imagine that some outcomes would be neutral; at least I know I am indifferent to many things that happen to me. And if I understand the expression 'contingencies of reinforcement' correctly, I would think that there would be stimulus changes that follow behavior that are not actually contingent on that particular behavior—*contingent* in the sense of *depending* on the behavior for their appearance. So what happens when something good happens after a response, but the response really had nothing to do with it? For instance if someone wishes for something and then gets it, would they be more inclined to wish for things? Didn't Frazier write something about this and call it superstitious behavior?"

"He certainly did," I answered. "Some reinforcers and punishers are not actually consequences of the behavior at all in the sense of being actually *produced* by the behavior; but they can nevertheless still strengthen or weaken that behavior; you understand, I hope, when I say that behavior is strengthened or weakened, I'm talking about an increase or decrease in the *frequency* of responding. We call stimuli that strengthen or weaken responses but were not caused by them, 'coincidental reinforcers,' or 'coincidental punishers,' respectively.

"An example of a coincidental reinforcer would be looking down and finding money on the ground; your looking down did not *cause* the money to be there; it was already there. Your looking down coincided with seeing it, even though looking down did not *produce* it. But you may begin to look down more often for some time because of this coincidence. The fact that seeing the money caused this behavior to increase meets the criterion for defining money as a reinforcer.

"This is quite different from the behavior of pulling on a drawer and having it open; here the operant behavior of pulling did produce the consequence of the open drawer—due to the mechanics of how drawers work—and is therefore a direct consequence of the behavior of pulling. To eliminate confusion, we can call all stimuli that immediately follow responses, 'postcedents.' This is in contrast to antecedent stimuli that precede responses. Postcedent stimuli may or may not be an actual *consequence* of the behavior; they may simply be coincidental, for instance. Antecedent and postcedent stimuli together comprise the context of behavior, and this context is what elicits, evokes, and reinforces or punishes behavior.

"Once again, in the case of the drawer, we say that the consequence is *contingent* on the behavior. That is, the consequence—the open drawer—*depends* upon the behavior; the drawer would not open without our pulling on it. Therefore, just as in evolutionary theory, behaviorologists have proposed a selection process as *the* causal mechanism in operant behavior. It is a selectionist theory of behavior. Just as those genes producing physical characteristics having survival value were selected, those behaviors that obtain food and water and avoid harm are *selected by consequences*. If you *push* on a drawer, or pull *up* on it rather than pulling out, the desired consequence of an open drawer will not follow; only the pulling out will produce the desired consequence of the open drawer; of all of the possible behaviors, pulling is the behavior that is selected by the consequence. It is important to note that *you* do not select this behavior for reinforcement, the environment does."

"If the environment selects behavior, where did the behavior come from in the first place?" Clifford asked. "Were we born with some of these 'operants,' as you call them? Or do they just appear?"

"I'm glad you asked that, Mr. Douglas," I answered. "Many people have asked that same question, and it is a good one: If operant behavior is not present at birth, what is its origin or provenance? Part of the answer to this again comes from the early work of T.E. Frazier. Casual observation of the behavior of any newborn will show that infants—of any species—will exhibit undifferentiated random movements. The infant's arms and legs will go this way and that, and the infant will jerk and cry and turn.

"Frazier found he could 'shape' new operant behavior from such undifferentiated movements. If his subject was fairly motionless, he may begin by reinforcing any movement in general in order to get the subject moving; you have to have some behavior occurring, you see, in order to begin further selection. Once his subject began to move he could reinforce those movements that more closely approximated the behavior he wanted. He would watch closely for responses that were necessary components of the final behavior he wanted to produce. Once these components became frequent, he withheld reinforcement until closer approximations appeared. And by continuing this procedure of successively reinforcing responses that more closely approximated the behavior he wanted, he discovered that he could produce novel behavior through careful selection.

"Frazier compared this procedure to a sculptor shaping a lump of clay into a work of art. The sculptor begins with an undifferentiated lump of clay. He may know what he wants the finished product to look like, say, the figure of a horse, for example, and begins gradually removing, adding, and shaping the clay until he shapes it into that final product. Analogously, a behaviorologist must begin with the existing responses of an organism and selectively reinforce only those responses that are components of the final behavior. For example, if Frazier wanted a pigeon to turn in a counter-clockwise circle he would first select any movement of the pigeon's head to the left for reinforcement with food. Once these movements became frequent, he would withhold reinforcement until the bird turned its head further, perhaps moving more of the upper body. He would then reinforce these more drastic turns to the left with food. Once these responses became frequent he may watch the feet and reinforce movements of the feet that turn the bird to the left. He would continue this 'shaping' until the bird turned a complete counter-clockwise circle. This shaping process has been demonstrated in all organisms that exhibit operant behavior.

"That reminds me of selective breeding in a way," Paul observed.

"It does," I agreed. "Their familiarity with selective breeding allowed Darwin and others to understand how physical characteristics could have been selected by their survival value. And behavior shaping allows us to see how successful behavior during the lifetime of an organism can be selected for similar reasons. I hope to give you a small demonstration of 'shaping' in the nursery. Even though the immature nervous systems of our very young infants are still developing, we can nevertheless shape *some* operant behavior, just don't expect to see the infant tap dancing."

He did not look up, but I saw a flicker of a grin cross Clifford's face.

An hour had passed since we first sat down and the sun was now lighting the table at which we were sitting. I looked at a sundial built into the middle of our table; it was designed and constructed by some of our older children. There are many different designs; some of the dials are horizontal, and others vertical. Several are in other orientations. There are many of these around the community and they add a touch of nostalgia for cultures past. They are instructive in helping the children understand the implications of the tilt of the earth on its axis, its rotation, the movement of the earth around the sun, and the latitude of our community. Their construction involves trigonometry and a good deal of craftsmanship. Some are on median time, while others are on local time and clearly marked as such. The shadow of the style told me it was a good time to enter the nursery.

4

Itook my guests through our nursery and showed them the aircribs I had spoken of, while explaining their function. Clifford immediately took out his cell phone and began taking pictures and video of the occupied aircribs.

"I'm sure you have read about our aircribs," I began. "They were originally designed by Frazier, but we have updated them significantly. We have added many interesting features that I will explain in a moment, but if you are not familiar with them, let me explain what they are and what they are not. First, what they are not: they are not experimental operant conditioning chambers, as many people seem to believe. We are *not* experimenting on our children, but we *are* applying known principles of learning."

We walked slowly through the nursery so my guests could view some of our infants in the occupied aircribs. Most cribs were empty at this time. We stopped now and then so they could examine them and see how they operated. Occasionally, colored lights would come on and go off and musical tunes would play in the occupied cribs. A few of the new mothers were nearby nursing their infants.

"I take it, these are the mothers," Martha asked, indicating the nursing women.

"For the most part, yes," I answered. "Parents are free to work in the nursery if they choose but this is not required of them. We like to have our mothers breast-feed if possible, both for good health and human bonding, but if for some reason they can't, we use bottles with their breast milk or, if this is not possible, we use donor milk."

I allowed our guests to observe all of this in silence before explaining the functions of the aircrib.

"What these are, essentially, are temperature-controlled sleeping chambers that keep the infant's immediate environment within an auspicious range of temperature, humidity, noise, and comfort. They permit the infant to wear a diaper only and therefore blankets are really unnecessary. They are comparable to most infant-cribs except they are enclosed by unbreakable glass on all four sides and are equipped with touch controls that operate various functions. The glass is a combination of 'smart glass' that can be made opaque if the outside light is too bright, and LCD glass that, like any computer screen, can also display images. The aircribs have sounds, mobiles, and lights of various colors that are computer controlled and behavior actuated. There is a computer screen on the ceiling of the crib, visible to an infant lying in the supine position, which displays interesting geometrical patterns and visual images contingent on certain behaviors. Once some operant behavior reliably emerges, it can then be selected by us to summon a caregiver for feeding, holding, diaper changes, removal for playtime, or anything else the infant may need or want."

"What does the infant actually have to *do* to get something to happen?" Paul asked. "Or should I ask, 'What are the contingencies?'" he added with a wry smile.

"Very good!" I said, quite pleased with Paul's progress. "This is actually the first environment that introduces engineered contingencies to the infants. At first, the behaviors can be anything from simple movements of limbs, to contact with, or movement of, various pliable manipulanda that are available to the infant. We especially look for non-crying verbal 'coos' and vocalizations that approximate human speech sounds. We want them to learn that these behaviors can produce good things, and that parts of the environment are under their control. We have found that when an infant can reliably produce favorable consequences with acceptable behaviors, unacceptable behaviors either disappear or rarely appear in the first place. And once the child can *reliably* summon a caregiver with acceptable behavior, all remaining unacceptable behaviors are deliberately extinguished; by 'extinguished' I mean these behaviors are not reinforced and they generally disappear."

I explained to my guests that behaviorologists have discovered that for operant behavior to be strengthened, it must be followed by the reinforcing consequence nearly immediately after the response to be most effective. I told them that neuroscientists have found that only those synapses that have very recently "fired" can be strengthened through the operant conditioning process.

I then continued, "All of the colored lights, sounds, geometric patterns, and changes in ambient lighting meet this immediacy requirement. Computerized motion sensors feed into a program that will activate these stimuli when particular movements are detected. These stimuli have been demonstrated experimentally to reinforce certain human operant behaviors over time. We even have the aircribs' computers programmed to 'shape' behavior—for example, into more vigorous movements.

"But the summoning of a caregiver necessarily has a lag time since it takes a few seconds to a minute or more for the caregiver to get to the aircrib. What this delay means, in essence, is that only the behavior that happens to be occurring *when the caregiver arrives* will be strongly reinforced, so this delay can cause problems; inappropriate behavior can be strengthened if the caregiver happens to arrive while the child is beginning to cry, for instance. This would be another good example of a coincidental reinforcer; we do not want to increase the frequency of annoying behavior—this is actually for the child's own good, as everyone loves to hold a happy baby.

"Fortunately, however, we can bridge the time gap with stimuli that *are* produced immediately, and these stimuli will eventually be used to strengthen the desired behavior. You can think of these as precursor, or bridging stimuli, and we can arrange for them to reliably precede the appearance of a caregiver. These bridging stimuli can be anything from a colored light, a tone, a bit of music, or some combination of these, to changes in ambient lighting. But whatever stimulus, or combination of stimuli, is chosen, will from then on exclusively precede the appearance of a caregiver; that is, they become exclusive caregiver precursors.

"Technically these bridging stimuli are called *conditioned reinforcers*, since their effectiveness as reinforcers is *conditional* upon the procedure of pairing them with other reinforcers; in this case the arrival of a caregiver. Of course, we are assuming the arrival of a caregiver is a reinforcer, and this can be easily tested. We have studied the conditions necessary to bridge this gap, and we can eventually get infants to summon their caregivers. Just like any parent, the caregiver must then try to determine why the child is summoning them. This takes a little practice. They check the baby over for any obvious problems such as a needed diaper change. If it is feeding time, they feed the infant. They may just take the baby out to hold, rock, or for playtime."

I noticed Martha avidly taking notes and looking perplexed as I was explaining the workings of the aircrib, so I stopped at this point and asked, "Does anyone have any questions?"

Martha did.

"I'm not sure I understand how an infant *this young* can learn to associate a particular light, say, with a caregiver, if it takes several minutes for him or her to appear. You talk about 'bridging stimuli' but could you give us an example of these. Won't other things have happened in this time interval that could be misconstrued by the infant as the precursor? Can you explain this procedure a little better? Also, what if the infant accidentally turns on some sound or light and can't turn it off?"

"Ah, you are very astute in your concerns. Have you studied any behaviorology?" I asked.

"Well," she replied, "you could say that; I'm sure we all read up on it a bit before coming here; and yes, I did take a one-semester course in behavior analysis in college as part of my psychology credit. This included a little lab work with small animals, and I have tried to train my cat. It was all very interesting, but I never thought at the time—rumors of your communities notwithstanding—that we would actually be applying these principles to the full design of communities. And by the way, why don't 'behavior analysts' call themselves behaviorologists? Or vice versa? It sounds to me like your philosophy of science and your scientific methodology are exactly the same."

"You were certainly taking the right courses, in our view," I said as we continued to walk slowly past several aircribs. "Behavior analysis and behaviorology are practically equivalent. Behaviorology is really just behavior analysis divorced from psychology. We share the same philosophy of behavioral science called 'radical behaviorism'—and now, by some, 'behavioral naturalism.' I might just say parenthetically that one of the defining features of that philosophy is that it regards all behavior as lawful. This includes the behavior within the skin, such as thoughts, feelings, emotions, and all internal reflexes. We have determined that these private behaviors follow the same principles of respondent and operant conditioning as our overt, or *public*, behavior.

"But, you see, problems arose when some behavior analysts wanted to keep their connection with psychology, while some of us wanted to make our rejection of metaphysical explanations for behavior more explicit and assume our place as a natural science. We believe it is imperative that other natural scientists understand that we are all speaking the same common scientific language, making it easier for us to work together to help solve humanity's problems. To do this we had to completely disassociate from psychology; Dr. Jensen alluded to this split with psychology in her talk yesterday. The reason many 'behavior analysts' remain under the psychology umbrella is mostly political and involves the benefits conferred to them by being affiliated with a well-established institution. Some of these conferred benefits involve university practices, grants, licensure and certification. If you are interested, we can discuss these in more detail later.

"Behaviorologists are, of course, adamant about maintaining their integrity as a natural science. Perhaps you have seen the cartoon drawing of a scientist working at a chalkboard filled with complex mathematics? Right in the middle of the chalkboard, between scores of equations, is written, 'Here a miracle happened'—this part in his chain of reasoning he could not explain."

"I have seen it," Paul said with a chuckle. "Very funny."

"And the very reason it is funny," I said, "is because it makes an important point: We cannot incorporate mystical solutions anywhere along the line in any scientific discipline; no matter how much scientific reasoning we do elsewhere. All of the reasoning that follows the metaphysical portion of the chain is pointless. Behaviorologists have worked with practically every species now from squid to human and the same learning principles are at work without exception, implying common ancestry. We find this continuity with other species fascinating and, as one might expect, all of the biological sciences are observing this continuity also. We homo sapiens are just super-learners. One behaviorologist has called us humans the 'marvelous learning animal.' We can play chess, read books, design buildings, airplanes, and space ships, build and program computers, make the exquisite movements of ballet, sing songs, make supercolliders that split atoms, and an astonishing panoply of other behaviors. You can think of our Walden Two communities as self-sufficient, minimally consuming and polluting, super-learning environments.

"Now, Martha, to answer your other question about how an infant this young learns to associate a particular stimulus—I believe you said a light in your example—with a caregiver. To be precise, the *infant* does not associate the light with a caregiver; *we* do, by setting up the contingency between the light and the caregiver. You see, 'to associate' means 'to put things together,' and it is *we* who put them together, not the infant. The infant's nervous system is changed by this association and will respond differently to the light in the future.

"Previously unconnected or weakly connected neurons are now 'wired together,' as they say, but the infant did not cause this to happen; the environmental contingencies did. I don't mean to be pedantic about this, but these seemingly small details highlight a major difference between behaviorology and cognitive psychology. Cognitive psychologists might claim that they are teaching *the infant* to associate the two, where we merely state the fact that it is the behaviorologist who associated them via the contingency he or she had set up between them. The difference can be profound since we are describing *what one needs to do* to produce the behavior change. We do not directly change behavior, we change the contingencies, and then the contingencies change behavior. That is why our applied efforts are technically called 'contingency engineering' instead of 'behavior engineering.'"

"And what about the infant accidentally turning on a light that it can't turn off?" Martha repeated.

"Oh yes," I said, "we have all of the stimuli set to time-out after a short duration, and these durations can be lengthened if we desire. As the infant's operant repertoire expands, we can arrange contingencies to condition the behavior that will return the stimuli to their former state—light off, for example.

And to your interesting observation about the delay in the re-inforcer: We first choose a stimulus that will impinge on the infant's sensory receptors regardless of how the infant is oriented in the crib; so, for example, we might pick a unique musical tune, or a change in ambient lighting. These can be heard or seen anywhere in the crib and it doesn't matter where the infant's eyes are oriented. This is necessary to meet the immediacy-of-the-reinforcer requirement; remember, the reinforcer must occur very soon after the response to be most effective and also to prevent an intervening response from being inadvertently reinforced. So, for example, we can begin by activating some stimulus change—say, a unique musical tune—a second or two before the arrival of a caregiver. Having the caregiver activate this musical tune immediately before approaching the infant in the aircrib will accomplish this. After several such pairings the musical tune will come to signal the arrival of a caregiver. Again, assuming the *arrival* of a caregiver is a reinforcer, the tune—being associated with the arrival—will eventually become a conditioned reinforcer and can then be used to reinforce responses. But we must eventually begin to gradually lengthen the interval of time between the onset of the musical tune and the caregiver's appearance. This is accomplished by having all caregivers remotely activate the musical tune for gradually increasing intervals of time before approaching the infant in the aircrib. They are to do this any time they need to approach the infant for any reason. After a number of such pairings of the musical tune with the caregiver, it becomes a reliable precursor to a caregiver, and also, more importantly, it becomes a conditioned reinforcer. That is, the musical tune can now also be used to reinforce some bit of operant behavior.

"We can now make the musical tune, as a conditioned reinforcer, contingent on some class of responses, say, cooing sounds of a given volume, or the pull on a suspended plastic ring; but it can be any arbitrarily chosen bit of operant behavior. From that point forward that response will produce the musical tune and a caregiver soon follows that. This whole procedure is a mixture of respondent and operant conditioning."

"And what if the chosen response does not increase as a result of being followed by the musical tune?" Clifford asked.

"Then the musical tune is simply not a reinforcer for that response," I said. "We may try another potential reinforcer for that response, or, we may choose a different response to reinforce."

"What if you do not find one?" he persisted. "What if you cannot reinforce the behavior of a particular infant?"

"Then the infant will not survive without the help of others," I answered solemnly. "Without this mechanism of reinforcement, humans and non-humans alike will not survive without intervention. They will fail to produce the necessities of life by their own efforts."

At this point, Traci Jensen entered and approached us affably.

"Good morning!" she said cheerfully. "I was just on my way to the children's educational center and wanted to swing by and say hello. Will you make it to the string quartet tomorrow, Fred? Perhaps our guests would like to attend?" she added invitingly.

"Oh, that would be wonderful!" Martha said enthusiastically. "And I want to thank you for that very informative talk you gave yesterday. Could I possibly get a copy of it for my article?"

"I'm sorry, I do not have a verbatim transcript," Traci said. "To keep my talks fresh, I only consult my notes to make sure I hit all of the important points I want to cover. But you are certainly welcome to a copy of them."

"I would like to have a copy too, Dr. Jensen," Paul added with a coy smile. "If it's not too much trouble."

"None at all," Traci answered. She showed no signs of noticing Paul's flirtation, but then Traci's demeanor was typically placid and inscrutable.

The aircribs are equipped with hand-held computer devices that can directly turn on and off various stimuli in the crib, such as colored lights and sounds. I asked Traci, who was very adept at what we call "hand-shaping behavior," to demonstrate the effects of contingent stimulus change on an infant's behavior. She said she had only a little time, but was more than happy to give a brief demonstration.

"Have you explained anything about this procedure, Fred?" she asked, and then continued before I could answer, "Well, perhaps I will just explain as I demonstrate." She removed the remote control device from a holder on the side of the aircrib. A four-month-old Asian girl was lying on her back and moving her arms and legs in a jerky fashion. The child's name, parents, and other relevant information were displayed on a small computer screen on the side of the aircrib. The child's name was Xiu Mei, which, I was told, means "beautiful plum" in Chinese.

After Dr. Jensen made a selection on the hand-held device, she pushed on a touchpad and the dark ceiling of the crib above the infant lit up with a slowly moving colorful pattern. The child froze for a moment and her eyes opened wide as she stared up at the ceiling of the crib. Then she began to vocalize as her arms and legs flailed briefly, displaying what most people would describe as excitement, interest, or happiness.

Traci explained, "You can clearly see that the stimulus change has captured the attention of this child. Now watch what happens when I turn it off."

As the ceiling of the crib went dark, the infant stopped moving, but her eyes were still fixed upon it. Traci waited a moment and then pressed on the pad to reactivate the colorful display. Again the child briefly froze and stared wide-eyed at the pattern before kicking her legs. While a child of this age is limited in its capacity to exhibit coordinated patterns of movement— most likely due to an immature nervous system—we can still select some movements for reinforcement.

"What I am going to do now," Traci explained, "is to try to get the child's left arm to raise well above her body. I will watch for movements of the left arm and then reinforce any movements that bring the arm above her body. I am arbitrarily defining a contingency; that is, I am defining what responses will produce the reinforcer—the reinforcer, in this case, is the colorful light display. I'm sure Fred has explained 'contingencies' by now, haven't you, Fred?" She gave our guests a wink, knowing full well that I most likely did. "The first contingency I will define is simply this: the colorful patterns will appear above the child if, and only if, she raises her left arm *upward.* "

Traci turned off the colorful display and we waited. After a short time the left arm moved slightly upward and Traci immediately turned on the display. More activity followed. After approximately five seconds the display was again turned off. But when the arm came back up, the pattern was activated once again. This cycle was repeated a few times until the arm-raising response became more frequent and happened more quickly after the colorful pattern was turned off.

"Now," Traci said, "I want you to observe what I am about to do. I am going to begin to wait until the left arm is raised *even higher*; notice that I am introducing a *new* contingency; I am shifting the criterion for reinforcement. The reinforcer will now be contingent on slightly *higher* arm movements. Also notice that I am reinforcing the movement on the way *up*; if I wait just a second too long the arm may be moving *down* when I deliver the reinforcer, in which case downward movements will increase in frequency.

"If this happens, I may have to return to an earlier stage in the procedure and again reinforce upward movements, even if they are not as high as some earlier movements. This whole procedure of continually changing contingencies in order to gradually shape behavior in an arbitrary direction, is called 'behavior shaping,' or simply 'shaping.' Frazier actually discovered this procedure while doing some government research for the war effort in the 1940s. He had a more colorful name for it then; he called it 'response differentiation by successive approximations,' but eventually, and more colloquially, simply called it 'shaping.'"

Traci continued selecting more and more vigorous upward arm movements for the delivery of the reinforcer until the child was reliably raising her left arm high above her body. This whole shaping episode took place within ten minutes.

"You might be tempted to say that *the child has learned* to move her arm in order to turn on the display—but you would be going beyond the facts," Traci said. "We need not postulate an internal learner to account for this behavior. You witnessed the contingencies that brought this behavior into existence, and they were outside of the child, in the environment. You have witnessed the shaping of a very simple motor response in an infant. The contingencies we arrange in our teaching environments for older children are, of course, much more complex and involve the kind of behavior many people call 'cognition.' I'm sure Fred can explain the procedures that bring about this behavior as well as anyone. I really must be going now, but I hope to rejoin you later this evening. Good day."

She placed the remote control device back in its holder, was well thanked for her demonstration, and she departed as abruptly as she entered.

"Verbal behavior can be shaped in a similar manner," I told my guests after Traci had left. "Parents do not wait until their child enunciates a word perfectly before delivering a reinforcer. Instead, a shaping procedure similar to the one in Dr. Jensen's demonstration is used. If a parent did not give a child a cookie until the child said 'cookie' perfectly, the parent would have a long wait indeed. Typically the parent enunciates a word like 'cookie,' and then gives the child a small piece of cookie for vocalizations that approximate that word.

"It may be necessary at first to reinforce *any* vocalization the child makes. Later, something like 'cuh' may occur and be reinforced. The parent usually repeats the word, and then may require a closer approximation before delivering another piece of the cookie. As closer approximations increase in frequency, the parent may withhold the reinforcer until even closer approximations appear before delivering the reinforcer. We can build a basic echoic repertoire by a similar procedure. We usually say a word and reinforce rough approximations to it; we then repeat the word and withhold the reinforcer until even closer approximations appear before delivering it. An echoic repertoire is slowly built up until the child can echo the many different phonemes made within a given verbal community, then many different morphemes and *words*.

"It is important to note that the parent's reinforcer-delivering behavior is also shaped by its successes in conditioning the child's behavior. There is always reciprocal control in social interactions. The parent's behavior-shaping procedure is also being shaped by its effectiveness on the child's behavior, just as Dr. Jensen's behavior was being selected by its effectiveness in shaping Xiu Mei's.

"The reinforcer-delivering behavior of all effective teachers and parents has been shaped by their successes in shaping behavior in this way. An effective teacher is one who knows when to deliver the reinforcer and when to withhold it. If a parent tries to increase the behavior too quickly, before earlier responses have been strengthened adequately, earlier approximations will extinguish due to lack of reinforcement. The parent may need to recapture the behavior by reinforcing earlier approximations again before moving on. A good 'behavior shaper' will keep the behavior moving in one direction, so to speak, without having to recapture it.

"I won't go into the details, but there is a higher-order class that involves moving behavior in a certain direction or intensity.

In other words, we can essentially reinforce *increasing intensity* itself. With speech recognition software, we can actually program our computers to shape various vocalizations into acceptable speech; by this I mean speech that will eventually be reinforced by one's verbal community. All of our aircribs are equipped with speech or parts-of-speech recognition software. When turned on, this software will activate various stimulus changes contingent upon these sound patterns. The software is also programmed to reinforce this behavior on different schedules of reinforcement. For example, the reinforcer may be contingent on several separate short vocalizations, or on one sustained vocalization."

"I don't know," Martha said doubtfully. "All of this seems a little too contrived and cold to me. Do you take them out to hold and play often?"

"Of course we do," I said amiably, understanding her concern. "We want to socialize them early and let them learn that people are warm and caring. We want close human bonds to form between the children and ourselves. We cannot just let these bonds form by accident. Good parents and teachers often can, and do, socialize a child; but we now know much more about this process and precisely what contingencies will bring about socialization. We cannot afford to let this happen by accident. Our children are our next generation and our highest priority. A culture must transmit itself to the next generation or perish as a culture.

"This transmission is what our communities do best. We do not want our children to become loners and behave in selfish ways, we want them to socialize and cooperate with others. Everything we do with children demonstrates our care and concern for their welfare. Contact with many warm and caring caregivers produces a more social infant. As I mentioned, these aircribs are mainly for sleeping and comfort, but in addition they teach the infant that they have some control over their nonsocial environment. Once we begin seeing reliable operant be-havior emerging, that is, once they can turn on and off various stimuli and summon caregivers in acceptable ways, we consider introducing them to more complex learning environments."

Martha smiled and appeared at least slightly satisfied with my answer. Many books have been written by pediatricians and psychologists willing to give childrearing advice, but when people think that childrearing practices are informed by sci-ence and may be too effective, they balk. Many children from wealthy families are raised by nannies and later sent off to boarding school to get the best education that money can buy. And a special class of tutors—those who understand the edu-cation necessary for royalty—tutor royal children. However, when we use added—what used to be called "positive"—rein-forcement in the most effective way possible to educate *our* chil-dren, people seem concerned. Unfortunately, methods informed by science do not seem "natural" to many people, as if science itself was not a natural product of human behavior.

"As you can see, we have about a hundred aircribs outfitted with these computers," I said, concluding our visit to the nurs-ery. "Now, if you will, please follow me across the hallway to the children's educational center."

We left the nursery and headed to the educational center.

5

Once in the children's educational center, our guests immediately wanted to know how our children compare academically with the children outside of Walden Two. This is a common question, and the only answer I can give them is how our children's standardized tests scores compare with children outside of our communities. We would not normally administer standardized tests in any of our communities, but some states in the U.S. have mandated that all children in the state meet that state's educational criteria. Where these tests are mandated, our children's standardized test scores are consistently shifted toward the upper end of the general population's normal curve.

As we approached the learning center, I offered the following opening comments:

"The education of all of our children relies on the best, most scientifically grounded teaching procedures available. These include, but are not limited to, *programmed instruction* developed by Frazier, *personalized system instruction* developed by Fred Keller, and what we call *precision teaching* developed by Ogden Lindsley. I will briefly explain some of these as we continue our tour. An enormous advantage to a learning community like Walden Two—and that, in essence, is what Walden Two is, a learning environment—is that we don't have to undo what poor parenting skills have wrought. Some parent-child interactions are notoriously appalling, and even many 'good' parents leave too much to accidental contingencies, often 'spoiling' the child by reinforcing unwanted behavior with coincidental reinforcers.

"Too many children enter into public schools with behavioral deficits; they do not have the prerequisite behaviors necessary for learning in that environment. These behaviors include good listening skills, being able to sit quietly and follow instructions, the dexterity needed to use writing or drawing implements, and so on. Other children enter the school system with maladaptive behaviors such as hitting others, talking at inappropriate times, showing off, and other offensive behaviors.

"Therefore, much time is wasted in public schools trying to undo what poor parenting has done, and in teaching the basic prerequisite behaviors that should have been in the child's repertoire before the child entered the school system. By the time a child starts school, for instance, attention, approval, and signs of success should already be well-established conditioned reinforcers. These are behaviors that could have easily been inculcated into the child's repertoire by anyone familiar with the rudiments of behaviorology. These basic skills are shaped early and consistently in all of our communities, and the transition from infancy to adolescence to adulthood is seamless."

"Do any of your children have learning disabilities?" Martha asked as we entered the learning center. "Autism, for example?"

Clifford Douglas looked up with interest. I wondered if he might have a child with autism, or knew someone close to him who did.

"Permanent learning disabilities are very rare among our children," I explained. "This is because we catch the few outliers that do occur very early and correct them with remedial contingencies known to be most effective. Many psychologists have usurped the techniques developed by behaviorological scientists and practitioners. Sadly, they have watered down our explicit terminology, but our techniques are much more effective than anything they have come up with from their non-natural science perspective. Several of our communities are certified in the treatment of autism spectrum disorders and offer services to parents with autistic children outside of our communities. We work with the parents of these children and teach them procedures that have proved to be very effective in overcoming or significantly mitigating this condition. Currently these procedures are effective in about 90 percent of cases."

As we walked around the learning center I pointed out the children's personal workstations. These are individualized depending on the child's interests, and they contain materials consistent with their personalized curriculum.

"Once our children leave the aircrib, they move on to these learning environments. This may begin as early as age two or three. As you can see, these environments are designed for the younger children; everything is scaled to their size, and interesting materials are available for them that engage all of their senses. If you look around carefully, you will notice that it is very safe, and there is nothing here that our children cannot interact with. Each child is allowed to explore the materials in these environments and our teachers demonstrate their use. Some materials are designed to teach very young children manual dexterity skills such as spooning a sand-like substance from one container to another, or manipulation skills such as sequencing, stacking and categorizing various age-appropriate objects. The young children placed in these environments are learning to discern the properties of the physical environment.

"What young children are learning at this age are the behaviors we take for granted and often forget we had to learn, such as making contact with the environment and manipulating it. They are provided with various materials that require progressively more complex coordinated responses to manipulate. When they become proficient working with the easier tasks they are offered more complex tasks that are slightly more challenging. At no time are they offered tasks they are not ready for. This exemplifies the gradual shaping procedure that Dr. Jensen demonstrated for you earlier, but rather than Dr. Jensen shaping the behavior, the natural environment is selecting it; we are simply providing learning tasks to the child in a systematic order of complexity. These are, of course, the same kinds of behaviors that children learn everywhere, but often haphazardly. Our arrangements here enable this learning to occur in a much more scientifically grounded, systematic fashion."

"This sounds like the kind of stage-learning that Piaget studied," Paul said. "Do you find that you must wait for some of the children to mature before they move into these environments?"

"Piaget made too much of stages of learning," I answered. "His concepts were nicely descriptive, but not explanatory. We must all learn behaviors in the order of their complexity. We must stand before we walk, and walk before we run. But why say we are going through stages? By pouring a liquid from a short fat container into a tall thin one and asking children which container has more liquid, Piaget concluded that children of a given age do not have a sense of 'conservation of volume,' since they often choose the higher liquid level in the tall thin container instead of saying they have exactly the same amount.

"Behaviorologists understand that the child's response of saying 'more' to the higher liquid level is a verbal response— we call this type of response a 'tact'—that is under the control of just one property of a complex stimulus. The child has learned to say 'bigger' or 'more' to objects that are higher, since in many cases this property does accurately reflect 'more.' The fact that the child must learn to tact many simpler objects and the relationships between them, before he or she can tact the more complex concept of amount per se, is not surprising to behaviorologists; it is expected. I'm sorry—a 'tact' is one of our technical terms for a class of verbal behavior."

"Could you briefly explain your conception of language?" Martha asked. "I would like to better understand how you account for language and cognition so I can address this in my articles. Do you not believe that we generate our own speech? I mean, do you believe that even our *use of language* is determined environmentally?" Martha asked in wonder.

I didn't really want to get into a discussion about verbal behavior at this point; after all, there was still much to see in the children's learning center. But I found myself pausing to explain the rudiments of verbal behavior as seen in the light of behaviorology. Because of its technical nature, it would be better if they would just read Frazier's book on the subject. But I was willing to give them a preliminary account of our view.

"I'm sorry I brought in a technical term here," I said. "As you may recall, Dr. Jensen said we would keep them to a minimum. In case you are interested, we offer many free online courses about verbal behavior and behaviorology. But let me just answer your query by saying that, yes, we do consider verbal behavior to be just like any other operant behavior. And behaviorologists insist that we do not *use* language; language is not a thing, it is behavior, and more specifically it is operant behavior. And like any operant behavior, it is strengthened and maintained by its consequences. As I mentioned before, one of the defining features of the philosophy of radical behaviorism, which underlies natural behavior science, is that *all* behavior is determined by similar principles, and we have found no reason to exclude *any* behavior.

"If you are interested, Frazier has written extensively on the subject and published a book called *Verbal Behavior*, a book he considered his most important work. In it he carefully defines verbal behavior and describes various categories, or classes, of verbal behavior. Like all of behaviorology's technical terms, these categories are defined by the functional relations between the behavior and the independent variables determining that behavior. When one talks about a 'mand,' 'tact,' or 'intraverbal,' a behaviorologist immediately knows, in general, what variables are determining that behavior. In other words, Frazier defined various functional categories of verbal behavior by their controlling variables. The 'tact' is just one of them and I will explain its function in just a moment.

"But I would like to take a moment at this point to mention that the linguist Noam Chomsky, whose work you may have read, attacked Frazier's book in a critical review way back in 1959. Most of his arguments were pure straw man arguments having no substance; he attributed beliefs to Frazier that Frazier never held. Nevertheless, more people have read Chomsky's review— or, more likely, have heard about it—than have read Frazier's work. This was quite unfortunate for everyone because it set back, for many years, a general acceptance of a natural science explanation of human verbal behavior. This is too often the case when people read secondary rather than primary sources.

"Chomsky himself proposed a Language Acquisition Device—a hypothetical module in the 'mind'—to account for what we call verbal behavior. Here again we see how easy it is to invent an internal explanatory fiction possessing properties commensurate with the behavior to be explained. Chomsky has also falsely claimed that behaviorology cannot explain *novel* verbal behavior or the *generativity* of 'language.' He was quite wrong about this; it can.

"Behaviorologists have found the independent variables determining verbal behavior, and they are in the environment; but no one is foolish enough to say that the bodies we inherited are irrelevant to this; we assumed this was understood. And, if it turns out that what linguists and cognitivists have been calling 'symbolic language' cannot develop in non-human organisms, it will be the behaviorologists who demonstrate this experimentally, not armchair theoretical linguists. Incidentally, behaviorological scientists have since answered Chomsky's review, and his critique was shown to be unfounded.

"Well then," I went on, picking up where I left off, "in defining the 'tact,' let me begin by repeating that we define verbal behavior just as we define any operant behavior, by its function—that is, by its controlling variables. As with any operant behavior, we must ask: What is the *context* in which the behavior is occurring? The immediate context includes the contingencies of reinforcement that select and maintain the behavior, along with the antecedent stimuli that come to evoke it, and the postcedent stimuli that determine the future probability of that behavior recurring. The 'tact' is defined by the fact that some of our verbal behavior is controlled by evocative non-verbal stimuli important to a *listener*; and typically, the listener provides social reinforcers for this verbal behavior.

"For instance, one simple example of the 'tact' is my saying 'aircrib' in the presence of an aircrib; my behavior is evoked both by the aircrib and by you as a likely audience that will respond favorably to my saying 'aircrib.' It is important for you to know what that object is called so you can write about it. The fact is, audiences similar to you in my personal history have periodically provided reinforcing social consequences—such as 'signs of interest,' nods, eye contact, and so on—when objects foreign to them evoked my verbal behavior of tacting.

"You might say my audiences have wanted to know what something was called, and maybe how it operated, and they reinforced my verbal behavior of naming and describing the operation of such objects. Again, it is the reinforcing consequences that immediately follow my verbal behavior—in this particular case the consequences are signs of attention or interest—that maintains my tacting. Linguists often think of this as 'reference,' but behaviorology's strict lexicon highlights the determining variables. All other categories of verbal behavior are defined in this way, that is, by their function."

"But clearly we do not always receive positive feedback for this kind of behavior," Martha said. "Occasionally we get no reinforcing signs of approval, or we may even get signs of disapproval, yet we continue to talk about the world—to 'tact,' as you say—even under these conditions. So is reinforcement really necessary?"

"That's true," I agreed, "we do not always receive reinforcing consequences for every response of this type of behavior, or *any* operant behavior, for that matter. In fact, it is rare to receive a reinforcer for *every* operant response. But it is not necessary to reinforce every response—intermittent reinforcement is enough. Reinforcers delivered on various intermittent schedules have been studied extensively in the laboratory and we know which are most effective for strengthening behavior. In fact, intermittent schedules make the behavior much more resistant to extinction—that is, on some schedules, the behavior will continue long after reinforcement has been discontinued completely."

"What other kinds of functional verbal categories are there?" Paul asked.

"Let me give you an example of a class of verbal behavior that mostly benefits the speaker—maybe you could see how the 'tact' mostly benefits the listener?" I asked. "A class of verbal behavior called the 'mand' is a functional unit of verbal behavior in which the verbal behavior of the speaker is reinforced by the *actions* of the listener. Typically in the mand, the speaker specifies or, in some cases, implies, the reinforcer expected from the listener. The reinforcer can be an object or an action from the listener. The speaker could say, 'Salt, please,' and receive salt as a reinforcing consequence. But the speaker could also specify specific actions from the listener in addition to the object requested. He or she could say, 'Pass the salt,' or 'Toss the salt shaker to me,' or 'Roll the salt shaker to me,' or 'Slide the salt over here,' or 'Salt my mashed potatoes please.'

"In each one of these more complex mands, the speaker is not only specifying an item—the salt—but also an action on the part of the listener. The speaker could also mand verbal behavior from the listener, as in, "Tell me what you did today," or "What is the diameter of the moon?" A bully might shout in a threatening manner, "Get out of my way!" If the person moves, he or she will undoubtedly increase the frequency of the bully's threats. Incidentally, the listener's behavior of moving out of the bully's way is reinforced by the *removal* of the bully's threat; you may remember this is called 'negative' or 'subtracted' reinforcement.

"But like any mand, threats are reinforced by the listener's response to the speaker's verbal behavior specifying the reinforcer. In all of these cases I have mentioned, the listener's compliance to these mands reinforces the speaker's verbal behavior. And just as you witnessed the environmental contingencies that shaped Xiu Mei's arm-raising behavior, our verbal behavior is similarly shaped and maintained by consequences, and then brought under stimulus control. I would hazard to say, if no one had ever responded in any way to Mr. Chomsky's verbal behavior, he would be mute to this day."

This was as far as I wanted to go into this subject with my guests, and I continued explaining our educational philosophy.

"*Now*," I said in a manner that let them know I was changing the subject, "our educational approach encourages children to learn about the natural laws of nature, and we discourage all of the 'fantasy and magical' thinking young children are so prone to. Learning factual cause-and-effect relationships, and what is 'real' versus what is 'imagined,' is critical to mastering one's environment and being effective in it. So we keep the line between the two clear. That is not to say we don't encourage 'imagination,' we do. We accept it as a behavior that enhances survival, and is especially important in creative endeavors. But we want to encourage observation and critical thinking first, during critical development of the child's foundational repertoire, and we don't feel our children are 'missing out' by being taught the natural sciences early in their education. In fact, our young students are always commenting on the fascinating observations and the causal relationships they have discovered in nature.

"Once a solid foundation in reality is achieved, our students, like those outside of Walden Two, thoroughly enjoy imagining while reading, creating stories and art, problem-solving, and playing alone or in groups. Imagining is neural behavior and can be enhanced by conditioning. Through classical—or *respondent*—conditioning, words can come to elicit 'conditioned seeing'; we call these conditioned seeing responses 'images,' of course. These images eventually come to be elicited by the words alone without the real objects present. For instance, if a parent says 'cat' many times just before the family cat is visible to the child, the word 'cat' will come to elicit the firing of some fraction of the same neurons that fire when actually seeing the cat.

"And once verbal behavior—individual words—come to elicit many conditioned seeing responses, we can whimsically combine them in ways that will elicit images of *non-existent* objects or beings. If I describe a red humanoid with horns, a pitchfork, and barbed tail, it may elicit a conditioned seeing response consistent with a nonexistent 'devil.' Much of our mythology was originally generated by conditioned seeing responses elicited by verbal behavior. There would be no mythology without verbal behavior. Of course, through the ages, artists have depicted actual images of such nonexistent entities, and now, with special effects and computer-generated imagery, or CGI, movie-makers also generate actual images of realistic-looking yet nonexistent entities."

"Dr. Burris, I notice that some of the children are working with abaci or sorobans—I've forgotten which is which." Paul said. "I even saw some rather strange looking devices. Have you found these devices actually aid in their understanding of mathematics? Or is this simply a way to give them a hands-on historical appreciation of the mathematical instruction in other cultures and times?"

"Well, a little of both," I answered. "We have found them to be extremely helpful for understanding both place-value and the various bases in mathematics. And, yes, they do also give the children an appreciation of our mathematical roots. The strange-looking abaci you observed were probably those for bases above or below ten. We have abaci suitable for working in base sixteen, for example, and this is very instructive for our young computer engineers who sometimes have to work in this base. These simple mechanical devices are easy to construct out of wood, wire, and beads, and the children seem to love the fact that they themselves can construct these mathematical devices and perform basic operations on very large numbers without pencil and paper. Also, we do not want the children to rely too heavily on computer technology.

"The same goes for the sundials you see around Walden Two. They are fun to construct and they teach our young members about latitude and the tilt and spin of the earth. And they demonstrate how time was measured in ancient cultures. This leads to discussions of the purpose of timepieces and how they were originally used to synchronize the behaviors of people and groups. Some of our sundials have been designed to give local time, and others median time—these are clearly designated on the dials; they require no batteries, of course, only sunlight. Small adjustments have to be made, of course, for the time of year, but the adjustment charts are also included on the sundials. Some of our young members have started a sort of business, making sundials and selling them on the Internet."

"Creating little capitalists, are you?" Clifford asked with a smirk.

"We have nothing against capital itself," I said, "*if* it is used as a generalized reinforcer for behavior that comports with our values. The money the children earn most often goes into outside purchasing of materials for school projects of interest to all of the children. People purchasing these sundials provide the latitudinal information of their homes and specify which sundial orientation and design they want. They can also choose among several materials, including wood, brass, and copper. Many of these are made completely out of recycled materials. The children then construct very well-crafted sundials in many different styles and orientations; once completed they are inspected and approved by their teachers before being mailed out."

"Are there other educational differences that we should note?" Paul asked. "I also saw some students using what appeared to be slide rules. Now there's another anachronistic device," he said with a laugh. "I actually taught myself how to use one when I was in high school."

"Perhaps," I said. "But it does increase the understanding and appreciation of logarithms for our young mathematicians. They can give a quick and reasonably accurate 'back-of-the-envelope' type answer for practical calculations. When more accurate calculations are required, say in engineering, we use a computer. But sometimes, at least in the planning stages, only approximate figures are needed. Much of this has been lost in the computer age. You may also note that we, along with the scientific world and other advanced cultures, exclusively use the metric system. While we work and think exclusively in metric, when dealing with measuring systems of other cultures, conversions are typically done by specialized slide rules, or computer, depending on the accuracy required.

"Another thing of special note is that we have adopted, expanded, and are experimenting with an alphabet called 'Unifon' created by Chicago economist John Malone in the 1950s. Standard spoken English has forty-four discrete sounds, currently represented over two hundred different ways, making the acquisition of reading behavior unnecessarily difficult. The English language has been estimated to be only twenty percent efficient. Unifon is an isomorphic system, meaning there is one letter for each phoneme, and one phoneme for each letter. In an expanded version of this alphabet, every possible human phoneme is represented by a unique symbol. Therefore, in Unifon, and unlike the English alphabet that has various sounds for the letter 'A,' for example 'Aye,' 'Ah,' 'uh,' etc., in Unifon, each phoneme has its own unique symbol. For instance the 'hard' A-sound is represented with a triangle while the 'ah' sound is represented by an inverted 'V.' Hence, when one sees an inverted 'V,' one exclusively makes the 'ah' sound. With this alphabet a person can read and easily spell any word without trouble, and it can be used as an aid to pronunciation when using the standard alphabet. Some of our members are transliterating various works into this alphabet—this is mostly done by computer and then checked by these members for accuracy. While it looks foreign to those not familiar with it, once the alphabet is learned it makes reading much easier. In addition, it makes computerized voice reading much easier and it also makes computer dictation and transcription software much more reliable. We have virtually eliminated reading problems such as dyslexia."

We moved into the areas designed for slightly older children and my guests appeared to be very interested in this aspect of Walden Two; I knew Martha had children of this age, so I continued in detail.

"The best place to learn is in a classroom that resembles the environment in which the behavior will eventually be evoked. The classroom is just a controlled learning environment, but we make every effort to make it resemble the 'real' world. We don't teach subjects per se, we teach our children *how to learn*, by which I mean, we teach them *how to study*. We do, of course, teach some subjects like reading and writing, for example, but immediately allow reading material appropriate to the child's level to take effect.

"For example, we may have simple written instructions that lead the child to a toy or fun activity, or explain how to operate some simple device. These are very simple instructions that will become progressively more complex as the child's repertoire expands, but they do strengthen neural connections involved in reading behavior. In most cases, these instructions specify behavior that will lead the child to surprising consequences. The 'surprising consequences' are carefully chosen because of their known reinforcing effects—the reinforcers used are typically tailored to the child. These simple instructions are examples of rule-governed behavior, and the whole sequence strengthens both reading and rule-following behavior.

"Relatively older children here are actually involved in designing their own curriculum and are given more latitude. This makes it more likely that their behavior will be reinforced since they naturally tend to choose what they like, and what they like, of course, is typically what has reinforced their behavior in the past. But their interests naturally broaden as they are exposed to more and more reinforcing material. The lessons they choose are really just vehicles to teach them *how* to study and acquire new behaviors that will produce reinforcers. They are taught techniques of memorization, *recall* strategies and analytic skills, as well as how to record and track their own progress. This 'recording and tracking' is part of what we call 'precision teaching,' one of the teaching procedures I mentioned earlier.

"We encourage our children to analyze and discuss what they have read, even if it's just a story. Our questioning and signs of interest, at first, serve as social reinforcers for reading. When we see them spending more and more time reading on their own, it is a good indication that this behavior is being reinforced intrinsically—that is, by the reading material itself—perhaps by imagery generated by the words, or by greater understanding of some subject. When reading behavior reaches this point, it may require little or no social reinforcement. But if you want to *keep* children reading you must give them books within their range of difficulty about subjects known to interest them, and not force them to read about subjects that have not yet become reinforcing.

"We know that forcing early readers to read uninteresting material causes their attention to wane and can induce daydreaming; daydreaming is a form of escape behavior that is incompatible with reading. Therefore, we are not proponents of the Great Books programs. As Frazier pointed out many years ago, to force children to read and know the contents of a few celebrated works of literature is a trivial achievement; to keep them reading for a lifetime is a great achievement. But to accomplish this requires that the reinforcers coming from the reading material be scheduled to occur at just the right time to 'hook' the reader so he or she will go on reading more and more difficult materials and continue reading for the rest of their lives.

"Just as an inveterate gambler never knows when his or her gambling behavior is going to pay off, the reader never knows when something interesting is going to happen. To strengthen the reading behavior of the very young reader and keep them reading may require that something interesting happen on every page. Eventually these reinforcers can be gradually stretched out to occur less frequently, as it often does in advanced literature for seasoned readers; thus experienced readers may read many pages before their reading behavior pays off. This is a good example of the scheduling of intermittent reinforcement I spoke of earlier.

"Virtually none of our children are shy or reticent. You must remember that we began socializing them from birth and we liberally reinforce their verbal behavior. They are respected and listened to by all of our adults, so they learn to speak up and ask questions. We make sure that acceptable verbal behavior produces favorable consequences, such as respectful attention and good verbal responses in return. This is how verbal behavior is naturally reinforced. Remember, all of our older members understand at least the basics of behaviorology, and know how to shape and maintain the verbal operants of our children. After all, they grew up mentoring and being mentored themselves, as you will witness shortly."

At this point, I led my guests into a room measuring six by ten meters in which children of around five years of age were being mentored in the basic principles of operant conditioning. The mentors of these children were adolescents somewhere around the age of fourteen. This particular day the children were learning to 'clicker-train' some puppies. Auditory clicks from small mechanical hand-held devices called 'clickers' were used as conditioned reinforcers. These simple devices make an audible and distinctive click that cannot be mistaken for other sounds in the environment. After the sound of the click is paired several times with a primary reinforcer such as a small treat or petting, the sound of the click will become a conditioned reinforcer.

This distinctive sound is ideal for reinforcing the puppy's responses, since it can be heard no matter which way the puppy's sensory receptors are oriented. One of the puppies was sitting very still and attentively watching a five-year-old girl a few meters away. Obviously this puppy had been previously conditioned to sit. When the girl called the puppy by name and told it to come, it eagerly moved forward toward her and, after several steps, the child pressed the clicker and then delivered a small homemade dog treat as a primary reinforcer. When the puppy had consumed the treat, the child petted her saying, "Good girl!" Then the young girl raised her hand with her palm facing out toward the puppy and said firmly, "Stay!" The child moved a couple of meters away from the puppy to repeat the procedure.

The mentor then said to the child, "Very good, Lisa! You gave no other cues before calling the puppy, and then after calling her, you waited until she made several steps toward you before delivering the conditioned reinforcer. You also were careful to click when the puppy was still moving." The young girl smiled with satisfaction and moved confidently to her new position. Then she noticed me and called out, "Watch, Dr. Burris, Willow comes to me every time now!" Then she sat down and remained quite still before calling again to the puppy, "Come here, Willow," and Willow moved toward her once more.

"That is very impressive, Lisa," I said. "You and Willow are *both* very good students. Keep up the good work!"

"Thank you!" she said proudly. "I think Willow likes to learn too," she added. Then she seemed to notice my guests for the first time, she gave a wave of her hand toward them, and said, "Oh, hello." She turned her attention back to the puppy again, held up her palm, and told it to stay while she moved away.

As we left the room, I said, "These children have previously had experience shaping the behavior of smaller animals such as mice in enclosed chambers; now they are learning to hand-shape the behavior of larger free-moving animals. This is, of course, the same shaping procedure that Dr. Jensen demonstrated with Xiu Mei in the nursery. But in this case, the mentor not only reinforced the young girl's behavior, she also *verbalized* to the child what she had done correctly. This is a very important part of mentoring, articulating the behaviors of the mentee that will meet the contingencies, and then formulating all of this into clear rules.

"I hope you also noticed the several conditioning procedures that were happening simultaneously. In this case, the mentor was shaping the child's behavior, just as the child was shaping the puppy's behavior. But I hope you are aware that the puppy was also shaping the child's behavior. This is common in all interlocking social interactions; there are contingencies operative for each participant. And while we may be able to specify in advance what we want both Lisa and the puppy to do, the puppy's performance will determine Lisa's behavior, which will in turn determine the mentor's behavior as well. It's a closed system."

"And who reinforces the mentor's behavior?" asked Clifford with his characteristic sarcasm. "Doesn't someone have to tell the mentor that he or she is doing a good job too?"

"Most mentors of this age," I responded, indifferent to Clifford's tone, "have reached a point where signs of successful teaching have become conditioned reinforcers—just as this young girl's behavior will eventually be shaped and maintained by its effects on the puppy's behavior. Social bonds will form between the mentor and mentee, and the obvious signs of satisfaction coming from the child's success will also reinforce the mentor's behavior. Once the child becomes proficient at shaping, the natural contingencies will take over and begin to maintain her behavior and, most importantly, will continue to select better approximations of optimal shaping techniques. But this may occasionally be supplemented with further verbal instruction, if necessary.

"We have developed symbiotic relationships with many diverse species here in our communities," I continued. "Our cats, for example, keep the rodent population in our fields down, and our sheepdogs keep our sheep together and in designated areas. But like all life here, the number of each animal species is kept carefully in check by our biologists and surgical veterinarians. The children you just saw are learning how to condition the behavior of some of our companion animals without using coercion, and these techniques will generalize to their human social relationships as well, and will also help them become good mentors themselves.

"Our young children begin working with small animals from around the age of five. What best distinguishes us humans from the other animals—apart from our complex tool making—is our verbal behavior. Our private verbal behavior—our thoughts—is also what gives us the illusion of an internal homunculus—such as a 'mind' or 'personality.' And our extra-somatic verbal behavior—that is, the collective verbal behavior that is stored outside of our bodies in books, on recordings, and in computer memory, for example—facilitates the transmission of our cultural practices.

"If you'd like, we can discuss this later when dealing with some of the relatively new models or conceptualizations of language, such as equivalence relations and relational frame theory. I can direct you to some literature and resources if you are interested. By the way, some of our behaviorologists have written very good books for the general public on these non-coercive techniques of companion animal conditioning; I can give you some references for them if you like."

We next moved back into the more traditional teaching center for the older children.

6

It has been said that heredity determines the range through which the environment can modify the organism and its behavior. As the environmental contingencies become optimal, genetics plays a more prominent role in individual differences in behavior acquisition. Each child is unique and has unique learning abilities. We, that is, teacher and child, design a curriculum that is suitable to the child's current repertoire and will move this child at his or her own pace toward mastery of the behaviors that comprise the curriculum. Moreover, the children participate in the recording of their progress on special charts called "standard celeration charts," originally designed by Ogden Lindsley in the 1960s. These charts clearly show the child's progress and children eventually record and track their own behavior without help. This is a key part of 'precision teaching.' Seeing signs of progress is an important reinforcer for a student's behavior and virtually eliminates the need for contrived reinforcers such as stars, ribbons, and prizes. We are also adamant about not comparing the accomplishments of children to each other. As we moved around the room examining the individualized study stations and some of the teaching materials, I continued my explanation of our teaching philosophy for my guests.

"By carefully and explicitly specifying the *behavior*—or, in some cases, the behavior *product*—that we expect to appear by the end of the lessons, we can determine if it meets a criterion that shows mastery. Now remember, the child works at his or her own pace, but it is important that they show mastery before moving on.

Moving children on to more complex material before they have mastered the current material is asking for later problems."

"And how do you define mastery?" Paul asked. "How do you determine whether they have met the criterion for a particular subject? And how do you decide when it is time for them to move on?"

"Our data tell us, Mr. Johnston," I answered. "And the mastery level for many subjects has been empirically determined from carefully kept records over the years. These data have shown us that children who do not meet this mastery level will most likely develop problems with more advanced material, while those who have met this level will not. We don't move children on if they have only half-mastered a subject, as is too often done in the American school system. Even if they are only having minor troubles in mathematics—say they are having trouble dealing with word problems in algebra or geometry—we do not just rate them with a grade and then move them on to more advanced material. They must get the equivalent of an 'A' rating. If it takes them a little longer than average, so be it."

"Can you give us an example of your criteria?" Martha asked.

"Certainly," I said. "We may require older children to identify artistic styles, periods, and artists, and have them correctly match an artist to a period with say, 90 percent accuracy—an accuracy they will eventually learn to calculate on their own. Or we may have them create art and music in one of these styles. The behavior must be observable, measurable and repeatable. This is not to say that some of this behavior doesn't eventually become covert, that is, it becomes the purely private neural behavior called 'thinking' or 'imagining.' But this covert behavior is typically *acquired* at the *overt* level.

"We also require that the behavior, or the behavior products, be capable of being objectively measured and evaluated by independent observers. And by specifying observable behavior that has a definite beginning and ending, we can count the responses and determine a rate of responding. The rate is an indication of fluency or 'automaticity,' and can be an extension of the criterion defining mastery. Fluency is defined as being able to exhibit the behavior to criterion without hesitation while making few or no errors, and within a specified time interval. Determining the rate of responding is also an important aspect of the feedback coming from behavior recorded on standard celeration charts.

"A student who can solve, say, twenty math problems with 100 percent accuracy will not see improvement over time if we simply measure accuracy. By timing the performance, however, the student may see improvement in performance *time*. By requiring students to be able to solve twenty two-digit multiplication problems in a set number of minutes, she can compare her performance time to her *own* previous performance time, not how she compares to others. These charts make improvement in performance conspicuous and provide feedback that reinforces a student's behavior.

"Children are also taught how to establish criteria that define mastery. They will eventually be learning new behaviors on their own, and they must be able to establish their own criteria for mastery. They are taught how to break a subject into small units, how to make their own study aids with which to practice, such as flashcards, and how to periodically stop and think about what they have just studied—to make sure they can recall it and put it in their own words—and how to remember material or behaviors by periodically probing themselves at random intervals to evoke the newly acquired verbal or motor behavior. We discourage them from going back to the material too quickly if they can't immediately remember something they have learned, at least not before they have tried various recall techniques that we have also taught them. We have found that evoking one's own latent behavior strengthens recall."

"But will his or her self-criteria be to the same standards as those in their formal education?" Clifford asked. "I remember studying hard in college, thinking I had mastered a concept only to find that I did not meet the standards set by my professor."

"You'll just have to take my word for this, Mr. Douglas, but yes, it will be," I answered. "One of the important things our children are taught is how to establish what it means to master a subject. This is the difference between good students and bad; good students know when they have learned something well—and I don't mean this as a slight to you, Mr. Douglas, but rather to your professors. Your professors come from various backgrounds and teaching philosophies; there is little uniformity in teaching methodology coming from cognitive models of learning.

"The problem of defining mastery of a subject will be the same for any person who continues on with his or her education once they have finished with their formal education. Everyone who continues to learn, whether inside or outside of our communities, must define what it is they expect to be able to do once they have learned it. Once they have explicitly defined the behaviors they expect to see, they will know when they have learned those behaviors. This should be clear before one begins to learn new behaviors. One of the problems in many educational settings is the vagueness of the criteria resulting from putting it in mentalistic or cognitive terms.

"Teaching children how to put the to-be-learned subject in behavioral terms is a big step toward objective assessment of mastery; it makes it much easier to determine when they have met the criterion for a subject. So they must first decide what it is they expect to be able to do after they have been exposed to a subject.

"But it is useless, for example, to say, 'I want to master calculus,' or 'understand the meaning of Shakespeare's *Macbeth*,' or 'develop an appreciation for great art or music.' These descriptions of learning outcomes are too vague to be of any use. Therefore they must learn to specify which *behaviors* demonstrate 'mastery,' 'understanding,' and 'appreciation,' and then design their own customized materials that break the subject down into easily digestible units that they can study at a rate that works best for them.

"Again, our focus is not necessarily on subjects per se but on how to think, study, remember, analyze, practice, rehearse, recall, find materials suitable to one's level, and so on. These skills produce more rapid learning and therefore become an important part of their repertoires on into adulthood. Once children 'learn *how* to learn' well, they are offered a large selection of subjects to pursue in many different fields, rather like electives in college. After they experience the advantages that acquiring new behaviors confer, there is no stopping them. While we do monitor the studying behavior of the young, our goal is to allow them to study anything they are interested in. Practically any subject under the sun is available to them."

I was afraid my guests were a little overstimulated and also tired of standing, so we moved into a small teachers' lounge outside the teaching center and took a much-needed break. There were sandwiches available, along with healthy vegetable chips and fresh apples from our orchard. In the wall facing the teaching center was a large one-way glass window looking into the classroom, and we could see some of children wandering in from an outdoor recess break.

I learned from talking with the journalists that, sadly, outside of our communities, a course in behaviorology is not considered a prerequisite course for teaching; here it certainly is, for it is the most relevant and effective science for improving teaching. We believe public schools have wasted much time and money trying to improve everything except their teaching methods. Many conventional teachers are credentialed on subject matter expertise alone. The most brilliant physicist or mathematician can make a very poor professor.

Teachers outside of our communities have limited training in mostly non-behaviorological pedagogical techniques and they simply *present* the material to be learned. This teaching "strategy" assumes that the student already has a study skill set. Just presenting material is not teaching, by our definition of the word. Too many teachers just assign material to be read, or problems to be solved, and then test students to measure what was retained. They then grade on a curve and use this data to produce a distribution purported to show that they are teaching. Testing "on a curve" this way will separate student performances no matter how poorly the teacher is teaching.

But in essence these students are simply stratified by test; that is, teachers will get a normal distribution this way, but is it teaching? Or are they just testing what students can pick up from assigned materials with the skill sets they already happen to have? If all students in conventional schools were to get 100 percent of the answers correct, the tests would deliberately be made more difficult so this could not happen.

While practically all teachers want their students to learn, these teaching arrangements allow them to blame poor performance, not on these barren arrangements, but on the students' "lack of effort" or on genetic shortcomings. Outcomes for poor performers are usually final, in the sense that children rarely have a chance to go back and relearn any material they haven't truly mastered. They are simply rated on their performance and then moved on—even if that performance falls far short of mastery. Although in serious cases, a student might be held back a grade, this is an action that raises its own set of problems. While some students may learn something despite bad teaching, this is far from what can be accomplished with precision teaching methods.

In contrast to the conventional rating system, if a child in one of our communities writes an essay that contains errors, we give the essay back to the child for correction. We may say,

"See if you can find the five misspellings that are in this essay," or, in other cases, we may have the student read his or her essay to the class and let the class ask questions that the essay raises. The student can then rewrite the essay to answer these questions or to clear up misunderstandings.

We also have our children write instructions or directions for some task and let them watch others try to follow them. This way they can see where others are having difficulty following their instructions or directions, and try to clear them up. Clear writing meets criterion when people can *respond* effectively to it. This is what *demonstrates* that the writing criterion has been met. By having them find and fix their own errors, rather than having teachers just mark them incorrect, they learn to spot them by themselves much earlier in the process.

If there are too many errors, then we have failed somewhere earlier in the teaching process. We must then reassess *our* shortcomings and introduce remedial educational programs that will condition the requisite behaviors needed to remedy the deficit. This rarely happens here since we keep very close track of our children's current 'capabilities' and do not go far beyond them. Likewise, we do not compare students to each other or show special approval to those who acquire behavior more rapidly. Many conventional teachers think that comparing children's performances can be a motivating factor, that holding up some exemplary students as models will evoke emulation. And while it may for some, we have found it to be counterproductive for others.

For my guests, however, I continued with a different concern. I returned to public education outside of our communities, and after consuming our snacks and small talk, we were ready to continue.

So I began thus: "Many children in conventional schools only get results from their efforts days or weeks after responding, much too late to serve as effective reinforcement for their study behavior; remember the 'immediacy' rule I spoke of. Practices like precision teaching and programmed instruction remedy this problem.

"But before I proceed further, please let me clear up some more terminology that I think is necessary in order to give you a better understanding of our lexicon. We use the more technical word 'conditioning' rather than the informal 'learning,' primarily because 'learning' implies an internal metaphysical 'learner.' This is just another kind of mystical inner agent; therefore we say 'conditioning' because it clearly denotes the *procedures* that bring about behavior change, but without implying any non-natural variables or entities inside or outside of the person. That is, 'conditioning' clearly denotes the arrangement of *contingencies*. And when we say that someone *was or has been* 'conditioned,' we are saying that the arrangement of contingencies was effective in bringing about behavior change in this person's repertoire."

"'Conditioning' sounds so sterile," Martha said. "Can we not just say 'teaching' and 'learning'?"

"Yes, of course we can," I answered. "As long as we know precisely what we mean by these words. We often say 'conditioning' as shorthand for 'operant conditioning.' But, to be clear, our learning centers or 'teaching centers' are technically called 'conditioning centers.' I have been using the less formal word 'learning' because I suspect you are more familiar with it. Also, I know 'conditioning' has *Brave New World* connotations for many people outside of our communities—and apparently for you also, Ms. Thompson—and I hope to disabuse you of that notion.

"But I also hope you understand that *your* schools too could accurately be called 'conditioning centers' since they *must* be arranging contingencies if behavior change is occurring. From our vantage point, however, we observe that contingencies in traditional schools are too often far from optimal and, in fact, are arranged very poorly in your average school. I hope this clarification will allow you to write a more accurate account of our lexicon—a lexicon we believe leads to clear thinking about behavior concerns. From now on, I will mostly be using the more technical word 'conditioning,' and will only use 'learning' if I think its familiarity will make you more comfortable yet nothing is lost.

"Now, with that caveat out of the way, what we are teaching our children essentially—as I hope I've made clear by now—is how to acquire new behavior on their own, and how to assess this new behavior and know when she or he has met established criteria said to demonstrate mastery. This is very close to what some other researchers have called 'self-efficacy'—by which they mean learning to evaluate or discriminate the effectiveness of one's own behavior. Therefore, we don't simply teach children subjects, we teach them how to acquire new behavior and how to determine whether that behavior is effective in the environment for which it was intended. Human-made environments are changing rapidly and we must continually acquire new behaviors that will be appropriate to them. As our environments change, so must we."

Paul looked at me and said with a concerned voice, "We all seem to accept without question these days that education has become the be-all and end-all of parenting. People in many countries, not just the U.S., are pushing their children harder and harder to out-compete their cohorts in order to vie for quickly diminishing well-paying jobs. How did it come to this? It has become another example of Darwinian selection involving winners and losers. Whose genes will be successful in an increasingly cognitive world?"

"Oh, I agree with you, Paul," Martha added. "We all want our children to outperform the children of others. Isn't it ironic that to call someone's child 'average' would be taken as an insult? I can imagine if I said this to one of my friends, they would storm off in a huff! Every parent wants his or her children to be superior to other children, even though it is clearly logically impossible for all children to be above average."

"I can see that," I said, agreeing with both of them. "This is plainly the result of the competitive contingencies of capitalism. Abundant monetary reinforcers accrue to those at the top. But the real value of learning has been lost in many societies today. Children should never think that learning is only necessary in order to acquire a respectable vocation. If teaching is done properly, children will actually enjoy the learning process itself. And this is what we should strive for.

"Acquiring new behavior keeps life interesting and can provide new ways to produce reinforcers directly by one's own efforts. None of our members will ever need to work for a large corporation—or any business for that matter—in order to live. We should not have to meet the learning criteria of corporate America. American schools, especially universities—which have themselves become profitable businesses—have become training and screening tools for corporations. Unlike most schools outside of our communities, we do not want our children to work for high grades or test scores just so they may compete in an academic marketplace. We want them to acquire behavior that produces our reinforcers more directly.

"We believe all of our children, due to the contingencies we have engineered into our teaching environments, are working to their full potential, and therefore they all receive equal attention and approval. Most reinforcers that will eventually result from newly conditioned behavior will come not from our teachers or from high grades, but from the newly acquired behavior itself; the children can now do things they could not do before the conditioning took place. If they enjoy computer programming or astronomy or medicine, they will engage in behaviors that bring them into contact with these disciplines, not with money. A famous astronomer once said that he could not believe that he was being paid to do astronomy, he loved it so much, you see. Do people not yet understand that happiness and contentment come mainly from successful responding and not from material things?"

"If your children do not compete," asked Martha, "then do you find they are more inclined to help other children learn as well? I remember—and I am embarrassed to admit—that I did not want to help a good friend of mine in school for fear that she would outperform me. We were very competitive."

"Yes. Our children are actually non-competitive and enjoy teaching others the skills they have learned," I answered. "This practice is good for the entire community. Children occasionally even mentor adults; we do not find it at all demeaning to learn from the young. When I mention this to older visitors, they are often quick to admit their own children have given them computer instruction on more than one occasion, although that's about all. But typically, slightly older children mentor younger children in an apprenticeship system that continues on into adulthood.

"New repertoires also get strengthened in the mentor by this mentoring system, since it requires the child to *verbalize* what he or she has learned, and then either model the behavior or describe it to others. Mentors are taught to provide just enough cues to evoke the behavior in the mentee, and then to gradually fade out the cues. This has been shown to foster behavior acquisition and allow the mentee's new behavior to come under control of the natural stimuli that will eventually evoke it. This is the same principle involved in programmed instruction, which I will explain in a moment. Because our children are not graded on a curve, or graded at all for that matter, they need not fear that helping their fellow classmates will reduce their place on the curve.

"Academic competition in schools, in many ways, breeds a desire to see others fail, and a reluctance to help others learn.

Think of the benefits that would follow if people would just teach others what they can do. Would your plumber teach you how to plumb? Or would he be afraid of putting himself out of a job? We have found that teaching is one of the best ways to rehearse newly acquired behavior since we must remember and articulate clearly what we can do in a way that allows others to follow our verbal instruction. Mentoring also shapes up good communication skills that are important for social communities like ours. An added benefit is that it strengthens human bonding, as mentors themselves become generalized reinforcers in the process."

"How does a generalized reinforcer differ from other reinforcers?" Clifford asked.

I was beginning to notice a change in his manner. The sarcasm was diminishing, but I was not sure what had changed his behavior. It was most likely not anything I had done. I was consciously ignoring his sarcastic remarks, but there was as yet little desirable behavior to reinforce and shape—until now.

"A generalized reinforcer is a stimulus that is associated with many *different* reinforcers," I explained, making good eye contact with Clifford. "Money is a good example of a generalized reinforcer since it can be exchanged for many other reinforcers such as food, clothing, services, entertainment, and so on. Attention is another example, and the reason that most people's behavior is reinforced by it. Children, for example, do not normally receive good things from parents unless the parents are looking at, or smiling at, or paying attention to, the child in a particular way. A scowling parent usually will not provide reinforces for the child's behavior. People who show friendly signs of approval are usually those who will provide other reinforcers, either primary reinforcers, like food, or secondary reinforcers, like conversation." Clifford did not realize it, but I was showing signs of approval for his behavior at that moment.

"So how does this apply to mentoring?" Clifford asked with apparent interest. "How does a mentor *become* a generalized reinforcer?"

"Well," I said, again mostly directed to Clifford, but also looking at the others occasionally, "since mentors facilitate behavior acquisition in a mentee, the mentor is closely associated in time with the reinforcers that any new behaviors produce. Imagine a person who has just been taught to properly play some beautiful sonata passage on the piano, a passage he or she could not play well before. The mentor who taught him or her to play this passage is necessarily present when this happens, and, through respondent conditioning, he or she becomes a conditioned reinforcer.

"Remember, in *respondent* conditioning, we are always pairing *stimuli*. In this case, the mentor is being paired with the beautifully played passage, which itself is eliciting pleasant emotions. This is similar to the process that happens in advertising, where vendors' products are paired with pleasant stimuli, but here they are being paired in a good way and for the benefit of all. Now, if you will, imagine that this same mentor has cleared up a problem that has caused this mentee much consternation, maybe an intractable mathematical problem. By reducing the consternation that this problem has caused for this person, the mentor again becomes a conditioned reinforcer—*but this time due to a different outcome*; the mentor is now being paired with the diminution of aversive emotional stimuli.

"After many such *diverse* experiences with this mentor, the mentor becomes a *generalized* reinforcer—he or she has not just been associated with *one* reinforcer but with many. These are the kinds of people we want around us because good things seem to happen when they are present. Any behavior that brings us into contact with them will be reinforced. We may visit them, or call them on the phone, or go to places where they are known to go. In fact, mentors *in general* can become generalized reinforcers; that is, we can come to like or respect *all* teachers and mentors.

"But here, and in our other communities, the mentor can, and often does sooner or later, become the mentee as the roles are reversed; these relationship are interchangeable and are never hierarchical. One person may teach another how to write some tricky lines of computer code one day, while the next day the other teaches the first how to correctly finger the strings of a cello. Close bonds form in these reciprocal relationships, as each becomes a generalized reinforcer for the other. But sadly, many teachers outside of our communities who are unfamiliar with our science, and who constantly dole out criticism and other punishments, can become generalized *negative* reinforcers, inducing all kinds of escape behaviors.

"If a child has many such unfortunate experiences with teachers, teachers in general will become generalized negative reinforcers, and the child will often avoid them through truancy, dropping out, feigning illness, or even by acting up in order to be sent to a time-out area where they can escape from such teachers and the educational environment in general. So perhaps you can see how, without well-engineered contingencies, some children can 'fall through the cracks' and get further and further behind. We want all of our children to reach their full potential. You could say that they are 'Walden Two actualized,' that is, brought to their full potential by the carefully engineered contingencies that prevail in our communities."

We had finished our refreshments in the teachers' lounge and moved into an adjacent classroom that was unoccupied at the moment. While I was showing them some of the classroom materials, Paul asked, "How do you keep your children motivated to learn—and to learn on their own? My son is only five—he'll be starting first grade next year. He loves his computer and playing video games, but he does not seem to be overly interested in books. When my wife and I read to him, he is usually playing some video game as we read. When we take his computer away, he pouts."

"This has become a common problem," I said. "Video games often provide much more immediate reinforcement than events in the 'real world.' Things are quickly happening in these games that make them especially exciting. They are quite addictive, but maybe not more so than the old pinball machines, for instance. The difference may just be the compactness and portability of them, although software is designed to keep the user playing."

"Yes," added Martha, "and the parents paying for the latest software."

"Sure," Paul agreed. And then he addressed me again: "But what do you do differently? How *do* you keep your children motivated to learn?"

"First," I said, "in addition to all of the aforementioned efforts, we also teach our slightly older children what we call intellectual self-management, which involves managing the variables in our own proximate environment to evoke optimal intellectual behavior. For example, children are taught it is best to study in the same or similar places and at the same time in order to take advantage of the fact that these stimuli come to 'set the occasion' for learning over time. You could say that certain places—such as libraries or the home study—put us in the mood for studying or reading by allowing us to concentrate better. Most of these places are specialized environments designed to eliminate distracting or competing stimuli. Responses to other minor distractions in these environments—such as fans or other room noises—eventually extinguish through habituation.

"Young children are also taught to avoid or eliminate distracting stimuli such as toys or media—such as that which you mentioned, Paul—that evoke responses incompatible with studying. Some distracting stimuli can be gradually introduced later in order to foster concentration skills in distracting environments. They are taught to recognize when they are not in a good state for learning, for example if they are anxious, distracted, or tired. Moreover we teach them how to get back into a learning state, sometimes by using Progressive Neural Emotional Therapy, or PNET for short, which is a behavioral technique developed by one of our behaviorologists for reducing stress and anxiety and improving focus.

"We teach them to gather together all of the materials necessary for their lessons and to keep them within easy reach; this way, they don't have to stop to go get something, breaking their focus. The workstations that I mentioned earlier are well equipped with the most common learning aids. These include globes, dictionaries, thesauruses, computers, notepads, writing implements, and other such materials.

"The student's own standard celeration charts are hung on the walls of their stations to display their progress and provide that all-important feedback. You know, behavior weakens if it doesn't get reinforced periodically. One rarely forgets *how* to learn because this is the kind of behavioral skillset that will always be useful, that is, it will produce reinforcing consequences in the world outside of these learning environments that will last a lifetime. After all, that is the whole point of learning, is it not?

"We teach our children the importance of getting good rest in order to prepare themselves for peak studying. Of course, our food here provides optimum nutrition, and we teach our children to avoid foods, or large quantities of food, that might spike insulin and cause drowsiness. In a nutshell, we teach our children how to put themselves in the optimal condition for learning. Our children are also indirectly taught 'perseverance' by scheduling reinforcers to occur on gradually stretched variable ratio—or VR—schedules of reinforcement. This is one of the intermittent schedules I spoke of earlier. The variable ratio schedule of reinforcement produces its effects by delivering reinforcers unpredictably on a gradually *increasing* schedule of reinforcement.

"At first, reinforcement comes liberally; maybe every response is reinforced. Once responding begins to occur regularly, the reinforcer may be delivered for every other response, then, for every third or forth response on average, and so on as the schedule is gradually 'stretched' to some final average ratio. The person never 'knows' which response will be reinforced; it may be the next response, or it may be the tenth or twentieth response. But under the contingencies of this schedule, reinforcement tends to occur most often after *rapid* responding, and this is what produces the high rates.

"This variable ratio schedule is built into gambling devices such as slot machines and accounts for their effectiveness in generating high rates of responding. Just go to any casino in Las Vegas and watch people pulling levers on slot machines to witness the effects this schedule has on human operant behavior—in this case, putting coins in a slot and pulling on a lever.

"But I hasten to add that as effective as they are, the VR schedules in these gambling devices are not optimal. Behaviorologists could actually design machines that would be much more effective in extracting money from gamblers, but of course they would never do so; just as they would never help advertisers. Behaviorologists have seen in the laboratory the effects this schedule has on the behavior of many different species. It is a very powerful schedule for producing what has traditionally been called 'perseverance' or 'persistence.'

"When we observe children working diligently on their own, we can safely assume that reinforcers are being produced naturally on a variable ratio schedule, and they are left undisturbed so that these natural contingencies can select and maintain their behavior. As I mentioned, behaviorologists could easily engineer much more powerful VR schedules than those that happen more randomly. This is why it is illegal to intentionally program such a schedule into gambling devices such as slot machines."

We moved over to the workstations and I showed my guests the computers provided for the students. I explained the software that was used for the programmed instruction for the learning modules. I also told them that several of our other Walden Two communities specialize in making these programmed-instruction modules and they also write the code for the software applications that present them.

"I have heard much about programmed instruction," Martha said. "What exactly is it, and how does it work?"

"Anything that can be verbalized can be taught using programmed instruction," I answered, while bringing the group's attention to a modern teaching computer displaying one of the teaching programs. "Behaviorologists have found that learning—again, to be precise, we say 'conditioning' since it implies arranging contingencies—is much more effective if the child actually emits the behavior, or at least part of the behavior, to be acquired. This way, synapses actually mediating the behavior are strengthened. One way to accomplish this is through programmed instruction in which the child moves through material broken into small units called 'frames.'

"These are typically no larger than a small paragraph. The child is exposed to just one of these frames at a time and must read the frame and supply some missing material, usually just a word or two, into a blank space provided. After the answer is supplied, the program then immediately displays the correct answer and moves to a new frame, allowing the child to continue. Notice that this consequence of displaying the correct answer and presenting another frame follows the response immediately. This is one of the requirements of optimal operant conditioning, as you may well remember, and is one of the defining features of programmed instruction."

I paused for a moment at this point, and Paul asked, "But how does the program ensure that a child will be correct? And what actually reinforces the response? Being correct?"

"Yes," I replied. "The frames are arranged in a sequence in such a way that the answer, or answers, to the frame they are working on was given in a previous frame. Of course the *first* frame either provides its own answer somewhere in the question, or else the answer is obvious and generally known. The material is designed in such a way that the child most often provides the correct answer. Matching, or 'being correct,' has become reinforcing through prior conditioning procedures. I think it is safe to say that people everywhere enjoy being correct, and this is undoubtedly due to social reinforcement that was given in his or her educational history. So, to answer your question definitively, yes, we have demonstrated experimentally that matching the correct answer reinforces responding."

"But what if the student's response is wrong in some *trivial* way," he asked, "such as incorrect spelling?"

"That is a very good question," I said. "This was a real problem for early programs that were more unforgiving than our modern programs. As you suggest, answers could be marked incorrect due to improper spelling. *Incorrect* responses to questions often become conditioned aversive stimuli for many people. This is usually due to contingencies involving ridicule or censure. While we avoid using these contingencies here, too many wrong answers can still actually punish responding and create the aversive emotional condition we all know as 'frustration,' and the child may escape from the aversive contingencies by quitting the program module and doing something else. So it is very important that the child be correct approximately 90 percent of the time.

"This is easily accomplished in more recent teaching programs simply by directing the child into a subroutine that will break the material into smaller steps, some of which may involve correcting spelling errors. They are then returned to where they left off. But if too many incorrect responses are made—the ratio of correct to incorrect responses is computed by the software—the child will be directed into a more extensive remedial program that teaches the prerequisite behavior needed before continuing in the main module. Conversely, children who are already familiar with parts of the material may be directed to instruction using frames that may take larger steps and use less prompting. All of our teaching software is self-adjusting based on learner performance.

"Our research has shown that requiring an *overt* response from the student also involves the neural behavior you might call attention or awareness. Unlike simple reading, where the student's attention can easily wane before he or she becomes aware of it, in programmed instruction the student must continually pay attention in order to answer questions in subsequent frames; therefore, attention rarely diminishes. And to answer your first question, Paul, there are plenty of prompts built into the early frames so the student's responses are correct almost all of the time. But these prompts are gradually faded out in later frames as the correct responses become more probable and are reliably evoked by the questions alone.

"Though the child is rarely asked a question in a frame that he or she cannot answer, the complexity of the repertoire keeps increasing in small steps. Children move through these programmed modules at their own pace and appear to work busily and happily. After they have finished a sequence of frames, they have been taught to stop and think about the material for several minutes, and to question themselves about it until they believe they understand it well. This is a most important step and a valuable technique for remembering the lesson. They are also taught to try to recall the material periodically, and to assimilate it into related areas to which they are familiar; and perhaps, if possible, to apply newly learned material when they can."

"Why is programmed instruction not being used more often in public schools?" Clifford asked.

"The short answer is the prevailing cultural contingencies," I told him. "Some of our culturologists have studied these as they pertain to the educational establishment in America, so I should direct you to them for a more informed and definitive answer. But programmed instruction has been around since the 1950s," I said despairingly, "and many other effective methods have also been available for some time as well. It's a shame they haven't been put to better use in American schools; after all, behaviorology was founded here in America. Many administrators must expend their efforts getting funding for computers, higher teacher salaries, new books, desks, buildings, and so on, while remaining uninformed about low-cost proven teaching methods. Industry, on the other hand, which is always watching for low-cost effective methods to train employees, has shown much more interest in these technologies."

"But why have software companies not capitalized on these teaching technologies?" Paul asked. "Surely they could profit heavily by providing educational software to schools."

"Well," I said, "as budgets are continually being cut for public education, the money is just not there to provide the profit margins needed to attract investors to such ventures. With the public education shortfalls, software developers can make much more money in the private sector. Outside of our communities, profit-driven companies are producing the more lucrative video games—such as first-person shooter games—that are teaching children how to kill, while simultaneously desensitizing them to violence.

"This is not a skill we find useful in our communities. When and where would this 'skill' ever be used in a peaceful world? Not to mention the time that is spent learning this behavior, time that could be used much more productively. Why not instead produce fun, game-like programs that teach valuable prosocial and educational repertoires in a wide range of subject matters? These could even be sold outside of the school system in the more lucrative private market. Given the importance of education, the developer is assured the product will sell. For this reason, some of our communities produce these *educational* computer software programs, both for use by our communities and for others. They are designed to be every bit as fun as games.

"Another important thing to note is that acquiring new behavior and expanding one's repertoire continues in our communities; it does not stop after school age. The studying behaviors that have been shaped by our behaviorologists will continue to be reinforced throughout the lifetimes of our members. All of us here are teachers or mentors. And, as I have already mentioned, when we teach others, it improves our *own* performance. I'm sure you've heard the adage: the best way to learn is to teach. Since there is little or no competition here, and we know we are not vying for limited resources or positions, we are happy to help others learn skills that we can all share.

"Understanding that all operant behavior is conditioned—whether socially or by the non-social environment—we realize that asking for help is no weakness. Giving an individual more credit for learning something on his or her own than we would for learning with help causes people to resist asking for help from others. This may be why many people outside of our communities are offended if you offer to help them. The reluctance to accept or provide help is a remnant from agential thinking and it has no place here.

"How can there be no competition here?" asked Clifford. "I find this hard to believe. Competition is a motivating factor for many of us. Do people here not want to get ahead?"

"Get ahead of whom?" I asked. "Does getting ahead mean that people must always endeavor to outperform others? I'm sure it is hard to believe," I said, completely understanding the contingencies responsible for the question, "but individuals here are not trying to amass great wealth so that they may live luxurious, sumptuous lives, while others flounder, if this is what you mean by getting ahead. We cannot see how philosophies that promote individual self-interest or selfishness can produce a better society, but modern capitalism seems to propose just this.

"In fact, these philosophies have made things worse for much of the population where they are in effect. Disregarding all the religions of the world over the ages that have attempted to teach selflessness, compassion for others, and love and understanding, much of the West instead adopted the philosophy of individual self-interest as the path to happiness and prosperity. This philosophy goes hand-in-hand with unfettered capitalism, which too often permits overwhelming wealth to accrue to a small fraction of the population, most often at the expense of the working class.

"Kings and other supreme leaders have, in both the past and present, through armies and other henchmen, used coercion to acquire their great wealth; with unfettered capitalism, coercion is unnecessary in accomplishing the same end. And this is the beauty of this system from the perspective of those benefiting the most from it. While this economic system favors particular people or groups, they cannot be held accountable for the inequitable distribution of the nation's wealth, for it is the markets, devoid of human values, that have bestowed wealth upon the few. It's obvious who to oppose when kings and other supreme leaders usurp the wealth of the nation, but whom does one oppose when it is abstract market forces that shift excessive wealth to them?

"Well, I think we have had enough for one day," I continued. "So let's relax now and agree to meet later. Because of your science backgrounds, I have gone into much more detail explaining our educational system than we normally do with our visitors. I hope I haven't gone too far? But if you do need more information, please let us know and we will provide resources for you. Our educational system is at the core of our success, and similar contingencies are built into all facets of our communities."

As we were leaving the Educational Center, I tried to bring closure to my commentary.

"Too many people seem to revel in the unplanned society and despise communities that are planned, exhibit complete cooperation, distribute the resources fairly, and have what these people derisively call collective goals. They would be willing to sequester a science of behavior—or use it selfishly to exploit others for their own aggrandizement—rather than use it to lift up all of humanity.

"Our communities have adopted the sort of *ethics* that would be envied by most religions, yet many despise us for being godless. But our ethics go even further than most religions and extend to other sentient animals that inhabit this planet with us. We believe we must be good stewards of the planet and leave it habitable for the many generations that will follow us. Teaching our children these values and passing on our culture is paramount to the survival of humankind.

"But for many religions, Earth is just a temporary way station on the road to an afterlife. Consequently, many religious people are not concerned about polluting it or changing weather patterns that might prove to be detrimental to our descendants. To them, changes to the planet must be the result of God's will. But we can no longer afford such ignorance. We, as rational humans—and as the 'marvelous learning animal'—must begin to use our science to enhance the lives of all of humanity, and increase our survival chances as a species. We need to eliminate the coercive practices that have been demonstrated over and over again to be so detrimental to human relationships and human happiness. If I may paraphrase Frazier: we have not yet seen what we can make of humankind."

7

After departing the learning environments, I took leave of my guests to attend to some business elsewhere. They were left free to roam about and ask questions of other members at their leisure. I did not want this to be, and I'm sure *they* did not want this to be, a completely guided tour of our community—after all, they were inquisitive journalists. I arranged to meet them later for tea near Walden Pond, a pond we had excavated and named in honor of Thoreau. We very much enjoy sitting along its shore in the evenings when we can relax and talk at the end of our day. We met at the pond after dinner around 8 p.m. Traci joined us along with her small group of journalists.

"Dr. Jensen, may I ask: do you think society at large is ready to adopt your ideas?" asked a man named Jeffery Simmons from Traci's group, a freelance writer for several magazines. "Although I don't doubt they are working successfully here in these smaller communities, do you believe you could ever get the current leaders of society to give up their way of life for yours? Societal structures and economic policies today seem so global and interconnected that we couldn't just eliminate them and convert everyone to Walden Twos without causing a massive economic collapse. Anyway, there are powerful people benefiting from the status quo who, unless they could find a way to *capitalize* on your communities, will not support them. I'm particularly speaking of those who espouse neoliberal economic policies, or free-market capitalism."

I was sitting near Traci, and we were all enjoying cold drinks of iced tea and watching the sun setting behind the pond.

"Well, I believe you hit the nail on the head there," Traci said. "Frazier began Walden Two as a pilot experiment, you see. It's not a good idea to apply any new technology on a grand scale and see if it works. It's just too risky. Frazier wanted to experiment on a much smaller scale so that he could create and develop model communities that others could emulate. We may not have an ideal community—if there could ever be such a thing, since they must continue to change and evolve—but our philosophy of experimentation allows us to try new ways of doing things and then select those that work best.

"We are continually improving by using this selection process. It is a very pragmatic approach and works exceptionally well for us. We had very few preconceived notions about what would work. While Walden Two originally adopted some basic practices from other cultures—we had to begin somewhere, you understand—we carefully chose only those practices that made sense in light of the science of behavior. But by adopting experimental practices, we have continuously improved upon them. We have found that the *ideal* community is one that can quickly adapt to change and produce highly educated people willing to work for its survival.

"If, for example, we find that our behavior is contributing to climate change or excessive waste, we can rapidly change the contingencies affecting our behavior to remedy this. We are, above all, realists, and are totally data-driven. We have no religious charlatans or corporate propagandists obfuscating our data. You know, having *collective* goals is considered a bad thing only under capitalistic contingencies. Societies composed of self-serving people unconcerned whether their culture survives after their death make poor societies."

Clifford shifted uneasily in his chair. He seemed to be uncomfortable with what Traci was saying. "The survival of the culture?" he said, somewhat astonished. "Since when should the survival of the culture take precedence over the individual? This seems to me to be the main problem with collectivist societies."

"I did not mean to imply that the culture *should* take precedence, Mr. Douglas," Traci answered in her casual manner. "And I do *not* believe it should. But Frazier once made a good point about culture while speaking to a group of university students about behaviorology and cultural design. This was back in the late '60s or early '70s when there was a strong anti-establishment movement among the young.

"During the question-and-answer session, one student stood up and asked defiantly, 'Why should I give a *damn* whether my culture survives?' to which Frazier responded, 'There may be no good reason, but if your culture has not convinced you to work toward its survival, so much the worse for your culture.' You see, Mr. Douglas, it is the culture that is going to survive and pass on the accumulated values and knowledge of humankind; no individual lives more than a hundred years, with rare exceptions. But an egalitarian culture that produces productive and happy people is probably worth perpetuating— for it will improve the lives of not only the countless people comprising it, but of their descendants as well.

"Therefore, we must be careful *not* to design a culture at the expense of the individual. We must take into consideration that the collective repertoires of individuals *are* the culture; the two are inseparable. When you strengthen either, you are strengthening both. But a culture composed of people not willing to work toward its survival, or working toward its destruction, can be *defined* as a poor culture. I'm afraid there are far too many disenfranchised groups in large societies that are not concerned whether their culture is perpetuated or not. I will leave it to others to determine whether their grievances are warranted."

Clifford sat back in his chair shaking his head.

"Now," Traci continued, "to return to Mr. Simmons' question: Do we think society at large is ready to adopt our ideas?

The answer is no, we do not expect large societies to emulate Walden Two, because they probably couldn't even if they wanted to. They are too cumbersome and inflexible to take advantage of the selection process I'm talking about. We think states, and even most cities, are too large. Governors and mayors, like most 'leaders,' seem to think of the governed as an aggregate mass to be controlled through political propaganda, mainly at election time. This control consists mostly of negative propaganda that denigrates the politician's opponents.

"We have studied these propagandistic techniques using some new findings in the domain of behaviorology called equivalence relations and relational frame theory; I hope to discuss these with you later if you are not already familiar with them. While for the most part political leaders of large populations are unresponsive to the *needs* of the many, they *are* responsive to the *desires* of a few very small private sectors—those wielding wealth and power. The downside to representative democracy is that the populace itself can be blamed for voting these 'leaders' into office. Most people do not realize that the pool of candidates from which they are to choose has already been well vetted by groups working on behalf of the privileged sectors."

Clifford sat up again, "This is only natural, isn't it? After all, we couldn't realistically allow true representatives of the masses to run things, could we? They would simply attempt to redistribute wealth by taxing the rich. Some of our Founding Fathers were well aware of this tendency and therefore divided and layered our government to prevent unchecked popular influence. I see nothing wrong with these people protecting their wealth; it's surely better than handing it over to the shiftless."

Martha looked at Clifford, obviously a little surprised to hear him speaking this way; he was clearly not wealthy and had not come from wealth, yet he was an apologist for the position of the wealthy. What had influenced his thinking?

"Oh, I do not see it that way at all!" Martha disagreed. "And I do not think most people—at least the people *I* know—want to take wealth from the affluent to distribute to the indolent. But we do believe the wealthy should be the first to support the society that permitted them to accrue such wealth. Let's not think of taxation as wealth redistribution, rather we should think of it as subsidizing our commonwealth: infrastructure, scientific research, educational facilities, salaries for public employees, and yes, programs for the less fortunate among us, and even our military. Unfortunately, I think too much wealth has moved into gated communities, and, since these people no longer use public resources, they do not wish to support the public commonwealth."

"I agree," added Paul. "We are not punishing the wealthy by making them pay their fair share. After all, they are still left with more than enough wealth *after* paying taxes. It actually hurts the average person more to pay taxes than it does the wealthy; even though we pay less, we also have less afterwards.

"I think we may agree that, with the ascendancy of global corporations and markets, capitalism has morphed into something quite different," Martha said, "and a truly global empire is finally on the horizon, but it will no longer be controlled by one nation, but rather by a multinational banking and business class."

"Yes," Traci said. "It is the neoliberal economic model that allows vast wealth to accrue to small segments of society. We should realize a society is in jeopardy when its ruling class is also a member of the acquisitive or avaricious class. These are people who are primarily interested in amassing as much wealth and material possessions as possible. Too many rulers live orders of magnitude above the standards of those they govern. Saudi kings and crown princes live in plush palaces and ride in gold-plated Rolls-Royces, and the current Russian president is purported to be among the richest men on Earth—and it is important to note, he was not so before taking office.

And the current U.S. president owns luxury hotels, casinos, and golf courses in many countries around the world."

"And," Paul added, "some fear he is taking advantage of his presidential position to make connections with leaders—some quite corrupt—of other countries that will one day pave the way for the expansion of his personal business empire into autocratic countries such as Russia, Saudi Arabia, and even North Korea."

"I think the current president is an extreme aberration as U.S. presidents go," Traci said, somewhat dismissively, "Not that other presidents have not benefited greatly from the position, but, all speculation aside, we do know that many political leaders have used their positions of power to change tax laws and relax regulations in such a way that will further enrich themselves and the small privileged sectors they represent. And even some modern religious leaders enjoy lifestyles well above the standards of their followers.

"Some of our American politicians, at the behest of the wealthy and business classes, argue that we need to *further* deregulate banks and other financial institutions, while they revel in profits therefrom. But, when expectations go awry, they turn to the masses for bailouts, using laws that were specifically crafted and implemented just for this eventuality. Here, in our communities, we all have the same standard of living and rise or fall together. Perhaps, due to the prevailing contingencies under materialistic capitalism, it is understandable—by which I mean, *scientifically* understandable, not justifiable—that people want to live these sumptuous lives, but the fact is, we do not have the planetary resources needed to allow Earth's current population of nearly eight billion people to live this way.

"Until the population is reduced benignly through careful child planning, this is a luxury granted only to the few. While our communities' standards of living are constantly rising, we do not allow our desires to exceed our resources. And, unlike some societies, we do not use others as scaffolding to support a privileged class that may want to exceed the limits. As you can see for yourselves, our standard of living is more than adequate for human health and happiness.

"All of our communities are responsive to the needs of the people comprising them. We have found that what is good for our individual members, is also good for our communities, and vice versa. Therefore, we don't propose trying to change large cities or states, for example. They are a product of an Industrial Age that will someday probably go the way of the dinosaur. The Industrial Age attracted rural people into the cities to work in factories with the promise of a new and better way of living—wage living. Perhaps someday our descendants will be looking at the skeletons of these behemoth buildings and wondering what they were used for.

"How many large buildings in cities are dedicated to banking, insurance, real estate, or retail? All of these are completely unnecessary in our communities and would be a waste of space and energy. We are advocating the creation of smaller communities, like ours, that are flexible, experimental, accountable to their populations, and networked to share information and take advantage of each other's ideas and efforts. This open sharing and cooperation can only happen in societies that are not competing for limited resources.

"So, alas, to answer your question, Mr. Simmons, no, we do not expect large societies to model themselves after us. They could easily adopt some of our practices piecemeal, as they have already done, but we do not expect them to address the needs of the people on an individual level—only in aggregate. Current trends suggest that they will continue to integrate further into a global corporate plutocracy, dominated by elites unresponsive to the needs of the majority of humanity. We are offering an alternative to that. We are showing others how to gradually decouple and eventually secede from the corporate state by establishing self-sufficient communities that will permit them to live the one precious life they will ever live. You cannot become truly independent until you have locally controlled, self-sufficient infrastructures in place. But, on the other hand, we can never, of course, completely ignore larger societies outside of our communities; the collective behavior of their large populations is now affecting the entire biosphere."

At this point, one of our members rolled out a metal serving table with some small snacks that consisted of cheeses, nuts, and frozen grapes, and large pitchers of iced tea and water. Our glasses are made of a colored recycled plastic and they were placed in fitted jackets. They have handles—only needed for carrying—that are removable, and since we would not be carrying our glasses, the handles were left in a bin near the glasses in the cafeteria.

Martha turned to me and asked, "But don't all cultures continue to evolve, Fred? What do you think sets yours apart?"

"Societies in general evolve, that is true," I said. "But evolutionary change does not guarantee improvement. Warring societies can evolve new weapons of war that permit them to dominate other, more peaceful, cultures; but they may eventually turn these weapons and the warring tactics they have learned onto their own populations. History and archeology are replete with examples of cultures that have perished. But our communities have one great advantage over larger societies. We can more easily and intentionally introduce variation by changing our sociocultural practices, and we can do this relatively quickly. This flexibility facilitates the selection process I spoke of and helps to winnow out less effective ways of doing things.

"It is analogous to animal breeders who watch for variation in members of a species, and then select and breed only those possessing the trait or traits the breeder is looking for. She doesn't wait for this final variation to appear naturally; she selects certain individuals from large litters, or from different litters, and mates those possessing the desirable trait. She most likely won't get what she wants in the next generation or two, but with ample variation she can select those animals with traits that more closely approximate what she wants.

"Through many iterations of this process, the breeder can derive something quite different from what she started with. And she may not have known *in advance* what she was looking for. But with variation and selection you don't need to know. That is the great advantage of it. We humans, and all extant life forms, arrived at our current biological form by a similar selection process, of course, but in our case it was those traits that allowed us to survive *long enough to reproduce* that were naturally selected. But varying our practices and selecting the most effective ones is only part of our success; our educational and incentive systems, informed by a science of behavior, are our main strengths."

"Would it be accurate to say that you don't agree with those historians, political philosophers, and judiciary scholars, who believe that the U.S. Constitution is one of the greatest documents ever penned?" Clifford asked. "Do you have a constitution for Walden Two?"

"Of a sort, we do," I replied. "However, it is based on broad missions and philosophies and contains much about our guiding principles of behaviorology. It is probably closest in philosophy to modern secular humanism. Any member can suggest modifications or changes for consideration. It's an ever-evolving document and is a record of how to replicate our successes for all communities in the network to share.

"Now, regarding the U. S. Constitution, we should start by recognizing that, compared to the constitutions of many of the world's nations, the U.S. Constitution has remained operational for an uncommonly long time, and it may remain operational for quite a long time to come. But some scholars have convincingly argued that the U.S. Constitution was a document written by aristocrats to protect the interests of the wealthy. I believe you alluded to these protections, Mr. Douglas, and I think James Madison's contemporaneous notes bear this out.

"The aristocratic classes have always been worried about democracy and what they derisively call 'mob rule.' They deplore true democracy and fear that the poor may rise up and attempt to claim a share of the wealth of the nation. They believed that those who own the country—meaning large landowners and the wealthy—should control it. Therefore, the U.S. Constitution was written taking this into account.

"Women could not vote and blacks were considered three-fifths of a person. The Electoral College added another layer of protection—as you have indicated—and offered a safeguard in case voters tried to elect a popular leader whose interests conflicted with that of the wealthy; the electors would be a stopgap. The House of Representatives, which putatively represents the common people, was only added—along with the Bill of Rights—because without some representation for the people, there was no other way to get all of the states to ratify the document. But with the effectiveness of modern propaganda, these concerns are now allayed.

"The U.S. Constitution has succeeded to a small measure," I continued, "but the point we need to consider here is not its successes, but the kinds of problems that it, and any constitution, raises. You can't write the rules for a society in stone and not expect major issues to arise. Societies are changing at an accelerated pace. They eventually evolve to a point where some of the issues the original framers of the document addressed do not apply well to contemporary issues.

"Things exist in modern society that the framers could not have imagined. And problems will always arise when rules are too rigid and intractable. The framers could not have anticipated some issues, such as *in vitro* fertilization, artificial intelligence, stem cell research, or modern weaponry, because nothing like them existed at that time. Of course, some Supreme Court justices think they can peer into the minds of the framers to see what they intended. We should not expect that the framers—over two hundred thirty years ago—could have could have imagined the lethality and capacity of modern hand weapons, or diagnostic methods that allow us to look at a fetus while still *in vivo*, but we are still adhering to their written words as if they were edicts from the gods."

"But we can change the constitution, and have changed it," Clifford said, somewhat petulantly. "The point of a constitution is to keep stability in a society. There are different levels of legislative change happening in our society; when we pass new bills, for example. We just don't want to change policies *too* quickly, hence a recalcitrant constitution and a more flexible legislature."

"Oh, of course," I agreed. "But that is my point, you see? Realistically, you can't just experiment by making large-scale changes to a society composed of hundreds of millions of people; there are just too many unknown factors involved, and the ramifications are unpredictable and possibly dangerous. This is perhaps the main reason for the Constitution's intractability. But this intractability can cause problems when changes *do* need to be made rapidly."

"Well, I for one, do not want rapid change," Clifford said. "Many of us happen to like things as they are."

"But you cannot keep things as they are, Mr. Douglas," I said. "New private institutions, as well as new technologies and products, are rapidly changing the way we live. The problem is that government cannot keep up. And government cannot be expected to solve all our problems. Politicians often propose changes by introducing new bills, that, even if they could get them passed through Congress unaltered, are usually far from perfect, and even these smaller-scale changes can produce unforeseen consequences.

"But they have to pretend that they know what they are doing if they want to get re-elected. They can't be honest and say, 'I *think* this is a good policy change; let's try it and see.' The greater the change, the more likely it is to cause problems. Trade agreements are a good example. How can anyone predict all of the ramifications of something so grand? These agreements affect millions of people and myriad institutions in many countries.

"The politicians too often rely on the predictions of economists and social scientists with their statistical correlational science of group behavior, using the economic and mathematical models they are so fond of. They don't see or care about the behavior of individuals, just the net effect of aggregate behavior: voting behavior, purchasing and consuming behavior, and opinions. To the plutocratic elites, 'the people' are one behaving mass, hence, 'the masses.' Manipulating the masses through propaganda is a highly perfected art form in the United States.

"As Noam Chomsky has pointed out, since leaders in 'free' democracies cannot openly use force to control the behavior of the population, they must use propaganda to pacify, and manufacture the consent of, the governed. In large societies, what is good for one group is likely to be bad for another. And what is good for the population is not likely to be what is good for the elites. *Our* science is about the behavior of the individual, and in smaller communities every individual matters. There seems to be an inverse relationship between the size of the group and the concern for the individual; as the population increases, the value of each individual seems to diminish."

"But our society is continuing to improve conditions for many people," Clifford said. "I will admit that it is not a linear path and more like a zigzag, but people now have access to things that their ancestors did not. Sure, there is inequity, but show me a society that does not have inequity. And by the way, there are programs like Medicaid to aid the poor."

"I'm sure we are all for helping the poor," I answered, "but but many well-intentioned programs have miscarried because of unforeseen by-products. Take welfare for example; a well-meaning program that, while temporarily helping some, as intended, also produced a small subculture of non-productive people. Any first year behaviorology student could have predicted this; non-contingent reinforcement can easily produce this effect.

"There was no science behind programs of this kind, just goodwill. Politicians from opposing parties use such failures to discredit the policies of their rivals, but then introduce their own untested solutions with their own unique sets of problems. Supply-side economics and trade agreements have each had detrimental effects on the working and middle classes. They have had the overall effect of shifting wealth to the moneyed and investment classes.

"Supply-side economics was supposed to expand businesses and create new jobs for the middle class. Instead, businesses spent their windfall tax cuts on new technologies that actually eliminated more workers, another example of unforeseen and unpredictable consequences. But perhaps I am being too naïve and generous; maybe this actually *was* predicted and the by-products were deemed not only acceptable, but also desirable. We may never know for sure. In any case, it is the vast majority of people who are caught in the middle of, and hurt by, these grand political experiments."

"What would you suggest?" Martha asked.

"Behaviorologists would be happy to sit down with policy makers and explain contingency management to them. We could at least make informed suggestions that would benefit society at large. But I'm afraid there are powerful private interests benefiting from the status quo that are not interested in our suggestions for improving working conditions, for example, if it means cutting into profits. On the other hand, our small communities are ideally suited for experimentation, and it is much easier to reverse any programs that might prove to be detrimental or ineffective. Besides, some of our methods are indeed being applied piecemeal, if unsystematically, outside of our communities, in areas such as education, clinical settings, and industry, to name a few. We can't say we agree with much of what larger societies are doing, but we would—with scientific justification—definitely like to see fewer coercive practices used in them."

Paul was sitting close to Traci—by design I'm sure. He looked at her with a broad smile and asked, "Dr. Jensen, I would like to hear what you believe to be the problem with our society. I'm sure you have thought long about this, haven't you? How would you improve our society?"

She looked directly at Paul and said, "It would take a team of our culturologists and behaviorologists working together before we would make specific suggestions, of course. We would begin by making small proposals known to improve certain conditions; this way we could build confidence in our methods. But the problem is not for want of viable solutions, but rather because of the powerful conflicting interest groups over which we would have little control, especially their representatives in government.

"Unfortunately, outmoded philosophies of humankind—both religious and secular—are preventing the natural science of behavior from being applied on the scale needed to make the behavior changes necessary to prevent likely global disasters. Some of these—for example nuclear war—are potentially existential threats to humankind. And some of these changes must be made *now* if we want to avoid the problems that will ensue. Science should not be thought of as a cold uncaring philosophy, but rather as an extremely effective method for understanding how things in our world work.

"We are only proposing more effective ways of doing what any good culture should be trying to do, and that is building the support of the population by eliminating most—if not all—of the punitive and coercive practices in the culture, and designing contingencies using positive reinforcers for desirable behavior. When you switch control from coercive practices to what behaviorologists call 'additive' or 'positive' reinforcement, people feel freer and happier; they learn better and enjoy what they are doing. We are offering more effective methods to educate people and hopefully pass on cultural practices worth passing on."

"I can imagine some critic asking why—if you have such powerful methods—you can't just condition *everyone* to accept your science and its implications," Clifford said to me. "Isn't this a fair criticism?"

"No, it is not," I objected, "because we have control of only a very tiny subset of the reinforcers in any given person's life. Also, behavior most often has multiple determinants, and we seldom have access to very many of these determinants. Governments do not need to have control of the added—or positive—reinforcers in a person's life; they have the power to coerce and punish people's behavior. If you do something illegal, like not paying your taxes or jaywalking, governmental forces can fine you or put you in jail. And most people blithely accept the fact that their governments have these powers.

"But if you are using additive reinforcement only, as in our case, you usually have control of only a small subset of a person's reinforcers; I'm speaking mostly of adults here because children are more dependent on others for their reinforcers. The physical world naturally reinforces certain behaviors, but I cannot, for example, make your physical contact with a reinforcing object contingent on some arbitrary behavior—only your reaching will produce that contact. Teachers do not make classroom laughter contingent on the deviant's showing-off, only the other children in the classroom can do so. And we certainly cannot make Juliet's affection contingent on Romeo's behavior, only Juliet can. And depending on Romeo's hormonal state, Juliet's affection can very well supersede most of the reinforcers that we could present!"

I believe Paul looked at me when I mentioned Romeo, but I did not look his way.

"My point is, of course, that behaviorologists operating in larger societies usually have access only to weak social reinforcers. These may or may not be capable of reinforcing a person's behavior, depending on his or her social conditioning history. For example, if we are attempting to use attention and approval as reinforcers, we are assuming that attention and approval have already become reinforcing through a particular conditioning history. Attention and approval will not reinforce the behavior of those without this history. Unless someone is having behavioral problems that bring him or her into therapy, it is difficult to change a long-held worldview just by making social reinforcement contingent on a different worldview, but of course, it can be done. People with strongly held beliefs about a supreme being and divine creation, for instance, will not easily give up these long-held beliefs just because others make some weak social reinforcer contingent on their verbal behavior expressing the opposite belief."

"Do people's personal beliefs really have that great an impact on how a society operates?" Martha asked. "I can see where religious voters may influence public policy, but is this really a bad thing? Banning abortion, for example, would not be the worst thing in the world, would it?"

"Perhaps not," I said, "but some beliefs can conflict with reality and hamper effective solutions. And remember, a culture does not exist outside of the collective behavior of its members. When large fractions of the population hold false beliefs, it can have an unfortunate impact on a society. For example most people believe the ubiquitous philosophical writings claiming that everything is determined *except human behavior*—and maybe the behavior of some subatomic particles. And just because behaviorologists now understand how these and other behaviors are acquired, does not mean we can just arrange people's environments to change that belief; we are not omnipotent.

"People's behaviors are constantly exposed to conflicting contingencies from many sources—philosophy and religion are just two of them—that are telling them the opposite. Now we can, and do, educate the public through our courses and writings, just like any other natural science does, and we believe we present good arguments and *testable* theories of behavior that will eventually win out. The question is, can we do it in time to effect the changes in behavior needed to save ourselves?

"Max Planck once said 'A new scientific truth does not triumph by convincing its opponents and making them see the light, but rather because its opponents eventually die, and a new generation grows up that is familiar with it.' I think this is a little too dire, but it is not far off the mark. It will be quite some time before larger societies produce the learning environments necessary to mitigate the propagation of supernatural and metaphysical beliefs that interfere with the development and occurrence of more appropriate, reality-based beliefs."

Traci set her empty glass aside and added, "With ever increasing population growth, we must begin dealing with the problems created by human behavior: overconsumption, excessive waste, pollution, overpopulation, exploitation of one group by another, personal violence, and the cultural violence that arises when people with different ideologies clash in the globalization process, and so on. We must look at this with clear heads. I am sure you have noticed that in the last several decades there has been a push for rapid globalization, have you not? Much of the current cultural violence in the Middle East results from the rapid changes happening to Third World cultures in our push for globalization. This also emphasizes Fred's earlier point that you can't change large societies quickly and not expect unforeseen repercussions. The West is hastily attempting to introduce values into cultures currently holding far different values. What reinforces *our* behavior is not necessarily what will reinforce *their* behavior.

"People have a wide range of differing conditioned reinforcers, as a visit to any other culture will demonstrate. Some of these become the *values* of a culture. This globalization process is being imposed on many societies by a small fraction of the world population whom we could call the 'global elites.' The policies they make are made literally behind closed doors with little or no input from major sectors of the societies affected.

"Some have argued that there could be as few as six thousand people who are making the major decisions that will affect the lives of the nearly 8 billion people on this planet. They are the people who run governments, the major corporations and financial institutions, the media, the higher courts of our judiciary, and our world religions. These people are currently making decisions for the rest of humanity with little input from any field other than economics. Should we be letting a relative handful of leaders make the major decisions affecting the lives of millions or billions of people? And I should add that most of these decisions are made with little regard for the interests of the billions of major stakeholders affected by them.

"We have seen what has happened in every country where this has occurred. The wealth of nations too often accrues to the leaders and their wealthy supporters; perhaps some of the wealth is shared with other power players in order to accomplish this, and a small amount trickles down to the population, but the rule stands. This is a lesson we should have learned by now. We need input from all of the stakeholders affected by these decision makers. What Americans currently think of as democracy is somewhat of a travesty: Every couple of years, the electorate can vote in—from a carefully preselected pool of candidates—some rotating fraction of their leaders; they are then expected to remain dormant until the next voting cycle. A true democracy would not only welcome input from its entire people, it would involve them in the decision-making process. With modern computers this is more possible than ever."

"Do you agree," Clifford asked, "that while it may not be a good idea to 'nation build,' Western culture should assist other cultures in their transition to more modern and democratic— even if imperfect—societies?"

"If it is done with care and respect for the values of these other cultures," I answered. "But we cannot foist *our* values upon them using weapons or threats of embargoes, or by fomenting coups in those countries that do not succumb to western cultural values. After much blowback, I think the U.S. may finally be learning this lesson. It is also very important that we not try to impose western values on cultures that don't have the proper contingencies in place. The U.S. itself went through a relatively slow cultural evolution in its short history. For example, it once countenanced slavery, its women and minorities were subjugated to second-class citizenship and could not vote, workers—many of them children—were mistreated, underpaid, and overworked, not unlike the sweatshops the U.S. now condemns in other cultures—even though some of our corporations are happy to take advantage of these sweatshops when they can do so surreptitiously.

"But now that U.S. values have changed, it will not tolerate its old values in other cultures—cultures that are not evolving rapidly enough and on a timetable necessary to satisfy the interests of U.S. and global elites. These elites cannot understand why these Third World cultures will not immediately succumb to their materialistic values. They are using coercive techniques to try to remedy this through threats of military action, arranging or supporting coups, occupations, embargoes, blockades, economic sanctions and so on. These are purely coercive techniques using negative reinforcement. You motivate the population of a target country by creating shortages or threats, and then offer to relent if they will comply with your demands.

"These coercive tactics not only hurt innocent populations, they also generate unwanted emotional by-products that will cause us problems both now and in the future. Coercion breeds counter-coercion; terrorism is only one example of this. Our government is much like the newly reformed smoker or 'born-again Christian' who wants to lecture to the unenlightened. It is not willing to let these cultures go through a similar slow cultural evolution or modeling process. The United States and some other western powers are trying to impose their most highly held values onto these very different cultures: free-market capitalism, materialism, consumerism, and rugged individualism.

"Here in Walden Two, we think it is best to *model* our cultural practices and let others decide whether they want to emulate them. We do it on a scale that demonstrates the possibilities that derive from adopting behaviorology to improve the human condition. While our people are healthy, happy, well educated, productive, and prosocial, we do not expect, say, highly religious cultures to immediately adopt our model. And we are not saying we currently have the answers to all of humankind's problems, but we are suggesting that we know how to find them.

"You may recall that Szilard and Einstein wrote to President Roosevelt warning him that Germany was possibly working on the construction of an atomic bomb. They in essence proposed that, while our scientists did not currently know how to build an atomic bomb, they had the science to find out how to build one. And this, in essence, is what we are saying; we cannot design the ideal society *in advance*, but we now have the science to help do so through a selection process. We believe we have produced an algorithm that will move us much closer to—if not an *ideal* society—at least a much more peaceful, less punitive, and better society."

Clifford moved uneasily in his seat before asking, "How can you be sure that you are going in the right direction? Even if you could engineer behavior, and I'm not saying that you can, what behaviors will a culture need, and who will decide?"

"I believe we can all agree on some prerequisites to happiness," I answered in what I believe was a kindly manner. "For example, most people will agree that good health and freedom from pain are necessary for happiness. People whose behavior produces mostly positive reinforcers on a favorable schedule of reinforcement, seem to be very happy. We describe this by saying that their 'GLR,' or general level of reinforcement, is high. In layman's terms, we might say that a happy person is one whose behavior produces good outcomes fairly frequently and regularly. And of course, the converse is also true; bad outcomes should occur quite infrequently. I think that we can also agree that people should be well educated and as free from coercion as is practicable. Relatively complex behavior patterns that produce positive reinforcers seem to be more gratifying for some people than simple behavior; this may explain why many people spend time solving puzzles, doing mathematics, and scientific research."

"Any truly viable society must begin by building prosocial behavior into the repertoires of its members," Traci added, "starting with healthy cooperation. American individualism may be preventing people from joining together to form cooperating groups with common concerns, for example. It is necessary that people work *conjointly* to resist the current power structures that dominate many societies. You may have noticed that political elites from *both* major political parties in the United States are no longer truly supportive of labor unions or third-party political groups, while both parties have no qualms about business roundtables, chambers of commerce, or elite think tanks and foundations.

"It is only the popular organizations that are hindered. Small popular organizations are often falsely deemed 'radical,' 'socialistic' or 'communistic,' and are quickly stamped out. Therefore, it is imperative that we begin building prosocial repertoires and getting people cooperating very early in life in order to combat this; it cannot be accomplished by a fractured population. Unfortunately, many wedge issues are deliberately used to fracture the population and prevent them from working in concert to address common concerns."

"I recall reading one of Alvin Toffler's books when I was in high school," said Simmons. "He reminds us that throughout most of humankind's history, we lived in small bands, or tribes, as hunter-gatherers where the small numbers allowed members to know and interact with one another on many levels. Agriculture brought this nomadic lifestyle to an end and brought extended families together in the common enterprise of farming.

"Ten thousand years later, the Industrial Age began to draw people to the cities and away from their farms—much like what is happening now in China—and broke extended families composed of grandparents, parents, aunts, uncles and children, into nuclear families consisting only of parents and children. Toffler has called these large sweeping changes to our way of life 'waves'; hunter-gathering was our way of life for most of human existence until the first wave of change, agriculture, came along.

"Agriculture occupied most of our efforts for about ten thousand years until the second wave of change, the Industrial Age, occurred. This drastically changed the way humans have lived for the last three hundred years. The industrial society brought many disparate people and groups together to work in factories and shops in the cities that grew around industry. The family unit became much smaller, consisting of just parents and children. As cities grew, more people were brought together who had no real common connection with each other. While hunter-gathering and farming required cooperation to produce a common outcome, this commonality was lost in the Industrial Age."

"Yes," I said, "and as the population of cities grew larger, 'alienation' was one effect; why make friends with or be nice to people you will probably never see again? In our Walden Two communities, we have populations of between two to five thousand people. This number is small enough to allow us to get to know each other fairly well. Here we know that we will possibly be working alongside one another at some future time. This close contact and need for cooperation produce the contingencies that keep our behavior in check. But as I told you earlier, being educated, and especially educated in behaviorology, we have learned to interact in positive ways, and rarely is there what you might call acrimonious or vitriolic disagreement; in fact, I have not seen this in our Walden Two community in my personal experience."

8

I was hoping my guests would become more contempla-
tive here at Walden Pond, and they had. As we finished our
snacks and drinks, we watched a group of young people pad-
dling small canoes on the pond. Some elderly members of our
community were walking on a trail that encircled the pond,
talking, and occasionally laughing quietly. Our solar lights are
shielded from above to reduce light pollution; this allows the
stars and other heavenly bodies to be seen more clearly. The
lights can, of course, be switched off to provide even better
viewing, and a few small removable telescopes sit on tripods
nearby for our amateur astronomers.

There are several permanent benches around the pond, but
we were sitting on more comfortable wooden lawn chairs made
here in one of our workshops. Various designs had been tried,
but members found that chairs with body-conforming canvas
seats and backs were the most comfortable; they recline and
have side levers that raise a leg support. There are small sheds
nearby in which to store them. Traci's and my group appeared
to be familiar with each other professionally or by reputation,
and all listened respectfully to whoever was speaking.

The sun had set long ago and a myriad of stars were clearly
visible in the night sky. Simmons appeared to be studying them
pensively when he spoke to no one in particular. "Are any of
you familiar with Carl Sagan's Cosmic Calendar?" he asked.
"I keep a copy of it on my office wall and I am always amazed
at the perspective it provides of our place in this universe. It
was in his book *The Dragons of Eden.*" He looked down from

the stars and turned toward me. "We tend to think of ourselves as the culmination of an evolutionary process, rather than just an intermediate stage in it," he said. "And while many of us have relinquished belief in a divine creator, there are still those who see evolution as purposeful and ourselves as the end product. Sagan's calendar went a long way toward dispelling that myth, for me at least. I read all of his books after that."

"Oh I agree," I responded. "I felt the same way when I first saw it. What a brilliant device to put things in perspective. Is that why you became a science writer?"

"You know, I think so," he said. "I developed such a wonder for the universe at a young age, and want to understand all I can about it before my time is up. I just turned thirty-seven last month. Sagan wrote that book four years before I was born. I think I read it when I was around fifteen or so. His writings stirred something in me and that calendar has always stuck with me."

Martha looked from one of us to the other and then said, "I'm afraid I'm not familiar with it. Could you enlighten me?"

"Well," Simmons began, "it's a calendar Sagan created by compressing the roughly 14 billion years that have elapsed since the Big Bang into one calendar year. The major events of the universe are then placed proportionally onto this calendar. One second of time on the calendar is equal to approximately four hundred seventy-five Earth years. So, for example, the formation of the Earth would have occurred on September 14 on this compressed Cosmic Calendar, fairly late in the year."

"I see," Martha said. "How interesting."

"Well, I only mention it, as I said, because of the perspective it gives to our place in this universe." Simmons looked back up at the stars again as if contemplating our insignificance to the universe, and then he began again. "For example, Earth's life—and we're talking about *microbes*—would have arisen on this calendar on September 25, almost ten months into the calendar year. But what astounded me is the fact that humans arrived in this universe on December 31, *at 10:30 pm*! This gives us quite a different perspective of our place here than our mythologies give. Now, if I recall correctly, all of recorded history takes place within the last ten seconds on this calendar; Christianity arose in the last four seconds, and science within the last second of the Cosmic Calendar! A human life is less than one fifth of a second."

And the science of behavior too, I thought as he continued to speak, occupies about one-fifth of a second on Sagan's calendar, the proverbial blink of an eye. What can we accomplish with such a science? Our leaders want to unfetter capitalism but not a science of behavior. Will it be too late to save humanity from itself? Can we lift ourselves by our own bootstraps, as they say? Can we become truly intelligent peace-loving stewards of the planet, preserving, nurturing, and balancing the life forms that exist here? Are we fit to be called the pinnacle of the animal kingdom?

Religion has been in existence for thousands of years. Christianity has been around for two thousand. When will it improve humankind? How many more centuries can we wait for it to change us? Frazier once quipped that if he were God, he would *not* have used heaven as the final reward for living a good life; he would have instead broken heaven up into little pieces and made them contingent on good behavior during the person's lifetime. That is how our science would inform him to be the most effective way to produce good behavior.

But, like capitalism, Christianity has often emphasized saving only certain select individuals, not humankind in general. There is as much dissension between various religious sects as harmony. Religion has produced unnecessary guilt, and the fear of eternal damnation has created undue anxiety for millions, if not billions, of people. In addition, valuable information—for example, information that could have averted venereal diseases—was withheld by early Christianity to ensure that the sinful would be justly punished here on Earth by these diseases. Even today some Christians withhold information about 'safe' sex to preclude the young from engaging in this putative 'sinful' behavior.

Venereal and other microbial diseases must have been frightening and perplexing to our ancestors, and the superstitious avoidance behavior we call 'rituals' abounded as a result. Any behavior that was thought to produce these diseases was labeled sinful. Without the scientific instruments needed to see and understand the microbes causing them, diseases must have seemed to be caused by supernatural forces displeased by these sinful behaviors. Therefore, certain meats were proscribed—such as pork—that in today's light we know would have been more likely to contain pathogens.

Religions codified these early behavior-disease correlations into edicts that forbade certain behaviors, calling them sinful and punishable by God, both here on Earth through disease, and then in the afterlife with hellfire. Here we have a type of superstitious practice that, while false, has overall survival value for those adhering to it, because those adherents actually *did* avoid the diseases. They were right about the correlation between the risky behavior and the disease, but wrong about the supernatural cause.

Even today, sex education cannot be taught in many schools in the United States because current religious dogma forbids sex before marriage. And if young people know how to copulate yet prevent pregnancy, or masturbate and preclude it, they may be tempted to engage in sexual activity. During the Inquisition, agents of Christianity meted out torture, and even death, for heretical behavior so that the heretic might begin his punishment here on Earth. Early Christians could not even spare the sinner his few remaining years on Earth unmolested, before he was consigned to Hell for *eternal* torture.

You cannot just expose people to religious—or any philosophical—tenets and expect to remake humanity; effective contingencies must be in place to reinforce rule-compliance. But then you must not just eliminate religion from contemporary life without replacing it with a more rational secular philosophy, and then arranging contingencies to support it. Whether we like it or not, the threat of eternal hellfire may be preventing some people from committing egregious criminal acts through avoidance conditioning. Until people are educated and given positive reasons for behaving well—that is, until contingencies based on added reinforcers are in effect— we may have to tolerate these superstitious beliefs for a few more generations in societies at large; but not here in our communities. We have engineered alternative secular contingencies that operate to keep people behaving well. We have broken heaven into little pieces.

I came out of my reverie in time to hear Simmons sum up. "My point is, I guess, that being a science writer has allowed me to see that the scientific method has allowed us to begin on a new journey. It has proven to be the most effective way to produce reliable information about the universe we live in."

"Yes," I concurred, "and now we must take our next step and apply it to ourselves. We must abandon the false philosophies and religions that stand in our path and have caused so much harm to humanity. I have often used as an analogy, the dichotomy between religion and science and that between bacteria and antibiotics. Just as antibiotics can destroy some bacteria while leaving more resistant strains, scientific explanations continue to refute *many*, but not all, superstitious explanations.

"And just as bacteria evolve and become resistant, so too do religious arguments. The 'god of the gaps' argument is always present; by which I mean, of course, that various gods have historically been used to explain the gaps in our scientific knowledge—but these 'gods' appear increasingly impotent, and become unnecessary once these gaps are filled. Early science would eventually explain the weapons of the gods: lightning, thunder, wind, earthquakes, volcanic eruptions, comets, disease, and so on—but not all at once!

"As science encroached on religious ground and began to explain more and more of what religion was trying to explain with mysticism, religion retreated and took refuge in those areas not yet lighted by science. The gods, once thought to exist high on Mount Olympus, became more and more remote until they unified into one god and entered the heavens, becoming an un-falsifiable abstraction. We have finally stripped them of their worldly powers of producing lightning, wind, thunder, and disease, but now, for some, they have become the very laws of physics.

"Religious verbal behavior kept evolving along with that of science in a sort of arms race. But while science has marched relentlessly forward, explaining observed and natural facts in our world—and even some facts, such as black holes, quasars, and an expanding universe that these religions never dreamed of—religion has retreated into the metaphysical realm of the 'soul' and the 'mind.' For instance, religion has tried to explain morality by saying it is the soul's God-given sense of right and wrong.

"Behaviorology has abandoned *all* mysticism and is explaining quite well naturally, what 'souls' and 'minds' were invented to explain mystically. We are relentlessly closing the gaps. If science had come out all in one piece, so to speak, religion would not have had a chance to adapt to the onslaught. Each generation scoffs with disbelief at the ignorance of their predecessors while reveling in their own. Simply put, religion has always thrived because of our ignorance of alternative natural explanations of our universe and ourselves; and it is harbored in that ignorance.

"Ironically, it may be the very success of science that has forced religion to evolve into such an abstract philosophy; it divorced itself from reality and became an un-falsifiable belief system trying to explain the nonexistent mystical entities of mind, spirit, and soul. When religion relinquished its attempts to explain natural phenomena in a useful way, physicists, biologists, and cosmologists bid religion adieu. But many of these very scientists seemed unconcerned that religion retained its claim on human nature and human behavior. Even though religion failed to advance our understanding of other natural phenomena, most people, including many scientists, thought it might still apply in the human realm. This is due to *their* ignorance of the natural science of behavior and its expansion of our understanding of human behavior."

"I'm sure you've noticed the recent spate of books on atheism by public intellectuals," Martha said.

"Oh yes, of course." I answered. "I believe these authors have seen the writing on the wall—if you'll excuse the religious metaphor. I imagine they wrote these books in part because they were aware that politicians, and others, were using people's religious beliefs to further their own agendas. Religious people vote. And they vote for candidates who promise to ban 'sinful' behavior through legislation. Or in some cases they just vote for those candidates who promise not to condone sinful behavior. I'm talking about abortions, euthanasia, same-sex marriages, homosexuality, doctor-assisted suicide, and so on. Parenthetically, religious people often vote for those candidates who promise to put prayer back in schools, as if this will solve some of humanity's problems."

"But if this is what people want," Clifford said, "well . . . that's democracy. What do you think politicians get out of all of this?"

"Notice that these bans and changes do not cost anything," I answered. "The politicians are simply pandering to people's superstitious beliefs in order to get votes. But once elected, they may begin cutting social programs that help the poor, reduce capital-gains taxes for the wealthy investment class, and weaken labor unions that provide a countervailing force to corporate power. Practically all of these policies squarely run counter to values that religious people support, but this is the power of modern propaganda.

"Also, if one's worldview is based on false beliefs, one can easily be persuaded—mostly by public relations propaganda put out by the fossil fuel industry—that climate change is a hoax or just natural, or perhaps is even in their God's plan. When the global population was much smaller than it is today, and when fewer people were consuming energy from these sources, some false worldviews could be overlooked or even countenanced. But with the global problems that are now occurring as a result of the aggregate behavior of an ever-growing population, it is imperative that people be educated, at least to a moderate degree, in the sciences, and have a worldview based in reality."

"If that is the case," said Clifford, "I would argue that scientists need to do a better job of communicating with the public."

"I think they have done what they can," said Paul. "I'm quite proud of our publication, and others like *Scientific American*, and, of course, yours, Martha, *Discover*. Many earlier science writers such as Carl Sagan, Isaac Asimov, and now contemporary writers like Richard Dawkins and others, have done a great service by taking the time to educate the lay public about science."

"I agree with that completely," I said. "But I submit even *they* have overlooked the key science that may now be needed to save us. While we continue to understand more and more about nature, maybe it is time to learn about our own behavior: Where does it come from? How can we produce it? What is 'good' behavior and how do we maintain it? We can no longer condone religious philosophies that just consider the Earth to be a way station for souls before they move on to some imaginary ethereal realm.

"In fact, we cannot condone *any* philosophy that purports that the Earth is expendable. And we especially cannot condone the behavior of those that are trying to hasten—what they believe to be—an impending apocalyptic end of humanity. Some religious zealots see global existential threats such as nuclear self-annihilation, catastrophic global climate change, or an asteroid strike, as divinatory biblical prophecy. We have reached a critical tipping point where we can no longer afford such irrational beliefs. Extremely destructive and lethal weapons are now in the hands of an increasing number of people around the world. Some of these people truly believe they are working as agents of a supreme being. *That*, I suspect, is why these authors have written their books attempting to dispel religious belief. But imagine, if you will, that everyone was suddenly converted to atheism, would this *alone* solve many of humankind's major problems? We think not.

"I know these writers meant well, but as I've already suggested, I wish we had alternative contingencies in place to reinforce prosocial behavior before dispelling some of these myths. As I alluded to before, the fear of supernatural sanctions may be the only thing keeping some people from committing serious crimes; and the promise of heaven may even entice some to treat their fellow humans well. And yes, we see the irony here: even superstitious belief can have a positive side. That is another reason we have endeavored to employ behaviorology on a larger scale; to ensure that there will be contingencies in place to support the prosocial behaviors that currently rely on superstition."

Martha gave me a wry smile. "You are not trying to tell us that you think modern religions still believe in the old explanatory creation myths are you? I realize that there are still Creationists and fundamentalist Christians who do, but I think some religions have made progress in keeping up with reality. After what you have said, I'm afraid to admit that I still attend a Catholic church, one that I have attended since childhood. I can't say that I am a believer anymore, but it does make me feel better when I attend. I am sure I don't have to tell you that the Catholic Church is trying to reconcile their religion with science. They have vindicated Galileo for holding the heliocentric view, and the Vatican has met with neuroscientists, and even cosmologists like Stephen Hawking. They are trying to keep abreast of new knowledge and they look at much of the Bible more as allegorical moral instruction than historical fact."

I was not sure if she was speaking tongue-in-cheek or not. When someone says that the Pope or the Church vindicated so-and-so, as if scientific findings need the imprimatur of religion, I usually think they are joking, and I'm usually wrong. So I proceeded as if she was not.

"Well," I said, "I believe you have made my earlier point; many major religions have begun to defer to the physical sciences; but not to the science of behavior. They insist on being the arbiters of morals and ethics. Even many scientists working in other fields or disciplines do not realize that there is a natural science of behavior that has grown steadily over the last hundred years. We have begun to shed much light on human values, rights, ethics, and morals.

"But I don't want to give you the impression that religion was originally conceived only to explain natural phenomena. Humans are the only species that understands that they will someday perish. There must have been a time in our early verbal history when it was necessary to say, 'all living things perish, and therefore I will perish too.' It is feasible that after the death of a loved one or friend, they sometimes seemed to reappear in dreams. Dreaming itself was an unexplained phenomenon, and it is not much of a stretch to imagine that our ancestors believed this was a netherworld that the departed inhabited.

"It is understandable that our ancestors may have jumped to the conclusion that we went to this 'other world' after this one. Dreaming and thinking are purely neural behaviors that can often be evoked by external stimuli, as when our alarm clock goes off and evokes more neural behavior that becomes a part of our dream. Let me just say this about religion and see if you agree with me: If only *one person* held currently accepted religious beliefs, he or she would be diagnosed as schizophrenic according to the American Psychiatric Association's Diagnostic and Statistical Manual of Mental Disorders, and they would be treated for this condition. But since many people hold these beliefs, and many others have at least been exposed to them, they have become socially acceptable delusions, even though they contradict scientifically acknowledged reality.

"But to get back to your original question, I think this is why these books on atheism came out at this time. We have to dispel these myths if we truly want to save humanity. We have to begin dealing with reality and stop allowing false beliefs to take us down the wrong path. All branches of knowledge, without exception, should be subject to challenge. If statements about reality cannot be tested and are not potentially falsifiable, they are useless. For someone to say they believe something on faith alone, and therefore they should not be challenged, is preposterous.

"Almost every religion warns its adherents to be wary of infidels who will assail their belief system. They do this in an attempt to make it invulnerable to challenge from the outside. Cults are notorious for this and often go further by prohibiting their adherents from even associating with disbelievers, including family members. But even conventional religions have some built-in safeguards against challenge. This insulates religious believers from other philosophies.

"Imagine any other branch of knowledge getting away with this. Scientific and religious views, like the very different views taken by psychology and behaviorology, are incommensurable paradigms; by which I mean that these paradigms or worldviews are philosophically incompatible and therefore cannot be reconciled in any reasonable way. This is because one is measurable and verifiable and the other is not. But isn't it a shame that such able thinkers have to spend so much time dispelling ancient myths," I said at last. "In our communities, we avoid perpetuating the mythologies of the past. They are dealt with in our course on mythologies and verbal behavior."

It was getting late, and only a few members of Walden Two remained near the pond. Others had put their chairs in the shed and had gone to their rooms. We agreed to meet the following morning for breakfast and we called it a night. As we were putting our chairs away, Simmons approached me and said, "Dr. Burris, I would like to speak with you and Dr. Jensen tomorrow about a proposal I'd like to make, if that's all right. I'm not sure who needs to approve it, but I'll begin with you two."

"Certainly," I said. "I'll join you and Dr. Jensen tomorrow at breakfast. Good night."

9

The next morning, I joined Traci and the journalists for breakfast. After we had served ourselves and were seated, Jeffery Simmons broached his proposal. He proposed that he come to live in Walden Two for an extended period of time—and in possibly a few of our other communities if necessary—as an embedded journalist in order to write an ethnography about us. He thought it might be necessary to move among several of our communities to note any variations that may exist. He told us there was a period during his college years when he was quite interested in planned alternative communities and had, at that time, read quite extensively about them. None of them, he said—except Walden Two—was based on a natural science of behavior. Traci and I thought it would be an excellent project and agreed to run it by our planners and try to work out the logistics. The next leg of our tour was to the prosthetic environments for the elderly at the Lindsley Center.

Early behaviorologists, and even some contemporary behaviorologists, do not believe it is necessary to discuss the nervous system in the analysis of behavior. They are perfectly content exploring the functional relations between the independent variables in the environment, and behavior—the dependent variable. They are quite content to leave neurophysiology to neuroscientists. But there are some behaviorologists working in the nascent field of neurobehaviorology who are eager to understand the physico-chemical underpinnings of behavior.

They believe that neuroscience can better explain the causes of some of the aberrant behavior not apparent at the level of observation by the behaviorologist. For instance, a diseased or stroke-damaged nervous system that can no longer mediate particular operant behaviors can help explain the inappropriate behavior that occurs in those suffering from aphasia or ataxia. Moreover, many behavior-distorting diseases, like Alzheimer's, Parkinson's, and dementia, are best understood at the level of brain physiology.

Neuroscientists have recently developed instruments that allow us to investigate and record the activity of individual neurons and networks of neurons. At one time, neuroscience was too speculative to be of much use to behaviorologists, but recent progress has proved to be both interesting and enlightening. Neuroscientists are using new methods to eke out the brain structures and brain regions mediating many behaviors of interest, and many of us believe they are providing information that may be useful to us.

We have no objection to utilizing any *natural* science, since, and by definition, they must be studying real events. But Frazier often warned about theories of behavior that borrow from other disciplines or fields of study, or hypothesize internal entities in order to account for their own theoretical shortcomings. Frazier persuasively argued that our theories should only be based on observations of real, and therefore measurable, events. At the same time, he was clearly admonishing psychology about a type of psychological theory still prevalent to this day.

But neuroscientists, when they are not wasting time looking for the dubious internal mechanisms of cognitive psychology— the "ghosts in the machine"—are beginning to satisfy this criterion, and we are anxious to work with them. Darwin's theory of evolution by natural selection was not fully accepted until the science of genetics helped explain the mechanism needed to account for it. This merging of genetics with evolutionary theory has been called the "Modern Synthesis." Neuroscience is now supplying the mechanisms needed to account for the findings of behaviorology in a new and different kind of synthesis, and we are anxious to work with them.

As we approached the geriatric center, Traci started things off.

"In the aged," she began in her clear and inimitable manner, "we can surmise—and in many cases, demonstrate—that the body and nervous system are changing in ways that fail to mediate previously effective behavior. While behaviorology can tell us the environmental conditions responsible for the acquisition, maintenance, and elimination of behavior, physiologists can tell us how and why the mediating nervous system is failing in disease and old age. And while we behaviorologists can *describe* this failure at our own level of observation, neuroscientists can better explain, in some cases, why environmental control is gradually being diminished or lost.

"For example, synaptic connections may be weakening between neurons, myelin may be thinning, brain cells in essential areas may be dying, and dendrites may wither and shrink. Some of these neural structures can be those that mediate components of complex motor behavior; others may involve sensory areas of the brain. As a result, sensory input is often diminished, deficient, or lost completely. Consequently, stimulus control of behavior is also reduced or lost, and behavior that was once evoked or elicited by these stimuli either does not occur, or occurs inappropriately.

"Decreased vestibular sense leads to falls and, in senility, behavior, or important components of behavior, may be inappropriate or lacking altogether. The behavior we call 'remembering' becomes unreliable and less vivid, and it becomes more difficult to acquire new behaviors, or to bring previously acquired behavior under the control of new stimuli. Short-term memory loss and confusion are notorious symptoms of the aging process. When once effective operant behavior reduces in frequency, and the general level of reinforcement—or GLR—falls below a certain minimum, boredom, apathy, and possibly depression and even suicide, can follow."

Paul politely inquired, "May I interrupt you for a moment, Dr. Jensen? Would you explain once again what you mean by 'general level of reinforcement?' Dr. Burris mentioned this yesterday, I believe. May we assume it means the amount of reinforcement?"

"You are quite right," Traci answered, smiling pleasantly; she was always quick with reinforcing feedback. "It is the amount, quality, and duration of the added reinforcers. I know that some of these terms are unfamiliar to you and I apologize; so please feel free to ask for clarifications at any time. But, as you can surely imagine from your own experience, when many good things are happening often throughout your day, and lasting for a good period of time, your mood is said to be good. Many of these good things are the result of our own operant behavior. But older people often cannot do the things they once could. Operant behavior is the very behavior required to produce some of these reinforcers, and when the behavior cannot occur for *whatever* reason, the general level of reinforcement will decline.

"The elderly also cannot hear or see stimuli clearly that were once pleasant—music and speech, for instance. And, in some cases, many friends from their age group have passed, so interactions with those who knew them well and provided distinctive social reinforcers, are also lost. Some of the operant behaviors that produce our reinforcers require an agile and pain-free body. So we sometimes have what is called a 'response cost.' Not too many people will play a game they love, such as tennis, with a broken leg or even with a headache. And most people give up these beloved games as their joints begin to hurt and their reaction time slows. But these are often the kinds of ailments that our geriatric folks have to contend with daily."

As we entered the Lindsley center, Clifford removed his phone from his belt and began to take pictures and video. Occasionally he would move away from us and speak in a low voice into recording software on his phone.

"What do we know, and what can be done, about the declining brain?" asked Martha. "And what do your communities have to offer the elderly that nursing homes do not?"

"We know from lesion and experimental ablation studies with animals," Traci replied, "which areas of the brain are involved in the mediation of certain operant behaviors. Though these areas often deteriorate more gradually in the aging process, the result is much the same. Prosthetics are often used to remedy sensory impairment. But while hearing aids can be given to the hearing impaired, eyeglasses for failing eyesight, and canes and walkers are provided for those unsteady on their feet, little has been done to modify the mechanical and social environments of the elderly. We need to do more than just amplify the *stimuli* affecting the elderly.

"I believe what you are asking, Ms. Thompson, is: What can be done about the loss of memory, behavioral complexity, and social reinforcement? You see, little can be done at this time about the declining brain itself. Knowing what mediating neural structures have failed may or may not help us to design the kinds of environments that will compensate for these failures. When permanent or semi-permanent changes are made to a person's environment to remedy *behavioral* deficits, we call it a *prosthetic environment*. Prosthetic environments can be engineered to remedy or mitigate many of the behavioral deficits affecting the elderly."

"May we assume that these prosthetic environments are individualized?" asked Paul, and then he quickly added, "Well, of course, they *must* be."

"Yes," Traci said. "Personal living spaces are tailored to the individual's deficits, of course, but the common rooms are designed to take into account the most common problems of the elderly in general. I will show you some of these as we move about. As our members age, they receive regular evaluations for sensory and behavioral deficiencies. And just as sensory deficits are remedied with sensory prosthetics, behavioral deficiencies are remedied with environmental prosthetics."

"Who actually designs these prosthetic environments?" Martha asked.

"A behavioral-medical staff," Traci answered. "But first, of course, they must make functional behavioral assessments of the repertoires of our aging members to determine what behaviors are deficient or lacking altogether. For example, a particular member may no longer respond appropriately to questions or may show fewer signs of social or environmental engagement. We also watch for inappropriate or aberrant behaviors, such as talking to imaginary people, referring to—again, we say 'tacting'—objects that are not present as if they were, and we look for signs of emotional disturbance. I am happy to report that these types of symptoms are extremely rare in our communities due to our proactive health care.

"In some cases, otherwise appropriate behavior may occur at inappropriate times and may need to be brought back under proper stimulus control. This can often be remedied by providing more conspicuous cues, and I'll give examples in a moment. Our behaviorologists carefully define the problem behavior—a behavior deficit, or excess aberrant behavior, for instance—and then determine the cues for it. Technically, we call these cues, '*evocatives*,' since they are stimuli that *evoke* the behavior. And finally, we try to determine the consequences that are maintaining or no longer maintaining the behavior. These are, of course, the contextual variables analyzed by contingency engineers, including those who go by the label 'applied behavior analysts.'"

"Contextual variables?" Paul asked.

"Yes," Traci explained, "behavior necessarily occurs in some context. There are antecedent stimuli, the behavior itself, and then postcedent stimuli—that is, stimuli that follow the behavior;

these antecedent and postcedent stimuli comprise the immediate context in which behavior occurs. Operant behavior can be 'cued' by antecedent stimuli, and strengthened or weakened by postcedent stimuli. The postcedent stimuli—again, the stimuli that follow the operant behavior—are often contingent upon that behavior only when certain antecedent stimuli are present.

"Let me give you a very simple everyday example of behavior in context. Picking up a fork will only be successfully executed when a *real* fork is stimulating us in some way—visually for instance—before the operant behavior occurs. In other words, only when a fork is actually present can picking it up be followed by fork-in-hand. We can make the same movement in the absence of stimulation coming from a real fork, but the reinforcer—fork-in-hand—will not follow this operant movement. The antecedent visual cues from the fork, and the postcedent tactile stimulation coming from the fork in one's hand, all comprise the contextual variables for the behavior. Does this make sense to you?"

"Yes," Paul said. "I suppose the contact with the fork is contingent upon reaching and grasping, but only when we actually see the fork?"

"That is absolutely right," Traci said ardently. "Contact with the fork would not occur without *both* the antecedent stimuli *and* the operant behavior of reaching; the postcedent stimulus—or consequence of the operant—is contingent upon *both*. As I said, this is a very simple everyday example. There are many other antecedents of behavior—including a reinforcement *history*—that determine whether the behavior will occur and be successful. My original point though, is that the aging nervous system and other body structures that mediate the contextual variables—that is, come between the antecedent and postcedent stimuli—can deteriorate due to the aging process and interfere with both the evocation of the response and the reinforcement process."

We moved into a room with a large round table under a circular skylight and sat down. Traci signaled me to pick up where she left off. Martha sat nearby with pen and paper for note taking. I began to explain to them that we first attempt to remedy physical sensory deficiencies to the fullest extent possible before designing behavioral prostheses.

"As Dr. Jensen was saying," I began, "often, and due to sensory impairment, cues for some behaviors seem to progressively weaken. Actually, the cues themselves are not weakening, of course, as they are still physically present and unchanged; it is the functional relationships between the cues and behavior that is weakening. People can't engage in conversation if the requisite sensory receptors are not responding properly to the verbal stimuli of others. Therefore, it is only after all *sensory* deficiencies are remedied to the fullest extent possible, that a careful behavioral assessment is made. If behavioral problems are noted, a *behavioral* prosthetic prescription to remedy them is considered, proposed, implemented, and finally evaluated for effectiveness. I'll discuss some examples, but to be sure, the aged are often fully engaged in this process and work closely with our geronto-behaviorologists. Of course, this process of assessment evaluation and prescription is repeated if necessary."

"My grandfather has lost so much of his hearing that many people no longer engage in conversation with him." Martha said. "Even family members get tired of shouting and repeating. He cannot hear the television without having the volume blaring. What do you do about something like this?"

"Obviously, some sensory deficiencies may warrant a combination of prescriptions," I replied. "For instance, for a severely hearing-impaired person such as your grandfather, watching videos may require that sensory prosthetics such as hearing aids be used together with headphones; it may also be necessary to supplement this with large and clear subtitling.

We actually have software here that will slow down the video motion and sound slightly for those who show an increase in comprehension by a more protracted stimulation. The sounds of phones and doorbells can be supplemented with flashing lights as cues for answering them.

"But for everyday conversation, I would suggest you try a simple procedure that often works surprisingly well; and that is to make sure your grandfather is attending to you before you begin to speak to him. Sit down in front of him when you want to converse with him. This will soon begin to serve as a cue that you are going to speak with him and will prepare him to listen. It also allows him to read your lips to some degree. I would suggest you speak more slowly and clearly, rather than loudly. Those with hearing loss often miss the initial consonants of words, and these are very important for responding correctly to what was said. Therefore, these initial consonants may need to be exaggerated or emphasized. Many people talk to the hearing impaired from across a room and with their faces turned away. And they often begin talking before having the full attention of the hearing impaired person."

"I will definitely try that," said Martha.

"I've read that it is very difficult to get older people to remember to take their medications," said Paul. "Have you found you must remind them?"

"Typically no," I replied. "That is the whole point of designing the prosthetic environment, we want the environment to cue the behavior if possible. We strive to return some of the person's independence to them. Therefore, unlike sensory or bodily prosthetics, behavioral prosthetics may add additional reminders and conspicuous cues—again, what we technically call 'evocatives' or 'evocative stimuli.' These serve to evoke those operant behaviors that fail to occur to the usual evocative stimuli. If you can't change the failing brain, modify the environment instead.

"Timers can actuate a synthetic voice to evoke the taking of medications at the appropriate time, or alert the person for a scheduled engagement. After all, our elderly are not trying to be defiant by not taking their medications; they simply need more salient cues. Why depend on the aged person to remember when the environment can be engineered to accomplish the desired outcome? Often elderly people forget whether they have taken their medication for that day; we must therefore provide more conspicuous feedback. If a person must take a regimen of pills four times a day, a simple remedy may be to have her black out one quadrant of that calendar's day after taking each regimen of pills; or a button can be pushed on a small device that accomplishes the same thing.

"In either case, when the square is completed, she knows she has taken them all. A conspicuous cue I'm sure you are familiar with is a pillbox containing several closable sections for each time of day into which the pills can be placed. Each day's empty sections show which of that day's pills have been taken. Multiple containers for each calendar day can be labeled with the relevant time to take the contained pill and can be programmed to remained locked until that time. This is a simple but important example because it shows how effective even small environmental changes can be. The section of the container can even light up when it is time to take a pill, or change to a different color once the lid is unlocked, and change again when the pill is taken and the lid is closed.

"Along with more conspicuous cues and amplified feedback, it may be necessary to reinforce the behavior of the elderly on a smaller ratio schedule of reinforcement. Young nervous systems may be able to support smaller reinforcers on larger ratio schedules, where elderly nervous systems require more frequent feedback. This was pointed out by an early behaviorologist named Ogden Lindsley, after whom this building is named."

"Do your staff assist in some of the everyday activities of these elderly members?" Paul asked. "Or do you find that the elderly take offense to offered help? The reason I ask is because I believe you said earlier that people here were not offended by offers of help."

"That is true," I said. "They are not offended by offers of help; but I believe what I said earlier is that our members are not reluctant to *ask* for help. As far as offering unsolicited help, it is usually better for all if we wait until we are asked before stepping in. If a person is contending with a problem but making good progress, we feel it is probably best to leave the person alone and let their own signs of progress shape his or her behavior. The same is true for the elderly; we encourage them to perform all behavioral activities within their ability. Too often, well-meaning people step in to do things for the elderly that they could do for themselves. This may be due to impatience or to misplaced goodwill, but we must permit and even encourage them to do as much as their infirmity will permit. We must allow them to retain their dignity, and activity is good for people of any age."

"And what about those who can no longer do the things they once enjoyed?" he asked, "What kind of prosthetic environment can assist them?"

"Ah," I said, "just because a failing body can no longer mediate certain operant behaviors that once produced particular reinforcers, this does not mean new behavior cannot be learned that will produce reinforcers in other ways. For example, a person who once received much social approval and intrinsic reinforcement for his or her athletic behavior, may find other activities that are just as enjoyable but within his or her limitations. Interactive virtual reality video games—adjusted to the user's reaction time—may satisfy this. In addition, he or she can also switch to light exercise, dance, yoga, or tai chi, to provide some of the physical proprioceptive reinforcers provided by movement. This is where our exceptional ability to acquire new behavior comes in; this is precisely what we teach in our formal educational environments. We have found that learning new behaviors and seeing signs of progress are very reinforcing at any age. We continue to learn new ways to produce reinforcers throughout our lives. But even when we are no longer able to *do* the things we once did, we still may enjoy teaching others or writing about them.

"Recreation is important for happiness because it usually produces reinforcers on a favorable schedule. Here again we see the value of the GLR. For instance, good literature describes characters and situations, and builds tension that is periodically dissipated, or even heightened. It may then begin a new cycle and repeat this to a denouement. But the vicissitudes of life constantly change the reinforcing value of both unconditioned and conditioned reinforcers. Just as hormones bring new sexual reinforcers into play for adolescents, the diminution of these hormones along with the attenuation of sensory receptors in the elderly, diminish them.

"As complex neural behavior—what psychologists call 'cognition'—begins to falter in the elderly, they may be encouraged to relax their personal standards a bit. For example they might try reading lighter material that they may have once thought beneath them. They have plenty of leisure time to read those mystery, adventure, and humorous novels that they may have scoffed at before. While some of these novels can be quite complex, others provide reinforcers on a smaller ratio schedule; that is, one doesn't have to read far before something interesting happens. These novels seem to better hold the attention of the very young and elderly.

"Some of our folks here have written quite good novels for various age groups, with interesting themes relevant to our way of life. Writing may prove to be even more entertaining as we age and can no longer do those things that require an agile body. Part of our success involves trying to do things in new ways, and older people are encouraged to do the same; it has been shown to have a positive effect on the hippocampus, which, I'm sure you know, is vital to memory. If you have always worked crossword puzzles, switch to Sudoku for a while; if you are right-handed, try using your left; take lessons to play a musical instrument such as the piano or guitar. The point is to keep mildly challenging yourself to keep life interesting and the brain healthy."

I walked them over to a group of computer simulators and encouraged them to put on the virtual reality headsets to experience the special software designed specifically for the elderly. Some of these were attached to treadmills with handrails and safety straps, and when in motion, the user appeared to move through various virtual worlds of one's choosing. Others had hand-held devices shaped like rackets or any other sports equipment used in that particular sport. The participant could select among many different activity programs that auto-corrected to the person's level of proficiency. Some programs featured famous vacation spots; others simulated hang gliding or sailing. As they tested the simulators, I explained a little about the development of the programs.

"Computer and virtual reality applications designed specifically for the elderly can also provide interesting challenges, entertainment, educational material, and games, with age-appropriate scheduled reinforcers programmed into them. Also, as I previously mentioned, our software developers may, where necessary, slow down the motion to compensate for declining reaction times. Each user logs on with a user name, and reaction times are recorded and tracked over time. This way we can clearly note and graph waning performances. These records are also useful for our epidemiological studies. Our computer software, by the way, is written both here and in some of our other communities by software developers who work closely with our behaviorologists, children, the elderly, and other members of various age groups. I can assure you it is very user-friendly and age-appropriate.

"They have also developed very good event calendars showing upcoming events and activities occurring in Walden Two; I hope to show you some of these events and activities later. By the way, these calendars are programmed with synthesized voice reminders to cue the behavior of going to the event or activity. We do not discourage sexual material or devices for those who enjoy them, but libido-reducing prescriptions are available for those whose health will not permit sexual activity. Large-print books and audio books are available in both computer format and in hard copy. We provide what Ogden Lindsley called 'response force amplifiers'—including voice amplifiers—to augment waning operant behavior. After all, due to motor neuron disease, Stephen Hawking was almost completely devoid of normal operant behavior, yet with very weak operants—some involving small eye movements—he could operate computer-controlled devices, and remained a vital asset to humanity to the end of his life."

I thought we were going to have to physically remove Martha from the simulator area; she became quite engaged in viewing the Grand Canyon from a glider plane that she herself was piloting. But after several minutes, she gave up the controls and we moved on.

"Remember also that, unlike elderly people in society at large, who are often thrown together with strangers from different walks of life, the aged in Walden Two communities have *much* in common due their history of working and living together in the community. And most of us are committed to humanitarian efforts and enjoy discussing political, economic, and philosophical topics.

"Many reinforcers depend on simple behavior such as locomotion. When elderly people find it difficult to get around, they miss out on many reinforcers that movement could bring them into contact with. With mobility problems, reinforcers that would accrue from visiting family and friends, or going to interesting places or events are lost. What behaviorologists call the 'response cost' can increase dramatically for disabled people. Response cost is the net reinforcement value of a response; that is, the reinforcing value of the response outcome, minus the effort or energy expense needed to produce the response's reinforcer. In a very real sense, that effort is aversive, and the aversiveness of the response effort combines with the reinforcement value algebraically

"For example, it may not be worth it to go to the theater if it entails getting into a wheelchair, and then back out of it to get into a car, then back out of the car and into the wheelchair, going through theater doors, finding a seat and storing the wheelchair, and so on, just to watch a ninety-minute play or movie; the response cost may be too high. Elderly people often forgo these high response cost reinforcers. This is not to mention that modern movies sometimes depict unfamiliar themes and new colloquialisms that the elderly may be unprepared to appreciate; that is, their conditioning history can be very different from that of the younger target audience for which the movie was made. Therefore, there is a theater room available with a nice selection of movies chosen by the elderly. Of course, this selection will change as new cohorts age and replace older members who have passed.

"In short, we engineer environments for the elderly that help them to produce those things that they once enjoyed, or to produce new things to enjoy. Our goal is to maximize reinforcement by compensating for their disabilities to the extent possible. Too many nursing homes for the elderly just provide the basic needs for them and try to make the person comfortable. Some simply provide the elderly with non-participatory entertainment. But they do the person a great disservice by not allowing them to produce their own reinforcers. They too often treat the elderly like children and rob them of their dignity. It has been shown that many of the adverse emotional reactions of the elderly are a result of their progressing loss of independence."

"So, Dr. Burris, would it be accurate to say that these are therapeutic environments for the elderly?" Paul asked.

"No, not really," I replied. "Therapeutic interventions are temporary and are designed to rehabilitate and eventually return the person to their normal environments. Prosthetic environments are more permanent arrangements designed to support or supplement deficient or failing repertoires that are not expected to return. They are more like eyeglasses. Eyeglasses do not remedy the eye condition; glasses are meant to be worn permanently. When the geriatric patient begins to lose functional behaviors and we do not expect them to return, we must arrange a supporting environment to supplement that loss. But we have found that it is essential that, rather than us just doing everything for the person, we allow the person to produce her or his own reinforcers, even if that involves an apparatus that will allow weaker operants to produce them, as I mentioned in the case of Stephen Hawking.

"Also remember that in smaller communities such as ours, with our people working together closely as we do, we are familiar with the repertoires of our members—what most people might think of as their personality. In larger societies the elderly are placed in nursing homes where nursing staffs are not familiar with each particular person's personal history, therefore they don't know what behaviors are absent from their repertoire and they must rely on verbal accounts from family and significant others. These are usually incomplete for prescriptive purposes. The aged are too often placed together with others whom they do not know or with whom they have little in common. These other people usually also have failing repertoires and are hard to interact with.

"Here at Walden Two, we all have much in common since we have often interacted and worked together on shared goals or outcomes. Our elderly are given useful tasks within their capability that give them a sense of purpose, and their behavior is reinforced by signs that they are still contributing to common goals. I imagine it is the same good feeling that most people outside of Walden Two get when they collaborate with others on community projects; you are working for something greater than yourself. Sadly, for many people conditioned outside of Walden Two, there *is* nothing greater than one's self.

"Furthermore," I continued, "we foster relationships between the generations so that people of all ages, including our elderly, have friends of all ages; we believe it is important to have enthusiastic young people around to raise spirits, so to speak. In this way we have recreated the extended families of the past, and some of the benefits these extended families conferred. When the elderly in many larger societies begin to lose their friends due to illness or death, and their families—children and grandchildren—have all grown and moved away, many familial social reinforcers are lost. In these circumstances we often say that the elderly lose purpose and no longer feel valued or needed.

"As I previously mentioned, as the response cost of ambulatory behaviors increases and the infirm move about less, contact with many other reinforcers are also reduced or lost. We keep our older people here as active as their conditions permit, but supply prosthetics if necessary to ensure maximal ambulation. As you can see, we have designed our buildings, entrances and sidewalks taking this into consideration. There are various mechanical devices that allow them to move about Walden Two as they please. We do not sequester the elderly by placing them out of sight from the young, and where they will receive infrequent visits from friends or relatives. They remain active and involved. We believe it is important for young and old to interact and learn from and respect one other, just as people have done in many older cultures throughout history."

"And what happens to those people whose health fails to the point of no return?" asked Martha. "How do you deal with this concern?"

"Surely you don't euthanize them?" Clifford asked.

"Of course not." I said. "But all of us are aware that we will eventually reach a stage where we can no longer take care of ourselves—if we live long enough. We provide for these people and make them as comfortable as possible. As long as the aged are happy, we couldn't care less if they put puzzles together all day. But options are available for those who have reached a point where living is not the best alternative. I'm not talking about people who become mildly depressed or have minor handicaps. And I'm not talking about people who you might suppose have become a burden to us. Remember, we have known these people intimately. They are our friends and family.

"I'm talking about those with terminal conditions that severely restrict that person's ability to experience happiness and quality of life ever again, or people who are in rapidly declining health and may be experiencing unrelieved pain, with no hope of recovery. Alternatives are available whereby they can self-administer a lethal injection through an intravenous line inserted for this purpose, and forgo any further unrelievable suffering. Believe it or not, just knowing we have this option alleviates a lot of anxiety, not only for people in this condition, but for all of us who understand that we too may one day have to suffer this fate.

"You see, while we are not afraid of death, we are afraid—and rightfully so, we believe—of the suffering that sometimes accompanies the dying process. We all must die, that is certain, but we do not have to die miserably and in an undignified manner. How many of us worry about *how* we will die? We wonder if we will have a stroke or heart attack and die immediately, or will we suffer and linger for months or years? It's probably best not to think too much about these things, but we must also be realistic and not deny that our own demise is inevitable."

"Have behaviorologists also analyzed the behavior of the dying person?" asked Martha a little incredulously. "I assumed behaviorologists only studied the behavior of the active living."

"We have analyzed behavior from cradle to grave," I said. "One behaviorologist in particular, Dr. Lawrence Fraley, has summarized, in behavioral terms, much of what we know about the complexities of the dying process. He has published a book on this subject called *Dignified Dying—A Behaviorological Thanatology*. Much of what I am about to relate to you comes from his analysis. He has pointed out that death, particularly the slow death that accompanies terminal illness, can sometimes occur in distinct stages. One stage he calls 'person death,' which is a kind of behavioral death where the body's nervous system will no longer support the operant repertoire that we call the person or personality.

"This can be the result of degenerative neurological disease or of progressive deterioration of the nervous system due to the aging process. Another kind of death may be called social death. This is the process by which the social contingencies that maintain the social interrelations between the dying person and his or her loved ones deteriorates to a point where the previously available mutual responses and reinforcers are lacking. This is the point in the progressive demise of a person when they must say goodbye to friends, acquaintances, and loved ones before their social repertoire deteriorates beyond recognition.

"These final farewells can involve a series of ritualized celebrations of the person's life and recognition of his or her accomplishments. Or it may just be visitations from significant others to say their last goodbyes. In both cases, these events occur with the understanding that this is the last time they will see this person alive. As the person's behavior deteriorates further, they may no longer be able to put on a good face during the dying process, and out of respect we must allow them privacy to die with some dignity. People who have known the person must understand that the failing body and nervous system will no longer support that person they once respected or loved. A small group of loved ones may be present during this process to assist the person as he or she dies.

"The final stage of death is the death of the body when it reaches a point where it no longer supports life-sustaining activities. Complete deterioration and decomposition follow body death. Usually, until bodily death occurs, people have historically considered the person to be alive, even when it is the machines connected to the body that are performing the missing bodily functions. Behaviorologists, and increasing numbers of medical practitioners, believe *death* actually occurs at *behavioral* death, or *person* death, when physical deterioration guarantees that no stimuli can ever again evoke operant behavior from the body—either overt activity or covert thinking or consciousness.

"But the behaviorally dead body—necessarily being closely associated with its behavior—continues to evoke strong emotions in those people who knew the person well, even though behavioral death may have occurred some time ago. We must try to separate the body from the person and rationally accept the fact that behavioral death *is* the death of the person—'person' being completely defined by the body's operant behavior. For many people, all three stages of death occur concurrently, but of course, in this case, there are no last goodbyes said.

"The slow death of a friend or loved one is very unpleasant to watch, and may elicit negative emotions and images that are later re-elicited when thinking of that person. This can taint the pleasant emotions that would otherwise have been elicited when thinking about that friend or loved one. People should not, but often do, expect the dying person to behave with dignity right up to the end as they suffer through sustained pain and failing bodily systems. As people die and can no longer maintain the operant behavior that they were known and loved for, we cannot expect them to continue behaving in that same manner. In our communities, we give ourselves alternatives that allow the person to avoid the slow and painful dying process. We have found ways to allow ourselves to die peacefully with some remaining dignity. After people with terminal conditions have made all final arrangements, and have said their last goodbyes to friends and family, they are then free to end their lives *before* behavioral death occurs and severe physical suffering ensues."

"And may we safely assume that each person must make that determination for themselves?" Martha asked.

"Of course," I answered. "People who have made it clear beforehand that they wish to be allowed to die physically in the event that behavioral death has occurred are granted this. I should also tell you that we do not just present these options at the end of a person's life, we are educated on the subject well in advance, so there is very seldom a need for a rash decision. We have educated our members on this issue and they are aware of—and have carefully thought about—the various alternatives available to them.

"We also have an advantage over many unfortunate people outside of our communities—our decision is not complicated by superstition. Moreover, most, if not all of our adults, have made out living wills and have let the appropriate caregivers and friends know what their end-of-life wishes are. Each person must make her or his own decision about these things and, while sometimes unpleasant, they are necessary for peace of mind. The decision to end one's life is completely in one's own hands, so to speak. Family, friends, and doctors may counsel them to make sure their decision is justified and unhindered by false beliefs. We do not want them to submit before their time.

"Outside of our communities, people must worry about their financial needs after the death of a loved one, especially if that person was a primary provider for them. People outside of our communities, unless otherwise provided for, must try to calculate the proper amount of insurance to purchase in the event of that provider's death. Insurance companies are profit-driven businesses and try to sell life-insurance policies that maximize these profits. Many families are not competent to do the necessary calculations needed to determine the amount of death benefits that will sustain them adequately in the event of the death of their provider. For this reason, they are often taken advantage of by some of these self-serving companies.

"Here, at least, we know that our needs will continue to be met after the death of anyone. At least we can rest assured that our standard of living will not change due to the death of another. A grieving person should not have the added burden of having to worry about his or her own economic survival. We have very supportive social networks, and research has shown that people who have close social relationships with others do much better after the death of a loved one than those with few friends. We are all grounded in reality here. We look at death as a natural event to be expected, and we do not try to deceive ourselves with a false belief in an afterlife."

We walked through a recreation area where several elderly people were playing bridge. A few others were teaching chess strategies to some of the younger members. The room was brightly colored and well lighted, and I pointed out some of the small details such as nonslip floors and the complete elimination of tripping hazards. Doorframes and steps were painted with a highly contrasting color to make them more salient. The playing cards were slightly larger and thicker than usual, and made with large numbers to aid failing eyes. Being longtime friends and members of Walden Two, the bridge group was talking animatedly and was quite jovial. An elderly man turned toward me and said, "Hello, Dr. Burris! Another tour?"

"Oh yes," I said, "and if you could take a moment I'd like you to meet our guests; they are writing about our community. This is Martha Thompson, Clifford Douglas, and Paul Johnston." I introduced the players in turn and when I got to the last couple, I turned to my guests with a smile and said, "Folks, I would like you to meet Steve and Mary Jamnik. As you may recall, they accompanied my grandfather to Walden Two many years ago."

10

"**W**ell, well," Paul said, shaking the Jamniks' hands, "it is a pleasure to meet both of you. I would love to have you join us this evening if you're available. I think I can speak for all of us when I say we would enjoy hearing all about your time here and the changes you've seen. Could that be arranged, Fred?"

"I don't see why not," I said, "If that works for Steve and Mary, of course."

We already had planned to meet near the pond that evening, and Steve agreed to join us there, but it was uncertain whether Mary could as she had a prior commitment. Steve, now in his 90s, is still in good health, as is Mary. We departed the recreation area and I took our guests around to other areas that I thought might be of interest. After looking over the exercise facilities and entertainment center, I took them through a room that served as an informal library and study area outfitted with walking desks, sometimes called 'treadmill desks.'

These are desks upon which a person can study or write while walking on a slowly moving treadmill. The importance of actively burning calories throughout the day has been shown to lead to a longer and healthier life. There were also conventional sitting desks equipped with adjustable-resistance pedals that allow a person to slowly move the large quadriceps muscles while engaging in otherwise neural activity. They are ideal for reading magazines and journal articles and for working at a computer. It is not necessary to exert oneself to the point of distraction while working at these desks in order to enjoy the benefits of slow movement; more vigorous exercises are usually done separately, perhaps with accompanying music or video.

As everyone knows by now, our ancestors were much more active than modern humans and it is our relatively sedentary lifestyle—along with poor nutrition—that is harming our health. There are similar workstations in several other areas of Walden Two, all containing walking or standing desks alongside conventional desks; but the walking desks are quite popular. We discovered that simple 'standing desks' that keep one upright but stationary, allow the blood to pool in the legs if one stands too long, so we are gradually phasing them out. Several older members were slowly walking at these desks with headphones, listening to self-selected music while perusing sundry reading material as we passed through.

I explained to our visitors that our communities are collecting longitudinal health data on our members for epidemiological studies to be shared among our network of communities and published in the proper journals. None of our members smoke. Few drink alcoholic beverages, and then only occasionally and in moderation. All eat healthy nutritious food, which is prepared in our community. And everyone is quite active, well educated and engaged. By eliminating these unhealthy variables, it is much easier to tease out other important variables without relying too heavily on factor analysis. We are quite happy, with few worries, and we have excellent proactive healthcare. Our neurobehaviorologists examine the brains of deceased members looking for lesions or other abnormalities that might help explain any deficient or aberrant behavior noted before the person's death. The databases from our collective communities rival that of any scientific cohort study.

"We have come to some interesting conclusions about aging and dementia," I said to them. "Our epidemiologists have teased out a few new *environmental* variables sufficient to produce dementia I am told, but I'm afraid I will have to wait until our investigators publish their findings in the proper journals before speaking more on this."

We left the Lindsley Building and headed to the cafeteria for lunch, and afterward I again left them to their own devices, as past experience suggested that they would appreciate some writing time at their computers. They seemed interested in trying out the workstations, so I directed them to those I thought would give them the most privacy, and I left to meet with Dr. Jensen and go on to a planners' meeting.

Our group of planners meets twice a month, or more often if necessary, to share observations and discuss issues concerning the community. Traci and I sit in on one of these monthly meetings and apprise the other members of any behavioral concerns. Our culturologists attend, of course, and provide an assessment of the overall health of the community. They sometimes suggest engineering new contingencies or modifying existing ones, if warranted. This information is also shared with all other communities in the network. This particular meeting was uneventful, but we did bring up Simmons' proposal to embed himself here as an ethnographer. After a brief discussion it was accepted without objection. We rejoined our guests late in the afternoon near the pond as was arranged, and Traci and I opened ourselves to questioning.

Martha began the questioning.

"Can you tell us a little about *yourself*, Fred? What was your education like here at Walden Two? I imagine the educational system has changed quite a bit since you were a boy, for, as you've suggested, it constantly evolves, does it not?"

"It certainly does," I answered. "Though there are many similarities with the current educational system, the *curricula* have changed quite a bit over the years and have become much more flexible. When this first Walden Two community began, the founders had adopted much of the curricula from the standard American educational system. This has all changed, as our culturologists have concluded that many of the courses in public and private schools outside of Walden Two were really unnecessary. This is undoubtedly obvious to many adults who do not remember much of the material covered in some of the courses they were required to take. If the behavior strengthened in a controlled environment—such as a school—is applicable to the world outside of school, it will be maintained by natural reinforcing contingencies. If the behavior is not applicable, it will either extinguish or, in some cases, incompatible behavior will be strengthened that will interfere with it."

"I took many required courses that I did not like at the time," Clifford said, "but I'm glad now that I was forced to take them; I would not have taken them otherwise."

"I'm sure you are right, Mr. Douglas, but when you use the word 'forced,' it troubles me a bit. You see, if there *are* certain subjects known to be important for all to learn—and by the way, we believe this to be true—it is our job to motivate the student to *want* to explore these subjects. We must prepare the ground for the student, so to speak, so he or she will want to learn more about these subjects on his or her own. Not all children will be ready for a particular subject at the same time, although this does not cause the chaos you might imagine; with our computerized teaching technology, each student can progress in a given subject on his or her own. If other children talk about a subject that another child is not familiar with, and they find this subject interesting, this can also motivate them to learn more about it. But I'm afraid even the use of mild coercion in education is antithetical to the enjoyment of learning—and the enjoyment of learning is what we seek. It is the foundation upon which expansive repertoires are built.

"What is just as important to our success as our flexible curricula, is our embrace of new teaching technologies such as virtual reality simulators. These educational simulators can be programmed to condition various operant behaviors and deliver reinforcers on schedules optimized by our behaviorologists. The software for the simulators is designed to track errors, sense waning performances, and adjust the teaching program accordingly. And, just as in our other teaching machines, the simulators will automatically switch to subroutines that will condition lacking prerequisite behavior before progressing to condition more complex patterns of behavior.

"These simulators, and the well-designed educational programs that run on them, have revolutionized our educational instruction. But I must admit, I still have many fond memories of using the early simple teaching machines that were in use when I was young, and of the dedication of my teachers. My father was in the first generation that you could actually say was a product of Walden Two's educational system. Grandfather Burris was, of course, like Frazier, not a product of Walden Two's educational system. Like many at that time, he had behaviors that had been shaped outside of our community. We call these *legacy behaviors*. Legacy behavior also includes the *values* one brings to a new environment. This was the hardest thing to deal with in *starting* a new community—dealing with behavior shaped in a culture that reinforced behaviors and endorsed values different from, or even antithetical to, the values of the new community."

"So are you saying that your engineered contingencies are not as effective with people coming from outside of your communities?" Clifford asked. "I would think contingencies are contingencies."

"That is a fair question, Mr. Douglas," I answered. "But it takes a certain amount of time for new contingencies, in any new environment, to have their effect. When Walden Two first began, many people—coming from a more competitive culture—wanted to step in and begin taking control. In their culture, leaders amass more power and wealth. Just look at some of our American politicians.

"Now in my grandfather's case, being a Harvard professor, his legacy behaviors happened to be mostly benign. For example, I was told that he was a little arrogant and overly decorous, though not unpleasantly so. And he had been exposed in childhood to the kind of contingencies we would call religious indoctrination. By this I mean that his local culture—family and religious community—made social reinforcers contingent on certain religious verbal behavior and rituals.

"This all occurred during his formative years and he held religious beliefs—like many of his generation—from an early age, though he later renounced them some time before entering college. He could not reconcile them with what he rationally knew to be true about the universe, you see. Here again, I want you to notice the conflicting contingencies to which he was exposed. But these beliefs are often hard to eradicate completely.

"Grandfather was not a *natural* atheist but rather a converted one, and there is a noticeable difference. Early beliefs are not just wiped out completely and the person returned to the state of a natural atheist—a natural atheist being a person who was *never* conditioned to hold these beliefs to begin with. But while he refrained from mentioning his early beliefs to my father, he did occasionally speak of the problems they produced for rational thought. Some psychologists refer to the effects of such conflicting contingencies as *cognitive dissonance.* I only mention this to contrast our views with those of psychologists; where they speak of *cognitive* dissonance, we point out that the dissonance is in the contingencies that produce the effect.

"Now I, on the other hand, was brought up without any mystical or metaphysical beliefs. I am truly a natural atheist. But I dislike defining people this way. This whole business of categorizing ourselves by what we *do not* believe in, strikes me as extremely odd. The contingencies to which I was exposed were carefully engineered to strengthen more scientific and pragmatic behavior, and I must say I am very grateful that I was exposed to these contingencies that brought about my rational thinking. My father later told me of some of the religious tribulations that my grandfather experienced as a child, which makes me even *more* grateful that I had the educational training that I had."

"Can you say that you are *happier* than you would have been had you been, um, conditioned, as you might say, outside of one of your communities?" Martha asked. "Is there any way to determine this?"

"Well, judging from the subject matter of much of your popular literature and movies, along with my studies of world governments and culture, I would say I am much better off and happier," I said. "It seems to me that contemporary mass culture is consumed with doomsday and apocalyptic scenarios of the future. Many of today's young people seem to be preoccupied with either extravagant lifestyles or doom. They also seem to have a shortened timeline, as if their days are numbered, so to speak, so why should they think long-term and try to build a future? We simply don't have these dismal visions of the future in our communities. You cannot totally appreciate the value of working in close cooperation with others unless you have experienced it firsthand. I imagine you have worked closely with your colleagues and editors on joint projects and felt a significant amount of satisfaction with your collaborative efforts, but to work toward the good of one's culture, and to truly feel like you are a vital part of it, is quite different. Imagine what you have experienced but on a grand scale. It's extremely gratifying."

"But you are obviously a bright man," said Clifford, clearly missing my point. "You could have done anything you wanted and lived at a much higher standard of living than most people. I will admit that your community is nice and even peaceful, but couldn't you have been just as happy, or maybe even more so, living elsewhere?"

He seemed genuinely uncertain about my values and motivations, but I believe he was also questioning his own.

"It is certainly possible that I would have been just as happy somewhere else," I said, "but I seriously doubt it. And you must know that happiness is only one indicator of living a good life. Many people can still be happy even while their actions are actually hurting others. There is no objective way to prove that I am happier here, of course. I mean—how can one know?

"But consider the classic motion picture *Citizen Kane*. Kane's life took a drastic turn when he was removed from his mother and his simple life and sent away to get a 'proper education.' He became famous, wealthy, and powerful, far beyond the norm, and many people would envy his fame, fortune, power, and extravagant lifestyle. But the mysterious utterance of 'rosebud' at the end of his life tells us a different tale; we have to wonder if he would have been truly happier with a simpler life and a loving mother. Good art oftentimes reveals an obscure truth.

"But I do know that my life here is very fulfilling, and contingencies here have fostered my belief that we should also work for the good of humankind. This would include working toward a more peaceful world and one that educates all people to their full potential. We are not only producing educational technologies here, we are producing clean technologies that we hope to export to other cultures. These will benefit us all. But I am quite aware that altruism is anathema to some Western philosophies."

Traci was sitting with her legs crossed, drinking coffee. Paul was seated beside her and would occasionally direct a question to her, which she always answered most cordially.

"I'm interested to know if you ever have reservations about your beliefs?" he asked. "How do your members reconcile their beliefs and values with those of most people outside of your communities? Surely they must be aware that there are lots of people holding irrational beliefs about many issues, from alien conspiracy theories to a number of incompatible religions. In fact, some have even combined these two by imagining that the gods spoken of by our ancestors were really extraterrestrial visitors with advanced technologies. I would think some of this would create internal conflict and doubt in some of your members," he added.

"And you, Mr. Johnston? Do you as a science writer have conflicting beliefs about such things?" she asked.

"No, of course not," he laughed. "But I always wonder how so many otherwise normal and even *intelligent* people can hold such conflicting beliefs in the first place. After all, they seem to function well in their jobs and home lives, so they must be somewhat rational in these other areas. I have friends, for instance, who actually believe our government was involved in bringing down the World Trade Center. It's ludicrous, yet one of these friends is an engineer from a prestigious engineering school! Of course, he no longer mentions this nonsense to me because I just laugh. He takes this in a good-natured way, but I actually think he believes it."

"I don't doubt it," said Traci solemnly. "I can only tell you that we do not have the inconsistencies in our behavior that result from conflicting contingencies. *People* are often said to be in conflict, but the conflicts are not in us, or even in our behavior, they are in the contingencies. In many societies incompatible behaviors and beliefs are reinforced by different sectors of the social environment. For example, one sector is telling them that the universe is lawful and understandable while another professes mysticism and miracles. Conflicting contingencies can compel some people to compartmentalize, so to speak, their incompatible beliefs, since different audiences usually evoke these beliefs. That is, they behave one way in the presence of one audience and another way in the presence of another audience. This is a clear example of stimulus control.

"Think of an adolescent child whose peers may reinforce behavior that would be unacceptable to the child's parents. And the parents may have previously reinforced behavior that would be derided by the child's peers. A conflict only occurs when the two audiences are brought together, in which case the stimuli for incompatible behaviors are present simultaneously. The child may behave more politely and subserviently in the presence of the parents, a behavior that the peers may not have seen in their friend before and may deride. Or the child may be more disrespectful or impertinent to the parents, gaining the approval of his peers, a behavior the parents have not seen in their child and may punish. But again, notice that the conflict is in the *contingencies*; incompatible behaviors are being evoked by different *audiences* that have previously reinforced or punished these behaviors. When the two audiences happen to come together, the child may become confused and anxious, as he or she has learned to anticipate punitive sanctions from one of these audiences.

"We do not have that problem here. The contingencies are very consistent and carefully engineered by educators to shape our behavior in one direction; that of a rationally informed, well-educated, prosocial person grounded in reality. And while we may want diversity and originality in our thinking, we want homogeneity in prosocial behavior—that is a constant. We must always deal respectfully with one another. We know that current and long-term contingencies drive these behaviors, so we do not blame the person when behavior goes awry. We examine and, if appropriate, alter the contingencies in the contextual variables responsible for the behavior. Many of our beliefs have been repeatedly tested and upheld with such overwhelming support that we would be fools not to accept them as working hypotheses. But we also realize and appreciate the provisional nature of our scientific findings and theories, and have no illusions of perfect knowledge. We understand that our verbal descriptions of reality will evolve as new evidence accrues."

At this point, Steve Jamnik drove up rather quickly in an electric cart, or 'e-cart' as we call it, and placed it in a parking area equipped with a small recharging station. He plugged a cable from the e-cart into a recharging port, and, after obtaining a folding chair from the shed, joined us, sitting in a position opposite our guests. He was in very good shape for the age of ninety-three. Mary could not join us at this time, but Steve said she would make an effort to join us later. Steve was a careful and thoughtful speaker who chose his words carefully, and though his voice was easy to understand, he spoke rather softly, as many elderly people tend to do. After the initial cordialities, Simmons began to speak.

"This is quite exciting to speak with an early member," he said. "I read *Walden Two*, as I'm sure we all have, and would enjoy hearing how things transpired for you. Have you had any regrets? Or is that a silly question since you surely would have left, if there were? And can you tell us what became of Rogers? Did you keep in touch with him?"

"As far as regrets," Steve replied, "if you mean about living here, the answer is a resounding 'No!' Mary and I have found peace and fulfillment here and I have pursued many things I would never have had time for under more, let us say, capitalistic contingencies. I'm more convinced than ever that the exigencies of life and work required to survive outside of our communities prevent most people from reaching their full potential. Since our communities encourage all members to mentor one another, I have learned about many things, from many people, that I would never have had time to pursue had I not come here. Helping, sharing, and cooperating with others has an unbelievable effect on repertoire building, whereas competitive behavior has an isolating and deleterious effect on one's behavioral expansion. In competitive cultures, many people do not want to see others improve. So not only do they not help them, they may actually resent them and try to *undermine* their endeavors.

"Mary and I helped design, build, and later remodel, our own house," Steve said in his quiet voice. "And we have helped many others to build theirs, as they did ours. This was very gratifying, even though we do not swing hammers too often these days," he added with a smile. "We have two wonderful children. Our son moved to one of our communities out west, near Los Alamos. We keep in close contact via Skype-like video conferencing software written by some of our software developers. And, as Mary and I choose not to travel far due to our advanced ages, he comes here to visit a few times a year. Our daughter lives here in Walden Two."

"I would love to meet her," said Martha, "What can you tell us about Rogers and his girlfriend? Wasn't her name Barbara?"

"Yes," Steve said, "well, we kept in contact by letters for many years, but he never came back to Walden Two. Barbara, his girlfriend and later wife, for they married soon after he graduated from law school, never liked the idea of communal living. And why would she? Her personal history was such that she wanted to pursue what was then fondly thought of as the 'American Dream.' Upward mobility was a very fashionable thing among the working and middle classes in the '40s and '50s and on into the '60s, and I suppose even now for some. I've read reports from political scientists and social commentators asserting that the American Dream is virtually dead for the middle class, having died sometime in the 1970s. But that should have been expected. A society dependent on continuously increasing consumption for its economic growth cannot survive indefinitely. We cannot *consume* our way to prosperity; it is analogous to a pyramid scheme that benefits only those who enter into the arrangement early. Here we have learned to stabilize our consumption and have substituted cultural *improvement* for growth; they are two quite different things.

"But yes, Rodge and Mary had four children if I recall correctly," he continued. "Rodge told me that they moved into what sounded to me like a lavish neighborhood, had a beautiful house with a swimming pool for the children, and he had become a partner in a reasonably prestigious law firm in Philadelphia. It sounded like he was relatively prosperous, even for the upper middle-class neighborhood in which he lived. In most respects, he lived well above the material standards that Walden Two could provide, though we tend to judge *our* wealth using more non-materialistic standards.

"But years later, I began to get letters expressing discontent. Barbara, coming from an upper middle class family herself, was more socially conscious than Rodge, and her new family's station in life was quite important to her. Without divulging the private details confided to me, I can only say that they divorced when their youngest child reached middle school. Barbara obtained custody of the children and kept possession of the house, while Rodge moved into a condominium. He attributed the divorce to the long hours he worked to keep his family up to the standards to which they were accustomed and to pay for the children's private schooling, including later, of course, private universities. The year following their divorce she married a man who came from old wealth. Barbara had finally moved to her 'proper' station in life. I lost touch with Rodge not long after that, but I do know he has since passed."

I could detect sorrow in Steve's voice as he reminisced about his friend. They had become quite close during their stint in the Pacific and these were critical years in their young lives.

"You must remember," I said, "that those who visited Walden Two in '45 had values and behaviors shaped by more fortuitous contingencies. These are some of the troublesome legacy behaviors I spoke of before. It should not surprise anyone that Barbara held values from the upper-middle-class culture from which she came, and in which her behavior was conditioned. Signs of upward mobility and relative material superiority can become powerful conditioned reinforcers—values—just as anything can. These were the values for many in the United States at the time, and still are for some. Barbara's behavior and values are completely understandable and lawful, and are still quite prevalent among the middle class in the United States and elsewhere. We can no more hold Barbara responsible for holding these values than we can hold ourselves responsible for our own values. But we can reasonably assert that these values may not be the best ones for equitable communal living."

"And don't forget that Barbara was an attractive and intelligent young lady," Steve said, "and this gave her many advantages in life denied to others. She used her attractiveness to her advantage; and this too is understandable from a behaviorological perspective, as Fred has just alluded to. People bestowed with such natural gifts often come to feel more entitled and privileged than others, and may see themselves as somehow, well, for lack of a better word, superior. And they may not wholly appreciate that these 'natural' advantages are the result of coincidental contingencies involving natural and sexual selection, rather than from anything they have done."

"It isn't too difficult," Traci added, "to teach children having advantaged endowments to consider things from the perspective of others, but it does require special cultural and educational contingencies. This is part of our ethical training, and we condition empathic behavior rather early in the child's education. But without this training, feelings of superiority are completely understandable and are clearly the result of the coincidental contingencies responsible for them. Physically attractive people are often lavished with social attention non-contingently; that is, they receive much attention simply as a result of their physical beauty or other natural assets. People naturally look at and admire beauty, and this attention is generally reinforcing. But what *behavior* gets reinforced is another matter.

"Countless studies have shown that attractive people are treated differently and are more likely to be given special treatment throughout most of their lives. They are even judged as being more intelligent by their teachers, for instance. Similar contingencies in Barbara's life may have favored behavior that propelled her to always desire more; but I am only guessing based on what we know from studies done by empirical sociologists. Advantaged children usually have nicer things than their peers and learn to *value* this throughout their lives. Oftentimes it is not one's possessions that are reinforcing, it is having superior possessions *relative to others*. You see, relative superiority, like practically anything else, can become a conditioned reinforcer."

"And, along those lines," Steve said, "I am convinced that there will always be people who will become discontented with possessions that *currently* make them happy, if others can acquire them too. I saw this in Barbara back when I knew her, but I could not articulate it at that time. She apparently carried this throughout her life. Rodge and I had many discussions when we were in the Pacific and he told me, even back then, that she was more materialistic than him, and more driven to move up in the world. This is what seemed to motivate her more than anything. He thought this would change once they married and had children, but from his letters I gathered that it did not. I imagine she passed these same values on to her children, as people often do. I can only hope that they both found some kind of happiness after their separation. I learned a lot from Rodge; in fact I wouldn't be here if not for him. From what I knew of him he would have loved it here. Instead he wound up working in a law firm with people he did not respect, to provide for a wife who did not respect *him*."

"And what of Frazier and Fred's grandfather?" Martha asked. "What can you tell us about them?"

"Well, Frazier was quite prolific and productive up to and including his latter years," Steve said. "He published many important papers on behaviorology and wrote several books on the science and its applications to society. He guided research and worked with some of our young behaviorologists on experiments involving self-awareness and insight, demonstrating that contingencies of reinforcement can better explain much of what now passes as cognition. You know, John Watson is considered the father of what we now call behaviorology, but Frazier did the most to systematize, develop, and refine it.

"He was a brilliant experimentalist and isolated many important variables determining behavior. He also helped define and develop the philosophy called *radical behaviorism* that some call by other names, such as *behavioral naturalism*. This philosophy admits internal behavior—including emotions, feelings, thoughts, and so on—as *behavior* determined by the same laws that determine external, or public, behavior. If you're interested in this philosophy I would suggest you read, *Radical Behaviorism: The Philosophy and the Science* by Mecca Chiesa, or *About Behaviorism* by Frazier. Frazier was an avid note-taker and always had a notebook with him to 'catch his thoughts on the wing,' as he liked to say. He pondered on so many things. I could tell you many amusing stories about Frazier; he was certainly a genius.

"As far as Fred's grandfather, he was quite happy here and also lived a productive life. While Frazier chose to have no children, Fred's grandfather had two; a son Arthur—Fred's father—and a daughter, Julie. But I'm sure Fred can tell you more about them than I."

Martha asked Steve, "Why do you suppose Frazier left no offspring? As you say, he was a genius, was he not?"

"Well, I suppose only Frazier knew the answer to that, but he left a legacy he considered far more valuable than his genes,

I suppose; he left us a viable natural science of behavior. His genes would have benefited his offspring, but all of us can benefit from the science he helped advance."

"Why, then, do you think so many people have resisted behaviorology," asked Simmons? "I mean, after all, it has been demonstrated to be very effective in changing behavior."

"I would like to answer that, if I may," Traci said. "I have come to believe it is mainly because it conflicts with their strongly held prescientific beliefs about the determinants of behavior. Beliefs, like all other behavior, are the result of contingencies, but in this case, they involve verbal behavior. These include, for some, their religious beliefs. And, as Frazier learned quite early the hard way, behaviorology also challenges long-held notions of freedom and dignity. In fact Frazier wrote a book about these very notions in which he argued very cogently, I believe, that we must now move beyond our notions of freedom and dignity if we genuinely want to advance our understanding of ourselves. Behaviorologists are continuing to discover the causes of our behavior and have found them to be in the external environment, not inside the individual.

"What *are* inside the individual are the mediating biological structures that allow behavior to happen. That is all. There are no 'ghosts' inside us. These biological structures mediate the contextual variables responsible for the behavior that will allow an individual of a species to survive to reproductive age, and then pass on to their descendants the genes that code for those structures. But outside of our communities and a few institutions of higher education that teach behaviorology, people are exposed mostly to what Frazier has called the 'literatures of freedom and dignity,' and our language is infused with these notions. Unfortunately, they hamper a true understanding of human behavior.

"Much faulty thinking is a direct result of our language," she continued. "Orwell emphasized this in his book *1984*, in which he wrote a fictional account of a totalitarian government that controlled its population partly by manipulating the language of the culture, for example, by eliminating words for important concepts, or changing the very meanings of words that would otherwise help people to see their plight. But it is imperative that our verbal behavior comports with reality, and this includes the independent variables known to determine behavior. Having words for false ideas is as dangerous as lacking words for true ones."

"Have we reached a point where we can say for certain that all behavior is determined?" Paul asked. "Some people's behavior seems to be unexplainable."

"We believe it is absurd to think that the behavior of *any* biological system is free from determination," said Traci. "Ignorance of the controlling variables is not a good argument for non-determination. And neither is unpredictability due to complexity. We realize that the burden is on us, and we are continually finding determining variables of which we were previously unaware. This strengthens our belief that we are on the right track. We have also found that by refuting and dismissing prescientific concepts, we actually have less to explain than we thought. We consider the behavior of all organisms to be a fully determined system.

"Excluding some mystics, most people no longer believe that the weather is free, in the sense of being undetermined, yet it is often quite unpredictable with any considerable degree of accuracy. Behaviorology has developed a scientific lexicon that points to and explicates the independent and dependent variables of this natural phenomenon called behavior. The very *lexicon* of behaviorology has helped to facilitate our endeavors to understand behavior. That is why it is imperative that those undertaking to effect behavior change—parents, teachers, therapists, and others—take the time to learn about this science.

"Our communities are engineering the contingencies that will produce the behavior needed not only for the survival and happiness of our *current* members; we have also been successful in getting people to take the future of our culture, planet, and humankind into consideration. How do you get people to do this? We know from our research that behavior is more strongly reinforced by its immediate consequences than by deferred consequences. How does one get, say, the people controlling a fossil-fuel energy company to forgo immediate short-term profits and to consider instead the deferred consequences of the overuse of fossil fuels? Getting more people to take the future into account is one of humanity's most pressing problems in the world today. How do you clearly define behavior of this kind? How do you engineer contingencies to bring this behavior about? And who decides what behavior should be reinforced?

"I hinted in my talk on Monday that I would answer this question as it pertains to *our* communities. The answer is that *no one decides* what behavior to reinforce! The data collected by our culturologists determine what behavior is needed. The data collected may come from the other sciences; for example, data concerning the spread of particular viruses, or concerning our energy expenditures. The culturologists then inform our behaviorologists who then work with the culturologists to engineer the contingencies that will bring about any behavior change that will alleviate the problem. After all, what good does it do to have energy saving devices if people are not willing to use them, or are misusing them? And if people are consuming energy above the capacity to generate it, how do you get people to reduce their consumption? You see these problems in many modern societies. After we introduce new contingencies and give them time to take effect, we reassess and collate our data. If after making the suggested changes, the desired outcomes are not met, we reanalyze the system. It is data-driven systems analysis informed by the two sciences, as well as others.

"It is important to stress that, in our communities, the behavior that must be engineered is accomplished by using *positive* or *added* reinforcement; that is, every effort is made to engineer contingencies designed to make members *want* to behave in ways that support and advance our culture. This is not hidden from anyone. In fact members are often involved in the design of the contingencies. We call the study of the effects of cultural contingencies, 'Culturology'; I briefly mentioned this science in my talk on Monday. It includes the study of the cultural contingencies of many past and present societies. I should add that we view cultures very differently than conventional historians do."

"There will always be people outside of your communities," said Clifford, changing the subject, "and I'm thinking of *my* general readership now, who may tend to call a segregated community like this a cult. What is your argument for countering this belief?" he asked.

"I would argue vehemently that our communities are about as far from cults as you can get," Traci said firmly, but with full composure. "Can you think of a cult that does not have a charismatic or authoritarian leader—past or present? I can't. And, almost no cult can exist without one. We have no charismatic or authoritarian leaders of any kind in any of our communities. In fact, unlike many large societies with cult-like leaders, we have no one who could be called a leader of any kind."

"What about Frazier? Didn't he found and design Walden Two?" Clifford persisted.

"Yes, but founding a community does not mean that the founder ever personally controlled it," she answered. "While Frazier was the impetus behind Walden Two, he did not design it alone. He had many competent people working with him, providing suggestions about everything from building structures to energy systems. He originally had several of his graduate students, and a few colleagues in behavior analysis, making useful suggestions on how to motivate the original population. And Frazier knew that any community designed to survive must outlast its founder.

"He understood that there must be self-perpetuating *educational* contingencies in place that will strengthen behavior that is good *for all stake holders in the community*, not just for leaders or small subsets of the population. By the *community*, of course, I mean all people comprising it. If the people are well provided for, happy, and are directly contributing to what makes the community thrive and successful, then they will continue to support the community and want to see it perpetuated. If they are not happy, they are unlikely to support it, and may even work to undermine it, as rebels and revolutionaries in cultures everywhere exemplify.

"Also, we do not promise some wonderful *future* life to those who are willing to sacrifice themselves for others, or tolerate subsistence conditions now. Nor do we promise a life in a hereafter to those who submit to the will of a guru pretending to have divine insight or access to revealed truth. Our happiness and contentment is here and now, on this earth at this, our only time.

"And lastly, cults typically isolate their members from information that might challenge the beliefs of the cult. They forbid contact with outside sources, often isolating members from family and friends. Even many conventional religions have similar, if less stringent, constraints. People never suspect that their own religion is cult-like, but we beg to differ. I would also add that our communities are not segregated; we are in contact with many communities both inside and outside of our network. We work closely, and share data with scientists outside of our communities. Many have even come to visit and have used our data in their studies."

"How are *conventional* religions 'cult-like?'" Martha asked. "I don't understand what you mean when you say people don't suspect their own religions to be cult-like?"

"For one thing, most people do not want their religious beliefs questioned," Traci said. "He or she simply claims that they accept their beliefs on *faith* and they are not to be challenged by any evidence or counter-arguments. In fact, such people become extremely offended if you question their religious beliefs. In some cases, evidence would seem to cheapen his or her belief—they seem to believe they get more divine credit for believing without evidence, you see? All of this would imply to me that the belief came from a dogmatic person, document, or bible. This kind of thinking is antithetical to rationality and evidence-based belief. The unquestioned acceptance of dogmatic sources is common in most conventional religions."

"I don't see why a person cannot retain a spiritual side to help them cope with life's problems," Martha said. "I find solace in some kind of cosmic spirit and see nothing wrong with this—even if it *is* a false belief."

"Perhaps," Traci said, "some of these personal beliefs are relatively benign, I agree—as long as they remain personal. But consider," Traci continued, "that since the late 1950s, U.S. schools have stressed the teaching of science, technology, engineering and math—what are now called STEM programs—in an effort to keep *competitive* with other advanced nations. Note the operative word 'competitive,' and not 'cooperative'; historically, nations have tended to *compete* for resources or other advantages. The emphasis on science and engineering was largely the result of U.S. technological competition with the Soviet Union, especially after the launch of Sputnik in 1957. But even with the current emphasis on STEM programs, the U.S. is falling behind other nations due to, we believe, poor educational contingencies. STEM programs are supposed to help prepare present-day children to compete in the twenty-first-century global economy, a global economy requiring highly complex intellectual behaviors.

"Leaders of all advanced nations understand that these complex behaviors are necessary if they are to remain *competitive* in the world. Yet many religions in the U.S. are attempting to remove any science from curricula—especially in middle and high schools—that might challenge their religious beliefs. Religions are instead teaching people to believe in magic and all kinds of superstition, quite the opposite of science and rationality. Schools of higher learning, most of which attempt to dispel false beliefs of all kinds, are often labeled 'liberal' or 'atheistic' by religious believers and are attacked in conservative media.

"But science-oriented people do not insist that science be taught in churches, so why do religious people insist that religion be taught in public schools? In our view, all religions are essentially cults in that they perpetuate demonstrably false beliefs and encourage people to follow charismatic leaders or gurus—even dead ones. Whether these religious leaders are sincere or merely charlatans, makes no difference to the dismal outcome. In Christianity, the cult figure is Jesus, and various religious figures purport to be either 'channeling' Jesus, or claim to have special mystical powers allowing them to interpret scripture for the masses.

"So," Traci concluded, "to get back to Mr. Douglas's question, we do not behave in ways, or have any of the defining criteria of a cult. As scientific communities, we encourage challenges to all of our hypotheses and cultural practices. If critics took the time to learn about our practices, they would see they are based completely on data coming from the various sciences. We are exceptionally pragmatic. Our energy sector is based on physics, our medical services are based on biology, chemistry, physiology and pharmacology; and our educational and incentive systems are based on behaviorology. As you might expect, *we* believe this science is applicable to cultural concerns because we have *demonstrated* that it is. And that is the great thing about the sciences: they either produce testable theories that are pragmatic, or they don't. If the theories turn out not to be testable or pragmatic, then they are quickly abandoned and replaced. Science, by definition, is never accepted on faith, and we dissuade our members from accepting anything dealing with reality on *faith,* rather than on rigorous scientific proof."

"You know," I added, "the late physicist, astronomer, and philosopher Victor Stenger has asserted that the difference between science and faith is that faith is belief *without* supportive evidence, while science is belief *with* supportive evidence. In science, if the evidence does not support a belief you throw out the *belief.* In religion, if the evidence does not support the belief, you throw out the *evidence.* We have thrown out many of the false beliefs of psychologists, philosophers, and theologians, but we have kept the proverbial baby intact.

"All advanced cultures today base their practices on science. 'Science,' as you know, is from the Latin *scientia* 'to know,' and its methodology of careful observation and experimentation is undoubtedly the most effective way to know and understand how the world works. We have merely extended and applied this methodology to human behavior. In fact, behaviorologists apply their science to themselves as behaving scientists, which is another defining feature of the philosophy of radical behaviorism. You could say that, in a meaningful way, we are lifting ourselves by our own bootstraps."

It was getting late. It was obvious that Mary would not be joining us. Steve said goodnight to all, detached the charger from his e-cart, climbed in and returned to his room. Not long after, we all went to ours.

11

The next morning, Traci and I took our guests on a wider tour of the community. Everyone who visits seems more interested in the nuts and bolts of our infrastructure than in what we consider to be the real heart of Walden Two: the natural sciences behind it—mainly behaviorology. That is why I have spent little time detailing the structure of our community. We use energy-efficient technologies at all levels, but they are those that we can repair ourselves or replace easily.

While we are not Luddites, we do not rely on any highly advanced technology that would make us overly dependent on outside manufacturers and technicians. In the event of widespread national (or global) disaster or economic collapse, we can keep our communities up and running quite well on our own. We have an array of energy sources ranging from solar panels to windmills. In addition, we have propane gas and other fuels, but only as backups to run our generators in the event of an emergency. We occasionally even use very high-efficiency wood-burning stoves for heating. These stoves have been engineered to produce very little waste products. And we also have the means to fall back on even lower subsistence technologies if necessary.

Most structures in Walden Two are assembled in ways that will make future disassembly easier. Almost everything here is reused, repurposed, or recycled. Our biologists strive to balance the life forms in our ponds and surrounding woods as much as possible, and these are not over-fished or over-hunted. It is often said that we are composed of what we consume; but you can take this a step further and say we are composed of what our *food* consumes—be it plant or animal. So in many cases, our biologists know the history of our food down to the microorganisms that they consume and the nutrients in the soil of our plants.

We have a few hydroponic greenhouses in addition to our more conventional greenhouses where some of our food is grown. Much of our food is grown in our fields or in one of our many outdoor gardens. The children also have a nice multi-tiered raised garden next to the school in which they learn to plant and tend some of our vegetables using organic gardening techniques. They later prepare, cook, and consume these vegetables themselves. It is essential that everyone understands and shares in food production.

Like anyone can, we have benefited from the work of our scientific colleagues around the world. One of the great things about science is its cumulative nature. Another is the provisional acceptance of its theories, which are often tested in pragmatic applications. We have applied the findings and developments of the other sciences, as we hope they will apply the findings of our science in beneficial ways. We are also quite happy to take advice based on scientific research wherever and whenever we can. For example, we have employed the suggestions presented in the very helpful publications that the Union of Concerned Scientists produces, such as *Cooler Smarter: Practical Steps for Low-Carbon Living*.

Much of the wood we use for construction is a composite material made from compressed sawdust and shavings left over from the milling process. Some of our insulation is made from discarded newspapers, and our ceramic tiles are recycled from vehicle windshields. Energy conservation methods such as insulation, non-incandescent bulbs, weather stripping, and so on, are comprehensively used. Windows from dismantled structures can be reused in new structures, or perhaps repurposed as covers for plant-starting boxes, or disassembled and recycled. Any wood that cannot be reused may be burned in the higher energy-efficient wood-burning stoves available, and we are working to improve this efficiency. We are proud of the fact that nearly all of our structures meet "Passivhaus," or "passive house," standards.

Also all of our communities are doing research in various areas of science and are producing technological improvements in everything from longer-lasting batteries to robotics and windmill design. Of course we share our findings with all communities in the network, and we patent our designs as appropriate. While we believe in the open sharing of information—and therefore do not like the patent process—we must protect ourselves from those outside of our communities who *will* patent our designs. If the larger outside community can benefit from our patented designs, we use the size of license fees to encourage fair use and discourage price gouging. In this way we can fulfill part of what we see as our responsibility to "share the wealth," and hopefully assist the rest of humanity.

I know that this differs from traditional cultural practices, where patents are used as a get-rich-quick resource. But as I said, our patents also preclude others from patenting our discoveries first and then profiting from them, including by actually making us pay to use our own designs. Information is shared between our communities through an intranet using high encryption software developed by our software engineers. Certain computers are dedicated to this private intranet while others are reserved for access to the more general Internet where we access scientific and scholarly journals and major newspapers from around the world.

As we walked around the grounds of Walden Two looking at various structures, I explained the workings of some of the infrastructure of our community. Though I understand why this is so interesting to people, I did not want them to get caught up in descriptions of the material composition of Walden Two. Therefore, I offered the following.

"Visitors are usually already somewhat familiar with our labor credit system from reading *Walden Two*, the seventy-year-old account written by my grandfather. We have modified this substantially over the years and have supplemented it with other contingencies. The original question was, is it necessary to use explicit tangible generalized reinforcers such as money or other tokens in order to motivate, reinforce, and maintain communally productive behavior? We found the answer to be 'no.' With the proper educational contingencies, and by utilizing some ingenious feedback stimuli engineered into various activities by our behaviorologists, we have found people will continue responding or working if noticeable signs of progress are contingent on that behavior. This may sound elaborate, but it is no different than the behavior of any homeowner who works to produce desirable home-improvement outcomes without extrinsic remuneration. The challenge was to considerably expand, through conditioning, what people consider to be their personal property."

"How do you evaluate and assess the behavior of your workers?" Martha asked. "Do your behaviorologists need to follow them and watch to see that the contingencies are effective?"

"Not at all," I said, "It is no different here than anywhere else. In most cases, after initial assessment, we no longer need to assess the behavior itself; we can instead assess the *products* of behavior. This is no different than the practices used in business. Most often it is the output product that is important. Now, if the product is inferior, we may have to reassess the behavior to see what is going on. And I am glad you asked that question, Martha, you are getting close to the heart of our community. These days, visitors constantly ask questions about our infrastructure, as if this is what defines a community. They want to know about our windmills, solar panels, geothermal systems, electric automobiles, hydroponic gardens, green houses, our sundry machinery, robotics, and so on. These things are interesting and I am happy to discuss them, but, as technology changes, so does our infrastructure. We update, replace, or retrofit our machinery as necessary; the operative word here is 'necessary.' If a technology is out of date by outside standards, but is still doing its job efficiently, we will only replace it when it fails.

"So, from our point of view, much of people's obsession with our infrastructure is somewhat misplaced; we believe that our infrastructure should be of subsidiary interest. Though we do hope others will adopt our energy-saving technologies and our parsimonious use of energy and materials, the technologies we employ will come and go. Most people in advanced societies have access to energy-saving devices and technologies, but how do we get people to use them and to use them wisely? For what good are innovative green technologies if you can't motivate people to use them? How do you convince people that it is good to turn off lights when they are not using them?

"There are ways to do this but it takes good educational contingencies involving instructional control. Saving energy can be made into a conditioned reinforcer through verbal instruction using what we have learned from equivalence relations and relational frame theory; these are recent developments in the domain of verbal behavior, which I hope to touch on during our tour tomorrow. So what is most unique about our communities, and what we believe people should be focusing on, is our educational system and our well-engineered cultural contingencies. These are the constants in all of our communities and they help to define us better than anything. We would have no infrastructure without appropriate constructive behavior, and no constructive behavior without well thought-out contingencies to shape and maintain it."

There are many benches around Walden Two and we sat down on one near an outdoor playground where a dozen or so five- and six-year-old children were climbing into tube-like structures leading up to a wooden fort. A slide on the other side brought them safely back to ground level. Loose rubber chips, covered with even softer wooden chips, were under any fall zones, which were few. In this case, both the tubes leading to the fort, and the slide on the other side, were mostly enclosed. We are very careful to protect little brains.

As we watched the children playing, Clifford remained silent and watched them with a pensive and distant look on his face. Was he thinking about his own children? Or was he perhaps remembering his own childhood? Children can have a strange effect on adults who rarely take the time to stop and see the world through children's eyes, especially when it occurs to them that their own eyes once looked at the world in a similar way. We watched them in silence for a few moments. Two of the children, a boy and a girl, were off to one side talking and not playing, but there was no budding romance here; they may as well have been of the same sex. Martha had a smile on her face as she watched them, while Traci studied them carefully with the inscrutable look and clear eyes she was known for. And we all laughed as several children popped out of the end of the slide at the same time, also laughing.

Paul broke the silence by asking us if we thought our incentive system compared well to those outside of our communities.

"Of course, people have always found ways to incentivize labor," I told him, "but they did not always have the information needed to do so without supplementing incentives with coercion. By applying what we have learned from a science of behavior, we can design and implement the contingencies that will produce all of the behavior needed for the innovation, construction, and maintenance of our infrastructure. Without this science we would be more like any other society, allocating time, energy, and funds, and hiring otherwise superfluous economists, managers and supervisors, to attempt to either incentivize an unhappy and overworked workforce or to coercively make them produce. Without a good understanding of the principles of a science of behavior, coercion is nearly always needed to supplement poorly designed contingencies."

Then I shifted gears by asking our guests more or less rhetorically, "Why do you suppose so many people—especially those in affluent materialistic societies—have so much anxiety and depression? Why does such a large proportion of your population have to take fluoxetine, diazepam, and other tranquilizers, anti-depressants and anti-anxiety prescription medications? Why are people self-medicating with alcohol, opioids, and other illicit drugs, and why has this become more prevalent even as material wealth increases? Are these drugs consumed to escape from aversive conditions and unpleasant emotions?

"We believe that most of society's problems emanate from poorly designed contingencies of reinforcement, the uncertainty about job security, and fear of not being able to provide for family and self. A large fraction of the U.S. government— that part working directly for business interests—is wanting to remove or reduce any remaining economic safety nets that are in place to help displaced or unemployed citizens. In short, they want to completely dismantle the 'welfare state.' They have used propaganda to turn the middle class, or what is left of it, against the poor, depicting them as healthy but lazy people riding on the coattails of the working class—and this public relations campaign has been very effective. Even one of the U.S. presidents spoke of 'welfare queens' wearing designer jeans, further incensing hard-working people.

"We believe this campaign to dismantle the welfare state may be an attempt to benefit the business sector by the *literal* production of hungry workers uncertain about their future. In our natural science of behavior, these deliberate deprivations are technically called 'motivating operations' or 'establishing operations,' and they increase the *effectiveness* of a reinforcer such as money and make any behavior that has produced that reinforcer in the past more likely to occur. Because money is the predominant generalized reinforcer in capitalistic societies, making it more difficult to obtain can increase its effectiveness as a reinforcer.

"But there are other underhanded methods used to increase the effectiveness of money as a reinforcer. Perhaps counterintuitively, you can increase its effectiveness to motivate workers by decreasing the value of the currency, for example, through inflationary measures using various economic manipulations. Workers, therefore, would have to do more work and earn even more money in order to purchase the same products they once bought for less. Similarly, you can increase taxes or raise the price of the products, or eliminate good-paying jobs in a higher labor-cost market by outsourcing them to cheaper labor markets, while simultaneously removing economic safety nets. This can force remaining workers to make disadvantaging concessions they otherwise would not make. This seems to be what is happening in the U.S. as the globalization process advances and social safety nets are removed. As you increase the number of people in a labor market by *any* means, the cost of labor goes down dramatically, a real boon for those businesses that require human labor.

"People will work harder and for longer hours, and will succumb to harsher treatment and working conditions, if they realize there are fewer jobs and no programs in place to tide them over between jobs. In 1997, Federal Reserve Chairman Alan Greenspan once told Congress that the reason that the economy was so strong at the time was because of, and I quote, 'worker job insecurity.' The *New York Times* reported that Greenspan said that 'workers have been too worried about keeping their jobs to push for higher wages.' To him, and to business, this insecurity was a *good* thing. Here again we see the conflicts—contradictory contingencies that are affecting the major stakeholders involved—between these major sectors of society. But could unhappiness, depression, and anxiety also emanate from what we've been told so many times before, that just having more material possessions does not necessarily make one happier? People see how the affluent, privileged sectors of society live, and may feel inadequate as a result, even though they themselves have more than enough to be happy. This could be another example of happiness coming from the amount or quality of our material possessions *relative to others*.

"Most people already have what is needed for happiness. Our ancestors were probably quite happy with much less than what most people now possess. Many people now have access to technologies that the most powerful ancient kings could not have imagined. What would a king have given for a handheld device that can store the information from literally tons of books, play high-fidelity music, record and display video, and communicate with others around the world? What would he give to travel in an automobile that could take him sixty miles in one hour? Or fly in a jet to distant countries in a few hours? And yet there are many people in your society and others who have access to all of this but are not content. Doesn't this suggest that a corporate-dominated society is not working for the whole populace, but instead for a small subset of it?

"Could this be an indication that something about corporate capitalism is not conducive to equanimity and happiness for everyone? Even many people holding executive positions in major institutions procure prescription drugs to reduce anxiety caused by the aversiveness of stress produced in these competitive environments. Poorer segments of society turn to cheaper illicit drugs for relief. But tell me," I asked, "what do *you* think we actually *need* in life to be happy?"

"Security would be paramount, of course, as in food, shelter, and clothing," Martha offered. "And love," she added. "But I must admit that I really haven't spent too much time analyzing what makes people happy."

"To that, I would add intellectual stimulation and entertainment," said Paul.

"I believe that here in our communities, at least, we have met those prerequisites with ease," I said. "But I thought you might also mention close social relationships and feelings of freedom and accomplishment. Very close social bonds have been shown to lead to happiness, and people with many close friends report being happier than those with few. Contingencies here enable and encourage very close social bonds. While we are composed of a heterogeneous ethnicity, we are homogeneous in values and goals. The fact that we have shared values and feel that we are all working toward truly common goals, establishes the contingencies needed in order to form close social relationships with others. We have broken the unseemly tribal bonds that have plagued many cultures in the past and are plaguing many cultures even today. And we certainly do not believe that sacrificing the individual for the good of small sectors of society—or even for the promise of some *future* ideal society—is a good idea.

"I should add one other very important factor. All of our people derive satisfaction from the natural reinforcers emanating from their own successful behavior, and this produces a sense of accomplishment. When operant behavior produces positive reinforcers on a favorable schedule—that is, when the general level of reinforcement is high—people say they *feel* happy, fulfilled, inspired, and enthused. And they also say that they feel free. Our educational contingencies strengthen the behavioral skills needed to be successful; our curricula are designed to produce the basic behaviors needed for success in virtually *any* environment."

Martha asked, "Do you attribute any of your success to a rejection of capitalism? Or, am I assuming too much? Perhaps I should first ask you if you reject capitalism?"

"Marx," I replied, "understood that working for others created a surplus of value or profit that goes to those whom he derisively called the 'bourgeoisie,' by which he meant the capitalist class that owns most of the society's wealth and means of production. When people work for themselves, there is no profit and no one is taken advantage of."

"Do you consider yourselves Marxists then?" asked Clifford, with his phone recorder obviously activated.

"We do not label ourselves as anything other than realists informed by science. Political categories are usually defined by critics for propaganda purposes—they have whatever meaning is given them to suit the critics' arguments. And these categories constantly change. Most of them have lost their original meaning, and in many cases they are simply used to elicit emotions in order to sway public opinion. These comments are not cynicism but scientific realism.

"For instance, calling someone a 'socialist' in a predominantly capitalistic society puts that person in an equivalence relation or—to say it in a less technical way—in a relation of 'sameness' with previously conditioned aversive stimuli that elicit negative emotions; this is typically accomplished through propaganda. Many people support socialistic programs and policies without realizing they are socialistic. Social Security, Medicare, and guaranteed coverage of pre-existing conditions are good examples. Therefore we define ourselves instead by our policies; political categories are for rhetoricians. Ask about our policies and practices, if you like, which we are more than happy to share. In short, our communities are informed by the findings of science, not by ideology."

"What do you consider to be the main purpose of your communities; how would you characterize yourselves?" Martha asked.

"If we, and by 'we' I mean the majority of humankind, are *ever* going to free ourselves from plutocratic, kleptocratic, or oligarchical governments, we must begin by forming self-sufficient communities along the lines of our Walden Twos. It is wise, prudent, and—we would assert—imperative, that all communities produce most of their own food and energy *locally*—at a minimum, the amount necessary for survival for a substantial length of time. Without local communal control of food, water, and energy, people will always be at the mercy of predatory profiteers. Once you have control of the necessities of life, you no longer have to prostrate yourself to others. That is what we have done here in our communities.

"Some *individuals* in modern technocratic societies have chosen to become survivalists and to live off of the grid, as they say. But they miss the many advantages of communal life. We have used all of the natural sciences in designing our communities so that we can provide healthy, unadulterated food, shelter, clean water, healthcare, and the best education possible—since it is informed by behaviorology—and all without involving remote businesses or governments controlled by profiteering plutocrats. As long as people are attached by an umbilical cord to profit-driven corporations, they will never be free from coercive control or exploitation. This is because privately owned corporations and corporate controlled governments can always threaten to terminate the services to which one has become accustomed, and this too is coercion."

"Other journalists before us have written very positive things about your communities," Martha said. "You have a good reputation for working with surrounding communities to your mutual benefit. Have you considered helping other, let us say, non-behavioral, communities that may want to establish independence?"

"Certainly," I said. "We are very willing and eager to help others to set up self-sustainable communities. We can see that many problems in the U.S. are due to self-serving business elites and their investors looking out for their own interests at the expense of others. This problem is only getting worse as power structures merge and globalize. Again, the contingencies explain why this happens. These people are behaving quite lawfully, although by 'lawfully' I mean that they behave just as our culturologists would predict them to behave from analyzing the contingencies to which they are exposed.

"They are quick to build nuclear arsenals and missile systems that enrich weapons manufacturers and their investors, while risking nuclear annihilation for most of the larger life forms on Earth, and also much of the plant life. They support governments whose militaries destroy or undermine countries with cooperative societies, justifying their actions by calling these countries 'socialistic' or 'communistic'—two of the political categories known to elicit outrage from a 'properly' conditioned populace. They may even orchestrate coups in these countries in order to prevent viable alternatives to capitalism. Possibly the only way to eliminate their dominance of our culture is to decouple from the products and services they provide. We must make them realize that their very existence is completely dependent upon our continuing consumption of these products and services.

"Ironically, people often inadvertently empower their own masters. Our ineptitude in dealing with this can be considered a form of 'learned helplessness'—which is a debilitating behavioral condition that results from an exposure to uncontrollable and unpredictable contingencies. Fortunately, it is never too late to educate others on how to rein in these self-serving juggernauts. Most people have accepted these institutions without question, and have never acquired the behavior needed to escape from their domination. People have always had the ability to free themselves from their dominance, but either didn't know how, or could not organize the critical mass of people needed to exert countercontrol. All along, we had the power to boycott their products and services until they became more responsible and accountable. And that power has indeed sometimes been used to great effect, as in improving the living and working conditions of farm and factory workers. We hope to see this kind of progress expanded into many other areas."

We watched as the children moved in an orderly manner from the playground back to the educational center, accompanied by two of the teachers. They entered a side door that led into one of the classrooms. The young boy and girl who were talking earlier were still together as they walked a short distance behind the others. Traci watched them with her Mona Lisa demeanor as they disappeared through the doorway. I knew the little girl well. Her name is Sigrid; she is Traci's daughter.

12

After finishing showing them around the grounds of Walden Two, we again stopped and sat down, this time near one of our greenhouses. Paul Johnston was a tall, slightly overweight man with thick glasses. I guessed him to be in his mid-30s. He sat down next to me on the bench. "You know, I'm sure, that it will take more than your communities to make the kinds of sweeping changes you are hoping for," he said. "How will you recruit enough people outside of your communities in order to make a significant difference?"

"We hope," I said, "that our communities will serve as models for others so they may see how easy it really is to reorganize their own communities and return them to local control. It is not even necessary, of course, that they adopt our philosophy in order to do so. I'm sure you are aware that American towns, cities, and villages were not always dominated by corporate structures. But, as I said, the corporations that now dominate our society have little real power without us. They are run by economic elites, some of which either own and control major media outlets or sit on the boards of directors for those outlets.

"As I have mentioned before, they use very effective propaganda techniques—now called 'public relations'—to influence the opinions and voting behavior of the general public. Though these public relations campaigns were originally designed to influence voters to vote for 'business-friendly' politicians, recently they have been very effective in influencing voters to elect the corporate capitalists themselves to run the U.S. government. Or they elect politicians who surround themselves with these people. Our behaviorologists have been doing some very interesting work in the area of propaganda as a result of being advantageously informed by a recently developed and conceptually refined theory of verbal behavior called 're-lational frame theory.' As I said, I hope to touch on some of this tomorrow. We are currently offering classes in this area and hope to elucidate the techniques used by unscrupulous propagandists of any and all kinds.

"Americans have not heeded the warnings of men like Eisenhower who warned us many years ago of what he called the 'military-industrial complex.' It is now clear how our taxes are funneled through the Pentagon to large corporate weapons manufacturers and other high technology companies. Some of these weapons are sold to our allies, but the profits from arms sales are not distributed back to the taxpayers who funded them, but to stockholders. In other cases, the Iran/Contra scandal for instance, we have seen how profits from il-legal arms sales were used to fund covert CIA operations in Nicaragua—operations, incidentally, that funded the capital-ist-backed Contras over the peasant Sandinistas.

"And while many others have repeated Eisenhower's admo-nition, no one seems to know for sure how to rein in these peo-ple. Well, we believe we can at least quit supporting them by becoming self-sufficient and decoupling from their framework. We have networked our communities together and openly share information with each other, while showing others how to do the same. With the collective effort of a critical fraction of the population, predatory corporations could be van-quished or at least quelled. But before doing this on a large scale, you simply *must* build your own local infrastructures and provide your own necessities. Without this local infrastructure in place, as I said before, they can threaten to withhold the things they provide, some quite vital to the survival of those people who are dependent upon them. Ask yourself if you could continue to live well without your local supermarket? That is the critical question."

"Oh, I'm not sure I could," Martha said. "I shop for groceries at an organic market, when I'm not indulging in fast food meals," she added with a laugh.

"Well then," I said to her, "you need to do your grocery shopping here; as I've said, our food is organic by any definition of that word. In fact, it is organic several levels down."

I tried to stay on point, so I continued more seriously by saying, "The analyses of our culturologists show that the contingencies that prevail under capitalism tend to foster competition, self-interest, and 'rugged individualism' which can further divide people. The more people compete, and the more that people are divided by skin color, ethnicity, gender, religion, or whatever else demarcates tribal bonds, the more difficult it will be to work together to build the kinds of communities—along with the supportive infrastructures—that are needed to decouple from these privately owned, increasingly oligarchical, superstructures.

"While one competitive group, and then another, may gain some apparent minimal advantage over others, all these groups similarly suffer under the same capitalistic contingencies. Some of your more progressive thinkers have suggested that the idolatry of rugged individualism in America may be preventing people from working together to resist the relentless encroachment of corporate domination of society. Economic elites prevent people from organizing by fomenting discord and weakening labor unions and popular organizations. They have also endeavored to propose laws that will undermine the collective actions of workers, such as touting the euphemistic 'Right to Work' laws; this law is tantamount to saying workers have the right to work with fewer protections and less bargaining power. At the same time, these same elites fully support organizations such as chambers of commerce, corporate think tanks, and business roundtables."

"I don't see why we can't just choose better leaders," said Simmons. "I know you attribute some of this to the pre-selection of candidates by party elites who are looking out for the interests of wealthy donors, and some to propaganda, or 'manufactured consent,' or whatever you want to call it. But we occasionally have some good politicians who seem to slip through and at least appear to be working toward more common goals. Why can't we just concentrate on getting better information to voters? Get them to focus on issues rather than slogans: 'Change,' and 'Hope,' and 'Making America Great Again,' and all other similar claptrap? People can read into these vague slogans whatever they want to believe. We need to get people to focus and vote on *issues* that really affect them."

"You are undoubtedly right, Mr. Simmons," I said. "We certainly could put out, say, the voting records of politicians and specify the precise issues they do and don't support. But we must first get people to respond to this information and to this information alone. Many people today do not believe anything that does not have the endorsement of their party, or their religion, or whatever authoritarian dogma they attend to. And yes, we too have seen politicians whose behavior demonstrates integrity, and who have worked hard to pass legislation protecting peoples' rights and our planetary resources, for instance. But, unfortunately, the more remote the leaders, and the more complex the controlling government, the less responsive they are to the governed, and the more likely the graft, corruption, fraud, and malfeasance.

"We can easily predict this from a contingency analysis. Some of our culturologists have spent years analyzing the cultural contingencies operating in various political structures such as governments and some of the institutions that have dominated cultures around the world and over time. In our Walden Two communities, we no longer have to rely on remote and unconcerned 'leaders'; we make our own decisions locally, based on our own data and our own needs. People know their own needs better than remote politicians do. But this does not mean that we can't learn from other communities and share what works."

"I know you have not broken off commerce with the outside world," said Clifford. "And you have said that you offer services to the larger society outside of your communities. How do you justify your support for these institutions you believe are hurting others? By purchasing their products, you are supporting them, are you not?"

Traci turned to Clifford, and before I could answer him, she addressed him in a most pleasant manner, as if she did not want to offend him by sounding condescending.

"We can, and do," she said, "continue to purchase products from those businesses that we deem are operating in good faith. As consumers of their products, we make sure our purchases are contingent on fair business practices and responsible environmental practices, and we let them know this by writing letters and emails. Conjointly, our communities can have a small but appreciable influence. We would strongly suggest that those of you living outside of our communities do the same. You should also check to see that a reasonable amount of the profit they earn comes back into your communities in some manner. This may be in the form of paying their taxes without obscene abatements, or sponsorship of community projects. After all, it is your culture that is supporting them; all arrangements should be fair and reciprocal.

"But here, in our communities, they have lost their power; and since we do not need to offer our labor to them in any form, we needn't worry that they will replace us with computers or robotics, or exploit us in other ways. We have taken away their ability to threaten us if we don't submit to their demands. We use our computers and robotics to *our* advantage, by which I mean to the advantage of all members of Walden Two communities. Our young engineers are constantly working on innovative robotic technology, and our programmers are writing very good and useful code for them. The difference here is that we will free ourselves from drudgery without eliminating someone's livelihood. We do not use robotics, computers, or any technology to produce profits that are then distributed to a small subset of the community. So yes, Mr. Douglas, we do limited amounts of commerce with responsible corporations, and only responsible corporations."

"And," I added, "once our Walden Two communities came to full fruition and stabilized, by which I mean, once we had our local infrastructures in place, we could begin our total independence and step outside the plutocracy. We hope that someday, all of humankind can move away from privately owned and controlled corporate societies, where even life's *necessities*—not just food and water but also medicine and healthcare—are controlled and supplied for profit. For what is profit other than that amount over and above the actual expense of a commodity or service, including the labor that went into it? There is seldom a point where these profiteers will say, 'I have enough now; I need no more.' Conditioned generalized reinforcers such as money do not lose their reinforcing value when people's needs are met. This is why money is so effective as a reinforcer; people will continue to work for it long after their needs are met.

"So there is a strong contingency under capitalism to keep increasing profits to the maximum by squeezing it from consumers and workers. We have recently seen that some pharmaceutical companies are capable of arbitrarily raising prices on life-saving drugs for no other reason than to increase profits so the owners themselves can live more luxurious lives. Some businesses pollute our rivers, streams, and wells, while other corporations take advantage of this and sell us bottled water as a result. How much can they extract from you? How much are you willing to pay them to save your life, or your spouse and children's lives? The price of some of these life-saving drugs is based on your willingness to pay, not on their actual costs. And while you currently may have to succumb to their monetary extortion, you should not *have* to."

"Wasn't it Ralph Nader," Paul asked, "who pointed out that some of our tax dollars go to fund the research and development—the R&D—for some of these corporations? He said that while public tax dollars often underwrite, say, the R&D done by these pharmaceutical companies, any profits made from ventures coming to fruition go *not* to the unwitting subsidizing taxpayers but to the *investors*. Your mention of weapon sales to allies, where taxpayers subsidize these weapon systems but profits from arms sales go to investors, reminded me of this also. Nader called this 'socializing the costs and privatizing the profits,' and he gave many other examples of this. And if the U.S. has developed some of the best health-care *technologies* in the world—for it certainly does not have the best health-care *delivery* system—it is because the taxpayers and consumers paid for it one way or another, either through tax subsidies or through exorbitant prescription drug and health-care costs and insurance premiums."

"As you—or Mr. Nader—suggest," I said, "the U.S. is certainly producing good health-care technologies but not equal access to them. And as you say, this is being done at the expense of the current generation that is paying for it through taxes and health-care costs, while those benefiting the most financially are sacrificing relatively little."

"But," Clifford said, "would you agree that capitalism has moved us toward what you are calling, 'positive reinforcement' on a grand scale? After all, workers are *paid* for their work, and with their earnings can then purchase those things that they desire, whatever they may be. Isn't this a good example of positive reinforcement? And the nice thing about it is that all purchases are personalized to one's needs or wants. We can spend our income at our own discretion."

"Yes," I said, "monetary incentives were a step in the right direction, and they were certainly an improvement over forced labor. But the contingencies under capitalism leave a lot to be desired. For example, Frazier pointed out long ago that what sometimes *looks* like positive reinforcement can actually turn out to be negative reinforcement. For example, employees often *appear* to be working for money, and we know that money is a generalized positive reinforcer for people with the requisite conditioning history. But what often happens is that the person becomes dependent upon an established salary. The person is then made to work due to *the threatened removal of* that salary; the removal of the threat is made contingent on performance, you see; this is an example of negative—or *subtracted*—reinforcement.

"When a manager threatens to fire an employee if he or she doesn't work harder or produce more, the threat of loss of wages is an aversive stimulus from which the employee can escape only by complying with the threat. And this unfortunate arrangement only applies to those who were lucky enough to find a decent-paying job that one could be threated to lose. This is the same situation I mentioned with regards to our dependency on the products of large corporations, some of which threaten to withhold vital products and services while others threaten to move out of the country unless we relent to their demands—usually for cheap labor, tax abatements, and less regulation.

"But, let's face it, working for someone else is too often a one-sided arrangement that can easily deteriorate into an adversarial relationship. I'm not necessarily talking about small business owners here, although they too can become corrupted by capitalistic contingencies. The owners will always be trying to increase profits by increasing the worker's output or by reducing the worker's pay and benefits; profits are typically involved in the contingencies driving their behavior. Business owners do not begin a business in order to provide jobs and incomes for other people; businesses are set up in order to provide a profitable income stream for the business owner—workers are an expense.

"If we didn't already have the facts, we could have predicted all of this by analyzing the prevailing contingencies. What will happen to the worker when cheaper labor and robotics become widely available? If robotics or computers become cheaper than human labor, well, it's goodbye human laborer. No one's career is safe under the contingencies of stark capitalism. This includes doctors, lawyers, accountants, brokers, designers, engineers, and on and on. Actors and entertainers will one day be computer-generated. I know this has become an age-old admonition, but there is a good reason for it: It is most likely true. So when people as workers are no longer needed as wealth generators for the plutocratic class, it will be incumbent on people to fend for themselves. And that is why *here*, we do!"

"Let me ask a completely different question if I may," Martha said: "Do you make any effort to breed 'better' people, however defined? Are there any restrictions in your procreation practices that might result in positive or negative eugenics, for example?"

"To a small degree, yes," I answered. "Through education, we do dissuade those having known transmittable genetic diseases or severe heritable birth defects from having children. We will do so until the time we can safely modify or replace the defective genetic molecules involved, which we hope to do in the very near future. But you must remember that here, anyone can still enjoy children in other ways, by teaching and working in the nursery, for example, and by serving as mentors—which we all are. And no one here will ever be dependent upon his or her children to provide for them in old age, which is sadly a concern for many people who live in societies without affordable programs for the elderly. But as far as breeding the 'best and brightest' say, no. Intelligence, per se, guarantees little about the behavioral repertoire that will develop.

"How many intelligent people do you know who are arrogant, selfish, cruel, or antisocial? Or believe in a supernatural supreme being or silly conspiracy theories? Don't be fooled, there are many otherwise intelligent people who do. Ironically, it has been convincingly argued that exceptionally intelligent people are much better at rationalizing and finding arguments for their false beliefs. In addition, intelligence, in the sense of a having a nervous system conducive to rapid behavior change through experience, only guarantees that a person can quickly acquire and retain complex patterns of behavior under environmental circumstances that are also sometimes quite complex. But the patterns of behavior that are rapidly acquired are the result of the prevailing contingencies of reinforcement. An intelligent person can just as easily acquire ruthless and selfish behavior as any other behavior. We don't need more intelligent *people*—the average person is quite adequate—what we need are more 'intelligent' *contingencies*!

"We have all seen how many presumably intelligent CEOs, politicians, and other 'leaders,' have worked selfishly and for small subsets of society. The fact that they can rapidly acquire behavior that exploits others and pillages the planet—all for short-term reinforcement—does not bode well for intelligence alone as the most desirable characteristic needed to increase humanity's chances of survival. Much more important are those behavioral repertoires said to indicate compassion, co-operation, empathy, gregariousness, philanthropy, and other prosocial behaviors. Behaviors said to evince these qualities can be deliberately conditioned by arranging contingencies to strengthen them. As Dr. Jensen pointed out in her introductory remarks, 'intelligence' is the descriptor we use for a nervous system perfectly suited for rapidly acquiring complex patterns of behavior. But what behavior is acquired can be anything."

"What about scientists?" Clifford asked. "Don't they also succumb to the weaknesses of humanity? How are they different?"

"The scientific community has built-in sanctions that limit unethical behavior," I said to him. "Findings are published in peer-reviewed journals and distributed to other scientists for evaluation. If a scientist is caught cheating, or stealing another's work, he is essentially finished as a scientist and ostracized from the scientific community. It's not that scientists are necessarily more ethical than others; it's that they know their work will be scrutinized, tested, and possibly replicated or not by others just as bright as themselves. Scientific ethics are in the contingencies. How many politicians, CEOs, and celebrities must hire lawyers at some point, to attempt to absolve them of their unethical or questionable behavior? Lawyers cannot vindicate scientists of the unethical behavior of faking data, or help them to validate a false theory; human laws have no bearing on scientific findings.

"Experimental verification and pragmatic results are the final arbiters of science, not legal jurisprudence. Unlike some professions, the work of scientists is carefully scrutinized by their colleagues, and not just by their contemporaries but also by future scientists who will continue to examine and assess their findings. Again, scientific ethics are in the contingencies—the sanctions—and this is why scientists make heroic efforts to challenge their *own* findings before publication. And as Isaac Asimov, quite a good historian of science, once pointed out, in 1900, Hugo de Vries, Carl Correns, and Erich Tschermak—a Dutchman, a German and an Austrian, respectively— each independently worked out the laws of genetics. Afterward, all three of these scientists looked into the scientific literature and found that Gregor Mendel had worked out the laws of genetics in 1867. All three of these scientists reported their findings as confirmation of *Mendel's* findings. Not one of them tried to take credit for Mendel's work. This is unusual in many other human endeavors."

"You stated that you dissuade those with known transmittable genetic defects from having children," Clifford said. "Does it disturb you that Hitler used a distortion of eugenics—negative eugenics in his case—to justify the eradication of people and ethnic groups he deemed inferior to German blood? Are you prepared for similar criticism?"

"Of course it disturbs me a great deal!" I replied emphatically. "I think it disturbs most humane people. But such criticism would be so grossly misplaced as to call into question the motivations of the critiquer. Hitler believed the myth that the German people were descended from a superior lineage that had become bastardized due to interbreeding with what he deemed to be inferior people and ethnic groups. He was not trying to create a *new* superior group of people; he was trying to restore the German people to their mythical former superiority. He, as many misinformed ideologues are wont to do, began with preternatural and metaphysical beliefs, and when you begin with such beliefs, they can quickly take you down the road to hell.

"As I hope I've made clear," I continued, much more evenly, "we see no reason to concern ourselves with 'improving the human stock,' as they say. Ordinary people are quite capable of solving humankind's problems while living happy lives and producing the necessities they will need to do that. Anyway, as I've suggested, more effective methods than selective breeding are on the horizon, and they will hopefully permit us to directly alter the genome to correct genetic defects. We soon hope to use these methods to cure genetic diseases such as hemophilia, retardation, primary immunodeficiency disorders, sickle cell anemia, Tay-Sachs disease, physical birth defects, and so on.

"I think we can safely forego producing a so-called 'superior race,' because I imagine even *they* will be inferior in many ways to the future capabilities of robots. So I ask you, if we were to breed a superior race of humans, should we expect them to be our servants or our masters? If today's elites—or those who believe themselves so—are any indication, I think we have our answer. Anyway, it is quite likely that our future robots will eventually outperform 'superior' humans on a multitude of tasks, and they can easily be programmed to be the servants of all humankind. I'll put my money on the robots."

"Won't robots just be able to carry out preprogrammed routines?" asked Paul. "They will only be as good as their programmers, will they not?"

"There is little doubt that the behavior of future robots will most likely be shaped analogously to that of organic life," I said. "Stimuli will evoke behaviors that may increase or decrease as a result of outcomes. We define the behavior of the robot just as we do human behavior; robotic behavior is anything that the robot 'does.' It will, of course, be humans who program which outcomes will strengthen the behavior of the robot. If we are careful in selecting these, robots can be of great service to our communities. I believe Asimov's Three Laws of Robotics can serve as a starting guide. Are you familiar with them?

"The first one states that no robot shall ever harm a human, or, through inaction, allow a human to be harmed. The second states that a robot must obey the orders given to it by humans except when they conflict with the first law. And the third states that a robot shall work for its own survival as long as this does not conflict with the first two laws. All other reinforcing outcomes—that is, those outcomes that should strengthen the robot's behavior and cause it to repeat the behavior under similar conditions—should be those that are most favorable to humankind. After all, we built them for this reason. They are our tools, with logic circuits designed by humans. If robots are superior to humans in many ways, it is because we designed them to be so using our knowledge of physics and electronics. The logic built into them by humans and the fact that electrons move very near to the speed of light make for a magnificent and useful device.

"Let me make a final point on this, if I may," I said. "Under current competitive capitalistic contingencies in the U.S., there will always be 'haves' and 'have-nots,' at least as long as wealth and power accrue mainly to what some social scientists have designated as a 'cognitive elite'. This label is given to people capable of performing very complex thinking tasks, such as abstract higher mathematics and complex computer programming. People with these esoteric skills have become a valuable commodity in many societies these days as large societies move further into computer-controlled banking and markets. There is also a need for these skills in cyber-security and cyber-spying as we move into new realms of cyber-warfare.

"Where brawn was valued a century ago, wealth is currently accruing more and more to those considered very bright. But the uneven distribution of wealth based on genetics is completely unnecessary. Our culturologists have designed communities in which *all* people can be happy and productive and free from coercion. Intelligence and higher education can no doubt be good for humanity, but you must remember that many of our current elites are not 'using' their intelligence and education for the good of humankind but rather for the good of their own kind. We should expect this from the findings of sociobiology, culturology, and behaviorology.

"So let us return for a moment to Martha's query about selective breeding and pretend that selective breeding can produce more intelligent people in a linear fashion; in other words, imagine that the offspring of selectively bred people will always be slightly more intelligent than, or equal to, their parent generation. Now, we know this does not happen because there is what is called 'regression to the mean.' Remember, though, this is just a thought experiment about an idealized process in order to make a point. And let's also imagine that we will only breed the brightest of the lot and prevent those people with low IQs from reproducing. I say this because there are some social scientists, like Charles Murray for example, who seem to suggest that if we could just eliminate people of lower IQs and quit wasting resources trying to educate them, we could solve many of our social problems. Now if only those with the highest IQs—let us, along with Murray, call them 'the cognitive elite'—assume positions of power and run our major public and private institutions, what will happen?"

"Well, I assume that the population will become highly intelligent for one thing," said Clifford.

"And how do people usually formally define general intelligence?" I asked.

"By IQ tests," Clifford replied confidently.

"But intelligence can only be defined by comparing one member of a species to other members of the same species," I said. "For the sake of argument, imagine that a species contained only one member, we would not know whether that one member was intelligent or not, would we? We would have no other members of that species to compare it to. We could only look at its behavior and determine whether it was successful at surviving or not. We could compare its behavior to that of another species, but when we say, for example, that a dog is 'intelligent,' we mean relative to other dogs, not to humans.

"The intelligence quotient is by definition a relative metric, and IQ tests occasionally have to be re-normed; that is, an IQ test must periodically be re-administered to a random sample of our contemporaries to determine an average score. This is because people appear to be getting slightly more intelligent over time, not because of better breeding, but because of other factors that I'll explain in a moment. We then administer this newly averaged test to a person from that cohort and divide this particular test-taker's score by the average and multiply by 100 to get his or her IQ score—the intelligence quotient.

"Notice that we are always comparing a person's score to an average score for an *equivalent* group of test-takers. This is important. It is easy to see that by using this formula, the *average* score of any cohort group will always be 100. But if test scores continue to increase over many generations for our imaginary group of '*well-bred*' people, we will have to keep determining new averages as people continue to get smarter; again, this procedure is called 're-norming the test.' If we fail to do this, we will be comparing people of different time periods, and this is not permissible.

"So as IQ scores go up for our imaginary group of 'well-bred' people, we will have to keep re-norming the test back to 100 in subsequent generations—as we do now due to what is called the 'Flynn Effect.' This is what I was just alluding to as due to non-genetic factors. In the Flynn Effect, the scores on the IQ tests become ever so slightly higher for succeeding generations—it appears as if our descendants are becoming increasingly more intelligent. James Flynn, the man who documented this phenomenon, has suggested that this is *not* a result of improvements to the nervous system but rather is a direct result of the proliferation of *educational* contingencies that promote scientific and logical thinking.

"But in *our* imaginary breeding thought experiment, we are *indeed* hoping to improve the nervous systems of our subjects through selective breeding, and as we administer re-normed tests for subsequent generations, our contemporary elites, who are considered very bright on *our* 'pre-normed' test, may appear to be average, or even dull, if they were to take a future re-normed IQ test. This will happen not only because future people will be getting smarter as their nervous systems become more conducive to conditioning, but also because we have prevented lower IQ people from reproducing, and they will no longer be leaving offspring to bring the average down.

"A future test taker who may score high if he or she were to take one of today's IQ tests could very well score average on future IQ tests, as the population becomes relatively more intelligent. In other words, future people whose intelligence is commensurate with those we currently believe to be uniquely qualified to run our major public and private institutions will one day no longer seem competent."

"So, in essence, what you are suggesting is that even with selective breeding, we would have the same problem," Paul noted.

"Yes," Traci affirmed, taking over for me, "because if wealth is even *indirectly* distributed based on intelligence—roughly defined by scores on IQ tests—future people with IQs equal to those people we now believe to be uniquely qualified to run our major governmental and private institutions, will be relegated to a lower stratum. The intelligence problem is one of *relativity* and always will be, because for the most part, inequitable distribution of wealth results from *differential* intelligence, not from absolute intelligence.

"Breeding more intelligent people will not solve one of capitalism's most troubling problems—the unequal distribution of a nation's wealth; it would just shift the people we currently consider to be highly intelligent down the intelligence ladder; future people with IQs commensurate with our current 'haves'—as measured by today's intelligence tests—will be the future 'have-nots.'

"Historically," I added, "due to beliefs of entitlement, elites of all kinds seem to think that they alone can appreciate, and therefore deserve, the good things in life. They reason that the lion's share of wealth and resources should be apportioned to those with the most merit or value to the culture, namely, themselves. And I think it's fair to assume that merit is partly based on heritable biological structures. Somehow, societies must properly address this problem of the 'haves' and 'have-nots' that results from individual differences in 'ability' and 'intelligence.' Of course, those at the favorable end of the curve do not see this a problem at all."

"I have a question," said Paul; "Wouldn't the future cognitive elites produce art that our contemporary cognitive elites may not be able to appreciate? And wouldn't they be capable of performing more complex behavior than our contemporaries? And create professions that require such complexity?"

"Oh, of course." I agreed. "But don't miss our point: Under current competitive capitalistic contingencies in the U.S., and even under contingencies in many non-capitalistic countries, there will always be 'haves' and 'have-nots' as long as wealth and power accrue mainly to a cognitive elite. Selective breeding *will not* solve this problem; it will only create a *new* population with relative differences. And until we solve the problems created by this, we will have inequality.

"Do you agree with Marx then?" asked Clifford: "To each according to his need, from each according to his ability?"

"I do," Traci answered. "But Marx did not have the science needed to address some of the problems created by this: how to keep people productive and behaving well. He was simply trying to incite the working class to overthrow the bourgeoisie, but there were no contingencies in place to support the behavior needed to sustain the society once this was accomplished. Our culturologists, on the other hand, have solved this problem—for us, at least—by designing communities in which *all* people can thrive and be happy and productive. This takes carefully thought out contingency engineering by both behaviorologists and culturologists. Our 'wealth' is mostly nonmaterial; it is our *culture*, and as it steadily improves, so do we all."

"And, if I may jump in here again," I said, "as I've alluded to before, there is no evidence that high intelligence is necessarily correlated with other important qualities such as empathy, altruism, and philanthropy. And if high intelligence is just an organism's ability to rapidly acquire and retain complex patterns of behavior, the behavior rapidly acquired can be anything—even destructive behavior. How many intelligent politicians and CEOs have chosen to work for self-serving ventures and short-term profits that end up hurting humankind's overall survival chances?

"Take global climate change as an obvious example. Those already heavily invested in fossil fuel extraction equipment and techniques want to make as much return on their investments as possible before humanity shifts to clean energy sources, even if, in the mean time, our biosphere is being damaged irreparably. Sociobiologists have suggested that we will work harder to protect and nurture those carrying our own genes—such as our relatives—or those carrying similar genes—such as members of our own ethnic group—or even those bearing similar superficial phenotypes to our own. Just as we have induced people to consider our community to be their common property, through contingency engineering, we can 'short-circuit' the innate tendencies described by sociobiologists and increase the size of what people consider to be their 'human family'; we can thereby induce people to work for the overall good of humankind."

"But why, do you suppose, some of these otherwise intelligent people don't see that their actions will eventually hurt future generations—their grandchildren, for example?" asked Martha. "Many of us can see it; why not them?"

"The behavioral processes involved in decision-making have been thoroughly investigated by behaviorologists," Traci answered. "And it is well understood that immediate consequences have a much greater effect on behavior than deferred consequences. It is therefore not surprising that these individuals are more heavily influenced by immediate profits over a deferred and uncertain dismal future. It is also easy to rationalize one's abandon when there is doubt cast upon scientific projections by people paid to confound public opinion.

"Those who either manage or invest in companies that pollute our streams, rivers, and wells, and then turn around and invest in companies that sell us bottled water, have made similar decisions. How many of these people actually live in a neighborhood similar to your own? Or are they using their wealth to isolate themselves from the ramifications of their own actions? For example, some are using their wealth to literally wall themselves off from the rest of us; they have moved into gated communities situated in more habitable environments. And all of this is necessitated as a consequence of their own morally abject behavior."

"But what about Frazier?" asked Martha, "He was certainly a genius, was he not? Would Walden Two even exist if not for him? Isn't this a good argument for superior intelligence?"

"First," I said, "let me be clear, we too fully appreciate people of superior intelligence. Many people here and in our other communities, I would argue, have very superior IQs, including Traci here. I was not making a case against superior intelligence but against positive eugenics, at least at this point. But many geniuses are perhaps given too much credit. Einstein was a genius, and Darwin, if not a genius, was at least original, and persistent, and a meticulous observer who systematized his findings into a scientifically beautiful general theory. But I posit that we would have discovered their findings without them.

"Russell Wallace came to the same conclusion as Darwin. And other physicists as well as mathematicians were on the verge of discovering Einstein's famous equation. Watson and Crick were in a close race with many other competent scientists, such as Linus Pauling. If not for their advantage of seeing the x-ray diffraction plates of Rosalind Franklin, someone else could have easily been first to work out the three-dimensional structure of the DNA molecule. This has happened over and over in science and also with many inventions.

"Many discoveries are the result of the 'zeitgeist,' so to speak. The continuous accumulation of small findings, usually by researchers of 'normal' intelligence, build to produce the conditions necessary for new discovery and synthesis—what Thomas Kuhn called 'paradigm shifts.' Information accumulates and reaches a critical mass that provides the conditions propitious for producing major shifts in our scientific paradigms."

"But we *are* grateful for Frazier for reasons other than his high intelligence," Traci added. "Certainly he had the biological substratum needed to support his complex repertoire, but it also helped that he was trained in the physiology department at Harvard rather than in the psychology department. This was a happy accident. His scientific training led him to look for observable functional relationships between real variables affecting behavior change. When he realized the ramifications of this path, he endeavored to remake psychology into a natural science.

"Yet even *he* faltered a little along the way early in his scientific career—for example he originally called what we now call an 'operant,' a type of 'reflex,' and he hypothesized a 'reflex reserve' to account for responses that continue to occur after reinforcement has been discontinued. But at the suggestion of his close friend and colleague, Fred Keller, he saw that this might lead to confusion, or worse, the reification of these concepts; that is, some might assume that the 'reflex reserve' was a real internal entity. Frazier was a brilliant experimentalist and soon extrapolated his findings to benefit society, but was it necessary that he be a genius to systematize the science as he did? It's an open question, but I think not. Still, it certainly didn't hurt."

It was nearing dinnertime, so we ended our discussion at this point. We directed our guests to a nearby dining area and for the moment went our separate ways. I believe I saw Clifford Douglas push the stop button on his recorder.

13

stairway leading from a cafeteria in a lower level to an upper-level dining area overlooking Walden Two is edged on one side at specific levels with alcoves containing booths for dining. Large picture windows in each alcove look out onto Walden Two and into nearby woods. Across from but adjacent to these alcoves, on the opposing wall, are paintings in various styles done by members of Walden Two. They are set in shallow recesses so they do not get brushed loose when people pass them on the stairway. I was to meet Traci and a couple of technicians from the nursery at two o'clock to discuss the construction of some additional aircribs and the re-purposing of a few older models that we would be replacing. I was about an hour early so I thought I would have a cup of coffee and read an article or two from the *Journal of Behaviorology*. On my way up the stairway, I spotted Martha Thompson sitting alone in one of the booths, typing on her laptop computer. I did not want to disturb her, but when she saw me she insisted I sit and talk. She was working on her article for *Discover* and specifically wanted to know more about Frazier and his role in the founding of the first community. But it wasn't long before we began to discuss the engineering of human behavior.

"You know," she said, "I have heard you speak many times about engineering contingencies that will strengthen desirable behavior. But frankly this *deliberate* engineering of human behavior is what worries me. Personally, I would feel manipulated."

"Is that so?" I asked with a smile. "What if I told you that I would give you a small amount of money, a dollar, say, to pick up a discarded scrap of paper on the ground and deposit it in one of the recycle containers over there? Would you do it?"

"Knowing the point of this exercise, probably not!" she said lightheartedly.

"Then don't," I said. "You are under no obligation or threat from me and therefore you should feel free to pick it up or not. Now, I could try increasing the amount of my offer until it exceeds whatever reservations you have about 'feeling manipulated,' as you say. You see, it is our *responsibility* as behaviorologists to see that this kind of behavior occurs and is strengthened by the addition of positive reinforcers rather than by the removal of negative reinforcers, although we do not use anything as crass as money. But, I suspect—judging from your level of education and refined manner—that in actuality your ethical training would cause you to experience a twinge of guilt for not obeying a request of your host, and in that case your complying with my request would be the result of *your* cultural contingencies, not ours.

"You could escape from this guilt by picking up the scrap of paper, you see? But notice that in this case, you would not be picking up the scrap of paper to contact positive reinforcers, but rather to escape from the mildly aversive condition called 'guilt.' Here, in Walden Two and our other communities, we specialize in arranging positive reinforcers to strengthen desirable behavior. And once the behavior begins to occur regularly, the natural consequences take over. In the case of litter, the natural consequences are having a pristine area to admire. Also, putting trash in the proper container makes it easier for others—or the person him or herself—to later collect for recycling.

"But we have an advantage here that you may lack in your society: We do not have to compete with the kind of 'resistance behavior' that you are implying. Well-meaning people often condition resistance to, and suspicion of, all forms of behavioral control. You see, much of the literature concerning freedom has convinced people that *all* forms of control are wrong, that anyone who is deliberately engineering the behavior of others must be exploiting them; hence your resistance to being 'manipulated,' as you would say.

"But again, I must point out that there are times when we should *want* others—teachers, for example—to arrange reinforcing contingencies that will strengthen our educational behavior, for instance. When we are trying to acquire new behavior, say playing a new musical instrument, we want a music teacher who is proficient with the instrument to model proper technique, and to describe the proper way to play the instrument, and most importantly, to provide positive feedback when we are playing it correctly. Do you believe that people are being manipulated when a teacher arranges contingencies that will improve playing?"

"No, because I assume that the person has voluntarily entered into this arrangement," said Martha. "Just as those who come to a therapist with problems usually come voluntarily. Your communities just seem to be a little too contrived. You appear, to me at least, to be conditioning people's behavior without their informed consent."

"Do you believe it is contrived because we take the future consequences of our collective actions into account and foster those behaviors that we know—from our analyses of other cultures, and our own research—to be favorable to the overall behavioral health of our community? Do you find more virtue in the unplanned society? I suggest you look around you before you answer that. Please don't misunderstand me, we know that exploitation is a very real concern and we take it quite seriously. But it is not a matter of controlling behavior or not controlling it—as behavior is always one hundred percent determined—it is a matter of what kind of control, for what purpose, and for whose benefit. The very word 'control' has negative connotations and suggests coercion, and most people cannot imagine a society designed in a way that can eliminate this form of control. But there is a good alternative, I can assure you."

"How would you go about conditioning a simple behavior like depositing trash in a proper receptacle?" Martha asked.

"Well," I answered, "for those with the prerequisite educational history—our older children, for example—getting them to deposit trash in the proper receptacle may be as simple as pointing out the natural consequences of doing so; although these natural consequences were most likely not the original consequences that shaped this behavior. The original contingencies usually involve verbal instruction or modeling, followed by abundant social approval. If people are simply following rules because of the *social* reinforcers that follow, we call this kind of rule-following behavior 'pliance.'

"But eventually, the advantages of having a clear area to walk in and a more attractive natural space to admire begin to reinforce the behavior. These are some of the natural consequences that will eventually maintain the behavior. Would you say that we are still determining the child's behavior after these natural consequences have taken over? If there *are* no natural consequences for any behavior we have shaped, then we shaped the wrong behavior.

"Once the natural consequences of the behavior take over and begin to maintain it, we are essentially out of the picture. And when this happens, and the person can *verbalize the natural contingency*, we call it 'tracking.' We help our young children to verbalize the contingency—that is, we want them to describe the relationship between the behavior and the natural consequence of that behavior—and this also makes the behavior more likely to occur.

"That is what I meant when I said that we might only have to point out the natural reinforcers for behaviors. As children have more experience with rules, and these rules have often proven in the past to have reinforcing value, the rules describing the natural contingency may be enough to evoke the operant. We eventually learn to trust those who have given us helpful rules in the past and we take their advice more easily.

"Tidiness does not usually come about by accident. This behavior, like many other useful behaviors, is quite deliberately conditioned here. We have provided our children with experiences with messy areas where they could not find things, and then helped them arrange these areas in such a way that they could more easily find toys or other items sought. Even many adults outside of our communities, without this training, never learn the benefits of a well-organized personal environment. Therefore they continue to waste much time looking for misplaced items and never seem to learn the simple operant behaviors that can prevent this.

"But even this seemingly simple act actually involves a very long process that begins with the establishment of social reinforcers. We spend much time conditioning—again, arranging contingencies for—our infants and young children—as we suspect all good parents and teachers do—by pairing the attention and approval of parents, teachers, and mentors, with other positive reinforcers. That is, we quite deliberately make social approval into a conditioned generalized reinforcer.

"You might simply call this 'socialization,' and it is certainly a part of the socialization process. This socialization can come about by chance, as it often does outside of our communities, or it can come about more deliberately, as it does inside of our communities. Now, some people mistakenly believe that just making their approval contingent on their child's behavior will suffice to strengthen the child's behavior. They may say, 'I reinforced my child's behavior with approval but the behavior did not increase.' They do not understand that attention and approval are not innate—or primary—reinforcers; they are conditioned reinforcers.

"Social approval, like all conditioned reinforcers, must *become* reinforcing through a prior conditioning procedure before it can be used effectively as such. Most parents may do this naturally, and this is good, but some parents do not understand the prerequisite conditioning procedures needed to establish conditioned reinforcers. It is important to note that some children, such as those labeled 'autistic,' may require specially designed contingencies to establish the approval of others as social reinforcers.

"Once attention and approval have become conditioned reinforcers through this procedure, mentors can make their approval contingent on certain behaviors that are good for everyone, including the child. And like any child exposed to good parenting, the children soon discover that the newly conditioned operant behaviors will produce many other reinforcers for the child, and this strengthens the whole process.

"As I'm sure you noticed in our teaching center, our teachers spend many hours interacting with our young ones, playing with them and demonstrating how things work. Just as importantly, these educational interactions not only strengthen operant behavior needed to deal effectively with the environment, they also strengthen social bonding and help establish the attention and approval of teachers and mentors as conditioned reinforcers. This is all done quite naturally and a casual onlooker may miss what is happening. But several conditioning procedures are happening concurrently; establishing social approval as a conditioned reinforcer is one of them."

"But what do you say to people who are just not comfortable with the idea that someone is deliberately engineering some of their behavior?" Martha asked.

"Well, I would ask them if they do not think that their parents, teachers, religious leaders, governments, employers, friends, and countless others, are trying to influence their behavior." I said. "But most of these influences are in the form of verbal rules, rather than the actual arrangement of contingencies. For example, people will give advice or warnings that *describe* contingencies to others. A parent may give advice to their child by saying, 'If you study hard, you will get good grades that will eventually lead to a lucrative job that will support you,' while a government may warn its people, 'If you don't pay your taxes, you will be fined or go to jail.' Religious leaders tell us that eternal damnation awaits those of us who engage in biblically proscribed behavior.

"Notice that in all of these cases, there are no actual contingencies involved; what we are given instead are *descriptions* of contingencies. That is, we are told what particular behaviors will be followed by particular consequences, but there are no consequences contingent on the behavior mentioned in the rule, because the behavior is not currently occurring. People often begin following rules for the social reinforcers given for rule-following. As I said, this is called 'pliance.' At first, these rules are often weak and ineffective, but as people have more and more positive outcomes from following the good advice of others, rule-following gets reinforced. We learn that following certain rules can lead to good outcomes. But why do you find it more repugnant when conditioning is done by experts who understand the real causes of behavior, and then use this knowledge to effect behavior change?

"Our children interact with many different teachers and mentors who are using positive reinforcement, and this tends to generate pleasant emotions. The pleasant emotions that are elicited by these interactions generalize to other people; this is not accidental. But let us get back to something as simple as teaching children not to litter. In many societies, people who litter are punished with fines or, in some cultures, by flogging. Are they free? Or more accurately, do they *feel* free? Is it the fact that we are using educational technologies informed by scientific observation and experimentation that bothers you? Or maybe it is because we are *too* successful?"

"Perhaps that is it," Martha conceded.

"That concern is certainly warranted but somewhat misplaced—in our case at least. It is undoubtedly true that people who manipulate others often do it for exploitative and nefarious purposes, and the manipulated person can then end up serving the interests of the exploiter."

"Yes. Precisely," Martha said. "And that is what bothers many of us. We are leery of those who would deliberately try to engineer some of our behavior. Although after what I have seen here, I can now see that manipulation and exploitation are occurring outside of Walden Two rather than within it."

"Well then," I said, "let me ask you again if you think it bothers people that their government and employers threaten fines and firing, or offer tax breaks and bonuses for their behavior? Can you explain why *this* does not seem to trouble people? I would argue that people are exploited in other ways as well. It's true that people are working for money that can be exchanged for other good things at their discretion, and they are providing a service for their employer that benefits him or her, and hopefully the compensation is commensurate with worker output. But do people not know that the employer will terminate his or her employment if he or she finds a way to accomplish the service provided by the worker, but with less expense?"

"Unfortunately, that's the way it works. That's just life. There are no guarantees," said Martha. "People have to keep themselves marketable if they want to keep gainful employment. I consider myself lucky that I chose journalism; it is a profession that will probably remain relevant during my lifetime and I enjoy it. But we journalists must keep abreast of any new technologies germane to our profession. We must be proficient with the computer and the Internet, and we must be adept at garnering reliable information using any new technologies. If we don't keep up, we may be replaced by someone who can. I wouldn't like it, but I wouldn't fault my employer for replacing me, I would fault myself for not keeping up."

"We have yet to terminate the services of any one of our members," I replied gently but resolutely. "Our educational system has given us very extensive and versatile repertoires. Much of this will transfer to other areas. We have general behavioral skills. It is not difficult for us to work in many different areas.

"But I would like to bring your attention to something that seems to be a byproduct of the philosophies concerning freedom, dignity, and freewill," I continued. "Frazier noticed that people often give credit in inverse proportion to the conspicuousness of the causes of the behavior concerned. People generally give others more 'credit' for doing something good when they don't understand *why* the person did it. If people can't see a conspicuous cause of behavior, they believe it must be something inside the person, some free spirit.

"But this is only because the contingences that selected the behavior are in the past and are no longer apparent. It is difficult for observers of the current behavior of others to know the *historical* contingencies that one must know in order to account for the behavior. So if someone does something heroic, such as running into a burning house to save a family of strangers, risking her or his own safety in the process, we may give maximal credit simply because we cannot account for that heroic act. But this is only due to our ignorance of the historical contingencies responsible for this behavior.

"The behavior may be due to the person having seen a news story or movie that depicted a person saving a family and receiving much public praise for his or her heroism. Or it could be due to the person imagining someone suffering in a fire; this aversive imagery may motivate the person to try to extract the family in order to avoid this horrific outcome. This would be an example of what is technically called a 'motivating operation' generating avoidance behavior. You see, the person could avoid further thoughts of a suffering family if he of she removed them from the building. But due to our ignorance of the historical contingencies that account for the behavior of our hero, the *prevailing* contingencies seem to be *against* running into a burning house and risking burning to death!

"But I agree with you, people *should* worry about being exploited; it happens all the time in competitive cultures. What I hope people will understand is that we first arrange the contingencies needed to keep a child's behavior within an auspicious range. Then, like any good teacher, we condition new behaviors that will expand the child's repertoire as we condition values that are good for the culture. We do not attempt to engineer *all* behavior; that would be impossible anyway. But like any society, we want our members' behaviors to be within socially acceptable limits. The main difference here is that we know how to accomplish this."

"I suspect that letting go of the belief in free will would be incredibly difficult for most people," Martha said. "I think it is human nature for people to want to do what they want, when they want, as long as they aren't breaking any laws. No one wants to think that someone else is controlling their behavior, whether they really are or not. People want total freedom."

"Now, when you are talking about freedom, what are you imagining that people are free *from*?" I asked.

"From others determining their behavior, of course."

"And by 'others' you mean other *people*?"

"Yes. Of course."

"What about the environmental determinants of behavior that do not involve other people? Should people rebel against these too?" I asked. "Do you believe that if there were no one deliberately arranging contingencies for people, that their behavior would be free from determination? The environment can be even *more* unforgiving; if we step off of a cliff, gravity will determine our fate. And if we touch a hornet's nest or drive a car without brakes, we will most likely be punished by stings or an accident. We are still 'free' to do so, of course—in the sense that no *human* is stopping us—but we are never free from the natural *environmental* consequences of our behavior."

"I believe that more and more Americans want limited government and the freedom to pursue their *own* goals. Many of us think that this is what is great about America—our freedom." Martha persisted.

"And so do we," I said quite seriously, "to the extent that our 'freedoms' do not hurt us in the long run. We must be careful, though. Somehow we must guide the ship that we are all on together. We cannot just condone procreation until overpopulation causes dire and pernicious consequences. Many people may suffer and starve as a result. The food that will be needed to feed the additional billions of people, and the waste products from this population which will need to be dealt with, will only snowball and cause more problems.

"We must begin to reduce these numbers benignly and humanely, or nature will solve this problem for us, only less kindly. As Dr. Jensen made clear in her introductory remarks on Monday, the science has spoken: human behavior is determined just as is every other natural event. And do not for a moment believe that behavior is not a natural event. Do you not think the behavior of the other animals is natural? Ignorance of the controlling variables does not make our behavior any less determined. And while I understand your concerns, Ms. Thompson, I repeat, in our case at least, they are misplaced.

"We at Walden Two and our sister communities are not exploiting others or taking away their freedom. I would argue that people here feel freer than the most fervent libertarian. And in a sense we *are* freer because our repertoires are quite extensive, giving us many more opportunities to behave in ways that produce a wide variety of positive reinforcers."

"But surely you must limit some behavior?" she asked. "Do you prevent some behaviors from occurring?"

"Yes, of course, as do all cultures," I answered. "But we mainly preclude offensive behavior by not evoking or reinforcing it. Unlike most cultures, we have been able to reduce punishment in all its forms to a bare minimum. We have found that it helps considerably to begin strengthening desirable behavior very early in a child's development. And we do not expose our children to material that can evoke antisocial behavior, or to people who are modeling undesirable behavior; at least until the child has reached a point in her or his development where he or she can describe what is reinforcing the offensive behavior of others. We know from studying the contingencies in other cultures what is most likely to cause problems. You've surely heard the old saw, 'A smart person learns from his or her own mistakes, but a wise person learns from the mistakes of others.' We have learned much from observing the mistakes of other cultures. No culture worth its salt would strengthen antisocial behavior and expect to improve that culture."

"It's funny you should mention libertarians because I do consider myself one," Martha proclaimed. "As long we are not hurting others, we just want to be left alone to do as we please. We want very limited government and laissez-faire capitalism. We believe this is the path to happiness and independence. But at the same time, I must admit that sometimes I feel conflicted about giving unlimited freedom to everyone; some people will abuse this freedom, and of course, I realize that not everyone will behave prosocially."

"Well then," I said, "first let me point out that under limited government and laissez-faire capitalism, private corporations will begin to privatize the functions of government. The privatization of everything from schools to Medicare has already been proposed, and, of course, regulatory agencies working in the public's interest have been gutted, or staffed with people coming from the corporate sector. How would democracy even work in a society dominated by private corporations? Can we count on market forces to hold them accountable? Is it one dollar one vote? By which I mean, will they only take the public into account when they begin to lose money? I'm sure you realize that corporations are more like totalitarian, rather than democratic, institutions? I would not count on market forces alone to stem the havoc they could cause.

"But let us put that aside for a moment," I said. "I believe the kind of unlimited freedom you are referring to is quite different from what behaviorologists mean by 'freedom,' so let's make that distinction very clear. We believe that behavior can be virtually free from coercion, but that is all. I believe that, as a libertarian, what you are referring to as unlimited freedom, is really just the permissive society; a society that permits people to pursue practically anything without restriction as long as it does not violate any laws.

"A permissive society is all well and good, in fact, you could say that our Walden Two communities are permissive; but there must be contingencies in place to, let us say, encourage people to do the right thing. People normally move through life contacting reinforcers somewhat randomly, and all kinds of behavior can get strengthened, some good, some bad. Parents may guide their children in certain directions, and they may try to limit the child's exposure to certain unwanted influences. If the parents are affluent, they may send their children to private schools and universities where tuition costs may weed out poorer, presumably more troublesome contemporaries of the child.

"But otherwise, many reinforcers are contacted haphazardly. If troublesome behavior does develop, the parents and others may arrange punitive contingencies in an attempt to suppress the behavior. In some cases, the parents may seek professional help for that child; for instance, if the child gets involved with illicit drugs, the parents may enter the child into a drug rehabilitation program.

"Libertarians may even advocate legalizing certain currently prohibited drugs that are considered dangerous by the medical establishment, all in the name of freedom. Without punitive sanctions placed on behaviors such as drug usage, people *feel* freer. But this freedom is only an illusion; again, the removal of punitive sanctions only frees one from these *human* sanctions. We must realize that there are other non-human factors determining drug usage, such as the reinforcing or punitive effects of the drug itself. And as we have seen, these are sometimes more powerful than human sanctions, often leading to the person's death in some cases; but I suppose one could argue that this is a kind of freedom.

"A permissive society that allows any and all behavior to occur without carefully considering possible *deferred* consequences is not a viable society. In a debate concerning freedom and permissiveness, Frazier once made a literary allusion to make his point; he said, 'When Milton's Satan falls from heaven, he ends in hell. And what does he say to reassure himself? *Here, at least, we shall be free.* And that, I think, is the fate of the old-fashioned liberal; he's going to be free, but he's going to find himself in hell.' I would argue that this also applies to the libertarians who want a completely permissive and unplanned society.

"We are entering an untested realm, Ms. Thompson, new technologies have recently arisen that permit people to immerse themselves in sadistic and violent virtual reality worlds. These worlds can desensitize users to violence while teaching undesirable antisocial behaviors of all kinds. While it is undoubtedly an unintended by-product of these games, they actually provide a good example of systematic desensitization, a procedure behaviorologists use in therapy to gradually desensitize clients to fears and phobias. While some of the violent behavior resulting from this desensitizing procedure may occur relatively quickly in some small fraction of the viewing population, for others, violent behavior may only occur far in the future, when certain conditions or motivating operations evoke it.

"This delay may make it more difficult to establish a direct connection between early exposure to desensitizing violent media and later violent behavior, but why even take the chance? Why *teach* our children how to be aggressive while simultaneously exposing them unnecessarily to desensitizing images of human violence? Do violent skills transfer to any useful areas of human interaction or endeavor? We have found that our young people will just as enthusiastically engage in games that do not involve violence or weaponry. And our games teach values and skills that generalize to other prosocial human activities. Unfortunately, as Albert Bandura has pointed out, many of today's parents are also products of violent fare. They have been desensitized to violence to the point where they may not be the best judges of what is acceptable or in the best interests of society in general."

"I tend to agree, but gun rights advocates are adamant about teaching their children how to defend themselves," said Martha. "And some of these games do just that."

"Well, does defending oneself mean we must to learn to shoot others with lethal weapons?" I asked. "Why not first teach children de-escalation skills such as those used in FBI negotiation training? Or teach them how to handle or report bullies? Or better yet, as in our communities, why not teach potential bullies how to acquire what they want from others in non-aggressive ways?"

"As you have intimated," she said, "there are many children who watch or play violent video games who do not become violent; only a small fraction do. How do behaviorologists explain this? Why do only some children, or adults, mimic this violent behavior? And why should we prevent everyone from playing or viewing violence just because only a small fraction of disturbed people are adversely affected by it?"

"Oh, we are quite aware of the statistics," I said. "But if children, and adults are viewing this just for entertainment and excitement, why not substitute something just as entertaining and exciting yet instructive? Well-designed teaching software can have contingencies built into it that can produce much excitement; some can even elicit some of the emotions that are generated by escape and avoidance behavior; simulated mountain climbing and parasailing come to mind. These escape and avoidance behaviors are evoked by conditioned aversive stimuli, and are similar to those built into violent video games. There are many virtual reality games that can be just as exciting as games of violence, yet they do not desensitize viewers to violence, or teach the user that violence is the best solution. We believe it would be prudent to make every effort to reduce entertainment that involves human violence. We do not have to take people's rights or freedoms away; education can go a long way toward eliminating much of this."

"And what of all those who would not go on to commit violence as a result of watching?" Martha persisted. "Why should they not be able to enjoy these games?"

"Most people have been exposed to contingencies that have either punished violent behavior, or strengthened behavior incompatible with violent behavior," I said. "I'm speaking of 'ethical training,' of course, and it is intended to help inhibit violent behavior that may otherwise occur. This kind of ethical training can be provided by religious or secular instruction. In most cases, it is enough to inhibit violent behavior.

"But let's revisit the efficacy of advertisements for a moment. Not everyone who views a commercial will go out and purchase that product. But data collected by advertisers show that sales definitely do go up. I mentioned this earlier. So these advertisements are having an effect on *some* fraction of the viewing audience. And, as we have established, maybe this is just a small fraction of viewers—but *which* fraction? It is usually the case that various commercials are affecting the behavior of different people in different ways.

"The same goes for viewing of violence. Not everyone will commit a violent act as a result of being desensitized to violence, perhaps partly because of ethical instruction. But what fraction of the population becoming more violent would be deemed acceptable? Even if the acceptable fraction is small, as the population increases, the absolute number of violent acts will increase as well. How many mass shootings can occur before it begins to disturb the equanimity of the entire culture? Just one or two school shootings can be extremely disturbing for many sensitive—I would argue, behaviorally healthy—people. The lockdown drills that young school children must currently go through can cause unnecessary anxiety for them and generate emotions inimical to the ideal learning environment.

"So let me ask you, Ms. Thompson, how much absolute violence do you think a society can tolerate before it begins to disturb the tranquility of the population? If we can reduce the violence—even if it is only for that fraction of the population adversely influenced by viewing violence—why not do so? Why desensitize people to violence at all? What is to be gained? Behaviorally healthy people should find violence appalling. Just because there are children and adults who will not go on to kill or harm others, can they not be just as happy in other ways? Were they unhappy until violent software and other violent media came along to make them happy? Are there not alternative forms of gaming entertainment that require skills that *are* transferrable to other areas of a culture, yet do not involve simulated killing? Based on extensive research, our culturologists believe so. And our software engineers are working with our behaviorologists to design software that is just as exciting, yet teaches children and adults valuable prosocial behaviors."

"For the record, how much of this is actually based on science? And how much is pure speculation?" Martha wanted to know.

"Well, that is a good question." I responded. "But if you will permit me to make a long-winded analogy, I think I can answer it to your satisfaction. Our analysis is based on science in very much the same way that climate scientists are explaining how human activity is affecting our climate. We know, for example, that certain triatomic molecules such as H_2O and CO_2 enter our atmosphere and radiate some of the infrared radiation leaving the earth, back down to earth. As I imagine you know quite well, electromagnetic radiation coming from the sun strikes the earth, and some of it is reflected back into space as infrared radiation.

"But when this reflected infrared radiation happens to strike one of these molecules, it is reflected *back* to Earth causing it to warm. As we pump more molecules of CO_2 into our atmosphere, more heat will be 'trapped' in this way. This is, of course, the greenhouse effect, though that is somewhat of a misnomer. If not for these molecules, the radiation reflected from Earth would escape. Now, we do want *some* global warming. Without our atmosphere and *some* greenhouse gases, our planet would be somewhere around minus eighteen degrees Celsius. But with just the right amount of these molecules, the natural temperature of our planet is at an energy balance that suits us quite well.

"Many of these heat-trapping molecules are by-products of the fossil fuel burning process, although some are from other natural sources, such as volcanism, forest fires, and plant and animal respiration. But it is clear that we are adding heat-trapping molecules to the atmosphere *in addition* to those from these other sources, which we cannot control. Now, this understanding comes directly from science—including laboratory science—and we understand the *processes* involved in this radiation-trapping phenomenon quite well. We are mainly concerned with the effects of anthropogenic climate change, since this is something we can immediately do something about—if we choose to do so. Or, I should say, if contingencies compel us to do so. Yet global-climate-change deniers—some of whom are profiting from the use of fossil fuels—have convinced many people that physics somehow does not apply to our planet.

"Energy provision aside, we should ask ourselves who is *capitalizing* on the sale of fossil fuels? As I mentioned before, there are many people who are already heavily invested in fossil fuel extraction equipment and techniques, and in the refineries that process crude oil into usable fuels. They would like to squeeze out every last dollar from their investments before humankind switches over to cleaner sources. While there are some remaining uncertainties when it comes to something as complex as the climate, the overall picture is becoming clearer.

"Once we began to understand the physics *underlying* a phenomenon like global climate change, we should have taken advantage of this understanding and begun to mitigate these unwelcome changes to our climate. Climate scientists have provided us with the information we need in order to mitigate these effects; the changes that need to be made involve *human behavior*. But most people are unaware that the science of behavior has advanced to a point where we can provide very helpful information. We can suggest new contingencies that will change *the behavior* of the population in ways that will do so.

"This may involve new tax incentives for home-energy efficiency and the purchase of non-gasoline powered cars, and so on. If energy companies had communal concerns and a long-term regard for all of humanity—instead of more profit for investors—they would have reinvested much of their profits into newer low-carbon energy technologies. If there is reasonable science telling us what is causing the recent warming effect of Earth—and there is ample science pointing to fossil fuel—then why not be proactive and err on the side of caution? This is the old 'error of commission' versus the 'error of omission.'

What is to be lost by switching to clean energy sources that do not emit CO_2?

"I only mention all of this," I said, "to provide an analogy for the unnecessary exposure of people to human violence. I use this particular analogy because, just as there are people who don't believe the validity of the science behind global climate change, there are those who don't believe the validity of the science underlying human behavior change; in this case, the causes of the increases in certain forms of violent human behavior. Just as with fossil fuel, we should ask ourselves who is capitalizing on the sale of violent media, and are they the very people who are obfuscating the data showing a *causal* connection between viewing of violence and the increase in certain types of violence?

"Behaviorologists understand quite well many of the processes underlying behavior, just as physicists understand the processes underlying climate change. By analyzing the contingencies of a culture, we can make informed predictions of what should occur as a result of those contingencies. The kind of exposure to violence we are seeing in our society involves principles that we have investigated extensively in both the laboratory and in the clinic.

"As I said, the conditioning that takes place while watching violence is very close to how behavioral therapists desensitize clients to fears, anxieties and phobias. We desensitize people's fears, anxieties, and phobias through exposure therapy and systematic desensitization, using procedures very similar to those we find in modern gaming simulations and movies. We know from countless investigations how to desensitize people to various emotional stimuli; should violence be one of them? Does it make a society 'healthier' if the people comprising it tolerate and accept violence? Or should people be repulsed by it?

"Our data show that violence is not behaviorally healthy for a culture, and neither is acceptance of it. People who become desensitized to violence are less inclined to work to eliminate it. The underlying science can tell us what is likely to happen when people are exposed to these kinds of materials, and we believe we are seeing it. So, again, why not err on the side of caution? What is to be lost by reducing children's and adults' exposure to violence-desensitizing materials and preventing them from experiencing what it feels like to kill or harm others?

"It's ironic that purveyors of unbridled freedom and permissiveness do not also advocate video games that would teach children how to prepare methamphetamine, or how to build bombs, or embezzle money from a business, although I'm certain there are some—in the name of freedom and libertarianism—who would. While these skills may be useful for law enforcement officers, they are not skills that transfer to many other useful areas or activities."

"But how do you know which skills will and will not be useful?" Martha asked. "What if young people are sent off to war, for instance? Won't these skills be useful then?"

"The military," I said, "is quite adept at training soldiers to kill in a relatively short period of time. It has been pointed out by people like Dave Grossman, a former professor and military historian at West Point, that the military is using software very similar to the ubiquitous off-the-shelf first-person shooter games—now made easily available to children—in order to train their special forces how to kill."

"I can agree with you that some of these mass shootings could be the result of exposure to these types of games and other media," Martha relented. "And I'm quite aware, as a science journalist, of the science behind global climate change. While I majored in journalism, one of my minors was earth science. Climate change is happening just as climatologists predicted, in tandem with the rise of the heat-trapping triatomic gases that you mentioned. But are we ready to say definitively that the rise of mass shootings is a direct result of the increased exposure to violent media? You say this comes directly from the behavioral processes that you have studied in the laboratory and observed in the clinic?"

"Yes, we are extrapolating from what we know from laboratory research and from clinical applications of this research," I said. "Also, our culturologists have looked to other cultures for clues. We now know from the natural science of behavior how behavior is acquired, motivated, maintained, evoked, elicited, generalized, and so on. And remember also, we did not have violent games providing such high levels of verisimilitude until relatively recently.

"While children from previous generations may have acted out war games and pretended to be soldiers or cowboys shooting each other, they were not exposed to the nearly perfect simulations of real human violence. And they certainly did not have the kinds of virtual reality games that actually teach the behavior of killing and allow the user to experience the feelings that accompany the killing of humans. Now, if for some unforeseen reason our culturologists ever *do* find that desensitizing children to violence and teaching them killing skills is beneficial to a peaceful society, we can easily engineer the contingencies to teach these skills.

"As I've mentioned, we are quite flexible and can implement new contingencies relatively quickly. We don't believe this will ever happen, but we will let the data speak and we'll act accordingly. For now, we have eliminated this variable to good effect. Our children are simply not interested in killing, and, in fact, are appalled by it. Prosocial behavior flourishes in our communities because of this, and, of course, we have engineered contingencies that directly reinforce this prosocial behavior.

"Now, at the risk of belaboring my point," I said, somewhat ruefully, "and as you correctly mentioned, only a small fraction of the violence-exposed population goes on to commit mass shootings, so let me just add this: In a booklet called *After Columbine*, the author—Dr. Kelly Zinna, a clinical psychologist who specialized in violence prediction—cited some important factors that many of these mass shooters have in common. The typical mass shooter usually feels that he—yes, it is usually a 'he'—has been victimized, and he has a history of perceived injustice done to him, such as being bullied, teased, or rejected by others. He may begin to fantasize about, and formulate ways to avenge, not only those who offended him, but also other people who resemble those offenders in any way. These shooters typically have had exposure to violent videos, games, or music, and some kind of practice with, and obsession with, lethal weaponry. And finally, there is typically a precipitous triggering event, such as expulsion from school, rejection, arrest, divorce, loss of income, etc. Now, we can ask, why would anyone think it would be advisable to deliberately train such a person how to kill others? Wouldn't we do better to teach this person good communications skills and how to resolve problems peacefully? If the latter, our behaviorologists can provide you with some magnificent software and training materials that can accomplish this; they have been designed based on the latest science. But if one thinks it would be better to teach such persons how to kill, well, you can easily find software that will do so at your local superstore, or on the Internet. People should also be aware that the behaviors learned from violence modeling, training, and desensitization may occur when the person is quite behaviorally stable, but these learned behaviors may only be evoked later when circumstances change. One usually behaves in ways that have been reinforced in the past, even if those behaviors were learned in simulations at some former time. If there are few or no peaceful alternative behaviors in the person's repertoire, we may not like the result.

"Of course, both climate science, and our analysis of at least *some* of the causes of certain forms of violence, may be mistaken. This is the nature of all provisional knowledge. But I must confess that I hope they are not mistaken, because in both cases, science is telling us what we can do to alleviate these problems, and the solutions are within our reach. If we are wrong about the causes of climate change and violence, we must begin anew, and the solutions may prove to be more intractable."

14

I **looked at my watch, and it was nearly time to meet with** Traci and the technicians. I was about to excuse myself when Martha broached a different topic. "Surely you must have *some* people here who do not contribute, are lazy, or just plain antisocial—right? How would you deal with a sociopath, for instance?"

"I don't think you fully appreciate the power of contingencies," I said to her. "People often ask us what we would do with a Charles Manson or a Ted Bundy, or some other infamous person labeled as sociopathic. What they are asking, essentially, is what we would do with a person conditioned outside of one of our communities and then placed into ours—a person with extremely aberrant behavior conditioned by coincidental contingencies in another society. You are asking me what we would do with people having extremely aberrant legacy behaviors, to which I've previously alluded.

"These are people who fell through the cracks, so to speak. Most likely there were many accidental contingencies that shaped these behaviors and no one noticed, cared, or knew the proper way to treat these maladaptive behaviors. In too many cases, these people are passed on—in schools for example— for others to deal with or pass on again. If a teacher knows he or she will not be dealing with this child after the school year, he or she may tolerate the aberrant behavior or just try to mitigate it during the child's tenure in the teacher's classroom.

"This can easily happen in large cultures where people know they are unlikely to have future contact with such a person. But it is best to catch aberrant behavior as soon as possible and see that it is not strengthened by positive or negative reinforcement. We are a close-knit community. All members participate in everyday social activities of one kind or another, and aberrant or non-functional behavior does not go unnoticed for long. We watch for anomalies and make sure that antisocial behavior does not have reinforcing consequences.

"Moreover, and perhaps more importantly, we make certain that prosocial behavior incompatible with this type of behavior is reinforced very early in childhood. In the case of some, or perhaps most, sociopaths, there is often the semblance of prosocial behavior while in social settings, and he or she only behaves in aberrant or antisocial ways under certain conditions—for example when the behavior is not likely to be punished.

"So there is obviously stimulus control of this type of behavior. There are also many other factors involved, such as the accidental conditioning of sexual responses to inappropriate stimuli, as in fetishes; other factors involve motivating operations, and so on. Some, if not many, of these behaviors can be evoked by verbal stimuli, as in sadistic literature. This involves new findings in verbal behavior involving relational frames and equivalence classes.

"So I believe the question of how we would treat one of society's sociopaths is a little unfair. It would be like asking a doctor how to treat an advanced illness *after* all of the doctor's good advice has gone unheeded. While we could probably treat and abate extremely aberrant behavior conditioned outside of our communities, we have no desire to take on the problem people whom another culture has accidently created and perhaps discarded. We do not wish to divert our resources in order to correct behaviors resulting from the poorly designed or accidental contingencies of another culture.

"Our communities specifically engineer contingencies that will strengthen social behavior. In the case of strong antisocial or criminal behavior, new mediating neural connections can be strengthened, but the old connections may still exist in some strength. So, unfortunately, the undesired behavior may re-emerge under certain conditions—for example, when newly conditioned alternative behaviors no longer procure reinforcement. This is the problem of recidivism. Just as in the case of learning disorders such as autism, it is far better to catch these aberrant behaviors as early as possible and prevent them from being reinforced, while concurrently strengthening the socially acceptable behaviors that will supplant them."

"I can imagine that some of these socially acceptable behaviors would not produce the same reinforcers that the anti-social behavior did," Martha said.

"Yes, that is true," I answered. "But many reinforcers produced by antisocial behavior are *conditioned* reinforcers. Unlike unconditioned reinforcers like food, water, warmth, and sexual stimulation that are reinforcing from birth, conditioned reinforcers *become* reinforcing during the person's lifetime by being paired with unconditioned—or primary—reinforcers. Signs of intimidation can *become* reinforcing, for instance, if people who have shown signs of intimidation in the past have complied with the demands of the intimidator. Therefore we must be careful during the socialization process as to what *becomes* a conditioned reinforcer.

"There is no reason why the primary reinforcers—such as food, water, and sexual contact—cannot be procured with socially acceptable behavior. Many criminal behaviors are socially reinforced by a small criminal subset of the population. Gangs, for example, often reinforce the criminal behavior of their members with social approval. Signs of respect from other gang members can strengthen the criminal behavior that is required to enter into, and remain in, the gang. Young people who grow up in these environments will have criminal behavior modeled, described, shaped, maintained, and strengthened by signs of approval, admiration, status, respect, and even offers of sex and other reinforcers. All of these criminal behaviors are conditioned by known principles of learning."

At this time, Traci approached us and informed me that the technicians from the nursery would be delayed; she suggested that we try to meet them at a later time, and before she could leave, we asked her to join us. Paul Johnston also coincidently entered at this time and appeared quite happy to sit next to Martha and across from Traci. After a few cordial exchanges between Traci and Martha, Martha began to inquire about Frazier.

"I would like to write a little something more about Frazier," she said. "Can you tell me anything about him that might be important for my readers to know?"

"First, I highly recommend that you read Frazier's writings yourself," Traci suggested, "and not what others have written about him. Someone once said that he has had the worst press since Darwin—and that might very well be true. Both Darwin and Frazier came to understand the concept and importance of *selection* in explaining the form and function of biological systems, and both were overthrowing long-held prescientific views of humankind. Selection may seem like too simple a process to explain the complex subject matters that it underlies. But just as Darwin took this seemingly simple process of selection and used it to explain and account for the diversity of life forms—a diversity that up until then had been attributed to a divine creator—Frazier discovered that a similar selection process accounts for the diversity of operant behavior. While both processes involve the accretion, or accumulation, of small changes over time, when people observe the final product without knowing the historical processes involved, they see design or purpose.

"So, like Darwin, Frazier had discovered a natural process that could explain the diversity of behavior, but without hypothesizing an internal homunculus, like mind. What was heretofore thought of as voluntary behavior, but is now better described by the concept of operant behavior, is actually behavior that is selected by the consequences of that behavior. Now, there are many things that obfuscate this selection mechanism. For example, in humans, modeling and rule-governed behavior seem to short-circuit the contingencies that would normally select the behavior.

"So, if someone tells us how to behave effectively in a given situation—by giving us instruction, for instance—we may no longer need to be exposed directly to the contingencies in order to be successful in that situation. We do not learn to put a coin in a vending machine by accident—we don't normally go around putting coins in slots to see what happens; someone either models the behavior for us, or describes this behavior for us by giving us a rule. For example, someone may say, 'Put your coins in this slot and pull on one of the plungers below the item you want.' But we must always remember that rules describe contingencies, and we had to learn to understand and follow verbal rules through a long history of verbal conditioning, well before rules could have this effect.

"Something concerning Frazier that may be of interest to you and your readers is that he applied his scientific findings to improve his own behavior," I added. "He designed his personal study here at Walden Two in such a way as to optimize his own behavior, especially his own verbal behavior. He applied what he learned about operant conditioning to himself. For many years he had a clock wired into the switch that turned on his desk light. This allowed him to record the time he spent writing. He plotted the results of each session onto a cumulative record whose slope explicitly indicated his productivity. He ate only lightly before doing intellectual work, so as not to induce drowsiness, and he began his writing every day at the same time and place. These conditions—of time and place—were likely to set the occasion for the intellectual be-havior that regularly occurred there. He was an early riser and worked several hours upon waking; he considered these early morning hours his most productive. He could be considered his own best experimental subject."

"Has the science advanced since Frazier's original analysis of operant behavior?" Martha asked. "What more have we learned about behavior?"

"It has advanced, and there are many good examples, but I'll just mention one important one," I said. "The work of Dr. Murray Sidman has opened new lines of research into lan-guage, cognition, and what has traditionally been called sym-bolism or reference in language. As teachers and parents name and describe objects and ongoing behaviors to children, equiv-alence relations form between these words and objects and ac-tions. To put it succinctly, equivalence relations will form when stimuli—such as words—are paired with other stimuli, such as objects, or pictures of objects, or even other words. Under these contingencies, the stimuli combined in this way will form into functionally equivalent classes, meaning one will evoke the other, or in some cases, evoke or elicit a response evoked or elicited by the other; they can come to function in similar ways.

"The children are learning to describe—again, we say tact—objects and events in the environment, including their own op-erant behaviors and the contingent relations between these operants and the contexts in which they occur. The latter—the ability to describe the contingency between the behavior and the natural consequence—is, as I have mentioned before, called 'tracking.' Equivalence relations form after many such experi-ences. Very young children will eventually point to objects when given the name of the object—either audibly or in writing—and will also say or write the name when shown the object. There are explicit conditioning methods used to facilitate the formation of equivalence relations, but I will spare you the details."

"But after many such experiences," I continued, "the child's behavior will reach a point where behavioral relations will form between objects and spoken or written object-names; they are said to have become functionally equivalent. Notice that the relations are purely behavioral; there is no non-behavioral relation between the spoken or written word 'cat' and the animal; the relation or connection is purely arbitrary and is formed between synapses in the brain due to the conditioning procedure. After conditioning, if you say the name of the object, the child can point to the written word, or to the object itself, or maybe just to a picture of the object.

"Early researchers found that, after training just a few of these relations, other relations emerge without further training. This was unexpected at the time. For example, we may directly condition the child to point to a picture of a horse when the word 'horse' is spoken. And then we may directly condition the child to point to the written word 'horse' when the word horse is spoken. But after many such conditioning trials, the child may point to the picture of the horse when seeing the written word 'horse.'

"This new relation was something that we did not directly condition. The formation of equivalence relations was investigated and described quite meticulously by Dr. Sidman, and he went on to operationally define the equivalence relation by requiring that three conditions must be met before calling a relation an equivalence relation, but I need not go into these at this time. This research is very relevant to the teaching of reading, and we have taken great advantage of Dr. Sidman's work. We have many computers with touch-screens and the educational software needed to teach the prerequisite behaviors required before equivalence relations will form—incidentally, relations other than equivalence will form as well.

"A relatively new theory, called relational frame theory, or RFT for short, has come out of Dr. Sidman's work and has been extended, developed, and investigated by Steven Hayes and Dermot Barnes-Holmes. It is an area of active research in several of our communities, including this one. I should add that, up until now, humans are the only species known to derive new relations between stimuli. So, as I mentioned the other day, if it turns out that what linguists have been calling symbolic language, cannot develop in non-human organisms, it will be the experimental behaviorologists who actually demonstrate this, not armchair theoretical linguists. Since you are well versed in RFT, Traci, perhaps you would like to talk a little about this area?"

"I will be happy to," she said, turning away from me and toward the others, but before she could speak, Paul said, "Excuse me for interrupting, Dr. Jensen, but doesn't the fact that people can *derive* new relations they have not been taught suggest that there are special cognitive mechanisms in the brain that are needed to account for it? This seems like a different process than simple stimulus control of responses. Something else more complicated seems to be going on here," he added with a perplexed look on his face.

"No more so than any process of generalization requires a special cognitive mechanism," Traci said. "Generalization involves the fact that some stimuli can have common properties. If an organism's responses of, say, pressing a lever, have been reinforced only when a green light is present, they will eventually only press when the green light is on. This process and the procedures that bring it about are well understood: responses reinforced in the presence of the green light will increase and responses in the absence of the green light will extinguish. But the organism will also respond to a light of similar wavelength as defined by physicists, and will respond increasingly less as the wavelengths become more dissimilar either way, larger or smaller. Does this require an internal cognitive mechanism?"

"I . . . don't think so," Paul answered.

"What about imitation then? We learn to imitate others when our behavior is reinforced for matching the behavior of another behaving person. Someone raises his arm, we raise our arm; he pats his head, we pat our head, and so on. But then we begin to imitate behaviors that we have never imitated before; does this too require a special cognitive mechanism?"

"No, again, I don't think so," he said. "Our behavior seems to be matching the stimuli coming from another person's behavior. But it must be behavior of which we are capable, correct? If someone does a double backflip off of a diving board, I can't match that!"

"Yes, of course," said Traci serenely, "it must be previously conditioned behavior that is in our repertoire; my point is, though, that we have never *imitated* that behavior before, not that we can or can't perform it."

"Ah, I'm with you."

"Well, then," Traci continued, "if the spoken word 'cat' is paired with the picture of a cat, and the picture of a cat is paired with the written word 'cat,' and this is done many times, these stimuli will form a class, or set, and each stimulus in the class will come to evoke the others. This process of one stimulus in the class evoking the others in the class *generalizes*, but it is no different than the generalizations of others processes. So, bear with me now, if this same procedure is repeated many times with many different stimuli, this whole *process* will generalize.

"Once the spoken word 'cat,' the picture of the cat, and the written word 'cat,' all come to evoke each other, we say they have become functionally related or functionally equivalent, and that they form a functional stimulus class. After we have repeated this procedure with many other spoken words, pictures, and written words, *classes begin to form more easily*, do you see? The process itself has generalized. If a child is shown a picture of a cow for the first time, he or she may ask, 'What is that?' meaning 'what is the spoken word for that animal?' 'Deriving' is the name we give to the process when each stimulus in a class comes to evoke the others and this process has not been explicitly conditioned. Even class formation itself generalizes and it becomes easier to form new classes, but this is no different than any other generalization process; it requires no special internal mechanism."

"And if you think about it," Traci said, "*relations* between things are similar in that, if one thing is the same as another, the other is the same as the first. And there is typically a symmetric relation that goes with any kind of relationship between stimuli. Once we begin to respond to the relations themselves—that is, once we can tact relations between things instead of tacting the things—we soon learn that there are symmetric relations also. This whole process will generalize too. And this brings me to relational frame theory.

"The research on equivalence relations opened a whole new line of research called 'relational frame theory' or, as Dr. Burris has said, 'RFT,' for short. This has been a very active area of research in the last two or three decades. While Frazier focused mainly on the controlling variables determining the verbal behavior of the *speaker*, RFT focuses much more on the effects of verbal behavior on the *listener*. And while it can be daunting to the uninitiated, it is actually well within reach of anyone willing to take the time to understand it. As for now, it would be better if I explained it by giving an example. Much of our verbal behavior has a structure, or form, or syntax. Some of this structure actually helps to elucidate relations between various stimulus objects by providing contextual cues. For example, if I say that a cow is *bigger than* a cat, the relation 'bigger than' tells the listener something about size relations between cows and cats.

"But instead of talking about the *structure* or *form* of this kind of verbal behavior, it might help our understanding if we can use a metaphor for this structure or form. We can use the metaphor of a 'picture frame,' or just a 'frame,' to highlight the form of verbal behavior that deals with the relations between stimuli. We can call the *form* of verbal behavior dealing with *relations* between stimuli the 'relational frame.' And again, this is just a metaphor for the structure or form of our verbal behavior.

"Just as a picture frame can hold many different pictures, the structure of a verbal emission—the relational frame—can hold many different relata—'relata' being the stimulus objects or events that are being *related*—objects such as cows and cats, for instance. Now the verbal frame can remain the same while the stimuli being related can change. Take my example of a relational frame dealing with the size relation between a cow and a cat. Someone could have said instead, 'A cat is bigger than a cow.' The relational *frame* is exactly the same as in my original example, but the stimulus objects being related have changed places.

"People learn various relations between stimuli by being exposed to numerous examples of these relational frames. When people are given many experiences or *examples* dealing with various relations between stimuli such as cows and cats, we call these multiple experiences 'multiple exemplars.' We are taught relations such as under/over, inside/outside, larger/smaller, more/less, better/worse, and so on. Notice also in these examples, one of the relations 'entails' the other. If a cow is *larger* than a cat, then the cat is *smaller* than the cow. This is called 'mutual entailment' in RFT. I'm sure you can see why it is called this, as one relation implies or entails the other. These symmetric relations are learned through 'multiple exemplar training,' and after many experiences in dealing with them, when given one relation, we begin to look for its symmetric relation. There are countless relations that can hold between stimuli, relations such as hierarchy, cause-and-effect, temporal order, and so on.

"Just as in the case of equivalence relations, new relations can emerge without being directly conditioned. For example, after teaching the relation 'larger than,' as in 'A lake is *larger than* a pond, and an ocean is *larger than* a lake,' the listener may say that 'A pond *is smaller than* a lake' and 'a lake *is smaller than* an ocean,' and even 'A pond *is smaller than* an ocean.' In this last example, two or more relations are combined to derive a new relation that was not taught—at least, it was not taught in *this* situation; therefore it is called 'combinatorial mutual entailment' because the two relations are combined to entail a new relation.

"And, again, this happens without these relations being directly conditioned *using these stimuli as relata*; these derived relations appear to emerge as if by magic. Of course, this does *not* come about by magic. People have had a history of verbal conditioning involving these relational frames, and various permutations of these relations were conditioned in the subject's past. These relating behaviors have generalized to a point where new relata can easily be inserted into the old familiar frames—to stay with our metaphor—and the person will appear to derive new and other relations between them. As I have said, people usually have many conditioning trials involving these relational frames, so deriving new relations is really just a form of generalization.

"So, for instance, you could tell the readers of *Discover*, Martha, that Walden Two communities are *different than* other communities of the past in that they use the natural science called behaviorology to strengthen behaviors that are beneficial to both the individual and the community. 'Different than' is a contextual cue that tells the listener that the relation between Walden Two and other communities involves the relation of *distinction*. You are telling your readers that something sets us apart from other communities. But your readers may now derive new relations due to his or her past conditioning in dealing with this relation.

"Notice, too, that your verbal behavior can *transform* how our communities will function as stimuli for readers of your report, even though they have never been directly exposed to any actual contingencies involving our communities. This is called 'transformation of stimulus function' in relational frame theory. The way various stimuli will function for people can be *transformed* by the verbal behavior of others. For example, a persuasive politician or demagogue may call an opponent or a news organization that has been critical of that politician a 'liar' or 'fake news,' respectively, and this may change the way the defamed politician or news organization will function as a stimulus in the future for those who have been exposed to this verbal behavior.

"The person or news organization has been put in a frame of reference with liars or fake things, and from now on this political opponent or news organization will generate some of the same emotions that the words 'liar' and 'fake' generate. This can cause a listener to discount even *justified* criticism coming from that news organization, for instance. The way the defamed politician or news organization will function as a stimulus after a listener has been exposed to this kind of verbal behavior has been transformed solely by verbal behavior.

"Similarly, your readers of *Discover* may respond with either positive or negative emotions when they hear the name 'Walden Two' entirely as a result of the relational frames you have used in your report. Equivalence relations and RFT are very promising concepts and are also very pertinent to the study of propaganda. Relational frames that are true—that is, they accurately tact relations between stimuli—are very useful for a listener, but on the other hand, framing can lead a listener to behave inappropriately if he or she has been given false relations between stimuli.

"Politicians are notorious for verbalizing untrue relational frames about opponents in order to win elections. For example, by saying that their opponent is weak on crime, or perhaps just plain weak, they may falsely put their opponent in an equivalence relation with weak things. What is remarkable is that patterns of air vibrations caused by our vocalizations, or by our written marks on paper, can *transform* the way stimulus objects in the real world will function in the future for the listener or reader. And they can do so without the listener or reader ever being exposed to any actual contingencies regarding those stimuli.

"We have also discovered treatments for many problems involving language. We say 'languaging' instead of 'language' to emphasize that language is not something independent of behavior; languaging *is* behavior, but it is more accurately called 'verbal behavior.' But, as I hope I've made clear, as humans acquire verbal behavior, the words can become equivalent in certain functional ways to the things and events that they refer to. The words can come to have all of the emotional impact that those things and events would have on our behavior.

"This can be a good thing or a bad thing, depending on how the relational frame has transformed the function of the stimuli related. Humans are the only animals known who can sit in an otherwise safe environment that is supplying all of one's needs, yet the person can recall past adversity, or can imagine future calamity, through languaging. Humans can verbally recount events that took place decades ago and relive them, by which I mean that the stimuli from their own verbal behavior—usually the *private* verbal behavior we call thinking—can elicit images and emotions that the original stimuli elicited, and this is mainly due to the effects of equivalence relations.

"This can also happen if people imagine dire future events that may or may not occur. Verbal behavior concerning past and future events can generate negative emotions as if the events were occurring now. Some people constantly dwell on ominous past or future events, and this can eventually lead to severe anxiety and depression that may take them into therapy. This has been referred to as 'the dark side of languaging.'

"I am only scratching the surface of our research into relational framing," Traci concluded. "The relations can be between very abstract stimuli and involve large networks of relations. I won't overwhelm you with the details, but I hope you find time to further investigate this subject if you are interested. I might add, again, that it is extremely relevant to propaganda, a subject that is garnering much interest around the world these days."

As Martha closed her computer and gathered her things together, she said, "I sincerely want to thank you both for your hospitality. I have learned quite a lot about a subject I thought I understood. I have always believed that human behavior is, for the most part, beyond scientific explanation, but you have given me much to think about. And I can tell you truthfully that I actually do love your peaceful community and the people here. Everyone I have talked with has been kind and helpful, including the children. Whether some or all of your obvious success is due to contingency engineering or not, I cannot definitively say. But, for the first time in my life, I actually hope so."

Then, as she stood up, she added in a lighthearted, humorous, affected manner, "Tomorrow evening I will return to my disarrayed world with its haphazard contingencies that give one the illusion of freedom and continue to write about science and its impact on our lives." And then more seriously, "But at least now I can add a science that, you have convinced me, has remained obscure and misunderstood for too long. I know that psychology has always been considered by other natural scientists to be a 'soft' discipline with eclectic and cobbled-together theories about human behavior.

"And I'm sure this image has tarnished the discipline and hampered a truly natural science of behavior. I can tell you from speaking to many scientists that they do not realize how far your science has advanced. As you have said, even when people observe the unsophisticated behaviors of simple organisms in simplified environments, they often miss the controlling variables; so I can imagine what they miss *here* when they look around."

"Yes," I agreed, "contingencies go quite unnoticed in everyday life."

As Martha gathered up her computer and placed it into a carrying bag, she leaned toward me so the others could not hear what she was about to say, then she hesitated for a moment before saying, "It's none of my business, but you might want to keep an eye on Mr. Douglas. There is no publication called *Newstime*; also, I couldn't help overhearing him as he spoke on his phone the other day and . . . well, I will leave it at that."

She then abruptly turned around and departed.

15

On the morning of the last day for our visiting journalists, we took a final leisurely walk around Walden Two, showing our guests our wood and metal shops, one of our small robotics plants—this particular one wound the wire coils for our generators—and one of our two water towers equipped with various levels of filtration devices for our assorted water usages. We next walked into a building housing the clean rooms where several people were wearing what appeared to be spacesuits. Inside, software-driven robotic devices were etching onto sheets of silicon the layers that make up some of the integrated circuits for various devices.

The importance of computers in our lives cannot be overemphasized. We, along with a team of engineers from several other communities, design our own logic circuits and share these designs with others in our network of communities. The software that drives our robotic lasers is openly shared with all communities, but only a few of our communities manufactured these chips.

Finally, after the morning tour and lunch, we met for the last time in the same small conference room in which Traci had given her introductory remarks. We prompted our visitors to ask any final questions they may have, and we made clear to them that they could always contact us in the future for any further information they may need to complete their reports; to this end, we provided each journalist with a card containing our contact information.

Dr. Fredrika Johansson, one of our culturologists, joined Traci and me to take questions. We sat at a large oval table where the three of us were evenly spaced between the others. Jeffery Simmons directed the first question to Traci.

"Dr. Jensen, in your talk on Monday you clearly denigrated psychology, arguing that it was not a natural science. Do you see any value in psychology? For example, do you see value in the work of such people as Phillip Zimbardo or Stanley Milgram? And do you find any value in other psychological studies?"

"Oh yes, of course." Traci answered. "Although we account for their findings just as we do with any behavioral phenomena. For example, the research into authority can be accounted for by well-known principles of behavior—we look to the past and present contingencies. But Milgram's findings are certainly interesting, as are the findings of many other researchers. What we take exception to in many of these studies is the explanations for the behavior involved. We want to know what contingencies actually make one person an authority figure for another, and why do people comply with the mands of authority figures?

"You may recall that a mand is verbal behavior that specifies the reinforcer the listener is to provide for the speaker. In the case of an authority figure, the authority may ask the listener to do something the listener would not ordinarily do. For instance the authority figure may tell the listener to deliver an extremely aversive and possibly dangerous electric shock to a subject, and if the person then complies by delivering that shock, this will reinforce the verbal behavior of the authority figure.

"But why does the listener comply when they otherwise would not? What is it about authority figures that cause a person to violate their own code of ethics? We believe we can answer these questions with known principles of behavior. In this case we know that many people under these circumstances do not feel they will be held responsible for their actions; they often believe they will be spared from any punitive consequences, and the person in authority will be held accountable instead.

"Likewise, many psychological researchers also have found interesting regularities in behavioral phenomena, and we must look for the controlling variables. Only by determining the controlling variables can we find effective methods to effect behavior change. Behaviorologists explain the gross findings of psychologists without postulating fictitious causes.

"Take, for example, the so-called trait called persistence. Psychologists may say that a person sticks to a task because he *has* persistence. They may even design tests to measure such 'traits,' and they may argue that these tests have been validated. But what they are actually measuring, in our view, are correlations between behaviors, in this case between a subject's verbal behavior—answers on the test—and corresponding properties of their subsequent actions. Frazier has pointed out that these so-called 'traits' usually begin as adjectives, as in, 'that person sure is persistent.'

"This is a description of *behavior*. Unfortunately, the adjective is often made into a noun and put inside the person to explain the behavior. If asked why the person persists, we may be tempted to say it is because he *has persistence*. This is circular reasoning. The hypothesized cause in this type of explanation is inferred from the very behavior we are trying to explain and adds nothing to our understanding of why the person's behavior persists.

"But behaviorologists can *produce* persistent behavior by arranging for reinforcement to occur on a particular schedule of reinforcement called a *variable ratio* schedule. This schedule delivers a reinforcer intermittently after varying numbers of responses, as on a gambler's slot machine, and it produces a steady and relatively high response rate. Thus we have determined empirically that it is this intermittent *schedule* that produces the persistent behavior, not an internal trait called 'persistence.' The law of parsimony would require that we accept the behaviorologists' simpler yet adequate explanation, since it does not posit any superfluous internal entities.

The advantage is that we now know how to *produce* persistent behavior.

"And in some cases, where animals appear to behave aggressively from birth, we may be tempted to say this is because the animal has inherited a trait called 'aggression.' Yet aggressive operant behavior can also be shaped in the animal during its lifetime through operant conditioning. And whatever it is that changes in the nervous system after operant conditioning, could have been wired up in a similar but more permanent manner by evolution. In other words, evolution could have selected a similar hard-wired version of the mediating nervous system that operant conditioning can produce during the organism's lifetime. Either way, we end up with a changed organism—or a changed nervous system if you like—not some aggressive internal agent or trait.

"In this case, these two selection processes are redundant, both producing a topographically similar behavior with some survival value. After all, it is the nervous system that mediates—not originates—behavior, and whether it was evolution that selected the hard-wired version, or operant conditioning that produced a soft-wired version, these would be the most parsimonious explanations for the behavior, not an inferred inner trait called 'aggression.' To call certain behaviors 'aggressive' is merely a description of what is observed, not a cause. Again, I mention all of this because it is vital to your understanding of our communities; you must understand the sciences behind them; namely behaviorology and culturology. All of our members are taught behaviorology and culturology in addition to the other natural sciences such as biology, physics, geology, and chemistry."

"I believe some people are genetically predisposed to violence and aggression," Paul said, only half jokingly. "I have known some guys who are just plain bullies."

"In a sense, you are correct," I said. "Typically, larger more muscular mesomorphic children soon find that they can lift or move things that others cannot. They learn that they can easily take things away from smaller, ectomorphic children, move them out of the way, and bully them in other ways; and this bullying behavior can get reinforced if we're not vigilant. But in fact, an adult cannot always be present to guard against reinforcement of the behavior of bullies. Although the behavior itself is not inherited, the body that often permits aggressive behavior *is*.

"Arthur Staats has pointed this out. Just as a lion has powerful muscles and teeth capable of tearing flesh—and learns through early operant experiences how to use them—people can have physical advantages that allow aggressive behavior to be reinforced. It is really no different than a person operating a backhoe—a type of response magnifier—where it is lever-moving behavior that is reinforced by consequences. If you outfitted a small person with a powerful robotic exoskeleton that allowed them to bully others, over time they may become quite a different person, as occurs when they are given response magnifiers such as clubs or guns.

"Therefore, I'm not saying that all bullies are large, but some people just happen to be born with bodies that predispose them to bullying behavior. But remember, the nervous system that mediates aggressive behavior in the large person is just like the nervous system in all other people, and works the same way; it is *not* a more aggressive nervous system. It is just that powerful bodies make it more likely that more aggressive behavior will be strengthened. The nervous system that mediates such behavior is not larger, the musculature is. But with proper contingencies, this nervous system can also mediate prosocial behaviors that have been strengthened by reinforcement procedures.

"Now, as Traci alluded to in her introductory talk, there can be individual differences in nervous systems. Some people may have larger or smaller amygdala or hippocampi, or fewer connections between the prefrontal cortex and motor systems, but special contingencies can often be arranged to compensate for any deficiencies. One of the dangers of allowing the parents of larger children to arrange contingencies for them is that they want to see their children succeed in any way possible. They often do not see their own children's dominating behavior as bullying."

"Aren't psychologists simply inferring these innate traits from observable behavior?" Paul asked, turning to Traci. "How is this different from inference in the other sciences?"

"Psychologists," Traci answered, "too often believe they are modeling their methods on other sciences when, for example, they use inference to posit inner agents and traits from publically observable behavior. They may believe this is similar to astronomers inferring an unseen planet by noticing perturbations in the motions of other nearby celestial bodies, or to physicists inferring small subatomic particles in order to explain otherwise unaccountable nuclear forces. But when astronomers infer a planet from the perturbations of nearby bodies, a big difference here is that we already know that planets are real natural phenomena that do exist in nature. When earlier scientists in the nascent field of physics hypothesized an 'ether' or 'phlogiston,' these notions led them astray, because these things were not known to exist beforehand."

"I agree," Paul added, "but this was not always the case in physics; physicists did not know that subatomic particles existed until they inferred them from the behavior of atomic interactions; these subatomic particles were *not* known to exist beforehand. They were inferred and later proven to exist."

"We are not saying that all inference is useless or unwarranted," I said. "But the hypothesized subatomic particles in nuclear physics, where the particles are only detected by recording equipment, adhere to the tenet of parsimony, which demands that we posit the simplest explanation that is adequate to account for a phenomenon—often called Occam's razor. These hypothesized subatomic particles are the simplest explanation that accounts for the known facts, and other experiments eventually confirmed them. This is not so with hypothesized entities inside the person; here there *are* alternative explanations that are observable, measurable, testable *and* simpler."

"Dr. Jensen, do you see physiology as an important adjunct to behaviorology?" Paul asked. "I believe you referred to this fusion of the two sciences as neurobehaviorology, is that correct?"

"Yes, but let me be clear about this," she answered, "we believe the sciences of physiology and behaviorology will always work at different, albeit complementary, levels of observation. While informing each other, they will always remain separate sciences. Various levels of analysis are suggested by the *Law of Cumulative Complexity*, formulated by behaviorologist Stephen Ledoux in 2012, which states: *The natural physical/chemical interactions of matter and energy sometimes result in more complex structures and functions that endure and naturally interact further, resulting in an accumulating complexity*. This law implies that each new level of complexity needs to be studied at its own level of observation because, as more complexity arises, new variables are affecting the more complex structures.

"For example, you cannot completely understand behavior by studying the physiology of the organism alone. You must look at the *environmental context* of the behavior. Not taking the context of behavior into account is like trying to understand why a peacock has a colorful plume without knowing how sexual selection works. Sexual selection is taking place at the level of evolutionary science, and it is variables at that level of observation that must be taken into account. The female peahen doing the selecting is at a different level of complexity than the variables the physiologist is dealing with. The physiologists can tell us what proteins make up the colorful plume and perhaps which genes produce those proteins, but not *why* they got selected. To understand why the colorful plume was selected, we must enter the realm of the evolutionary biologist.

"Similarly," Traci continued, "the physiologists may be able to tell us what neurons and muscles mediate a particular bit of behavior—say, hand-waving when seeing a friend across a room—but not the context of the behavior and the functional relations between environment and behavior that account for that behavior. To understand the relations between behavior and environment, we must enter the realm of the behaviorologist. The explanation for hand-waving may include a personal history involving parents who modeled the behavior for this person as a child, perhaps even mechanically moving the child's arm to simulate a wave when someone was coming or going. As others smile and wave back, this can come to strengthen hand-waving behavior. This is an elliptical explanation but it will have to do for the moment. My point is that you must study behavior at *its* own level of complexity to understand the variables—the stimuli both inside and outside of the organism—that elicit, evoke or select it."

Martha jumped in at this point. "Fred, my research shows that there are a few hundred communities such as yours in the United States alone. Are they all self-sufficient, or do some require outside assistance?"

"To the extent that they provide the necessities of food, water, and shelter," I said, "they are completely self-sufficient. Many of our products—such as the materials for our computer boards—are currently purchased on the market, but we are hoping to change this. After extensive research, we buy what we need in bulk and can usually get items at a reasonable price. But we do make our own cotton thread and make practically all of our own clothing. And of course, we produce our own energy which, I hasten to add, we use very frugally."

"I know that some of your communities are more like research centers than simple communities," Martha said. "And I believe I read that a couple out west have fairly sophisticated astronomical observatories. I noticed that here in Walden Two you use high technology combined with lower technologies. Why not just complete the break with the past and computerize and mechanize as much of your community as possible? As you have suggested earlier, you do not have to worry about depriving people of their livelihoods. And wouldn't automation provide you with more even leisure time?"

"That is true," I answered. "Employment for employment's sake is not a concern here. And even without complete automation we have increased our leisure time considerably, mostly because everyone is productive and contributes to the community, including the children. By the way, it is very important to include children in all of the activities of the community. Not only do they feel like they are useful and vital members of the community, in addition, close social bonds will form. It is also good for other reasons that I needn't go into now.

"To get back to your question about leisure, we do not have the burden of sustaining a distinct leisure class supported by an overworked underclass. A separate leisure class cannot as easily be hidden in smaller communities like Walden Two as it can in larger societies. By having everyone contributing equally—again, including children to their ability—our workload is reduced considerably. We have equal leisure just as we have equal access to healthcare and property. We completely understand the contingencies that make this arrangement anathema to some outside of our communities who consider themselves more valuable and consequently feel more entitled to leisure.

"And to your point about our technologies, we do not want to become completely reliant on higher technologies that may fail at some point. Therefore we have lower technologies to fall back on. Many technologies of the past have been lost and cannot easily be duplicated by modern engineers. For instance, modern engineers are having trouble explaining how some ancient civilizations built their enormous structures with the resources available at the time. Now, admittedly, with modern recording devices, we do not have to worry so much about this. Carl Sagan has called the 'storage' of information outside of the body 'extrasomatic information,' by which he meant the information stored in books, computer disks, video recordings and so on.

"Incidentally, behaviorologists do not see this as stored information, but rather as stimuli that can later evoke our operant behavior, but that is beside the point. We have at least two reasons for retaining these lower level technologies. The first is to retain the ability to switch back to them in the event of a catastrophic event. I'm sure you are aware that strong electromagnetic pulses from solar flares or nearby nuclear explosions can play havoc with electronic devices. And it isn't out of the question that some natural catastrophe could occur, such as the eruption of a super-volcano somewhere in the world or a small asteroid strike, and either of these could result in the partial blighting of the sunlight to our solar panels.

"We have much of our food in greenhouses that are capable of filtering the air if necessary, and also backup ultraviolet lights. In the event of energy outages we can always switch to lower technologies, or in some cases, run them in parallel to supplement insufficient higher technologies. The second reason is to maintain the behavior needed to construct and use these technologies and pass them on to future generations. So it is best that we keep and use them along with our higher technologies."

"Is it safe to assume that *none* of your members hold religious views?" Martha asked. "Or any, what I'm sure you would call 'non-rational' views? Do they ever wonder what all of this is for? Is there any purpose to life other than just *living* happily and productively?"

"Are you asking us to tell you the meaning of life?" I asked, a little surprised. "I could answer your question, but I don't think it would satisfy you. My answer would first involve asking you what you mean when you say the meaning of life. Do you mean the purpose of life?"

"Yes, I suppose," Martha said. "Are we just here to pass our eighty years or so and then perish? Or are we, as a species, moving or evolving toward something greater? What is our human destiny? Are we hoping humankind will eventually become immortal? Or leave this planet and inhabit other worlds? It that our purpose?"

"Well," I began, "you are asking us questions that we may be in no better position to answer than anyone else. One thing is for sure: Before we propagate humankind to other worlds, we must be able to manage human behavior on *this* planet. Until we can demonstrate—if only to ourselves—that we can manage and control our own behavior, we may not be the proper species that *should* inhabit other worlds. But I should say at the outset, and this is not just wordplay, we have to carefully define what we mean by 'purpose' and 'meaning.' The word 'purpose' is often used to describe why some current behavior is occurring by inferring the consequences the behavior has had in the past.

"For example, if we see a response that has produced a particular reinforcer in the person's past, we may say that the *purpose* of current similar responses is to produce that reinforcer once again. But something that may or may not occur in the future cannot evoke responding in the present. What *does* evoke current responding are current stimuli—stimuli that were present when the response originally occurred and was reinforced. Now there is much regularity between behavior and its consequences; if there were not, we could not survive. Similar behavior is most often followed by similar consequences; but to say that this is the *purpose* of the response is to miss the contingencies that have selected the response, and they are in the person's history."

"But don't we *imagine* future consequences?" Martha asked. "I often think of what will happen if I do this or that, I then decide which outcome I prefer. I can weigh outcomes, can't I? I can even imagine what will happen long after I am gone from this Earth."

"That is the prevailing view of what is happening," I said, "but, again, behavior does not occur because of future consequences but rather because of past consequences. How can something that has not yet happened control a current response? To call behavior purposeful is just another way of saying that the behavior has had a characteristic consequence *in our past* when we have behaved in similar ways. Frazier described all of this beautifully in his book, *About Behaviorism*. Now, I am sure that you do imagine—in the sense of privately seeing . . . by the way, do you know what I mean by private seeing or private behavior?"

"Not really," Martha frowned, shaking her head.

"I'm sorry about that," I said. "What I'm calling private behavior are those responses or stimuli that stimulate only the behaving person; they are such things as toothaches, feelings of love, warmth, and so on; they are not public behaviors that others can see. Imaging is also a private behavior. How does such behavior come about? Well, just as the light coming from an object such as a chair will elicit a seeing response, so too will stimuli that often *accompany* the chair. If we say 'chair' often enough to a child who at that moment is actually seeing the chair, eventually the spoken word 'chair' will elicit a similar, but usually weaker, seeing response. This is called conditioned seeing, and it is the result of Pavlovian conditioning. We say the child can now imagine the chair when we tell him or her a story about chairs. Does this make sense to you?"

"Yes, I believe so."

"Very good. So what I was saying is that I'm sure that all of us can imagine what consequence has followed a particular behavior in the past when we have behaved in similar ways. But this imagining is not of a future event, but of past events, or possibly of what we have seen or heard should happen. It is really no different than any conditioned seeing-responses. Human language—verbal behavior—has drastically changed the way we humans respond to the world. Our verbal behavior allows us to imagine a future, usually one that at least somewhat resembles our past.

"This is a result of the operations that bring about equivalence relations and relational framing that Traci and I touched on earlier, and we are, so far as we know, the only species that does this. No other organism is worried about dying; they have no verbal behavior to even conceive of this. While animals may get sick and presumably feel miserable, they do not imagine death, or what death is like. To ask what death is like, we must imagine that death is like some prior experience. But death is not an experience at all, it cannot be experienced—it is the *absence* of experience.

"If you want to try to imagine what death is like, I would suggest that you try to imagine what you were experiencing for the 13.7 billion years before your nervous system ever formed to respond to stimuli. Of course, you cannot even imagine this. The atoms that now make up your body were, at one time, dispersed throughout parts the universe. Imagine that somehow every atom of your body was returned to where it was billions of years ago. Were you lonely then? Or cold? Of course not! Only an organism capable of verbal behavior and relational framing can even try to imagine something like this."

"So then, is *this* your heaven?" Martha asked me; she waved her hand around to embrace the whole community.

"I remember reading," I answered, "something Frazier once said about the concept of heaven. He pointed out that no one has depicted a universally desirable heaven. This is simply because different people have been exposed to different contingencies over the ages, and it is the contingencies one is exposed to that determine what kind of heaven they will imagine. The

American Indians imagined a happy hunting ground, something they enjoyed due to their contingencies of survival, while some Europeans imagined their heaven containing streets paved with gold. I suppose the elderly and sick may imagine a heaven where there is no pain or suffering and everyone is young and healthy. What people value is partly a result of the values of the culture from which they came, and from their own personal experiences. Frazier also pointed out that the Christian vision of Hell is really just a collection of all of the aversive stimuli that were available at the time it was first depicted in religious literature. These were not only the tortures *humans* inflicted on one another but also those that could be imagined. Electric shock was not mentioned because it was not available at that time. Today we could depict an even more terrifying hell.

"Our RFT folks can help explain how our verbal behavior about a nonexistent hell can elicit anxiety, and eventually cause this anxiety to snowball; this would be another example of the dark side of language. For example, if I were to say to you, 'Hell is worse than you can imagine,' the contextual cue 'worse than' could create an incremental loop of imagining behavior. A suggestible person could begin by imagining hell as they have been conditioned to think of it through religious instruction. But, if they are told and believe my verbal assertion with the contextual cue 'worse than,' they must now try to imagine a hell that is *worse than* what they first imagined. And if they *do* imagine a worse hell, they must now imagine an even *worse* hell, because the statement says that hell is 'worse than' one they *can* imagine.

"This cycle could continue on indefinitely, causing the person to ruminate in a downward spiral about a verbally elicited, but nonexistent place called hell. This can easily happen when people are dealing with imaginary abstractions. Obviously, the statement "Hell is worse than you can imagine" does not describe hell in any scientific way that can be tested. The statement really has no meaning in any real sense because any speaker verbalizing it cannot possibly know what a listener can imagine, therefore, there are no circumstances under which this assertion could be verbalized. And we can be quite certain that no human past or present has seen a real place called 'hell.' And this includes all lunatics and other fantasizers.

"So you asked me if this is our heaven?" I continued. "Well, all I will say is that we are moving in that direction."

"I think you partially addressed this,' Paul said, "but how do *your* communities avoid modern anxiety, Dr. Jensen? Surely you are not immune to stress and anxiety, are you?"

"Well, for one thing," Traci said, "the everyday stresses of living aside, people in modern societies are constantly inundated with the ubiquitous bad news coming from around the world. This is a truly modern phenomenon. Even in our relatively recent past, news from distant places was learned, if at all, from reading newspapers, and—before the invention of the telegraph—not until days or weeks after the news event occurred; but even then, it was not seen. With the increasing number of people now inhabiting virtually every dry niche on the planet, something bad is likely to happen to some group of people every day. Earthquakes, forest fires, tornadoes, hurricanes, tsunamis, droughts, wars, mass shootings, terrorism, and on and on, are now viewed virtually in real time. And with the omnipresence of recording devices, many horrific events are captured on video. Video clips of these horrific events are played over and over on twenty-four-hour news cycles, I am told. Once news programming was put into the ratings system, positive news that did not garner as many viewers was reduced or eliminated; people want to know where the danger lies, and news agencies took advantage of this tendency.

"You don't have to be a behaviorologist to understand what effect this oversaturation with bad news has on people. It can cause unnecessary fear and anxiety even in people who are in no danger at all and are unlikely to experience any of these events firsthand. That is why, in our communities, we see no reason to expose our members to all of this negative news; we instead focus on good news and those things we can act on. It has a much more positive effect. I should mention that our children are taught to be aware of the various states of their bodies. As a result of this training, they are quite aware of their anxious states and have learned how to avoid them. Special contingencies are needed to bring these private behaviors to awareness, but this is easily accomplished by our behaviorologists. It is no different than conditioning someone to talk about the private conditions that we call a stomachache, or feelings of love or sadness. But there are many other ways we avoid the fate of other cultures as well."

"Then how do you explain the fact that people in many cultures continue to watch all of this?" Clifford asked. "Why don't people just turn it off?"

"As I alluded to earlier," Traci answered, "all successful organisms with nervous systems have evolved to watch for and avoid, if possible, predators and other dangerous stimuli. Organisms that were indifferent to danger would have been at a great disadvantage and probably did not survive long enough to have offspring. Therefore it is important to our survival that we are aware of truly imminent threats and other aversive stimuli so we can avoid them. The problem we see occurring with global media is that they make us aware of threats that are not imminent and will most likely never occur to us in our lifetime; we are becoming hyper-aware of improbable events.

"Have you noticed that people seem to be more interested in bad news that occurs closer to home? If someone is murdered or terrorized in one's neighborhood or city, people may take precautions; they may begin to lock their doors or purchase firearms. Any unfamiliar or previously unnoticed noise in the house may startle them. People are typically more interested to hear about earthquakes in their own country than those in distant countries. There is an inverse relationship between the propinquity of an event and our interest or concern with it. So the problem, as we see it, is really that people are beset with images of aversive events that *appear* to be more of an imminent threat than they actually are and this causes undue anxiety. Since no one in our communities profits monetarily from bad news, our news tends to be much more useful and less provocative."

"Fred, are you telling us that your contingency engineers can get people to behave well just by arranging consequences?" Simmons asked. "There has to be more to it than that, right? It all seems too simple."

"Of course, we don't arrange contingencies to shape each and every behavior of concern," I said. "With verbal organisms we can *tell* others how to attain reinforcers. Once verbal behavior is well conditioned, it may only be necessary to *tell* others what behavior will meet the contingencies that are in effect. Exciting work has been done in rule-governed behavior and equivalence relations. There is no mystery here. Verbal behavior is itself a learned behavior, and being exposed to verbal behavior can change the way various stimuli will function for us in the future. Telling a man that there is a dangerous insect in his automobile will change the way the automobile will function as a stimulus; where the automobile may have evoked the behavior of opening the door and getting inside, it may—as a result of being told there is a wasp inside—now function as a stimulus to be avoided, purely as a result of verbal behavior and nothing else.

"There are many different kinds of rules and rule-governed behaviors, and people follow rules if following rules in their past has led to reinforcing consequences. We can verbalize rules that explain how to operate various devices, for example, but only *after* extensive conditioning has brought motor behavior under the control of verbal behavior. If you cannot follow instructions to turn the steering wheel of an automobile, or put on the brakes, then you cannot benefit from the verbal behavior of an instructor who is teaching you to drive.

"But take into consideration that there *are* contingencies involved in *complying* with verbal behavior; social reinforcers are contingent on compliance, and this is why we call the following of verbal instruction, 'pliance.' Pliance simply means, initially at least, that a person is simply following instructions for social approval; the compliant behavior of children is a typical example of this. Eventually the behavior will be evoked by the situation and maintained by the actual consequences. Verbal behavior, in all its forms, allows our species to pass on the valuable rules of our culture—the knowledge of our culture—so each person's behavior does not have to be shaped by nonsocial contingencies of reinforcement.

"Then too, there is modeling. In modeling, a person models for others the behavior that will produce the reinforcer. For this to be effective, the modelee must have an imitative repertoire that was previously conditioned, and must be able to imitate the components of complex behaviors in the order they were modeled. Also, the component behaviors that are modeled must be in the modelee's repertoire. If a ballet dancer, or musician, for instance, models a complex set of behaviors that are not in the prospective modelee's repertoire, then he or she cannot benefit from the modeled behavior; that is, the modelee's behavior will not meet the contingency. So, to put a fine point on this, social reinforcers may initially be made contingent on rule-following or modeling, but eventually the behavior will be maintained by the actual production of the natural reinforcers for the behavior.

"But Mr. Simmons, I believe you are suggesting that contingency engineering seems too simple of an explanation for our success, so I hasten to add that the apparent simplicity of arranging contingencies to effect behavior change is deceptive. Remember that selection processes also worked to produce the broad diversity of the complex life forms that inhabit the Earth. And this complexity led people to imagine an omnipotent creator or intelligent designer.

"Behavior, or at least operant behavior, is also selected—by its consequences. The complexity of the repertoire of the intelligent adult also appears to demand an intelligent creator— a creative 'mind.' But if this is so, now we must explain this 'mind' and how it came about. We have made our task more difficult than necessary. Unfortunately, there are still people to this day who are wasting their time trying to reconcile the paradoxes of an omnipotent creator god, so let's not make that same mistake with human behavior.

"Our operant behavior is selected by its consequences and can become increasingly complex, just as our bodies have become complex over time. The time scales involved in the two processes are different only because evolutionary processes have selected a nervous system capable of rapid modification. The rapid selection of behavior was, and is, necessary for our survival. Simple basic behaviors are strengthened in the child, modified, and built upon to produce the complex behavior of the adult.

"Behaviorologists understand that there are physiological structures that come between behavior and environment. Some of these mediating structures involve biochemicals such as hormones, but the mediating structure of special note is of course the malleable nervous system. As I've said, this complex structure can change rapidly as a result of our experiences. Rocks and other minerals, to give a trivial example, do not *behave* by our definition of that word, they move only as a result of external forces; they have no nervous systems, articulated limbs, or muscles to move them. Plants are composed of living cells that serve various functions for the life of the plant but they too, lack nervous systems that can mediate responding. But now enter the realm of the more complex species, those organisms with not only nervous systems, but also with limbs having articulated joints and the muscles to move them.

"All life is immersed in a sea of energy, and some life-forms have evolved specialized receptors that respond to various forms of this energy: photoreceptors, chemoreceptors, phonoreceptors, and so on. Of course, we call the energies capable of affecting these receptors 'stimuli,' and these stimuli form the context of behavior. Organisms with nervous systems respond to both antecedent and postcedent stimuli, and the nervous system is a mediating structure between these stimuli. But more importantly, the nervous system is changed by the outcomes of responding, and will link the antecedent stimuli with both the response *and its consequence.*

"In other words, the nervous system comes between the external energies that occur before and after responding and is changed as a result. This malleable nervous system evolved over eons of time and each incremental improvement increased our survival chances. But it is important to understand that the nervous system does not *originate* behavior, it is a *mediating* system. So, to answer your question, Mr. Simmons, our culture—which, incidentally, is also evolving through a selection process—is designed to strengthen behavior that is good for both the individual and the culture. The simple and basic behaviors of the child are carefully strengthened and then layered to produce the complex behaviors of the rational adult."

"How would you define the values of your communities?" asked Simmons. "At some point, you have to step outside of science, right? I mean science cannot produce values—do you agree?"

"Science can tell us what will increase our chances of survival," said Dr. Johansson. "The collective behavior the members of a culture, along with the artifacts and infrastructure, comprise a culture. The values of a culture are those things that reinforce the behavior of the members. These can change over time as new generations of people are exposed to new and different contingencies. Practically anything can be made into a value; that is, anything can become a conditioned reinforcer.

"If we say that a person values music or art, we simply mean that music or art will reinforce that person's behavior. It may just be the behavior of sitting quietly and listening to music. But the values of a culture become reinforcing through conditioning procedures. Practically anything can be made into a conditioned reinforcer—a value—through conditioning; that is, through respondent and operant procedures. Skin color, honesty, money, piety—all are valued in some cultures. People must learn to value money, for instance, through conditioning. Money can be exchanged for many primary and secondary—conditioned—reinforcers. The same goes for status and religious values and truthfulness. These all become reinforcing—again, valued—through conditioning, but typically, in most cultures, no one *explicitly* designs the procedures that bring these about; they happen naturally.

"Oh, there is religious instruction, and parents often reinforce or punish certain behaviors in their children that are in accord with the parent's values, but for the most part these values are learned by accident through modeling and verbal behavior. China, India, Japan, and the U.S. all have different things they value. Japan, for example, may value uniformity more than individuality, where the U.S. is the opposite.

"So what you are asking us is, what are the values of our communities and where did they come from; or equivalently, what reinforces our behavior? Walden Two actually was founded soon after Humanism had issued the Humanist Manifesto I in 1933. These influences were rife among intellectuals and scholars at the time of the founding of Walden Two, and are still in accord with our values today. Let me give you just two examples:

"The third tenet of the Humanist Manifesto I states: 'Holding an organic view of life, humanists find that the traditional dualism of mind and body must be rejected.' And the fourteenth tenet states: 'The humanists are firmly convinced that existing acquisitive and profit-motivated society has shown itself to be inadequate and that a radical change in methods, controls, and motives must be instituted. A socialized and cooperative economic order must be established to the end that the equitable distribution of the means of life be possible. The goal of humanism is a free and universal society in which people voluntarily and intelligently cooperate for the common good. Humanists demand a shared life in a shared world.'

"We began with similar rational precepts and have added others. For instance, we have virtually eliminated coercive practices of any kind and replaced them with positive reinforcement, to great effect."

"But why did behaviorologists find it necessary to completely dissociate from psychology?" asked Simmons. "You have admitted that some of their findings are interesting. Why not work together with them, sociologists and economists, to increase our understanding of human behavior and all of the influences on it?"

"Simply because those who subscribe to the philosophy that endorses the belief that we need to change opinions, beliefs, attitudes, and so on," Traci said, "propose very different interventions than those of behaviorology, ones that have not been very successful, in our view. Just look at the dismal data on clinical outcomes if you question this. Since behaviorologists look for the independent variables of which behavior is a lawful function, to the extent that we can manipulate these variables, they can be engineered to produce behavior to specification.

"One method of changing behavior commonly used outside of our communities is changing group-contingencies. Contingencies are the dependencies between independent and dependent variables. So group-contingencies are changes in the contingencies affecting the behavior of a large number of people without regard for the behavior of any *particular* individual. Economists and social scientists are often concerned only with the net result of the aggregate behavior of large numbers of people. Economists study some of these group-contingencies and develop economic laws. For example, when interest rates decline, they notice lawful changes in, say, group investment behavior.

"But the change in behavior brought about by lowering interest rates involves what behaviorologists call rule-governed behavior; a rule is verbal behavior that describes a contingency. For example, the rule 'invest in short-term bonds when interest rates are rising,' describes a behavior, 'invest in short-term bonds,' and an antecedent condition, 'rising interest rates.' Often, the consequences of following the rule are explicitly given, but, as in this case, the consequences—you will make or preserve more money—are merely implied. It is important that you realize that these investors have had a history of following rules, such as economic verbal-rules, before these lowered rates will affect their behavior.

"Therefore, note that these economists are coming in very late in the game, for they are observing lawfulness in behavior at another level of analysis—after contingencies in one's life have already produced a large verbal-behavior repertoire, and conditioned rule-following is well established. So notice that these kinds of economic behaviors are lawful and can be statistically predicted only if potential investors have already been conditioned to speak the language and they have learned the rule. This is not operant conditioning per se. It is investment behavior evoked by verbal rules, that is, by being told that the

U.S. Federal Reserve has reduced interest rates and 'knowing' that it is time to invest in short-term bonds. I should probably mention at this point that behaviorologists have been extensively investigating rule-governed behavior, and we have found that people who are given rules often continue to follow the rule long after the contingency described by the rule has changed.

"Here in our communities, we focus more on micro-contingencies. We focus on the independent variables that condition the behaviors of *individuals*—for example, the behaviors that make up basic pro-social repertoires, and then we build upon them to produce more complex repertoires.

"Economists and social scientists seem to love mathematics and the power of statistical prediction. This gives them a broad sort of control of human behavior by allowing them to change variables known to affect the behavior of a large group of people at once, without knowing or caring much about the behavior of any given individual. This is much like actuarial tables that tell insurance companies how many deaths to expect in a given population without knowing who in particular will perish. We, on the other hand, don't deal with people as an aggregate abstraction; we work with people as individuals.

"Sociologists too have been looking in the wrong place for solutions to social-behavioral problems. They imagine they are diagnosing, for instance, 'personality' disturbances, and then they try to correct these ethereal constructs. They talk about ways to reduce aggression or increase people's work ethic. When people develop patterns of behavior, due to principles well understood by behaviorologists, sociologists try to account for these patterns by inferring internal agents borrowed from psychology, like 'traits,' for example. For sociologists, these are what need to be reformed; that is, some *internal person* or *trait* needs to be reformed.

"In contrast, behaviorologists look to the environmental contingencies that, through species evolution, first selected the bodies and physiological structures that mediate behavior, and then through a similar selection process during the lifetime of the person, shape and maintain the behavior of the individual. You see, through evolutionary processes, a nervous system in which behavior could be changed by its consequences was selected. This kind of behavior is, of course, operant behavior and is called that because, when it is evoked, it *operates* on the environment, changing it in some way.

"Think about your own behavior and how it changes your immediate environment in beneficial ways. The ability of behavior to be affected by consequences was a great leap for the survival of innervated species, for as you know, there are many species without nervous systems—plants, for example—that lack the ability to operate upon and alter their environments to benefit themselves. Not only can they not alter them, they cannot escape from them, by moving out of inimical environments, for instance.

"The physiological underpinnings of these selection processes are becoming well understood, but this is not the time or place to discuss this. I might just mention here that the process of selection, in which behavior is selected by its consequences, in no way violates cause and effect order. Many people believe that the cause of a phenomenon must necessarily precede it. And while this is easy to miss in selection processes such as operant conditioning, it is still true. In operant conditioning, the consequences of a response do not strengthen *that* response; they cause a cascade of biochemical changes that strengthen synapses that were involved in the mediation of that response. Thereafter responses similar to the successful response are more likely to occur in the future. However, behaviorology concentrates on understanding the behavior-acquisition process *after* these necessary mediating structures have evolved. And we are well aware that real physiology-based individual differences in these structures can lead to different learning concerns.

"As I've said, behaviorologists begin by adhering to the principles of naturalism and by assuming that our subject matter is lawful. Of course, if our subject matter is not lawful, there can be no science of behavior. Unfortunately, because behavior and its causes are so complex—perhaps the most complex phenomenon subjected to scientific investigation—most people don't believe that behavior is lawful, and therefore they don't believe it can be submitted for scientific investigation. But unpredictability due to complexity does not mean that behavior is not lawful.

"Just ask a meteorologist to predict the weather for next week, or ask a physicist to predict the behavior of a falling leaf. Everyone, or almost everyone, believes that these natural phenomena are lawful even if not always predictable. But even when simple behaviors of simple organisms are isolated in simplified environments, the untrained observer, more often than not, misses the controlling variables. Behaviorologists have been very successful in isolating the independent variables that are responsible for much of behavior's complexity. It goes without saying that if you don't understand the underlying science, you can't take advantage of a technology produced by that science. Please don't take offense, but without that understanding you end up with the problems you're seeing outside of our Walden Two communities all around the world.

"Now, some effective practices in behavior management have arisen without benefit from our science and its precise lexicon, but they often have arisen by hit-and-miss, and the behavior change is frequently attributed to spurious variables. But we are quickly running out of the time needed to solve looming and potentially disastrous global problems; for example, problems that will emanate from climate change and overpopulation. Therefore, we can no longer afford to continue using these historically inept methods of behavior change while just hoping that somehow things will come out differently. With the rapid increase in population and recent advances in the technologies of other sciences—some potentially dangerous, such as space-based weapon systems—we must act quickly and begin to implement science-based behavioral solutions."

We talked on this way into the late afternoon. Our guests would be gathering up their belongings from their rooms soon and leaving us. We said our goodbyes and I shook hands with Simmons, Paul, and Martha, but when I looked around for Clifford, he was gone. Soon after the rest of the journalists had departed the conference room, I walked outside and spotted Clifford in the distance sitting alone near the pond, obviously in no hurry to leave. I would be going that way. . . .

16

I had estimated Clifford Douglas to be a man in his early to mid-30s. He was sitting alone on a bench near the pond, studying his cell phone. The sky was a deep blue, and a warm breeze blew lightly across the pond, but he didn't seem to notice. Instead, he was engaged—like so many of his generation—with an electronic device.

"Well, it certainly is a beautiful day, isn't it?" I said as I approached him from behind. I then stopped for what I expected to be a brief cordial handshake and farewell. "Yes, it is," he said, looking up from his phone and appearing a little surprised that someone was near. He apparently took my statement to be a trite greeting rather than a tact of the weather condition—either that or he really didn't care.

"Have you got a moment, Dr. Burris?" he asked, setting his phone down. "I would like to speak with you about something rather important to me . . . and maybe just as important to you, I suspect."

"Sure, I have a moment," I said, moving around the bench and sitting down near the end. "Have we provided you with enough information for your article?" I asked him.

He didn't answer but rather looked at me for a moment with a resigned look on his face before responding. "Dr. Burris, I want to be ... I want to be completely honest with you. I'm not who I said I was. Oh, I *am* Clifford Douglas all right, and I *am* a journalist of sorts, but I'm not ..." he stopped and seemed to change course before beginning again, "well, let's just say, I'm not in a good place in my life."

I looked at him with obvious concern, I'm sure, but said nothing at this point, waiting for him to continue.

"First, please let me tell you a little about myself that may help explain my original intentions for coming here," he said. "I attended Indiana University, and although I was not a great student, I eventually received a Bachelor of Arts in journalism with a concentration in investigative journalism and news reporting. In fact, I met my wife there when we were still in our late teens—I was nineteen and she was a precocious seventeen. I would say we were both pretty idealistic at that time, but we were not really happy with the way things were looking for our generation—all this business about being the generation that would not do as well as our parents, and all.

"While I tended to lean to the right, I really had no strong political beliefs at that time, but you would not be wrong to say that I was a staunch capitalist hoping to make lots of money. I just wanted to buy the things that most young people want and expect to earn without too much sacrifice; many of these are just things our parents could earn with menial nonprofessional jobs—things like a decent house and car. These days, we are constantly bombarded with images of extreme wealth, you know, and I don't think previous generations were exposed to this to the same degree, do you? Near-billionaire celebrities, athletes, musicians and such? So, after graduating as a mediocre student at best, I tried hard and found work here and there writing columns for small publications. But it was not steady work, and the money was not that great either." He looked at me as if to see if I was still interested. I was.

"Well, let me just cut to the chase. I found that while I was not a great journalist, I did have a knack for writing what are called 'hit pieces,' and I began to get offers to write these for a few local and state politicians. I could collect information about a politician's rivals and pretty much destroy—or at least severely undermine—their reputations. I could nearly always find something that would cast doubt on 'good' people. I could frame an unfounded accusation in the form of a question, thereby disguising it and making it sound more like an assertion.

"If unfounded rumors about an affair abounded about a rival candidate, I might write, 'Do we really need another philandering politician in office?' Notice I did not say he *was* a philanderer; I just took advantage of the rumors and then posed a general question. My job was to cast seeds of doubt. Even if my candidate's rival was proposing social programs that people liked, I would argue that my candidate would propose something even better, oftentimes knowing full well that my candidate detested these programs and would never implement them in the first place.

"I'm sure you can see how this 'talent,' if you will, would be highly valued among the political class, and I gained much respect among one particular political party; I happened to work mostly for a conservative group, but this same tactic is used on both sides. Politics is really just a propaganda battle these days; maybe it always was. I knew exactly what I was doing, and as things progressed, I began to *fabricate* stories under a pseudonym and upload them to popular social media platforms and websites. I was putting out 'fake news,' and yet ironically, I, along with many others, began to accuse good journalists of putting out fake stories. We found we didn't even need to offer convincing arguments in order to refute good journalism; the tag 'fake news' was always enough to discredit a story in the eyes of those who thought mainstream media had become too 'liberal.' I found that if people *wanted* to believe a story, they were not going to let truth get in the way. We had inverted the world of journalism, real was fake and fake was now real. I was Winston Smith in Orwell's *1984*.

"I was gaining a good reputation among political ideologues, and was often referred to others running for office or up for re-election. Eventually I was introduced to a group of people who were not politicians themselves but were powerful in their own right as members of think tanks or some other ideological cabal—my wife always jokingly called them 'cabals,' but she was not far off the mark. It was as though I had moved up a rung or two on the ladder. These people seemed to be the power behind the politicians, and I knew they sometimes actually drafted the bills they wanted passed. It was somewhat flattering to have these wealthy and obviously intelligent people coming to *me* for my services. And when you are mostly around such people, well, I suppose *you* would say that they selectively reinforce particular beliefs. Therefore, I actually began to accept some of their views and no longer questioned them or cared whether they were, in fact, true.

"It didn't take me long to understand what was expected of me. I was to write articles discounting the findings of climate scientists, for example, or promoting 'clean' coal, and offshore drilling and so on. I would frame my arguments in a binary fashion, where one outcome was draconian or a short slippery slope to it: You were either pro-life or you wanted to allow an innocent eight-month-old baby to be ripped from its mother's womb; you were either for freedom or you wanted to take all guns away from people; restricting military-style weapons would lead to . . . well, you get the idea. And other people were either *with* us or *against* us; there was no middle ground, and this made it quite clear to my readers which side they were on, and who was the 'enemy.'

"I was also expected to attack and undermine any views that might challenge the status quo—the logic being that if people are confused about any particular issue, they will usually do nothing and things will remain the same. It is only when people are accurately informed and have a clear understanding about issues that they can take effective concerted action. And for those benefiting from the status quo, inaction on the part of the common people is usually better than action. It was my job to see that popular action doesn't happen. I thought about this the other day when you were talking about the tobacco companies obfuscating data linking tobacco products to various life-threatening diseases; by making smokers uncertain about the hazards of smoking, they simply continued to smoke—even though, as you said, there actually was overwhelming evidence of the health hazards of smoking *even at that time.*

"This is precisely what I did. I was a proud member of Lies Incorporated, yet I helped to propagate the mantra—or meme—that professional journalists from the major media were constantly putting out fake news. I could assert this with no evidence. Have you ever seen the current U.S. president actually present tangible evidence countering supposedly fake stories? I even once wrote that many *scientists* were unscrupulous and were underwritten by people who simply wanted to control the lives of people, and so on. I'm ashamed to say, I could even make scientists—along with good journalists—into the bad guys, even though I knew in my heart that both were seeking truth."

I had a few questions at this point, and I thought I knew where he was going with all this, but I wanted to let his story unfold without interruption. I was also intrigued by his openness and honesty. I felt like a priest receiving confession, so I simply nodded occasionally to let him know that I was following him, but his penance would be out of my hands.

"My wife was, and still is, very idealistic," he continued. "While *my* values were changing, hers remained high and stable and have not changed much since college. I soon found that I was attacking people and ideas that she admired. I tried to assure her—and *myself*—that I was only doing it for the money, that I did not really believe what I was writing; it was just a game both political sides were playing, and neither side was any better than the other. And I tried to convince her that it was providing a decent income for our family, and this was what was important. However, I must admit, it began to taint my view of people. I began to *think* like I wrote. I became jaded about politics and politicians, but I still enjoyed the money and the challenge of finding 'dirt' on rival politicians and destroying them in the eyes of the public.

"I finally felt like I had a little power over things, and I was even making decent money for doing so. But I soon realized that the people I was helping were no better than those I was denigrating, and often they were worse—although when I was around them, they made me feel like I was doing important work. I was invited to some of their exclusive political parties and began to meet prominent people I had only read about or seen on television. *Some*, of course, I had never read or heard about; they worked behind the curtain, so to speak. When I was introduced to them, they patted me on the back and told me what a good job I was doing. But you yourself must know, because of people like me, other people no longer trust the media; in fact, they no longer know whom to believe. I thought this was amusing at the time. But now I realize that people like me are the real problem. How does one undo a false meme? With another meme? It's not that easy.

"I hope I'm not keeping you, Dr. Burris, but if I may, I would like to tell you just one more story before I get to my main point—one that will surely interest you. I was once commissioned by a very elderly oil and energy tycoon who was looking for dirt on a particularly popular female candidate who wanted to restrict offshore drilling. She was also opposed to the construction of a potentially lucrative oil pipeline that was to go through an area inhabited by a small group of indigenous people.

"I was invited to meet with him at a very exclusive restaurant in New York to discuss writing a book about this candidate. I was lavished with one of the finest meals I have ever had. I was beginning to like this more and more as I literally got a taste of the good life. When we were finished, he agreed to underwrite my book if I would suggest that this candidate was, among other things, homosexual—a lesbian. This would be enough to diminish her in the eyes of many voters and practically guarantee her defeat. I assured him I would look under every rock to find out, but I would not outright lie, only selectively distort, at least as long as I was putting my real name on the book. I know how bad this sounds, but again, I thought of it as a job.

"You see, I reasoned that I was no different than a doctor who must perform surgery to save the life of a dangerous criminal who may go on to torment others, or a lawyer who must do everything to see that an obvious felon is acquitted. As professionals, they don't judge the criminal; they just do what they are paid to do. Even so, I knew I was losing what little integrity I had left. I knew that a truly good journalist would not begin with preconceived notions of what to write. The desired conclusion should not guide the facts; the facts should guide the conclusion: 'Follow the argument wherever it leads,' you know?"

"Ah, Socrates," I said wistfully. "But at least you realized what was happening to you; some people do not. Their values change along with their behavior, as you have implied was happening to you, and they become and remain quite different people."

"Yes," Clifford said. "And this was definitely happening to me. It was an insidious process. As a result, my wife and I became estranged, and she left me at the end of last year. I had become a different person all right—much different than the one she married. I know you could probably better explain how this happened to me, Dr. Burris, but even *I* could see what was happening, though I never thought of it in your terms before.

"Now, having said all of that, what I'm about to tell you should really interest you. At one of the political get-togethers I attended last October, a man approached me whom I had seen many times before and knew to be a prominent member of an influential think-tank. He was not a politician, but I could see that many politicians deferred to him. At first, he only casually mentioned your communities and asked me if I knew anything about them. After a little discussion and a few drinks, he asked me if I would be interested in visiting your community and writing a report for his group. He told me that they believed your communities could eventually pose an existential threat to democracy and capitalism if they could be shown to provide a viable alternative to our current political system.

"I knew this was hyperbole, and by this time—especially after losing my wife—my conscience was beginning to bother me more and more. Conflicting contingencies you might say. But I told him I was willing to take on the assignment, and we agreed on some terms. I signed an agreement and was paid an advance. I really don't think your communities posed a threat to anyone when they were relatively spartan, but once you began to provide more amenities and began working with other scientists, well . . . it became a different story. They were afraid that egalitarian communities such as yours would begin to appeal to many people frustrated by the growing inequities in our increasingly corporate-dominated world.

"Of course, these inequities are only growing worse, and with all this talk about the one percent and all . . . . Anyway, he assured me, if my report was 'good,' they would provide a sizable stipend for me and make sure my article was published in the most popular media, and maybe even the chance for a few television appearances. So I began by reading *Walden Two*, your grandfather's account of the community as it was in the 1940s. I actually liked the community as he described it, and it now seems strange to me that I am sitting here talking to his grandson."

Clifford paused and looked up at me at this point; I only nodded and said, "Please continue."

"It's funny, but the other day, in the education center, when you were explaining to me how *people—mentors—*could become generalized reinforcers, it occurred to me that something similar was happening to me when I was with these people. But I realized that they were only flattering me about the things I wrote that benefited them—things I was becoming ashamed of, things that turned my wife against me, things I knew in my heart were untrue. Oh, it made me feel a little superior and, as I said, it gave me the feeling that I had some power. But I knew . . . I knew in my heart what I was doing was wrong. I have a young son who has a future beyond mine. And when you asked me how philosophies that promote selfishness and self-interest could ever produce a better world, I realized that this was what these people were promoting.

"I had read *Atlas Shrugged* in college, and I bought into Rand's philosophy. I thought that really competent people would always be advocates for capitalism, and only incompetent losers were advocates for some type of socialism. I had written as much. And like many people, I conflated socialism with totalitarianism. I believed that all of us should only be working for our own self-interest. But should we *really*? I mean, is selfishness really in our best interest? Short term, possibly, but long term? I no longer think so.

"There are so many definitions of socialism put out there by people like me. I was beginning to see that my readers were being duped. I was not giving them all the facts. And the 'facts' I was giving them were not reliable. I can see this even more clearly now. I want you to know that—even with my increasing reservations—I actually came here to write a scathing appraisal of your community. I had every intention of placing your communities in one of the pigeonholes known to frighten people. I was planning to call your communities 'socialistic,' 'communistic,' 'cultish,' and so on. Again, the desired conclusion had preceded the 'facts.' All I needed to do was skew them. And without question, people would discount your communities without even questioning my 'facts.'

"This is how things work these days; no one even tries to verify facts for themselves. Most people do not even know where to find accurate information or how to evaluate journalism for accuracy. They just accept it without question if it agrees with what they already believe. And they visit websites, or read or watch news sources in agreement with their worldview. I agree with what you said during breakfast on our second day here: Journalists should be trained to the highest standards of reporting and then should not be unduly influenced by outside forces. Accurate tacts, would you say?"

"Yes," I said, stopping him at this juncture. "Clifford, please do not think you are the first to be sent here to write a scathing report about our communities. So let me be clear about this: Behaviorology, one of the main sciences behind our communities, *has* no political ideology. In this regard it is no different than physics or chemistry. We have simply applied this science, along with other sciences, to design what we believe to be a better way of living. People must come to understand that behaviorology is no different than any other natural science. Perhaps someday you can help to convey this.

"But like all other sciences, it can be used for nefarious purposes, as physics was used to build the atom bomb, and chemistry, chemical and biological weapons. If our cultural practices happen to resemble one or more of your political categories, that is just the way it is. Of course, the practices of all communities must necessarily resemble some prior practices. If some people see our communities as egalitarian and want to label that as socialism, so be it. As I said before, we do not place our communities in any historical political category; we define ourselves by our practices, and these practices will change as new data come in. We *will* follow the argument wherever it leads. Our communities are non-coercive because we have found this to be the most effective way to build productive repertoires of behavior while simultaneously forming close human bonds. If you would like to write an accurate account of our community, I would be happy to provide you with data to support this."

Clifford looked out over the pond. "Do you think it might be possible for me to stay here for a week or two as I begin to write?" he asked. "I would be happy to work or anything el . . ."

He stopped before finishing, and I could hear his cell phone vibrating. He picked it up and read a text from its screen. "It's from one of my patron's assistants," he said. "He wants to know how things are going. Let me call him. Please stay." He pressed a few buttons and dialed the number.

"Hello, Jon," he said, after a moment. "I just got your text . . . yes, I'm fine, how are you? . . . Tell Mister . . . " he looked at me, suddenly realizing he had almost unwittingly divulged his benefactor's name, "um . . . please tell your boss that I'm gathering some very good information about the community. Now, that is the good news. The bad news is that I will be returning his advance and will not be writing his requested account of the community. . . . The agreement? Well, tell him we can litigate that in court if he wishes to do so. Or he can just find another lackey, there are many out there to choose from." With this, Clifford hung up and set the phone back down on the bench.

"As I was saying," he continued, "I would like to at least begin to write my account here. I can pull my own weight and will be happy to work for my keep. Maybe I could join Simmons and we could work together?"

"Since you will be staying for a much-shorter period of time, I think that could easily be arranged," I told him. "Perhaps you would like to have your ex-wife and son join you?"

"I would like that very much," he said. "I may ask her to join me later. You know, I'm still quite idealistic. I just never thought it was possible to work toward the improvement of one's culture as a whole, only for parts of it. I always thought we had to decide which group we belonged to and then work to improve conditions for that group. And maybe—for those so inclined—to work to slightly improve the conditions of others as well. But I agree with you, societies today are too cumbersome, the problems too unwieldy, and the leaderships are too remote to attend to the needs of *all* of the people. I would love to live with my wife and son again but in a culture where everyone matters and no one is excluded. Who knows," he said, with a laugh, "we may decide to live here in Walden Two, or one of your sister communities."

"If you are interested, we actually have communities that specialize in transitioning new members into our communities," I told him. "They can even help you clear up any outside obligations you may have as you transition. Unfortunately, a certain percentage of people want to live here because they have serious problems in society at large. I don't believe you fall into this category, but I think you can understand why we must evaluate and vet potential members? We cannot allow ourselves to be the dumping ground for dysfunctional societies."

"Of course," he said, smiling broadly.

We sat in silence for a moment looking out over the pond. Some other members were beginning to wander up after a day's work and began to remove chairs from the shed. A small group of elder members rode up together on e-carts. Some young members were lying on blankets reading books as the daylight began to wane. I saw Clifford look up at the clear blue sky above as a warm breeze caressed us. His cell phone began to vibrate, but he didn't seem to notice.

Epilogue

My grandfather wrote about his visit and recruitment to Walden Two nearly seventy years ago. He could be accurately described as a Walden Two hybrid. He spent most of the first half of his life in academics, teaching students who were mostly striving for high grades that might allow them to move into the higher echelons of society. He spent the last half of his life in Walden Two where, as he wrote, people of all ages continue to learn new behavior that will produce outcomes that benefit all, including themselves. It was interesting for me, as his grandson, and as a behaviorologist and product of Walden Two, to read his account of the fortuitous event that brought him here and changed his life—and mine.

My grandfather and Frazier became very close friends over the years. They were both very rational and well-informed men and had many pleasant philosophical discussions about society, science, civilization, and culture in general, among many other things. After being diagnosed with terminal leukemia, and carefully weighing the prognosis he was given by several concurring medical experts, my grandfather chose to end his life peacefully at the end of what was believed by his doctors to be his last hiatus from continuous pain and suffering. He understood that he had reached the point where the quality of his life would soon become unbearable. A ceremony was given in his honor where he spoke his last words to his friends before his suffering would distort his repertoire beyond recognition. All were aware that this was the last time they would see him as the Burris they knew, respected, and loved. Soon after this, and after making his final arrangements, he said goodbye to his family and administered a lethal mixture of chemicals that calmed and suppressed his nervous system; he died very peacefully within minutes. His last operant ended his life.

Grandfather Burris was cremated and, like all members of our community, his ashes were spread among the woods of Walden Two; there are no graves in Walden Two. People are remembered for the products of their behavior; these may be records of verbal behavior (their writings) or the effect they have had on others as their teachers, mentors, or friends. But with few exceptions, ordinary people *everywhere* are mostly forgotten after a generation or two. And why should we care? If we have lived happy, peaceful, and productive lives, we have done our part. No one should expect more from us. Our desire to be immortalized in memory is simply the generalization of our desire to be liked, but it is an irrational desire.

Frazier, again, also not a product of the contingencies of Walden Two, was not immune to thinking about his legacy, and he understood well the contributions he had made to science, and that his legacy was secure. But he later wrote in his autobiography, "If I am right about human behavior, I have written the autobiography of a nonperson. I have collected alms for oblivion, but not, I think, for no reason. There are consequences . . . an individual is only the way in which a species and a culture produce more of a species and a culture."

Fraziere knew that his behavior also was the result of the determining contingencies he so meticulously explored in the environments of other behaving organisms. He understood that there was no internal creative agential Frazier. Frazier will be, and should be, remembered as the person who first *behaved* the natural science of behavior, and defined, systematized, and articulated that science. He can be considered the locus where contingencies caused a human to behave this natural science into full existence. For all science is, and necessarily must be, only behavior; there can be no science without an organism to behave it. Frazier will be remembered many generations from now mostly for this, and Walden Two.

I've written this account to tell about the communities that are based on behaviorology, the natural science of behavior, first clearly outlined by Frazier. He saw that the science could improve the human condition by eliminating the coercive practices used in parenting, teaching, government, the workplace, interpersonal relations and international affairs. And he introduced in their place positive reinforcement to shape and maintain desirable behavior. I said at the outset that I wanted to bury Frazier not to praise him, but even Frazier knew the fruits of his labor would continue on, and this appealed to him, as it does to me.

Rogers and my Grandfather Burris kept in touch by letter for some time. Grandfather kept the letters, and we found them after his death among his many correspondences. Rogers never again visited Walden Two as far as I can discern from Grandfather's letters, and from speaking with Jamnik. And while he kept in close touch with Steve and Mary for a time, according to Steve, the intervals between letters increased and eventually slowed to a stop after several years. Rogers and Barbara lived, at least for a time, the "American Dream" in a small exclusive suburb in Philadelphia. Their children went to private schools and all did very well, according to Rogers. Barbara apparently moved them in all of the right social circles. Even so, some of his letters were rather plaintive when he discussed his life, marriage, and divorce, but he felt he made the right decision at that time by not staying in Walden Two.

Castle remained a Philosopher with a capital "P." To the end of his life, he was still trying to answer the same old questions: "What is it to be human?" "Why is learning necessary?" "What is Mind?" "Where do values come from?" He died in 1987 at the age of 83. As far as I know, he never answered these questions even to his own satisfaction.

We at Walden Two do not have to physically *fight* with others for our cultural survival, because we do not compete with others for our resources. But we do take our cultural survival into account and work to improve the contingencies generating our behavior. It is, of course, aggregate behavior that makes up any culture. And the behavior needed for our survival is of paramount concern. It is the job of our culturologists to look at long-term outcomes and meta-contingencies. That is, they look at the long-term consequences of our aggregate behavior and engineer contingencies to keep us on track.

I'm often struck with wonder at how I came to live in Walden Two, the many coincidences of history that brought me here. I think about my grandfather often, and what brought him here to father my father. How Rogers' and Jamnik's visit to his office in 1945 lured him away from his professorial life to bring him here. But isn't this true of all lives? Isn't most people's behavior the product of so many coincidences and fortuitous contingencies? One chance meeting or lucky break can change the course of our lives forever. Jamnik has said that had he not come to Walden Two on that fateful day, his life certainly would have been very different. He believes he most likely would have gotten a menial job, which was all his education had prepared him for, had children, and then probably struggled like so many others like him. Now, he believes, he has reached much of his potential here. He was relatively young when he came to Walden Two and has since been provided with many learning opportunities. He was the one who said that he was not *self*-actualized but rather *Walden Two*-actualized. I very much agree.

Coincidental contingencies of survival and reinforcement have been responsible for the human body and behavior up to now. One can't help looking back over the history of our universe and the series of accidents that brought us here to this moment in time: the forging of our atoms in the nuclear furnaces of stars, the formation of our planet at this "Goldilocks" location near the star we call the sun, the lucky asteroid strike that ended the millions-of-years reign of the dinosaurs to bring our mammalian ancestors to the fore to begin to be shaped by new selection pressures. The mutation adjustments of the hand, the eye, and our wonderful brain were selected only from those that reached reproductive age. And the brain! What a complex piece of matter. An organ changed by experience in such a way that our behavior is selected by its consequences, consequences that were also selected because of their survival value in a purposeless universe.

In humankind's last second on Carl Sagan's Cosmic Calendar, the collective behavior we call *science* has permitted us to glimpse the processes behind the formation of the universe and our biological beginnings. For the first time—but perhaps not—matter has come to understand its own origins and complexity. After many false starts, many wars and deaths, many false philosophies, religions, and theories, we have finally arrived at the point where we can begin seriously designing cultures that can engineer the behavior needed to prevent us from destroying ourselves, and we can greatly enhance humankind's chances of survival.

The sizes of our Walden Two communities were determined experimentally. We were trying to answer the question: What is the ideal number of people needed *in one location* in order to produce ample self-sustaining resources and produce valuable artifacts? This number may change as our communities evolve. We are currently realizing the advantages of communal life, and of fair trade, information sharing, and cooperation between our communities. Our recent ancestors lived in tribes that were small enough for members to get to know one another well and develop cooperation. Here we have greatly expanded our numbers to keep life interesting. For who has more than a thousand friends? Or even a hundred? The Walden

Two Network permits the open sharing of new practices that have proved successful in increasing those behaviors necessary for human survival and happiness.

We can be grateful for the variables that came together to produce people like Frazier, variables that permitted them to understand that the biological and behavioral sciences are underpinned with selection processes. Yes, we have reached another pinnacle. We can finally end ignorance and war, rid ourselves of hate and fear, and engineer our environments to produce behavior within an acceptable range of prosociality, productivity, and happiness. It's easy to see in hindsight how we got here, and hard for some to believe that destiny played no role. Our communities—without lying politicians, jails to lock up transgressors, thieves, warmongers, purveyors of religion and other false ideologies—are allowing us to advance rapidly; for what are we but behavior? Good riddance to the soul, mind, and spirit! The Abrahamic religions have predicted an apocalyptic end to humankind, and this is reflected in many artistic themes. Science, but especially behaviorology, has a different view: Rather than prepare for an apocalyptic end, we must roll up our sleeves and begin. Frazier once asked if we wanted our behavior to be determined "by accident, by tyrants, or by ourselves through effective cultural design." Our Walden Two communities are our answer to Frazier's question.

Suggested Readings

Walden Two, by B.F. Skinner
Beyond Freedom & Dignity, by B.F. Skinner

For more information about the natural science of behaviorology, consider the book *What Causes Human Behavior—Stars, Selves, or Contingencies?* by Dr. Stephen F. Ledoux. This book is a general-audience primer, and is fully described at www.behaviorology. org/books, where you can find many more options for further reading. Another resource is www.bfskinner.org, the website of the B. F. Skinner Foundation. Both website provide links to additional related sites.

About the Author

Michael Shuler, who resides in a small Midwestern town, has had a lifelong interest in B.F. Skinner and behavior analysis.

He was first led to the writings of Skinner and other behavior analysts by an unfavorable article about the noted psychologist titled "God Is a Variable Interval." After reading Skinner's Science and Human Behavior, Verbal Behavior, and Beyond Freedom and Dignity, and, over the years, Skinner's complete works (as well as the works of others), he became interested in the possible application of a natural science of behavior toward reducing coercive practices and solving a host of the most dire global problems. This led him to apply this science to his personal and interpersonal life. He received a Baccalaureate Level Behaviorology Certificate and is the archivist for The International Behaviorology Institute.

A retired railroad engineer, he also enjoys bicycling, spending quality time with his family, and reading science-related books and journals, especially those concerning relatively new developments in language research involving equivalence relations and relational frame theory. A World of Our Own Making is his first novel.

www.ingramcontent.com/pod-product-compliance
Lightning Source LLC
Chambersburg PA
CBHW070748190726
48292CB00002B/462